PENGUIN BOOKS

THE PENGUIN BOOK OF THE CITY

Robert Drewe was born in Melbourne in 1943, grew up in Perth, Western Australia, and has also lived in San Francisco, London and Sydney. He is the author of five novels, *The Savage Crows*, *A Cry in the Jungle Bar*, *Fortune*, *Our Sunshine* and *The Drowner*, and two volumes of short stories, *The Bodysurfers* and *The Bay of Contented Men*, as well as plays, screenplays, journalism and film criticism. His work has been widely translated, won national and international prizers, and been adapted for film, television, radio and the theatre.

The Penguin

BOOK OF
THE CITY

Edited by Robert Drewe

PENGUIN BOOKS

PENGUIN BOOKS

Published by the Penguin Group
Penguin Books Ltd, 27 Wrights Lane, London W8 5TZ, England
Penguin Putnam Inc., 375 Hudson Street, New York, New York 10014, USA
Penguin Books Australia Ltd, Ringwood, Victoria, Australia
Penguin Books Canada Ltd, 10 Alcorn Avenue, Toronto, Ontario, Canada M4V 3B2
Penguin Books (NZ) Ltd, 182–190 Wairau Road, Auckland 10, New Zealand

Penguin Books Ltd, Registered Offices: Harmondsworth, Middlesex, England

First published by Penguin Books Australia 1997
Published in Great Britain by Penguin Books 1998
3 5 7 9 10 8 6 4

The Acknowledgements on page 379 constitute an
extension of this copyright page

The moral right of the editor and authors has been asserted

Printed in England by Clays Ltd, St Ives plc

For Amy

CONTENTS

Introduction

The city – good or bad, civilised or blighted, source of enlightenment or vice? Samuel Johnson, Robert Herrick, Voltaire, Lewis Mumford and Woody Allen won't hear a word against it. Just about everyone else from William Cobbett to Neil Simon professes to knowing its evils only too well.

In their more ironical moments, London newspaper columnists still like to quote Dr Johnson's remark, *When a man is tired of London, he is tired of life*. These days, with deeper irony, they even complete his sentence – *for there is in London all that life can afford*. (As Fleet Street's Maggie Brown has grumbled, 'It's London I'm tired of, not life.')

Dr Johnson, like Herrick before him, was that rare English literary beast, the city-lover. (Wordsworth? While Wordsworth is well known for his hyperbolic appreciation of the beauty of London viewed at dawn – *Earth has not anything to show more fair* – he liked to stay up there beside the Lakes, well away from it.) In a cultural tradition which glorifies the countryside, Herrick and Johnson sounded a note seldom heard in English literature.

The tradition is that of Cobbett, who christened London 'the great Wen' – a wen being a sebaceous cyst, especially on the scalp, but in London's case a parasite on the countryside, which Cobbett saw as the fount of all health and reason. This tradition, based on the rejection of the insanitary nineteenth-century industrial metropolis, was enthusiastically exported to North America and Australia where, bizarrely, it still flourishes today, especially among poets.

But Herrick, vicar of Dean Prior, in the scenic parish of Exeter in Devonshire, was so keen for his career-long exile in the countryside to end that in 1648 he penned the poem, 'His Return to London'. Pining for the city, he began: *From the dull confines of the drooping West/ To see the day spring from the pregnant East,/Ravish'd in spirit, I come, nay more, I fly/To thee, bless'd place of my nativity.*

Woody Allen would only agree. Asked in 1993 why he hated leaving New York for a weekend in the country, he said, 'I don't trust air I can't see.'

Anticipating Dr Johnson – and, in the New World three centuries later, Mumford and Allen – Herrick was happy to swap the scones, jam and cream and pastoral tranquillity for the cosmopolitan vigour of London. As he exclaimed, rather breathlessly: *All nations, customs, kindreds, languages!* . . .

Allen the film-maker feels the same about the city whose more rarefied reaches he has helped immortalise: 'I could live in Paris, but it would be second choice. In no other city in the world but New York can you see, all on the same night, two operas, four different ballets and a dozen jazz bands. In the '20s, '30s and '40s New York was as great as a city could be. It's still the greatest city in the world.'

But for urban fervour the self-proclaimed 'child of the city' Lewis Mumford was streets ahead. This proudest of New Yorkers, lacking a male parent, went so far as to claim Manhattan as his spiritual father. Mumford it was who, as an aspiring young writer in 1917, experienced an epiphany one evening in early spring while walking to Manhattan across the Brooklyn Bridge:

Here was my city, immense, overpowering, flooded with energy and light ... And there was I, breasting the March wind, drinking in the city and sky, both vast, yet both contained in me, transmitting through me the great mysterious will that had made them and the promise of the new day that was still to come.

The world at that moment opened before me, challenging me, beckoning me, raising all my energies by its own vivid promise to a higher pitch. In that sudden revelation of power and beauty I trod the narrow, resilient boards of the footway with a new confidence ... The wonder of that moment was like the wonder of an orgasm in the body of one's beloved, as if one's whole life had led up to that moment and had swiftly culminated there.

I have carried the sense of that occasion through my life as a momentary flash reminding me of heights approached and scaled. That experience remains alone: a fleeting glimpse of the utmost possibilities life may hold for man.

Well, not quite alone. He soon had another one. (That he was going on leave in New York after several months of Navy service may have had something to do with it.) This epiphany also occurred as he approached the bridge 'under the slowly deepening violet sky'.

As he explained the sensation: 'I had for the second and last time an indescribable but exalted sense of my whole future spreading out before me ... In that breathless moment past and future, my past and the world's past, my future and the world's future, came together.'

Of course, the exciting combination of cityscape, harbour and sky has energised many imaginative men and women. If not an epiphany of Mumfordian magnitude, its effect is not too dissimilar: a flash of realisation that one is charged with the mysterious will and power that animate the city. On one hand you are filled with the wonder of technology, culture and the romance of city life; on the other, with a profound sense of confidence and purpose in your own potential.

Its force is even present in the love–hate relationship that many urban dwellers have with their city, well exemplified in the defiance New York arouses in Jack Lemmon in Neil Simon's *The Out of Towners*:

We don't surrender! You hear that, New York? We don't quit. Now how do you like that? You go ahead, and you can rob me, and starve me, and break my teeth, and my wife's ankles! I'm not leaving! You're just a city! Well, I'm a person, and persons are stronger than cities! This is George Kellerman talking! And you're not getting away with anything! I got all your names and addresses!

In any artistic rendering of the city theme alienation is a constant. Given the anonymity the city provides, it could hardly be otherwise. Artists, especially writers, have recognised this dichotomy, and that cities have always proved a source of freedom by providing anonymity, notwithstanding the estrangement and isolation that goes with it. Indeed, the city's impetus towards modernity is to be found in that narrow zone between loss of community and discovery of self.

As for the artistic potential of the city, the Australian critic Humphrey McQueen has said: 'As a source of wonder, cities are as varied as any creativity displayed in nature or in art museums. The neons of Tokyo are shamed by neither coral reefs nor Abstract Expression. The tonal range of trees is more limited than those of concrete and bitumen.'

It is a provocative and appealing remark. I see the stories in this collection like those unshamed neons: often teasing and inviting, perhaps fizzing with odd currents and connections, sometimes strangely sinister, always dazzling.

Some of these stories were familiar to me – indeed, they come from my own shelves. Some, published in magazines as recently as a few months before this publication, or written especially for this book, could hardly be newer. While place was kept in mind it was always the story that counted, not whether Rotterdam or Rome or Rio were covered. (They aren't.) This is not a travel book, yet travellers (those vulnerable souls with their discarded responsibilities and receptive fatigue) feature prominently here. While there is great diversity, it is not a particularly politically correct diversity. Not surprisingly, New York and London, the great cities of the English language, predominate.

The criterion for selection was simply the personal taste of a professional writer and amateur reader – and someone who, like many Australians, has lived in several cities and been a committed traveller. There is a remark by Ian McEwan in *A Move Abroad* that rings loud bells for me. 'Choosing a new form in which to write bears some resemblance to travelling abroad.' I go further: I used to see travelling and the writing of fiction not only as interchangeable occupations but as parts of the same emotional state.

As McEwan says, 'The sense of freedom is no less useful for being illusory or temporary. The new place has its own rules and conventions, but they are not really yours, not quite yet. What you notice first is the absence of the old familiar constraints, and you do things you would not do at home.'

People in these stories do things they would not do at home. They eat strange food, go to brothels, face their worst racial and sexual fears, have abortions, deal with hotel staff, punch a Disneyland bear. Others of them are firmly at home – in the ghetto, the apartment block, the bar, the restaurant, the street, the social event of the decade. All bar one of the stories are fiction. The one factual story, 'L.A. *Noir*' by Joan Didion, was chosen for its clever and incisive representation of a city and life-style beyond fiction as most of the world understands it.

Apart from the pleasure of being able to display the work of my favourite authors, the great joy in compiling this collection has been to choose stories that really speak of the city to *me*. That means shrewd and whim-sical and sometimes hard-edged stories that not only show us their characters coping with the tensions and exhilarations of city life, but also hint at the fierce eye and provocative imagination of the writer.

There are few eyes more intense and imaginations more stimulating than those of the illustrious authors represented here. My thanks to them all for their alacrity in participating in this anthology and for their readiness to accept my word that Australia is the most urbanised country in the world.

Robert Drewe
Sydney

JOHN UPDIKE

The City

His stomach began to hurt on the airplane, as the engines
changed pitch to descend into this city. Carson at first
blamed his pain upon the freeze-dried salted peanuts that
had come in a little silver-foil packet with the whiskey
sour he had let the stewardess bring him at ten o'clock
that morning. He did not think of himself as much of a
drinker; but the younger men in kindred gray business
suits who flanked him in the three-across row of seats
had both ordered drinks, and it seemed a way of keeping
status with the stewardess. Unusually for these days, she
was young and pretty. So many stewardesses seemed,
like Carson himself, on second careers, victims of
middle-aged restlessness – the children grown, the long
descent begun.

A divorced former business-school math teacher, he

worked as a sales representative for a New Jersey manufacturer of microcomputers and information processing systems. In his fifties, after decades of driving the same suburban streets from home to school and back again, he had become a connoisseur of cities – their reviving old downtowns and grassy industrial belts, their rusting railroad spurs and new glass buildings, their orange-carpeted hotels and bars imitating the interiors of English cottages. But always there was an individual accent, a style of local girl and a unique little historic district, an odd-shaped skyscraper or a museum holding a Cézanne, say, or a Winslow Homer that you could not see in any other place. Carson had never before visited the city into which he was now descending, and perhaps a nervous apprehension of the new contacts he must weld and the persuasions he must deliver formed the seed of the pain that had taken root in the center of his stomach, just above the navel.

He kept blaming the peanuts. The tempting young stewardess, with a tender boundary on her throat where the pancake makeup stopped, had given him not one but two packets in silver foil, and he had eaten both – the nuts tasting tartly of acid, the near engine of the 747 haloed by a rainbow of furious vapor in a backwash of sunlight from the east as the great plane droned west. This drone, too, had eaten into his stomach. Then there was the whiskey sour itself, and the time-squeeze of his departure, and the pressure of elbows on the armrests on both sides of him. He had arrived at the airport too late to get an aisle or a window seat. Young men now, it seemed to him, were increasingly corpulent and broad, due to the mixture of exercise and beer the culture kept pushing. Both of these specimens wore silk handkerchiefs in their breast pockets and modified bandit mustaches above their prim, pale, satisfied mouths. When you exchanged a few words with them, you heard voices that knew nothing, that were tinny like the cheapest of television sets.

Carson put away the papers on which he had been blocking in a system – computer, terminals, daisy-wheel printers, optional but irresistible color-graphics generator with appropriate interfaces – for a prospering little manufacturer of electric reducing aids, and ran a final check on what could be ailing his own system. Peanuts. Whiskey. Crowded conditions. In addition to everything else, he was tired, he realized: tired of numbers, tired of travel, of food, of competing, even of self-care – of showering and shaving in the morning and putting himself into clothes and then, sixteen hours later, taking himself out of them. The pain slightly intensified. He pictured the pain as spherical, a hot tarry bubble that would break if only he could focus upon it the laser of the right thought.

In the taxi line, Carson felt more comfortable if he stood with a slight hunch. The cool autumn air beat through his suit upon his skin. He must look sick: he was attracting the glances of his fellow-visitors to the city. The two young men whose shoulders had squeezed him for three hours had melted into the many similar others with their attaché cases and tasseled shoes. Carson gave the cabdriver not the address of the manufacturer of reducing and exercise apparatus but that of the hotel where he had a reservation. A sudden transparent wave of nausea, like a dip in the flight of the 747, had suddenly decided him. As he followed the maroon-clad bellhop down the orange-carpeted corridor, not only were the colors nauseating but the planes of wall and floor looked warped, as if the pain that would not break up were transposing him to a set of new coordinates, by the touch of someone's finger on a terminal keyboard. He telephoned the exercise company from the room, explaining his case to an answering female and making a new appointment for tomorrow morning, just before he was scheduled to see the head accountant of another booming little firm, makers of devices that produced 'white noise' to shelter city sleep.

The appointment jam bothered Carson, but remotely, for it would all be taken care of by quite another person – his recovered, risen self. The secretary he had talked to had been sympathetic, speaking in the strangely comforting accent of the region – languid in some syllables, quite clipped in others – and had recommended Maalox. In the motion pictures that had flooded Carson's childhood with images of the ideal life, people had 'sent down' for such things, but during all the travelling of his recent years, from one exiguously staffed accommodation to the next, he had never seen that this could be done; he went down himself to the hotel pharmacy. A lobby mirror shocked him with the image of a thin-limbed man in shirt sleeves, with a pot belly and a colorless mouth tugged down on one side like a dead man's.

The medicine tasted chalky and gritty and gave the pain, after a moment's hesitation, an extra edge, as of tiny sandy teeth. His hotel room also was orange-carpeted, with maroon drapes that Carson closed, after peeking out at a bare brown patch of park where amid the fallen leaves some boys were playing soccer; their shouts jarred his membranes. He turned on the television set, but it, too, jarred. Lying on one of the room's double beds, studying the ceiling between trips to the bathroom, he let the afternoon burn down into evening and thought how misery itself becomes a kind of home. The ceiling had been plastered in overlapping loops, like the scales of a large white fish. For variation, Carson stretched himself out upon the cool bathroom floor, marvelling at the complex, thick-lipped undersides of the porcelain fixtures, and at the distant bright lozenge of foreshortened mirror.

Repeated violent purgations had left undissolved the essential intruder, the hot tarry thing no longer simply spherical in shape but elongating. When vomiting began, Carson had been hopeful. The hope faded with the light. In the room's shadowy spaces his pain had become a companion whom his constant interrogations left unmoved; from minute to minute it did not grow perceptibly worse, nor did it leave him. He reflected that

his situation was a perfect one for prayer; but he had
never been religious and so could spare himself that
additional torment.

The day's light, in farewell, placed feathery gray rims
upon all the curved surfaces of the room's furniture –
the table legs, the lamp bowls. Carson imagined that if
only the telephone would ring his condition would be
shattered. Curled on his side, he fell asleep briefly;
awakening to pain, he found the room dark, with but a
sallow splinter of street light at the window. The soccer
players had gone. He wondered who was out there,
beyond the dark, whom he could call. His ex-wife had
remarried. Of his children, one, the boy, was travelling
in Mexico and the other, the girl, had disowned her
father. When he received her letter of repudiation,
Carson had telephoned and been told, by the man she
had been living with, that she had moved out and joined
a feminist commune.

He called the hotel desk and asked for advice. The
emergency clinic at the city hospital was suggested, by
a young male voice that, to judge from its cheerful vigor,
had just come on duty. Shaking, lacing his shoes with
difficulty, smiling to find himself the hero of a drama
without an audience, Carson dressed and delicately took
his sore body out into the air. A row of taxis waited
beneath the corrosive yellow glare of a sodium-vapor
streetlight. Neon advertisements and stacked cubes of
fluorescent offices and red and green traffic lights flick-
ered by – glimpses of the city that now, normally, with

his day's business done, he would be roving, looking for a restaurant, a bar, a stray conversation, a possibility of contact with one of the city's unofficial hostesses, with her green eye-paint and her short skirt and tall boots and exposed knees. He had developed a fondness for such women, even when no deal was struck. Their brisk preliminaries tickled him, and their frank hostility.

The hospital was a surprising distance from the hotel. A vast and glowing pile with many increasingly modern additions, it waited at the end of a swerving drive through a dark park and a neighborhood of low houses. Carson expected to surrender the burden of his body utterly, but instead found himself obliged to carry it through a series of fresh efforts – forms to be filled out, proofs to be supplied of his financial fitness to be ill, a series of waits to be endured, on crowded benches and padded chairs, while his eye measured the distance to the men's-room door and calculated the time it would take him to hobble across it, open the door to a stall, kneel, and heave away vainly at the angry visitor to his own insides.

The first doctor he at last was permitted to see seemed to Carson as young and mild and elusive as his half-forgotten, travelling son. Both had hair so blond as to seem artificial. His wife, the doctor let it be known, was giving a dinner party, for which he was already late, in another sector of the city. Nevertheless the young man politely examined him. Carson was, he confessed, something of a puzzle. His pain didn't seem localized enough for appendicitis, which furthermore was unusual in a man his age.

'Maybe I'm a slow bloomer,' Carson suggested, each syllable, in his agony, a soft, self-deprecatory grunt.

There ensued a further miasma of postponement, livened with the stabs of blood tests and the banter of hardened nurses. He found himself undressing in front of a locker so that he could wait with a number of other men in threadbare, backwards hospital gowns to be X-rayed. The robust technician, with his standard bandit mustache, had the cheerful aura of a weight lifter and a great ladies' (or men's) man. 'Chin here,' he said. 'Shoulders forward. Deep breath: hold it. Good boy.' Slowly Carson dressed again, though the clothes looked, item by item, so shabby as to be hardly his. One could die, he saw, in the interstices of these procedures. All around him, on the benches and in the bright, bald holding areas of the hospital's innumerable floors, other suppliants, residents of the city and mostly black, served as models of stoic calm; he tried to imitate them, though it hurt to sit up straight and his throat ached with gagging.

The results of his tests were trickling along through their channels. The fair-haired young doctor must be at his party by now; Carson imagined the clash of silver, the candlelight, the bare-shouldered women – a festive domestic world from which he had long fallen.

Toward midnight, he was permitted to undress himself

again and to get into a bed, in a kind of emergency holding area. White curtains surrounded him, but not silence. On either side of him, from the flanking beds, two men, apparently with much in common, moaned and crooned a kind of tuneless blues. When doctors visited them, they pleaded to get out and promised to be good henceforth. From one side, after a while, came a sound of tidy retching, like that of a cat who has eaten a bird bones and all; on the other side, internes seemed to be cajoling a tube up through a man's nose. Carson was comforted by these evidences that at least he had penetrated into a circle of acknowledged ruin. He was inspected at wide intervals. Another young doctor, who reminded him less of his son than of the shifty man, a legal-aid lawyer, who had lived with his daughter and whom Carson suspected of inspiring and even dictating the eerily formal letter she had mailed her father, shambled in and, after some poking of Carson's abdomen, shrugged. Then a female physician, dark-haired and fortyish, came and gazed with sharp amusement down into Carson's face. She had an accent, Slavic of some sort. She said, 'You don't protect enough.'

'Protect?' he croaked. He saw why slaves had taken to clowning.

She thrust her thumb deep into his belly, in several places. 'I shouldn't be able to do that,' she said. 'You should go through the ceiling.' The idiom went strangely with her accent.

'It did hurt,' he told her.

'Not enough,' she said. She gazed sharply down into his eyes; her own eyes were in shadow. 'I think we shall take more blood tests.'

Yet Carson felt she was stalling. There was a sense, from beyond the white curtains, percolating through the voices of nurses and policemen and agitated kin in this emergency room, of something impending in his case, a significant visitation. He closed his eyes for what seemed a second. When he opened them a new man was leaning above him – a tall tutorial man wearing a tweed jacket with elbow patches, a button-down shirt, and rimless glasses that seemed less attachments to his face than intensifications of a general benign aura. His hair was combed and grayed exactly right, and cut in the high-parted and close-cropped style of the Camelot years. Unlike the previous doctors, he sat on the edge of Carson's narrow bed. His voice and touch were gentle; he explained, palpating, that some appendixes were retrocecal – that is, placed behind the large intestine, so that one could be quite inflamed without the surface sensitivity and protective reflex usual with appendicitis.

Carson wondered what dinner party the doctor had been pulled from, at this post-midnight hour, in his timeless jacket and tie. Carson wished to make social amends but was in a poor position to, flat on his back and nearly naked. With a slight smile, the doctor pondered his face, as if to unriddle it, and Carson stared back with pleading helpless hopefulness, mute as a dog, which can only whimper or howl. He was as weary of pain and a state

1 7

of emergency as he had been, twelve hours before, of his normal life. 'I'd like to operate,' the doctor said softly, as if putting forth a suggestion that Carson might reject.

'Oh yes, *please*,' Carson said. 'When, do you think?' He was very aware that, though the debauched hour and disreputable surroundings had become his own proper habitat, the doctor was healthy and must have a decent home, a family, a routine to return to.

'Why, right *now*,' was the answer, in a tone of surprise, and this doctor stood and began to take off his coat, as if to join Carson in some sudden, cheerfully concocted athletic event.

Perhaps Carson merely imagined the surgeon's gesture. Perhaps he merely thought *Bliss*, or really sighed the word aloud. Things moved rapidly. The shifty legal-aid lookalike returned, more comradely now that Carson had received a promotion in status, and asked him to turn on one side, and thrust a needle into his buttock. Then a biracial pair of orderlies coaxed his body from the bed to a long trolley on soft swift wheels; the white curtains were barrelled through; faces, lights, steel door lintels streamed by. Carson floated, feet first, into a room that he recognized, from having seen its blazing counterpart so often dramatized on films, as an operating room. A masked and youthful population was already there, making chatter, having a party. 'There are so many of you!' Carson exclaimed; he was immensely happy. His pain had already ceased. He was transferred from the trolley to a very narrow, high, padded table. His arms were spread out on wooden extensions and strapped tight to them. His wrists were pricked. Swollen rubber was pressed to his face as if to test the fit. He tried to say, to reassure the masked crew that he was not frightened and to impress them with what a 'good guy' he was, that somebody should cancel his appointments for tomorrow.

At a point and place in the fog as it fitfully lifted, the surgeon himself appeared, no longer in a tweed jacket but in a lime-green hospital garment, and now jubilant, bending close. He held up the crooked little finger of one hand before Carson's eyes, which could not focus. 'Fat as that', he called through a kind of wind.

'What size should it have been?' Carson asked, knowing they were discussing his appendix.

'No thicker than a pencil,' came the answer, tugged by the bright tides of contagious relief.

'But when did you sleep?' Carson asked, and was not answered, having overstepped.

Earlier, he had found himself in an underground room that had many stalactites. His name was being shouted by a big gruff youth. 'Hey Bob come on Bob wake up give us a little smile that's the boy Bob.' There were others besides him stretched out in this catacomb, whose ceiling was festooned with drooping transparent tubes; these were the stalactites. Within an arm's length of him, another man was lying as motionless as a limestone knight carved on a tomb. Carson realized that he had been squeezed through a tunnel – the arm straps, the swollen rubber – and had come out the other side. 'Hey, Bob, come on, give us a smile. *Thaaat's* it.' He had a tremendous need to urinate; liquid was being dripped into his arm.

Later, after the windy, glittering exchange with the surgeon, Carson awoke in an ordinary hospital room. In a bed next to him, a man with a short man's sour, pinched profile was lying and smoking and staring up at a television set. Though the picture twitched, no noise seemed to be coming from the box. 'Hi,' Carson said, feeling shy and wary, as if in his sleep he had been married to this man.

'Hi,' the other said, without taking his eyes from the television set and exhaling smoke with a loudness, simultaneously complacent and fed up, that had been one of Carson's former wife's most irritating mannerisms.

When Carson awoke again, it was twilight, and he was in yet another room, a private room, alone, with a sore abdomen and a clearer head. A quarter-moon leaned small and cold in the sky above the glowing square windows of another wing of the hospital, and his position in the world and the universe seemed clear enough. His convalescence had begun.

In the five days that followed, he often wondered why he was so happy. Ever since childhood, after several of his classmates had been whisked away to hospitals and returned to school with proud scars on their lower abdomens, Carson had been afraid of appendicitis. At last, in his sixth decade, the long-dreaded had occurred, and he had comported himself, he felt, with passable courage and calm.

His scar was not the little lateral slit his classmates had shown him but a rather gory central incision from navel down; he had been opened up wide, it was explained to him, on the premise that at his age his malady might have been anything from ulcers to cancer. The depth of the gulf that he had, unconscious, floated above thrilled him. There had been, too, a certain unthinkable intimacy. His bowels had been 'handled', the surgeon gently reminded him, in explaining a phase of his recuperation. Carson tried to picture the handling: clamps and white rubber gloves and something glistening and heavy and purplish that was his. His appendix had indeed been retrocecal – one of a mere ten percent so located. It had even begun, microscopic investigation revealed, to rupture. All of this retrospective clarification, reducing to cool facts the burning, undiscourageable demon he had carried, vindicated Carson. For the sick feel as shamed as the sinful, as fallen.

The surgeon, with his Ivy League bearing, receded from that moment of extreme closeness when he had bent above Carson's agony and decided to handle his bowels. He dropped by in the course of his rounds only for brief tutorial sessions about eating and walking and going to the bathroom – all things that needed to be learned again. Others came forward. The slightly amused, dark Slavic woman returned, to change his dressing, yanking the tapes with a, he felt, unnecessary sharpness. 'You were too brave,' she admonished him, blaming him for the night when she had wanted to inflict more blood tests upon him. The shambling young doctor of that same night also returned, no longer in the slightest resembling the lawyer whom Carson's daughter had spurned in favor of her own sex, and then the very blond one; there materialized a host of specialists in one department of Carson's anatomy or another, so that he felt huge, like Gulliver pegged down in Lilliput for inspection. All of them paid their calls so casually and pleasantly – just dropping by, as it were – that Carson was amazed, months later, to find each visit listed by date and hour on the sheets of hospital services billed to him in extensive dot-matrix printout – an old Centronics 739 printer, from the look of it.

Hospital life itself, the details of it, made him happy. The taut white bed had hand controls that lifted and bent the mattress in a number of comforting ways. A television set had been mounted high on the wall opposite him and was obedient to a panel of buttons that nestled in his palm like an innocent, ethereal gun. Effortlessly he flicked his way back and forth among morning news shows, midmorning quiz shows, noon updates, and afternoon soap operas and talk shows and reruns of classics such as Carol Burnett and *Hogan's Heroes*. At night, when the visitors left the halls and the hospital settled in upon itself, the television set became an even warmer and more ingratiating companion, with its dancing colors and fluctuant radiance. His first evening in this precious room, while he was still groggy from anesthesia, Carson had watched a tiny white figure hit, as if taking a sudden great stitch, a high-arching home run into the second deck of Yankee Stadium; the penetration of the ball seemed delicious, and to be happening deep within the tiers of himself. He pressed the off button on the little control, used another button to adjust the tilt of his bed, and fell asleep as simply as an infant.

Normally, he liked lots of cover; here, a light blanket was enough. Normally, he could never sleep on his back; here, of necessity, he could sleep no other way, his body slightly turned to ease the vertical ache in his abdomen, his left arm at his side receiving all night long the nur-turing liquids of the I.V. tube. Lights always burned; voices always murmured in the hall; this world no more rested than the parental world beyond the sides of a crib.

In the depths of the same night when the home run was struck, a touch on his upper right arm woke Carson. He opened his eyes and there, in the quadrant of space where the rectangle of television had been, a queenly smooth black face smiled down upon him. She was a nurse taking his blood pressure; she had not switched on the overhead light in his room and so the oval of her face was illumined only indirectly, from afar, as had been the pieces of furniture in his hotel room. Without looking at the luminous dial of his wristwatch on the bedside table, he knew this was one of those abysmal hours when despair visits men, when insomniacs writhe in an ocean of silence, when the jobless and the bankrupt want to scream in order to break their circular calculations, when spurned lovers roll from an amorous dream onto empty sheets, and soldiers abruptly awake to the metallic taste of coming battle. In this hour of final privacy she had awakened him with her touch. No more than a thin blanket covered his body in the warm, dim room. *I forgive you*, her presence said. She pumped up a balloon around his arm, relaxed it, pumped it up again. She put into Carson's mouth one of those rocket-shaped instruments of textured plastic that have come to replace glass thermometers, and while waiting for his temperature to register in electronic numbers on a gadget at her waist she hummed a little tune, as if humorously to disavow her beauty, that beauty which women have now come to regard as an enemy, a burden and cause for harassment. Carson thought of his daughter.

Although many nurses administered to him – as he gained strength he managed to make small talk with them even at four in the morning – this particular one, her perfectly black and symmetrical face outlined like an eclipsed sun with its corona, never came again.

'Walk,' the surgeon urged Carson. 'Get up and walk as soon as you can. Get that body moving. It turns out it wasn't the disease used to kill a lot of people in hospitals, it was lying in bed and letting the lungs fill up with fluid.'

Walking meant, at first, pushing the spindly, rattling

I.V. pole along with him. There was a certain jaunty knack to it – easing the wheels over the raised metal sills here and there in the linoleum corridor, placing the left hand at the balance point he thought of as the pole's waist, swinging 'her' out of the way of another patient promenading with his own gangling chrome partner. From observing other patients Carson learned the trick of removing the I.V. bag and threading it through his bathrobe sleeve and rehanging it, so he could close his bathrobe neatly. His first steps, in the moss-green sponge slippers the hospital provided, were timid and brittle, but as the days passed the length of his walks increased: to the end of the corridor, where the windows of a waiting room overlooked the distant center of the city; around the corner, past a rarely open snack bar, and into an area of children's diseases; still farther, to an elevator bank and a carpeted lounge where pregnant women and young husbands drank Tab and held hands. The attendants at various desks in the halls came to know him, and to nod as he passed, with his lengthening stride and more erect posture. His handling of the I.V. pole became so expert as to feel debonair.

His curiosity about the city revived. What he saw from the window of his own room was merely the wall of another wing of the hospital, with gift plants on the windowsills and here and there thoughtful bathrobed figures gazing outward toward the wall of which his own bathrobed figure was a part. From the windows of the waiting room, the heart of the city with its clump of brown and blue skyscrapers and ribbonlike swirls of highway seemed often to be in sunlight, while clouds shadowed the hospital grounds and parking lots and the snarl of taxis around the entrance. Carson was unable to spot the hotel where he had stayed, or the industrial district where he had hoped to sell his systems, or the art museum that contained, he remembered reading, some exemplary Renoirs and a priceless Hieronymus Bosch. He could see at the base of the blue-brown mass of far buildings a suspension bridge, and imagined the dirty river it must cross, and the eighteenth-century fort that had been built here to hold the river against the Indians, and the nineteenth-century barge traffic that had fed the settlement and then its industries, which attracted immigrants, who thrust the grid of city streets deep into the surrounding farmland.

This was still a region of farmland; thick, slow, patient, pious voices drawled and twanged around Carson as he stood there gazing outward and eavesdropping. Laconic, semi-religious phrases of resignation fell into place amid the standardized furniture and slippered feet and pieces of jigsaw puzzles half assembled on card tables here. Fat women in styleless print dresses and low-heeled shoes had been called in from their kitchens, and in from the fields men with crosshatched necks and hands that had the lumpy, rounded look of used tools.

Illness and injury are great democrats, and had achieved a colorful cross section. Carson came to know by sight a lean man with cigardark skin and taut Oriental features; his glossy shaved head had been split by a Y-shaped gash now held together by stitches. He sat in a luxurious light-brown, almost golden robe, his wounded head propped by a hand heavy with rings, in the room with the pregnant women and the silver elevator doors. When Carson nodded once in cautious greeting, this apparition said loudly, 'Hey, man,' as if they shared a surprising secret. Through the open doorways of the rooms along the corridors, Carson glimpsed prodigies – men with beaks of white bandage and plastic tubing, like those drinking birds many fads ago; old ladies shrivelling to nothing in a forest of flowers and giant facetious get-well cards; and an immensely plump mocha-colored woman wearing silk pantaloons and a scarlet Hindu dot in the center of her forehead. She entertained streams of visitors – wispy, dusky men and great-eyed children. Like Carson, she was an honorary member of the city, and she would acknowledge his passing with a languid lifting of her fat fingers, tapered as decidedly as the incense cones on her night table.

The third day, he was put on solid food and disconnected from the intravenous tubing. With his faithful I.V. pole removed from the room, he was free to use both arms and to climb stairs. His surgeon at his last appearance (dressed in lumberjack shirt and chinos, merrily about to 'take off', for it had become the weekend) had urged stair climbing upon his patient as the best possible exercise. There was, at the end of the corridor in the other direction from the waiting room from whose windows the heart of the city could be viewed, an exit giving on a cement-and-steel staircase almost never used. Here, down four flights to the basement, then up six to the locked rooftop door, and back down two to his own floor, Carson obediently trod in his bathrobe and his by now disintegrating green sponge slippers.

His happiness was purest out here, in this deserted and echoing sector, where he was invisible and anonymous. In his room, the telephone had begun to ring. The head of his company back in New Jersey called repeatedly, at first to commiserate and then to engineer a way in which Carson's missed appointments could be patched without the expense of an additional trip. So Carson, sitting up on his adaptable mattress, placed calls to the appropriate personnel and gave an enfeebled version of his pitch; the white-noise company expressed interest in digital color-graphics imaging, and Carson mailed them his firm's shiny brochure on its newest system (resolutions to 640 pixels per line, 65,536 simultaneous colors, image memory up to 256 kilobytes). The secretary from the other company, who had sounded sympathetic on the phone five days ago, showed up in person; she turned out to be comely in a coarse way, with bleached, frizzed hair, the remnant of a swimming-pool tan, and active legs she kept crossing and recrossing as she described her own divorce – the money, the children, the return to work after years of being a pampered suburbanite. 'I could be one again, let me tell you. These women singing the joys of being in the work force, they can *have* it.' This woman smoked a great deal, exhaling noisily and crushing each cerise-stained butt into a jar lid she had brought in her pocketbook. Carson had planned his afternoon in careful half-hour blocks – the staircase, thrice up and down; a visit to the waiting room, where he had begun to work on one of the jigsaw puzzles; a visit to his bathroom if his handled bowels were willing; finally, a luxurious immersion in last month's *Byte* and the late innings of this Saturday's playoff game. His visitor crushed these plans along with her many cigarettes. Then his own ex-wife telephoned, kittenish the way she had become, remarried yet with something plaintive still shining through and with a note of mockery in her voice, as if his descending into a strange city with a bursting appendix was another piece of willful folly, like his leaving her and his ceasing to teach mathematics at the business school – all those tedious spread sheets. His son called collect from Mexico on Sunday, sounding ominously close at hand, and spacy, as long awkward silences between father and son ate up the dollars. His daughter never called, which seemed considerate and loving of her. She and Carson knew there was no disguising our essential solitude.

He found that after an hour in his room and bed he became homesick for the stairs. At first, all the flights had seemed identical, but by now he had discovered subtle differences among them – old evidence of spilled paint on one set of treads, a set of numbers chalked by a workman on the wall of one landing, water stains and cracks affecting one stretch of rough yellow plaster and not another. At the bottom, there were plastic trash cans and a red door heavily marked with warnings to push the crash bar only in case of emergency. At the top, a plain steel door, without handle or window, defied penetration. The doors at the landings in between each gave on a strange outdoor space, a kind of platform hung outside the door leading into the hospital proper; prepoured cement grids prevented leaping or falling or a clear outlook but admitted cool fresh air and allowed a fractional view of the city below.

The neighborhood here was flat and plain – quarter-acre-lot tract houses built long enough ago for the bloom of newness to have wilted and for dilapidation to be setting in. The hospital wall, extending beyond the projecting staircase, blocked all but a slice of downward vision containing some threadbare front yards, one of them with a tricycle on its side and another with a painted statue of the Virgin, and walls of pastel siding in need of repainting, and stretches of low-pitched composition-shingled roof – a shabby sort of small-town vista to Carson's eyes, but here well within the city limits. He never saw a person walking on the broad sidewalks, and few cars moved along the street even at homecoming hour. Nearest and most vivid, a heap of worn planking and rusting scaffold pipes and a dumpster coated with white dust and loaded with plaster and lathing testified to a new phase of construction as the hospital continued to expand. Young men sometimes came and added to the rubbish, or loudly threw the planking around. These efforts seemed unorganized, and ceased on the weekend.

The drab housing and assembled rubble that he saw through the grid of the cement barrier, which permitted no broader view, nevertheless seemed to Carson brilliantly real, moist and deep-toned and full. Life, this was life. This was the world. When – still unable to climb stairs, the I.V. pole at his side – he had first come to this landing, just shoving open the door had been an effort. The raw outdoor air had raked through his still-drugged system like a sweeping rough kiss, early-fall air mixing summer and winter, football and baseball, stiff with chill yet damp and not quite purged of growth. Once, he heard the distant agitation of a lawnmower. Until the morning when he was released, he would come here even in the dark and lean his forehead against the cement and breathe, trying to take again into himself the miracle of the world, reprogramming himself, as it were, to live – the air cold on his bare ankles, his breath a visible vapor, his bowels resettling around the ache of their healing.

The taxi took him straight to the airport; Carson saw nothing of the city but the silhouettes beside the highway and the highway's scarred center strip. For an instant after takeoff, a kind of map spread itself underneath him, and then was gone. Yet afterwards, thinking back upon the farm voices, the distant skyscrapers, the night visits of the nurses, the doctors with their unseen, unsullied homes, the dozens of faces risen to the surface of his pain, he seemed to have come to know the city intimately; it was like, on other of his trips, a woman who, encountered in a bar and paid at the end, turns ceremony inside out, and bestows herself without small talk.

BANANA
YOSHIMOTO

Newlywed

Once, just once, I met the most incredible person on the train. That was a while ago, but I still remember it vividly.

At the time, I was twenty-eight years old, and had been married to Atsuko for about one month.

I had spent the evening downing whiskey at a bar with my buddies and was totally smashed by the time I got on the train to head home. For some reason, when I heard them announce my stop, I stayed put, frozen in my seat.

It was very late, and I looked around and saw that there were only three other passengers in the car.

I wasn't so far gone that I didn't realize what I'd done. I had stayed on the train because I didn't really feel like going home.

In my drunken haze, I watched as the familiar platform of my station drew near. The train slowed down, and came to a stop. As the doors slid open, I could feel a blast of cool night air rush into the car, and then the doors again closed so firmly that I thought they had been sealed for all eternity. The train started to move, and I could see the neon signs of my neighborhood stores flash by outside the train window. I sat quietly and watched them fade into the distance.

A few stations later, the man got on. He looked like an old homeless guy, with ragged clothes, long, matted hair, and a beard – plus he smelled really strange. As if on cue, the other three passengers stood up and moved to neighboring cars, but I missed my chance to escape, and instead stayed where I was, seated right in the middle of the car. I didn't have a problem with the guy anyway, and even felt a trace of contempt for the other passengers, who had been so obvious about avoiding him.

Oddly enough, the old man came and sat right next to me. I held my breath and resisted the urge to look in his direction. I could see our reflections in the window facing us: the image of two men sitting side by side superimposed over the dazzling city lights and the dark of the night. I almost felt like laughing when I saw how anxious I looked there in the window.

'I suppose there's some good reason why you don't want to go home.' the man announced in a loud, scratchy voice.

At first, I didn't realize that he was talking to me, maybe because I was feeling so oppressed by the stench emanating from his body. I closed my eyes and pretended to be asleep, and then I heard him whisper, directly into my left ear, 'Would you like to tell me why you're feeling so reluctant about going home?'

There was no longer any mystery about whom he was addressing, so I screwed my eyes shut even more firmly. The rhythmical sound of the train's wheels clicking along the tracks filled my ears.

'I wonder if you'll change your mind when you see me like this,' he said.

Or I thought that's what he said, but the voice changed radically, and zipped up into a much higher pitch, as if someone had fast-forwarded a tape. This sent my head reeling, and everything around me seemed to rush into a different space, as the stench of the man's body disappeared, only to be replaced by the light, floral scent of perfume. My eyes still closed, I recognized a range of new smells: the warm fragrance of a woman's skin, mingled with fresh summer blossoms.

I couldn't resist; I had to take a look. Slowly, slowly, I opened my eyes, and what I saw almost gave me a heart attack. Inexplicably, there was a woman seated where the homeless guy had been, and the man was nowhere to be seen.

Frantic, I looked around to see if anyone else had witnessed this amazing transformation, but the passengers in the neighboring cars seemed miles away, in a totally different space, separated by a transparent wall, all looking just as tired as they had moments before, indifferent to my surprise. I glanced over at the woman again, and wondered what exactly had happened. She sat primly beside me, staring straight ahead.

I couldn't even tell what country she was from. She had long brown hair, gray eyes, gorgeous legs, and wore a black dress and black patent leather heels. I definitely knew that face from somewhere – like, maybe she was my favorite actress, or my first girlfriend, or a cousin, or my mother, or an older woman I'd lusted after – her face looked very familiar. And she wore a corsage of fresh flowers, right over her ample breasts.

I bet she's on her way home from a party, I thought, but then it occurred to me again that the old guy had disappeared. Where had he gone, anyway?

'You still don't feel like going home, do you?' she said, so sweetly that I could almost smell it. I tried convincing myself that this was nothing more than a drunken nightmare. That's what it was, an ugly duckling dream, a transformation from bum to beauty. I didn't understand what was happening, but I knew what I saw.

'I certainly don't, with you by my side.'

I was surprised at my own boldness. I had let her know exactly what I had on my mind. Even though the train had pulled in to another station and people were straggling on to the neighboring cars, not one single person boarded ours. No one so much as glanced our way, probably because they were too tired and preoccupied. I wondered if they wanted to keep riding and riding, as I did.

'You're a strange one,' the woman said to me.

'Don't jump to conclusions,' I replied.

'Why not?'

She looked me straight in the eye. The flowers on her breast trembled. She had incredibly thick eyelashes, and big, round eyes, deep and distant, which reminded me of the ceiling of the first planetarium I ever saw as a child: an entire universe enclosed in a small space.

'A minute ago, you were a filthy old bum.'

'But even when I look like this, I'm pretty scary, aren't I?' she said. 'Tell me about your wife.'

'She's petite.'

I felt as if I were watching myself from far away. What are you doing, talking to a stranger on a train? What is this, true confessions?

'She's short, and slender, and has long hair. And her eyes are real narrow, so she looks like she's smiling, even when she's angry.'

Then I'm sure she asked me, 'What does she do when you get home at night?'

'She comes down to meet me with a nice smile, as if she were on a divine mission. She'll have a vase of flowers on the table, or some sweets, and the television is usually on. I can tell that she's been knitting. She never forgets to put a fresh bowl of rice on the family altar every day. When I wake up on Sunday mornings, she'll be doing laundry, or vacuuming or chatting with the lady next door. Every day, she puts out food for the neighborhood cats, and she cries when she watches mushy TV shows.

'Let's see, what else can I tell you about Atsuko? She sings in the bath, and she talks to her stuffed animals when she's dusting them. On the phone with her friends, she laughs hard at anything they say, and, if it's one of her old pals from high school, they'll go on for hours. Thanks to Atsuko's ways, we have a happy home. In fact, sometimes it's so much fun at home that it makes me want to puke.'

After this grand speech of mine, she turned and nodded compassionately.

'I can picture it,' she said.

I replied, 'How could you? What do you know about these things?' to which she smiled broadly. Her smile was nothing like Atsuko's, but still it seemed awfully familiar to me. At that moment, a childhood memory flitted through my head: I'm walking to school with a friend, and we're still just little kids, so we're wearing the kind of school uniforms with shorts, instead of long pants. It's the dead of winter, and our legs are absolutely freezing, and we look at each other, about to complain about the cold, but then we just start laughing instead, because we both know that griping isn't going to make us any warmer. Scenes like that – smiles of mutual understanding – kept flashing through my mind, and I actually started having a good time, on my little train bench.

Then I heard her saying, 'How long have you been down here in Tokyo?'

Her question struck me as terribly odd. Why had she said it like that, 'down here in Tokyo'?

I asked her, 'Hey, are you speaking Japanese? What language are you using?'

She nodded again, and replied, 'It's not any language from any one country. They're just words that only you and I can understand. You know, like words you only use with certain people, like with your wife, or an old girlfriend, or your dad, or a friend. You know what I mean, a special type of language that only you and they can comprehend.'

'But what if more than two people are talking to one another?'

'Then there'll be a language that just the three of you can understand, and the words will change again if another person joins the conversation. I've been watching this city long enough to know that it's full of people like you, who left their hometowns and came here by themselves. When I meet people who are transplants from other places, I know that I have to use the language of people who never feel quite at home in this big city. Did you know that people who've lived all their lives in Tokyo can't understand that special language? If I run into an older woman who lives alone, and seems reserved, I speak to her in the language of solitude. For men who are out whoring, I use the language of lust. Does that make sense to you?'

'I guess so, but what if the old lady, the horny guy, you, and I all tried to have a conversation?'

'You don't miss anything, do you? If that were to happen, then the four of us would find the threads that tie us together, a common register just for us.'

'I get the idea.'

'To get back to my original question, how long have you been in Tokyo?'

'I came here when I was eighteen, right after my mother died, and I've been here ever since.'

'And your life with Atsuko, how's it been?'

'Well, actually, sometimes I feel like we live in totally different worlds, especially when she goes on and on about the minutiae of our daily lives, anything and everything, and a lot of it's meaningless to me. I mean, what's the big deal? Sometimes I feel like I'm living with the quintessential housewife. I mean, all she talks about is our home.'

A cluster of sharply delineated images floated into my mind: the sound of my mother's slippers pattering by my bed when I was very young, the trembling shoulders of my little cousin, who sat sobbing after her favorite cat died. I felt connected to them, despite their otherness, and found solace in the thought of their physical proximity.

'That's how it feels?'

'And how about you? Where are you headed?' I asked.

'Oh, I just ride around and observe. To me, trains are like a straight line with no end, so I just go on and on, you know. I'm sure that most people think of trains as safe little boxes that transport them back and forth between their homes and offices. They've got their commuter passes, and they get on and get off each day, but not me. That's how you think of trains, right?'

'As a safe box that takes me where I need to go, and then home?' I said. 'Sure I do, or I'd be too scared to get on the train in the morning – I'd never know where I'd end up.'

She nodded, and said, 'Of course, and I'm not saying that you should feel the way I do. If you – or anyone on this train, for that matter – thought of life as a kind of train, instead of worrying only about your usual destinations, you'd be surprised how far you could go, just with the money you have in your wallet right now.'

'I'm sure you're right.'

'That's the kind of thing I have on my mind when I'm on the train.'

'I wish I had that kind of time on my hands.'

'As long as you're on this train, you're sharing the same space with lots of different people. Some people spend the time reading, others look at the ads, and still others listen to music. I myself contemplate the potential of the train itself.'

'But I still don't understand what this transformation's all about.'

'I decided to do it because you didn't get off at your usual station and I wanted to find out why. What better way to catch your eye?'

My head was swimming. Who was this being, anyway? What were we talking about? Our train kept stopping and starting, slipping through the black of the night. And there I was, surrounded by the darkness, being carried farther and farther from my home.

This being sitting next to me felt somehow familiar, like the scent of a place, before I was born, where all the primal emotions, love and hate, blended in the air. I also could sense that I would be in danger if I got too close. Deep inside, I felt timid, even scared, not about my own drunkenness or fear that my mind was playing tricks on me, but the more basic sensation of encountering something much larger than myself, and feeling immeasurably small and insignificant by comparison. Like a wild animal would when confronted by a larger beast, I felt the urge to flee for my life.

In my stupor, I could hear her saying, 'You never have to go back to that station again, if you don't want to. That's one option.'

I guess she's right, I thought, but continued to sit there in silence. Rocked by the motion of the train and soothed by the rhythm of the wheels below, I closed my eyes and pondered the situation. I tried to imagine the station near my house and how it looked when I came home in the late afternoon. I recalled the masses of red and yellow flowers whose names I didn't know out in the plaza in front of the station. The bookstore across the way was always packed with people flipping through paperbacks and magazines. All I could ever see was their backs – at least, when I walked past from the direction of the station.

The delicious smell of soup wafted from the Chinese restaurant, and people lined up in front of the bakery, waiting to buy the special cakes they make there. A group of high school girls in their uniforms talk loudly and giggle as they walk ever so slowly across the plaza. It's weird that they're moving at such a leisurely pace. A burst of laughter rises from the group, and some teenage boys tense up as they walk past. One of the boys, though, doesn't even seem to notice the girls, and walks on calmly. He's a nice-looking guy, and I'd guess that he's popular with the girls. A perfectly made-up secretary passes by, yawning as she walks. She isn't carrying anything, so I imagine that she's on the way back to the office from an errand. I can tell that she doesn't want to go back to work; the weather's too nice for that. A businessman gulping down some vitamin beverage by the kiosk, other people waiting for friends. Some of them are reading paperbacks, others are people watching as they wait.

One finally catches sight of the friend she's been waiting for and runs to greet him. The elderly lady who walks slowly into my field of vision; the line of yellow and green and white taxis at the taxi stand that roar away from the station, one after another. The solid, weathered buildings nearby and the areas flanking the broad avenue.

And when I began to wonder what would happen if I never went back to that station, the whole image in my mind took on the quality of a haunting scene from an old movie, one fraught with meaning. All the living beings there suddenly became objects of my affection. Someday when I die, and only my soul exists, and my spirit comes home on a summer evening during the Bon Buddhist festival, that's probably what the world will look like to me.

And then Atsuko appears, walking slowly toward the station in the summer heat. She has her hair pulled back in a tight bun, even though I've told her that it makes her look dowdy. Her eyelids are so heavy that I wonder whether she can actually see anything, plus she's squinting now because of the glaring sun and her eyes have narrowed down to practically nothing. She's carrying a big bag instead of a shopping basket. She looks hungrily at the stuffed waffles in the little stall by the station, and even pauses for a moment as if she were going to stop and buy one, but then she changes her mind and walks into the drugstore instead. She stands for a long while in front of the shampoo section.

Come on, Atsuko, they're all the same. Just pick one. You look so serious! Shampoo is not something worth wasting time on. But she can't decide and keeps standing there, until a man rushing through the store bumps into her. Atsuko stumbles and then says she's sorry to the man. He bumped into you! You're not the one who should apologize. You should be as hard on him as you are on me.

Finally, Atsuko finds the perfect shampoo, and she takes it up to the cash register, where she starts chatting with the cashier. She's smiling sweetly. She leaves the store, a slender figure of a woman, becoming a mere black line as she recedes into the distance. A tiny black line. But I can tell that she's walking lightly, though slowly, and drinking in the air of this small town.

Our house is Atsuko's universe, and she fills it with small objects, all of her own choosing. She picks each of them as carefully as she did that bottle of shampoo. And then Atsuko comes to be someone who is neither a mother nor a wife, but an entirely different being.

For me, the beautiful, all-encompassing web spun by this creature is at once so polluted, yet so pure that I feel compelled to grab on to it. I am terrified by it but find myself unable to hide from it. At some point I have been caught up in the magical power she has.

'That's the way it is when you first get married.' Her words brought me back to my senses. 'It's scary to think of the day when you'll move beyond the honeymoon stage.'

'Yeah, but there's no point dwelling on it now. I'm still young. Thinking about it just makes me nervous.

I'm going home. I'll get off at the next station. At least I've sobered up a bit.'

'I had a good time,' she said.

'Me too,' I replied, nodding.

The train sped forward, unstoppable, like the grains of sand in an hourglass timing some precious event. A voice came booming out of the loudspeaker, announcing the next stop. We both sat there, not saying a word. It was hard for me to leave her. I felt as if we'd been together a very long time.

It seemed as if we had toured Tokyo from every possible angle, visiting each building, observing every person, and every situation. It was the incredible sensation of encountering a life force that enveloped everything, including the station near my house, the slight feeling of alienation I feel toward my marriage and work and life in general, and Atsuko's lovely profile. This town breathes in all the universes that people in this city have in their heads.

Intending to say a few more words, I turned in her direction only to find the dirty bum sleeping peacefully by my side. Our conversation had come to an end. The train sailed into the station, slowly, quietly, like a ship. I heard the door slide open, and I stood up.

Incredible man, farewell.

RON CARLSON

Reading the Paper

All I want to do is read the paper, but I've got to do the wash first. There's blood all over everything. Duke and the rest of the family except me and Timmy were killed last night by a drunk driver, run over in a movie line, and this blood is not easy to get out. Most of the fabrics are easy to clean, however, so I don't even bother reading the fine print on the Cheer box. They don't make this soap to work in all conditions anymore. Then I get Timmy up and ready for school. He eats two Hostess doughnuts and before he's even down the street and I've picked up the paper, I can hear him screaming down there. Somebody's dragging him into a late model Datsun, light brown, the kind of truck Duke, bless his soul, always thought was silly. So, I've got the paper in my hands and there's someone at the door. So few people come to the back door that I know it's going to be something odd, and I'm right. It's that guy in the paper who escaped from the prison yesterday. He wants to know if he can come in and rape me and cut me up a little bit. Well, after he does that, my coffee's cold, so I pour a new cup and am about to sit down when I see Douglas, my brother from Dill, drive in the driveway in his blue Scout, so I pour two cups. Douglas looks a little more blue this morning than a week ago. He started turning blue about a year before they found the bricks in his house were made out of Class Ten caustic poison or something. He's built a nice add-on or he and Irene, bless her soul, would have moved. But at least this morning, he's wearing an extra John Deere hat on the growth on his shoulder, so that's an improvement. He says he's heard about Duke and the three girls and he asks me, 'What were you all going to see?' I can barely hear him because I see two greasers backing Duke's new T-bird out the sidelawn. If they're not careful, they're going to hit the mailbox. They miss it and pull away; that car was always the prettiest turquoise in the world. I stir a little more Cremora into my coffee and turn to my blue brother. His left eye is a little worse, bulging more and glowing more often these days. You know, as much as I stir and stir this Cremora, there's always a little left floating on the top.

JUNOT DÍAZ

How to Date a Brown Girl

Wait until your brother, your sisters, and your mother leave the apartment. You've already told them that you were feeling too sick to go to Union City to visit that *tía* who likes to squeeze your nuts. (He's gotten big, she'll say.) And even though your moms knew you weren't sick you stuck to your story until finally she said, Go ahead and stay, *malcriado*.

Clear the government cheese from the refrigerator. If the girl's from the Terrace, stack the boxes in the crisper. If she's from the Park or Society Hill, then hide the cheese in the cabinet above the oven, where she'll never see it. Leave a reminder under your pillow to get out the cheese before morning or your moms will kick your ass. Take down any embarrassing photos of your family in the *campo*, especially that one with the half-naked kids dragging a goat on a rope. Hide the picture of yourself-with an Afro. Make sure the bathroom is presentable. Since your toilet can't flush toilet paper, put the bucket with all the crapped on toilet paper under the sink. Spray the bucket with Lysol, then close the lid.

Shower, comb, dress. Sit on the couch and watch TV. If she's an outsider her father will bring her, maybe her mother. Her parents won't want her seeing a boy from the Terrace – people get stabbed in the Terrace – but she's strong-headed and this time will get her way. If she's a white girl, you're sure you'll at least get a hand job.

The directions you gave her were in your best hand-writing, so her parents won't think you're an idiot. Get up from the couch and check the parking lot. Nothing. If the girl's local, don't sweat. She'll flow over when she's good and ready. Sometimes she'll run into her friends and a whole crowd will show up, and even though that means you ain't getting shit it will be fun anyway and you'll wish these people would come over more often. Sometimes the girl won't flow over at all and the next day in school she'll say, Sorry, and smile, and you'll believe her and be stupid enough to ask her out again.

You wait, and after an hour you go out to your corner. The neighborhood is full of traffic – commuters now cut through the neighborhood – making it hard on the kids and the *viejas*, who are used to empty streets. Give one of your friends a shout and when he says, Still waiting on that bitch? say, Hell, yeah.

Get back inside. Call her house and when her father picks up ask if she's there. If he sounds like a principal or a police chief, a dude with a big neck, someone who never has to watch his back, then hang up. Sit and wait. And wait. Until finally, just as your stomach is about to give out on you, a Honda, or maybe a Cherokee, will pull in and out she'll come.

Hey, she'll say.

Come on in, you'll say.

Look, she'll say. My mom wants to meet you. She's got herself all worried about nothing.

Don't panic. Say, Hey, no problem. Run a hand through your hair like the white boys do, even though the only thing that runs easily through your hair is Africa. She will look good. White girls are the ones you want most, aren't they? But the out-of-towners are usually black – black girls who grew up with ballet and Girl Scouts, and have three cars in their driveway. If she's a halfie don't be surprised that her mother is the white one. Say, Hi. She'll say, Hi, and you'll see that you don't scare her, not really. She will say that she needs easier directions to get out, and even though she already has the best directions on her lap, give her new ones. Make her happy.

If the girl's from the Terrace, none of this will happen.

You have choices. If the girl's from around the way, take her to El Cibao for dinner. Order everything in your busted up Spanish. Amaze her if she's black, let her correct you if she's Latina. If she's not from around the way, Wendy's will do. As you walk to the restaurant, talk about school. A local girl won't need stories about the neighborhood, but the others might. Tell her about the *pendejo* who stored cannisters of Army tear gas in his basement for years until one day they all cracked and the neighborhood got a dose of military-strength stuff. Don't tell her that your moms knew right away what it was, that she recognized the smell from the year the United States invaded your island.

Hope that you don't run into your nemesis, Howie, the Puerto Rican kid with the two killer mutts. He walks them all over the neighborhood, and every now and then the mutts corner a cat and tear it to shreds, as Howie laughs and the cat flips up in the air, its neck twisted around like an owl's, red meat showing through the soft fur. And if his dogs haven't cornered a cat, then he'll be behind you, asking, Is that your new fuckbuddy?

Let him talk. Howie weighs two hundred pounds and could eat you if he wanted. But at the field he'll turn away. He has new sneakers and doesn't want them muddy. If the girl's an outsider, that's when she'll hiss, What a fucking asshole. A homegirl would have been yelling back at him the whole time, unless she was shy. Either way, don't feel bad that you didn't do anything. Never lose a fight on a first date.

Dinner will be tense. You are not good at talking to people you don't know.

A halfie will tell you that her parents met in the Movement. Back then, she'll say, people thought it was a radical thing to do. It will sound like something her parents made her memorize. Your brother heard that one, too, and said, Sounds like a whole lot of Uncle Tomming to me. Don't repeat this.

Put down your hamburger and say, It must have been hard.

It was, she will say.

She'll appreciate your interest. She'll tell you more. Black people, she will say, treat me real bad. That's why I don't like them. You'll wonder how she feels about Dominicans. Don't ask. Let her speak on it and when you've finished eating, walk back through the neighborhood. The skies will be magnificent. Pollutants have made Jersey sunsets one of the wonders of the world. Point it out. Touch her shoulder and say, Isn't that nice?

Get serious. Watch TV, but stay alert. Sip some of the Bermudez your father left in the cabinet, which nobody touches. She'll drink enough to make her brave. A local girl will have hips and a nice ass but won't be quick about letting you touch her. She has to live in the same neighborhood as you do. She might just chill with you and then go home. She might kiss you and then leave. Or she might, if she's reckless, give it up, but that's rare. Kissing will suffice. A white girl might give it up right then. Don't stop her. She'll take her gum out of her mouth, stick it to the plastic sofa covers, and then move close to you. You have nice eyes, she might say.

Tell her that you love her hair, her skin, her lips,

because, in truth, you love them more than you love your own.

She'll say, I like Spanish guys, and even though you've never been to Spain, say, I like you. You'll sound smooth.

You'll be with her until about eight-thirty, and then she'll want to wash up. In the bathroom, she'll hum a song from the radio and her waist will keep the beat against the lip of the sink. Think of her old lady coming to get her, and imagine what she would say if she knew that her daughter had just lain under you and blown your name into your ear. While she's in the bathroom, you might call one of your boys and say, *Ya lo hice, cabrón.* Or sit back on the couch and smile.

But usually it won't work this way. Be prepared. She will not want to kiss you. Just cool it, she'll say. The halfie might lean back and push you away. She will cross her arms and say, I hate my tits. Pretend to watch the TV, and then turn to her to stroke her hair, even though you know she'll pull away again. I don't like anybody to touch my hair, she will say. She will act like somebody you don't know. In school, she is known for her attention-grabbing laugh, high and far-ranging like a gull's, but here she will worry you. You will not know what to say.

You're the only kind of guy who asks me out, she will say. Your neighbors will start their hyena calls, now that the alcohol is in them. She will say, You and the black boys.

HOW TO DATE A BROWN GIRL

You want to say, Who do you want to ask you out? But you already know. Let her button her shirt and comb her hair, the sound of it like a crackling fire between you. When her father pulls in and beeps, let her go without too much of a goodbye. She won't want it. During the next hour, the phone will ring. You will be tempted to pick it up. Don't. Watch the shows you want to watch, without a family around to argue with you. Don't go downstairs. Don't fall asleep. It won't help. Put the government cheese back in its place before your moms kills you.

NEIL JORDAN

Last Rites

One white-hot Friday in June at some minutes after five o'clock a young builder's labourer crossed an iron railway overpass, just off the Harrow Road. The day was faded now and the sky was a curtain of haze, but the city still lay hard-edged and agonisingly bright in the day's undiminished heat. The labourer as he crossed the overpass took note of its regulation shade of green. He saw an old, old negro immigrant standing motionless in the shade of a red-bricked wall. Opposite the wall, in line with the overpass, he saw the Victorian facade of Kensal Rise Baths. Perhaps because of the heat, or because of a combination of the heat and his temperament, these impressions came to him with an unusual clarity; as if he had seen them in a film or in a dream and not in real, waking life. Within the hour he would take his own life. And dying, a cut-throat razor in his hand, his blood mingling with the shower-water into the colour of weak wine he would take with him to whatever vacuum lay beyond, three memories: the memory of a green-painted bridge; of an old, bowed, shadowed negro; of the sheer tiled wall of a cubicle in what had originally been the wash-houses of Kensal Rise Tontine and Workingmen's Association, in what was now Kensal Rise Baths.

The extraordinary sense of nervous anticipation the labourer experienced had long been familiar with him. And, inexplicable. He never questioned it fully. He knew he anticipated something, approaching the baths. He knew that it wasn't quite pleasure. It was something more and less than pleasurable, a feeling of ravishing, private vindication, of exposure, of secret, solipsistic victory. Over what he never asked. But he knew. He knew as he approached the baths to wash off the dust of a week's labour, that this hour would be the week's high-point. Although during the week he never thought of it, never dwelt on its pleasures – as he did, for instance on his prolonged Saturday morning's rest – when the hour came it was as if the secret thread behind his week's existence was emerging into daylight, was exposing itself to the scrutiny of daylight, his daylight. The way the fauna of the sea-bed are exposed, when the tide goes out.

And so when he crossed the marble step at the door, when he faced the lady behind the glass counter, handing her sevenpence, accepting a ticket from her, waving his hand to refuse towel and soap, gesticulating towards the towel in his duffle-bag, each action was performed with the solemnity of an elaborate ritual, each action was a ring in the circular maze that led to the hidden purpose – the purpose he never elaborated, only felt; in his arm as he waved his hand; in his foot as he crossed the threshold. And when he walked down the corridor, with its white walls, its strange hybrid air, half unemployment exchange, half hospital ward, he was silent. As he took his place on the long oak bench, last in a line of negro, Scottish and Irish navvies his expression preserved the same immobility as theirs, his duffle-bag was kept between his feet and his rough slender hands between his knees and his eyes upon the grey cream wall in front of him. He listened to the rich, public voices of the negroes, knowing the warm colours of even their work-clothes without having to look. He listened to the odd mixture of reticence and resentment in the Irish voices. He felt the tiles beneath his feet, saw the flaking wall before him the hard oak bench beneath him, the grey-haired cockney caretaker emerging every now and then from the shower-hall to call 'Shower!', 'Bath!' and at each call the next man in the queue rising, towel and soap under one arm. So plain, so commonplace, and underneath the secret pulsing – but his face was immobile.

As each man left the queue he shifted one space forward and each time the short, crisp call issued from the cockney he turned his head to stare. And when his turn eventually came to be first in the queue and the cockney called 'Shower!' he padded quietly through the open door. He had a slow walk that seemed a little stiff, perhaps because of the unnatural straightness of his back. He had a thin face, unremarkable but for a kind of distance in the expression; removed, glazed blue eyes; the kind of inwardness there, of immersion, that is sometimes termed stupidity.

The grey-haired cockney took his ticket from him. He nodded towards an open cubicle. The man walked slowly through the rows of white doors, under the tiled roof to the cubicle signified. It was the seventh door down.

'Espera me, Quievo!'.

'Ore, deprisa, ha?'.

He heard splashing water, hissing shower-jets, the smack of palms off wet thighs. Behind each door he knew was a naked man, held timeless and separate under an umbrella of darting water. The fact of the walls, of the similar but totally separate beings behind those walls never ceased to amaze him; quietly to excite him. And the shouts of those who communicated echoed strangely through the long, perfectly regular hall. And he knew that everything would be heightened thus now, raised into the aura of the green light.

He walked through the cubicle door and slid the hatch into place behind him. He took in his surroundings with a slow familiar glance. He knew it all, but he wanted to be a stranger to it, to see it again for the first time, always the frst time: the wall, evenly gridded with white tiles, rising to a height of seven feet; the small gap between it and the ceiling; the steam coming through the gap from the cubicle next door; the jutting wall, with the full-length mirror affixed to it; behind it, enclosed by the plastic curtain, the shower. He went straight to the mirror and stood motionless before it. And the first throes of his removal began to come upon him. He looked at himself the way one would examine a flat-handled trowel, gauging its usefulness; or, idly, the way one would examine the cracks on a city pavement. He watched the way his nostrils, caked with cement-dust, dilated with his breathing. He watched the rise of his chest, the buttons of his soiled white work-shirt straining with each rise, each breath. He clenched his teeth and his fingers. Then he undressed, slowly and deliberately, always remaining in full view of the full-length mirror.

After he was unclothed his frail body with its thin ribs, hard biceps and angular shoulders seemed to speak to him, through its frail passive image in the mirror. He listened and watched.

Later it would speak, lying on the floor with open wrists, still retaining its goose-pimples, to the old cockney shower-attendant and the gathered bathers, every memory behind the transfixed eyes quietly intimated, almost revealed, by the body itself. If they had looked hard enough, had eyes keen enough, they would have known that the skin wouldn't have been so white but for a Dublin childhood, bread and margarine, cramped, carbonated air. The feet with the miniature half-moon scar on the right instep would have told, eloquently, of a summer spent on Laytown Strand, of barefoot walks on a hot beach, of sharded glass and poppies of blood on the summer sand. And the bulge of muscle round the right shoulder would have testified to two years hod-carrying, just as the light, nervous lines across the forehead proclaimed the lessons of an acquisitive metropolis, the glazed eyes themselves demonstrating the failure, the lessons not learnt. All the ill-assorted group of bathers did was pull their towels more rigidly about them, noting the body's glaring pubes, imagining the hair (blonde, maybe) and the skin of the girls that first brought them to life; the first kiss and the indolent smudges of lipstick and all the subsequent kisses, never quite recovering the texture of the first. They saw the body and didn't hear the finer details – just heard that it had been born, had grown and suffered much pain and a little joy; that its dissatisfaction had been deep; and they thought of the green bridge and the red-bricked walls and understood – .

He savoured his isolation for several full minutes. He allowed the cold seep fully through him, after the heat of clothes, sunlight. He saw pale, rising goose-pimples on the mirrored flesh before him. When he was young he had been in the habit of leaving his house and walking down to a busy sea-front road and clambering down from the road to the mud-flats below. The tide would never quite reach the wall and there would be stretches of mud and stone and the long sweep of the cement wall with the five-foot high groove running through it where he could sit, and he would look at the stone, the flat mud and the dried cakes of sea-lettuce and see the tide creep over them and wonder at their impassivity, their imperviousness to feeling; their deadness. It seemed to him the ultimate blessing and he would sit so long that when he came to rise his legs, and sometimes his whole body, would be numb. He stood now till his immobility, his cold, became near-agonising. Then he walked slowly to the shower, pulled aside the plastic curtain and walked inside. The tiles had that dead wetness that he had once noticed in the beach-pebbles. He placed each foot squarely on them and saw a thin cake of soap lying in a puddle of grey water. Both were evidence of the bather here before him and he wondered vaguely what he was like; whether he had a quick, rushed shower or a slow, careful one; whether he in turn had wondered about the bather before him. And he stopped wondering, as idly as he had begun. And he turned on the water.

It came hot. He almost cried with the shock of it; a cry of pale, surprised delight. It was a pet love with him, the sudden heat and the wall of water, drumming on his crown, sealing him magically from the world outside; from the universe outside; the pleasurable biting needles of heat; the ripples of water down his hairless arms; the stalactites gathering at each fingertip; wet hair, the sounds of caught breath and thumping water. He loved the pain, the total self-absorption of it and never wondered why he loved it; as with the rest of the weekly ritual – the trudge through the muted officialdom of the bath corridors into the solitude of the shower cubicle, the total ultimate solitude of the boxed, sealed figure, three feet between it and its fellow; the contradictory joy of the first impact of heat, of the pleasurable pain.

An overseer in an asbestos works who had entered his cubicle black and who had emerged with a white, blotchy, greyish skin-hue, divined the reason for the cut, wrists. He looked at the tiny coagulation of wrinkles round each eye and knew that here was a surfeit of boredom; not a moody, arbitrary, adolescent boredom, but that boredom which is a condition of life itself. He saw the way the mouth was tight and wistful and somehow uncommunicative, even in death, and the odour of his first contact with that boredom came back to him. He smelt again the incongruous fish-and-chip smells, the smells of the discarded sweet-wrappings, the metallic odour of the fun-palace, the sulphurous whiff of the dodgem wheels; the empty, musing, poignant smell of the seaside holiday town, for it was here that he had first met his boredom; here that he had wandered the green carpet of the golf-links, with the stretch of grey sky overhead, asking, what to do with the long days and hours, turning then towards the burrows and the long grasses and the strand; deciding there's nothing to do, no point in doing, the sea glimmering to the right of him like the dull metal plate the dodgem wheels ran on. Here he had lain in a sand-bunker for hours, his head making a slight indentation in the sand, gazing at the mordant procession of clouds above. Here he had first asked, what's the point, there's only point if it's fun, it's pleasure, if there's more pleasure than pain; then thinking of the pleasure, weighing up the pleasure in his adolescent scales; the pleasure of the greased fish-and-chip bag warming the fingers, of the sweet taken from the wrapper, the discarded wrapper and the fading sweetness, of the white flash of a pubescent girl's legs, the thoughts of touch and caress, the pain of the impossibility of both and his head digging deeper in the sand he had seen the scales tip in favour of pain. Ever so slightly maybe, but if it wins then what's the point. And he had known the sheep-white clouds scudding through the blueness and ever after thought of them as significant of the preponderance of pain; and he looked now at the white scar on the young man's instep and thought of the white clouds and thought of the bobbing girls' skirts and of the fact of pain – .

The first impact had passed; his body temperature had risen and the hot biting needles were now a running, massaging hand. And a silence had descended on him too, after the self-immersed orgy of the driving water. He knew this shower was all things to him, a world to him. Only here could he see this world, hold it in balance, so he listened to what was now the quietness of rain in the cubicle, the hushed, quiet sound of dripping rain and the green rising mist through which things are seen in their true, unnatural clarity. He saw the wet, flap-ping shower-curtain. There was a bleak rose-pattern on it, the roses faded by years of condensation into green: green roses. He saw the black spaces between the tiles, the plug-hole with its fading, whorling rivulet of water. He saw the exterior dirt washed off himself, the caked cement-dust, the flecks of mud. He saw creases of black round his elbow-joints, a high-water mark round his neck, the more permanent, ingrained dirt. And he lis-tened to the falling water, looked at the green roses and wondered what it would be like to see those things, hear them, doing nothing but see and hear them; nothing but the pure sound, the sheer colour reaching him; to be as passive as the mud pebble was to that tide. He took the cake of soap then from the grilled tray affixed to the wall and began to rub himself hard. Soon he would be totally, bleakly clean.

There was a dash of paint on his cheek. The negro painter he worked beside had slapped him playfully with his brush. It was disappearing now, under pressure from the soap. And with it went the world, that world, the world he inhabited, the world that left grit under the nails, dust under the eyelids. He scrubbed at the dirt of that world, at the coat of that world, the self that lived in that world, in the silence of the falling water. Soon he would be totally, bleakly clean.

The old cockney took another ticket from another bather he thought he recognised. Must have seen him last week. He crumpled the ticket in his hand, went inside his glass-fronted office and impaled it onto a six-inch nail jammed through a block of wood. He flipped a cigarette from its packet and lit it, wheezing heavily. Long hours spent in the office here, the windows running with condensation, had exaggerated a bronchial condition. He let his eyes scan the seventeen cubicles. He wondered again how many of them, coming every week for seventeen weeks, have visited each of the seventeen showers. None, most likely. Have to go where they're told, don't they. No way they can get into a different box other than the one that's empty, even if they should want to. But what are the chances, a man washing himself ten years here, that he'd do the full round? And the chances that he'd be stuck to the one? He wrinkled his eyes and coughed and rubbed the mist from the window to see more clearly.

White, now. Not the sheer white of the tiles, but a human, flaccid, pink skin-white. He stood upwards, let his arms dangle by his sides, his wrists limp. His short black hair was plastered to his crown like a tight skullcap. He gazed at the walls of his own cubicle and wondered at the fact that there were sixteen other cubicles around him, identical to this one, which he couldn't see. A man in each, washed by the same water, all in various stages of cleanliness. And he wondered did the form in the next cubicle think of him, his neighbour, as he did. Did he reciprocate his wondering. He thought it somehow appropriate that there should be men naked, washing themselves in adjacent cubicles, each a foreign country to the other. Appropriate to what, he couldn't have said. He looked round his cubicle and wondered: what's it worth, what does it mean, this cubicle – wondered was any one of the other sixteen gazing at his cubicle and thinking, realizing as he was: nothing. He realized that he would never know.

Nothing. Or almost nothing. He looked down at his body: thin belly, thin arms, a limp member. He knew he had arrived at the point where he would masturbate. He always came to this point in different ways, with different thoughts, by different stages. But when he had reached it, he always realised that the ways had been similar, the ways had been the same way, only the phrasing different. And he began then, taking himself with both hands, caressing himself with a familiar, bleak motion, knowing that afterwards the bleakness would only be intensified after the brief distraction of feeling – in this like everything – observing the while the motion of his belly muscles, glistening under their sheen of running water. And as he felt the mechanical surge of desire run through him he heard the splashing of an anonymous body in the cubicle adjacent. The thought came to him that somebody could be watching him. But no, he thought then, almost disappointed, who could, working at himself harder. He was standing when he felt an exultant muscular thrill run through him, arching his back, straining his calves upwards, each toe pressed passionately against the tiled floor.

The young Trinidadian in the next cubicle squeezed

out a sachet of lemon soft shampoo and rubbed it to a lather between two brown palms. Flecks of sawdust – he was an apprentice carpenter – mingled with the snow-white foam. He pressed two handfuls of it under each bicep, ladled it across his chest and belly and rubbed it till the foam seethed and melted to the colour of dull whey, and the water swept him clean again, splashed his body back to its miraculous brown and he slapped each nipple laughingly in turn and thought of a clean body under a crisp shirt, of a night of love under a low red-lit roof, of the thumping symmetry of a reggae band.

There was one intense moment of silence. He was standing, spent, sagging. He heard:

'Hey, you rass, not finished yet?'

'How'd I be finished?'

'Well move that corpse, rassman. Move!'

He watched the seed that had spattered the tiles be swept by the shower-water, diluting its grey, ultimately vanishing into the fury of current round the plug-hole. And he remembered the curving cement wall of his childhood and the spent tide and the rocks and the dried green stretches of sea-lettuce and because the exhaustion was delicious now and bleak, because he knew there would never be anything but that exhaustion after all the fury of effort, all the expense of passion and shame, he walked through the green-rose curtain and took the cut-throat razor from his pack and went back to the shower to cut his wrists. And dying, he thought of nothing more significant than the way, the way he had come here, of the green bridge and the bowed figure under the brick wall and the facade of the Victorian bath-house, thinking: there is nothing more significant.

Of the dozen or so people who gathered to stare – as people will – none of them thought: 'Why did he do it?' All of them, pressed into a still, tight circle, staring at the shiplike body, knew intrinsically. And a middle-aged, fat and possibly simple negro phrased the thought:

'Every day the Lord send me I think I do that. And every day the Lord send me I drink bottle of wine and forget 'bout doin' that'.

They took with them three memories: the memory of a thin, almost hairless body with reddened wrists; the memory of a thin, finely-wrought razor whose bright silver was mottled in places with rust; and the memory of a spurting shower-nozzle, an irregular drip of water. And when they emerged to the world of bright afternoon streets they saw the green-painted iron bridge and the red-brick wall and knew it to be in the nature of these, too, that the body should act thus –

HELEN GARNER

In Paris

The apartment was on the fourth floor. The building had no lift. On his day off the man lay on the mattress that served as a sofa and read, slowly and carefully, all the newspapers of his city. The tall windows were open on to the balcony. Every twenty minutes a bus swerved in to the stop down below, and the curtain puffed past his face. At two o'clock the woman came into the living room with her boots on.

'I feel like going for a walk,' she said.

'Bon. D'accord,' said the man.

'Want to come with me?'

'Tu vas où?'

'Up to Sacré Coeur and back. Not far.'

'Ouf,' said the man. 'All those steps.' He put one paper down and unfolded the next.

'Oh, come on,' said the woman. 'Won't you come? I'm bored.'

'I don't want to go down into the street,' said the man. 'I have to go down there every day. I get sick of it. Today I feel like staying home.'

The woman pulled a dead leaf off the potplant. 'Just for an hour?' she said.

'Too many tourists,' said the man. 'You go. I'll have a little sleep. Anyway it's going to rain.'

Late in the afternoon the man went into the kitchen and opened the refrigerator. He looked inside it, then shut it again. He walked across the squeaking parquet to the bedroom. The woman was lying on her stomach reading a book by the light of a shaded lamp. Her wet boots stood in the corner by the window.

'There's nothing to eat,' said the man. 'No-one went to the market.'

The woman looked up. 'What about the fish?'

'Yes, the fish is there.'

'We can eat the fish, then.'

'There's nothing to have with it.'

The woman marked her place with one finger.

'What happened to the brussels sprouts?' she said. 'Did the others eat them last night?'

'No.'

'Well, let's have fish and brussels sprouts.'

Before she had finished the sentence the man was shaking his head.

'Why not?'

'Fish and green vegetables are never eaten together.'

'What?'

'They are not eaten together.'

The woman closed the book. 'People have salad with fish. That's green.'

'Salad is different. Salad is a separate course. It is not served on the same plate.'

'Can you explain to me,' said the woman, 'the reason why fish and green vegetables must not be eaten together?'

The man looked at his hand against the white wall. 'It is not done,' he said. 'They do not complement each other. Fish and potatoes, yes. Frites. Pommes de terre au four. But not green vegetables.'

'It's getting on for dinner time,' said the woman. She turned on her back and clasped her hands behind her head. 'The others will be back soon.'

'I don't know what to do,' said the man. He moved his feet closer together and pushed his hands into his pockets.

'If I were you,' said the woman. 'If I were you and it was my turn to cook, and if there was nothing to eat except fish and green vegetables, do you know what I'd do? I'd cook fish and green vegetables. That's what I'd do.'

'Ecoute,' said the man. 'There are always good chemical and aesthetic reasons behind customs.'

'Yes, but what *are* they.'

'I'm sure if we looked it up in the *Larousse Gastronomique* it would be explained.'

The woman got off the low bed and went to the window in her socks and T shirt. She looked out.

'I'm hungry,' she said. 'Where I come from, we just eat what's there.'

'And it is not a secret,' said the man, 'that where you come from the food is barbaric.'

The woman kept her back to the room. 'My mother cooked nice food. We had nice meals.'

'Chops,' said the man. 'Hamburgers. I heard you telling my mother. "La bouffe est dégueulasse", you said. That's what you said.'

'I said "était". It was. It used to be. But it's not any more. It's not now.'

The man took a set of keys out of his pocket and began to flip them in and out of his palm.

'Aren't there any onions?' said the woman, still looking out the window.

'No. Not even onions.'

'I don't see,' said the woman, 'that you've got any choice. What choice have you got? Unless you cook the fish by itself, or just the sprouts.'

'There would not be enough for everybody.'

The woman turned round from the grey window. 'Why don't you go out into the kitchen and cook it up. Cook what's there. Just cook it up and see what happens. And if the others don't like it they can take their custom elsewhere.'

The man took a deep breath. He put the keys back in his pocket. He scratched his head until his hair stood up in a crest. 'J'ai mal fait mon marché,' he said. 'I should have planned better We should have – '

'For God's sake,' said the woman. She leaned against the closed window. 'What's the matter with you? It's only food.'

The man put his bare foot on the edge of the mattress and bounced it once, twice.

'Tu vois?' he said. 'Tu vois comment tu es? "Only food". No French person would ever, ever say "It's only food".'

'But it *is* only food,' said the woman. 'In the final analysis that's what it *is*. It's to keep us alive. It's to stop us from feeling hungry for a couple of hours so we can get our minds off our stomachs and go about our business. And all the rest is only decoration.'

'Oh là là,' said the man. 'Tu es – '

He flattened his hair with one hand, and let his hand fall to his side. Then he turned and walked back into the kitchen. He opened the refrigerator. The fish lay on its side on a white plate. He opened the cupboard under the window. The brussels sprouts, cupped in their shed outer leaves, sat on a paper bag on the bottom shelf. The man stood in the middle of the room and looked from one open door to the other, and back again.

JOYCE CAROL OATES

Happy

She flew home at Christmas, her mother and her mother's new husband met her at the airport. Her mother hugged her hard and told her she looked pretty, and her mother's new husband shook hands with her and told her, Yes she sure did look pretty, and welcome home. His sideburns grew razor sharp into his plump cheeks and changed color, graying, in the lower part of his face. In his handshake her hand felt small and moist, the bones close to cracking. Her mother hugged her again, God I'm so happy to see you, veins in her arms ropier than the girl remembered, the arms themselves thinner, but her mother was happy, you could feel it all about her.

The pancake makeup on her face was a fragrant peach shade that had been blended skillfully into her throat. On her left hand she wore her new ring: a small glittering diamond set high in spiky white-gold prongs.

They stopped for a drink at Easy Sal's off the expressway, the girl had a club soda with a twist of lime (*That's* fancy, her mother said), her mother and her mother's new husband had martinis on the rocks, which were their 'celebration' drinks. For a while they talked about what the girl was studying and what her plans were and when that subject trailed off they talked about their own plans, getting rid of the old house, that was one of the first chores, buying something smaller, newer, or maybe just renting temporarily. There's a new condominium village by the river, the girl's mother said, we'll show you when we drive past; then she smiled at something, took a swallow of her martini, squeezed the girl's arm, and leaned her head toward hers, giggling. Jesus, she said, it just makes me so happy, having the two people I love most in the world right here with me. Right here right now. A waitress in a tight-fitting black satin outfit brought two more martinis and a tiny glass bowl of beer nuts. Thanks sweetheart! her mother's new husband said.

The girl had spoken with her mother no more than two or three times about her plans to be remarried, always long distance, her mother kept saying Yes it's sudden in your eyes but this kind of thing always is, you know right away or you don't know at all. Wait and see. The girl said very little, murmuring Yes or I don't know or I suppose so. Her mother said in a husky voice He makes me feel like living again. I feel, you know, like a woman again, and the girl was too embarrassed to reply. As long as you're happy, she said.

Now it was nearly eight-thirty, and the girl was light-headed with hunger, but her mother and her mother's new husband were on their third round of drinks. Easy Sal's had entertainment, first a pianist who'd been playing background music, old Hoagy Carmichael favorites, then a singer, female, black, V-necked red spangled dress, then a comedian, a young woman of about twenty-six, small bony angular face, no makeup, punk hairdo, dark brown, waxed, black fake-leather jumpsuit, pelvis thrust forward in mock-Vogue-model stance, her delivery fast brash deadpan in the nature of mumbled asides, thinking aloud, as if the patrons just happened to over-hear, The great thing about havin' your abortion early in the day is, uh like y'know the rest of the day's uh gonna be fuckin uphill, right? There's these half-dozen people in a uh Jacuzzi, uh lesbians in a hot tub, hot new game called 'musical holes', uh maybe it just ain't caught on yet in New Jersey's why nobody's laughin', huh? the words too quick and muttered for the girl to catch but her mother and her mother's new husband seemed to hear, in any case they were laughing, though afterward her mother's new husband confided he did not approve of dirty language issuing from women's lips, whether they were dykes or not.

They stopped for dinner at a Polynesian restaurant ten

miles up the Turnpike, her mother explaining that there wasn't anything decent to eat at home, also it was getting late wasn't it, tomorrow she'd be making a big dinner, That's okay honey isn't it? She and her new husband quarreled about getting on the Turnpike then exiting right away, but at dinner they were in high spirits again, laughing a good deal, holding hands between courses, sipping from each other's tall frosted bright-colored tropical drinks. Jesus I'm crazy about that woman, her mother's new husband told the girl when her mother was in the powder room, Your mother is a high-class lady, he said. He shifted his cane chair closer, leaned moist and warm, meaty, against her, an arm across her shoulders. There's nobody in the world precious to me as that lady, I want you to know that, he said, and the girl said Yes I know it, and her mother's new husband said it in a fierce voice close to tears, Damn right, sweetheart: you know it.

SALMAN RUSHDIE

The Free Radio

We all knew nothing good would happen to him while the thief's widow had her claws dug into his flesh, but the boy was an innocent, a real donkey's child, you can't teach such people.

That boy could have had a good life. God had blessed him with God's own looks, and his father had gone to the grave for him, but didn't he leave the boy a brand-new first-class cycle rickshaw with plastic covered seats and all? So: looks he had, his own trade he had, there would have been a good wife in time, he should just have taken out some years to save some rupees; but no, he must fall for a thief's widow before the hairs had time to come out on his chin, before his milk-teeth had split, one might say.

We felt bad for him, but who listens to the wisdom of the old today?

I say: who listens?

Exactly; nobody, certainly not a stone-head like Ramani the rickshaw-wallah. But I blame the widow. I saw it happen, you know, I saw most of it until I couldn't stand any more. I sat under this very banyan, smoking this self-same hookah, and not much escaped my notice.

And at one time I tried to save him from his fate, but it was no go . . .

The widow was certainly attractive, no point denying, in a sort of hard vicious way she was all right, but it is her mentality that was rotten. Ten years older than Ramani she must have been, five children alive and two dead, what that thief did besides robbing and making babies God only knows, but he left her not one new paisa, so of course she would be interested in Ramani. I'm not saying a rickshaw-wallah makes much in this town but two mouthfuls are better to eat than wind. And not many people will look twice at the widow of a good-for-nothing.

They met right here.

One day Ramani rode into town without a passenger, but grinning as usual as if someone had given him a ten-chip tip, singing some playback music from the radio, his hair greased like for a wedding. He was not such a fool that he didn't know how the girls watched him all the time and passed remarks about his long and well-muscled legs.

The thief's widow had gone to the bania shop to buy some three grains of dal and I won't say where the money came from, but people saw men at night near her rutputty shack, even the bania himself they were telling me but I personally will not comment.

She had all her five brats with her and then and there, cool as a fan, she called out: *'Hey! Rickshaaa!'* Loud, you know, like a truly cheap type. Showing us she can afford to ride in rickshaws, as if anyone was interested. Her children must have gone hungry to pay for the ride but in my opinion it was an investment for her, because must-be she had decided already to put her hooks into Ramani. So they all poured into the rickshaw and he took her away, and with the five kiddies as well as the widow there was quite a weight, so he was puffing hard, and the veins were standing out on his legs, and I thought, careful, my son, or you will have this burden to pull for all of your life.

But after that Ramani and the thief's widow were seen everywhere, shamelessly, in public places, and I was glad his mother was dead because if she had lived to see this her face would have fallen off from shame.

Sometimes in those days Ramani came into this street in the evenings to meet some friends, and they thought they

were very smart because they would go into the back
room of the Irani's canteen and drink illegal liquor, only
of course everybody knew, but who would do anything,
if boys ruin their lives let their relations worry.

I was sad to see Ramani fall into this bad company.
His parents were known to me when alive. But when I
told Ramani to keep away from those hot-shots he
grinned like a sheep and said I was wrong, nothing bad
was taking place.

Let it go, I thought.

I knew those cronies of his. They all wore the armbands of the new Youth Movement. This was the time
of the State of Emergency, and these friends were not
peaceful persons, there were stories of beatings-up, so I
sat quiet under my tree. Ramani wore no armband but
he went with them because they impressed him, the fool.

These armband youths were always flattering Ramani.
Such a handsome chap, they told him, compared to you
Shashi Kapoor and Amitabh are like lepers only, you
should go to Bombay and be put in the motion pictures.

They flattered him with dreams because they knew
they could take money from him at cards and he would
buy them drink while they did it, though he was no
richer than they. So now Ramani's head became filled
with these movie dreams, because there was nothing else
inside to take up any space, and this is another reason
why I blame the widow woman, because she had more
years and should have had more sense. In two ticks she

could have made him forget all about it, but no, I heard her telling him one day for all to hear, 'Truly you have the looks of Lord Krishna himself, except you are not blue all over.' In the street! So all would know they were lovers! From that day on I was sure a disaster would happen.

The next time the thief's widow came into the street to visit the bania shop I decided to act. Not for my own sake but for the boy's dead parents I risked being shamed by a . . . no, I will not call her the name, she is elsewhere now and they will know what she is like.

'Thief's widow!' I called out.

She stopped dead, jerking her face in an ugly way, as if I had hit her with a whip.

'Come here and speak,' I told her.

Now she could not refuse because I am not without importance in the town and maybe she calculated that if people saw us talking they would stop ignoring her when she passed, so she came as I knew she would.

'I have to say this thing only,' I told her with dignity. 'Ramani the rickshaw boy is dear to me, and you must find some person of your own age, or, better still, go to the widows' ashrams in Benares and spend the rest of your life there in holy prayer, thanking God that widow-burning is now illegal.'

So at this point she tried to shame me by screaming out and calling me curses and saying that I was a poisonous old man who should have died years ago, and then she said, 'Let me tell you, mister teacher sahib *retired*, that your Ramani has asked to marry me and I have said no, because I wish no more children, and he is a young man and should have his own. So tell that to the whole world and stop your cobra poison.'

For a time after that I closed my eyes to this affair of Ramani and the thief's widow, because I had done all I could and there were many other things in the town to interest a person like myself. For instance, the local health officer had brought a big white caravan into the street and was given permission to park it out of the way under the banyan tree; and every night men were taken into this van for a while and things were done to them.

I did not care to be in the vicinity at these times, because the youths with armbands were always in attendance, so I took my hookah and sat in another place. I heard rumours of what was happening in the caravan but I closed my ears.

But it was while this caravan, which smelled of ether, was in town that the extent of the widow's wickedness became plain; because at this time Ramani suddenly began to talk about his new fantasy, telling everyone he could find that very shortly he was to receive a highly special and personalised gift from the Central Government in Delhi itself, and this gift was to be a brand-new first-class battery-operated transistor radio.

Now then: we had always believed that our Ramani was

a little soft in the head, with his notions of being a film star and what all; so most of us just nodded tolerantly and said, 'Yes, Ram, that is nice for you,' and, 'What a fine, generous Government it is that gives radios to persons who are so keen on popular music.'

But Ramani insisted it was true, and seemed happier than at any time in his life, a happiness which could not be explained simply by the supposed imminence of the transistor.

Soon after the dream-radio was first mentioned, Ramani and the thief's widow were married, and then I understood everything. I did not attend the nuptials – it was a poor affair by all accounts – but not long afterwards I spoke to Ram when he came past the banyan with an empty rickshaw one day.

He came to sit by me and I asked, 'My child, did you go to the caravan? What have you let them do to you?'

'Don't worry,' he replied. 'Everything is tremendously wonderful. I am in love, teacher sahib, and I have made it possible for me to marry my woman.'

I confess I became angry; indeed, I almost wept as I realised that Ramani had gone voluntarily to subject himself to a humiliation which was being forced upon the other men who were taken to the caravan. I reproved him bitterly. 'My idiot child, you have let that woman deprive you of your manhood!'

'It is not so bad,' Ram said, meaning the *nasbandi*. 'It does not stop love-making or anything, excuse me, teacher sahib, for speaking of such a thing. It stops babies only and my woman did not want children any more, so now all is hundred per cent OK. Also it is in national interest,' he pointed out. 'And soon the free radio will arrive.'

'The free radio,' l repeated.

'Yes, remember, teacher sahib,' Ram said confidentially, 'some years back, in my kiddie days, when Laxman the tailor had this operation? In no time the radio came and from all over town people gathered to listen to it. It is how the Government says thank you. It will be excellent to have.'

'Go away, get away from me,' I cried out in despair, and did not have the heart to tell him what everyone else in the country already knew, which was that the free radio scheme was a dead duck, long gone, long forgotten. It had been over – *funtoosh!* – for years.

———

After these events the thief's widow, who was now Ram's wife, did not come into town very often, no doubt being too ashamed of what she had made him do, but Ramani worked longer hours than ever before, and every time he saw any of the dozens of people he'd told about the radio he would put one hand up to his ear as if he were already holding the blasted machine in it, and he would mimic broadcasts with a certain energetic skill.

'*Yé Akashuani hai*,' he announced to the streets. 'This is All-India Radio. Here is the news. A Government spokesman today announced that Ramani rickshaw-wallah's radio was on its way and would be delivered at any moment. And now some playback music.' After which he would sing songs by Asha Bhonsle or Lata Mangeshkar in a high, ridiculous falsetto.

Ram always had the rare quality of total belief in his dreams, and there were times when his faith in the imaginary radio almost took us in, so that we half-believed it was really on its way, or even that it was already there, cupped invisibly against his ear as he rode his rickshaw around the streets of the town. We began to expect to hear Ramani, around a corner or at the far end of a lane, ringing his bell and yelling cheerfully:

'All-India Radio! This is All-India Radio!'

———

Time passed. Ram continued to carry the invisible radio around town. One year passed. Still his caricatures of the radio channel filled the air in the streets. But when I saw him now, there was a new thing in his face, a strained thing, as if he were having to make a phenomenal effort, which was much more tiring than driving a rickshaw, more tiring even than pulling a rickshaw containing a thief's widow and her five living children and the ghosts of two dead ones; as if all the energy of his young body was being poured into that fictional space between his ear and his hand, and he was trying to bring the radio into existence by a mighty, and possibly fatal, act of will.

I felt most helpless, I can tell you, because I had divined that Ram had poured into the idea of the radio all his worries and regrets about what he had done, and that if the dream were to die he would be forced to face the full gravity of his crime against his own body, to understand that the thief's widow had turned him, before she married him, into a thief of a stupid and terrible kind, because she had made him rob himself.

And then the white caravan came back to its place under the banyan tree and I knew there was nothing to be done, because Ram would certainly come to get his gift.

————

He did not come for one day, then for two, and I learned afterwards that he had not wished to seem greedy; he didn't want the health officer to think he was desperate for the radio. Besides, he was half hoping they would come over and give it to him at his place, perhaps with some kind of small, formal presentation ceremony. A fool is a fool and there is no accounting for his notions.

On the third day he came. Ringing his bicycle-bell and imitating weather forecasts, ear cupped as usual, he arrived at the caravan. And in the rickshaw behind him sat the thief's widow, the witch, who had not been able to resist coming along to watch her companion's destruction.

It did not take very long.

Ram went into the caravan gaily, waving at his arm-banded cronies who were guarding it against the anger of the people, and I am told – for I had left the scene to spare myself the pain – that his hair was well-oiled and his clothes were freshly starched. The thief's widow did not move from the rickshaw, but sat there with a black sari pulled over her head, clutching at her children as if they were straws.

After a short time there were sounds of disagreement inside the caravan, and then louder noises still, and finally the youths in armbands went in to see what was becoming, and soon after that Ram was frogmarched out by his drinking-chums, and his hair-grease was smudged on to his face and there was blood coming from his mouth. His hand was no longer cupped by his ear.

And still – they tell me – the thief's black widow did not move from her place in the rickshaw, although they dumped her husband in the dust.

Yes, I know, I'm an old man, my ideas are wrinkled with age, and these days they tell me sterilisation and God knows what is necessary, and maybe I'm wrong to blame the widow as well – why not? Maybe all the views of the old can be discounted now, and if that's so, let it be. But I'm telling this story and I haven't finished yet.

Some days after the incident at the caravan I saw Ramani selling his rickshaw to the old Muslim crook who runs the bicycle-repair shop. When he saw me watching, Ram came to me and said, 'Goodbye, teacher sahib, I am off to Bombay, where I will become a bigger film star than Shashi Kapoor or Amitabh Bachchan even.'

' "*I* am off", you say?' I asked him. 'Are you perhaps travelling alone?'

He stiffened. The thief's widow had already taught him not to be humble in the presence of elders.

'My wife and children will come also,' he said. It was the last time we spoke. They left that same day on the down train.

After some months had passed I got his first letter, which was not written by himself, of course, since in spite of all my long-ago efforts he barely knew how to write. He had paid a professional letter-writer, which must have cost him many rupees, because everything in life costs money and in Bombay it costs twice as much. Don't ask me why he wrote to me, but he did. I have the letters and can give you proof positive, so maybe there are some uses for old people still, or maybe he knew I was the only one who would be interested in his news.

Anyhow: the letters were full of his new career, they told me how he'd been discovered at once, a big studio had given him a test, now they were grooming him for stardom, he spent his days at the Sun'n'Sand Hotel at Juhu beach in the company of top lady artistes, he was buying a big house at Pali Hill, built in the split-level mode and incorporating the latest security equipment to protect him from the movie fans, the thief's widow was well and happy and getting fat, and life was filled with light and success and no-questions-asked alcohol.

They were wonderful letters, brimming with confidence, but whenever I read them, and sometimes I read them still, I remember the expression which came over his face in the days just before he learned the truth about his radio, and the huge mad energy which he had poured into the act of conjuring reality, by an act of magnificent faith, out of the hot thin air between his cupped hand and his ear.

TOBIAS WOLFF

Next Door

I wake up afraid. My wife is sitting on the edge of my bed, shaking me. 'They're at it again,' she says.

I go to the window. All their lights are on, upstairs and down, as if they have money to burn. He yells, she screams something back, the dog barks. There is a short silence, then the baby cries, poor thing.

'Better not stand there,' says my wife. 'They might see you.'

I say, 'I'm going to call the police,' knowing she won't let me.

'Don't,' she says.

She's afraid that they will poison our cat if we complain.

Next door the man is still yelling, but I can't make out what he's saying over the dog and the baby. The woman laughs, not really meaning it, *'Ha! Ha! Ha!,'* and suddenly gives a sharp little cry. Everything goes quiet.

'He struck her,' my wife says. 'I felt it just the same as if he struck me.'

Next door the baby gives a long wail and the dog starts up again. The man walks out into his driveway and slams the door.

'Be careful,' my wife says. She gets back into her bed and pulls the covers up to her neck.

The man mumbles to himself and jerks at his fly. Finally he gets it open and walks over to our fence. It's a white picket fence, ornamental more than anything else. It couldn't keep anyone out. I put it in myself, and planted honeysuckle and bougainvillea all along it.

My wife says, 'What's he doing?'

'Shh.' I say.

He leans against the fence with one hand and with the other he goes to the bathroom on the flowers. He walks the length of the fence like that, not missing any of them. When he's through he gives Florida a shake, then zips up and heads back across the driveway. He almost slips on the gravel but he catches himself and curses and goes into the house, slamming the door again.

When I turn around my wife is leaning forward, watching me. She raises her eyebrows. 'Not again,' she says.

I nod.

'Number one or number two?'

'Number one.'

'Thank God for small favors,' she says, settling back. 'Between him and the dog it's a wonder you can get anything to grow out there.'

I read somewhere that human pee has a higher acid content than animal pee, but I don't mention that. I would rather talk about something else. It depresses me, thinking about the flowers. They are past their prime, but still. Next door the woman is shouting. 'Listen to that,' I say.

'I used to feel sorry for her,' my wife says. 'Not any more. Not after last month.'

'Ditto,' I say, trying to remember what happened last month to make my wife not feel sorry for the woman next door. I don't feel sorry for her either, but then I never have. She yells at the baby, and excuse me, but I'm not about to get all excited over someone who treats a child like that. She screams things like '*I thought I told you to stay in your bedroom!*' and here the baby can't even speak English yet.

As far as her looks; I guess you would have to say she's pretty. But it won't last. She doesn't have good bone structure. She has a soft look to her, like she has never eaten anything but donuts and milk shakes. Her skin is white. The baby takes after her, not that you would expect it to take after *him*, dark and hairy. Even with his shirt on you can tell that he has hair all over his back and on his shoulders, thick and springy like an Airedale's.

Now they're all going at once over there, plus they've

got the hi-fi turned on full blast. One of those bands. 'It's the baby I feel sorry for,' I say.

My wife puts her hands over her ears. 'I can't stand another minute of it,' she says. She takes her hands away. 'Maybe there's something on TV.' She sits up. 'See who's on Johnny.'

I turn on the television. It used to be down in the den but I brought it up here a few years ago when my wife came down with an illness. I took care of her myself – made the meals and everything. I got to where I could change the sheets with her still in the bed. I always meant to take the television back down when my wife recovered from her illness, but I never got around to it. It sits between our beds on a little table I made. Johnny is saying something to Sammy Davis, Jr. Ed McMahon is bent over laughing. He is always so cheerful. If you were going to take a really long voyage you could do worse than bring Ed McMahon along.

'Sammy,' says my wife. 'Who else is on besides Sammy?'

I look at the TV guide. 'A bunch of people I never heard of.' I read off their names. My wife hasn't heard of them either. She wants to know what else is on. ' "*El Dorado*",' I read. ' "Brisk adventure yarn about a group of citizens in search of the legendary city of gold".' It's got two-and-a-half stars beside it.'

'Citizens of what?' my wife asks.

'It doesn't say.'

Finally we watch the movie. A blind man comes into

a small town. He says that he has been to El Dorado, and that he will lead an expedition there for a share of the proceeds. He can't see, but he will call out the landmarks one by one as they ride. At first people make fun of him, but eventually all the leading citizens get together and decide to give it a try. Right away they get attacked by Apaches and some of them want to turn back, but every time they get ready the blind man gives them another landmark so they keep riding.

Next door the woman is going crazy. She is saying things to him that no person should ever say to another person. It makes my wife restless. She looks at me. 'Can I come over?' she says. 'Just for a visit?'

I pull down the blankets and she gets in. The bed is just fine for one, but for two of us it's a tight fit. We are lying on our sides with me in back. I don't mean for it to happen but before long old Florida begins to stiffen up on me. I put my arms around my wife. I move my hands up onto the Rockies, then on down across the Plains, heading South.

'Hey,' she says. 'No Geography. Not tonight.'

'I'm sorry,' I say.

'Can't I just visit?'

'Forget it. I said I was sorry.'

The citizens are crossing a desert. They have just about run out of water, and their lips are cracked. Though the blind man has delivered a warning, someone drinks from a poisoned well and dies horribly. That night, around the campfire, the others begin to quarrel.

Most of them want to go home. 'This is no country for a white man,' one says, 'and if you ask me nobody has ever been here before.' But the blind man describes a piece of gold so big and pure that it will burn your eyes out if you look directly at it. 'I ought to know,' he says. When he is finished the citizens are silent: one by one they move away and lie down on their bedrolls. They put their hands behind their heads and look up at the stars. A coyote howls.

Hearing the coyote, l remember why my wife doesn't feel sorry for the woman next door. It was a Monday evening, about a month ago, right after I got home from work. The man next door started to beat the dog, and I don't mean just smacking him once or twice. He was beating him, and he kept beating him until the dog couldn't even cry any more; you could hear the poor creature's voice breaking. It made us very upset, especially my wife, who is an animal lover from way back. Finally it stopped. Then, a few minutes later, I heard my wife say, 'Oh!' and I went into the kitchen to find out what was wrong. She was standing by the window, which looks into the kitchen next door. The man had his wife backed up against the fridge. He had his knee between her legs and she had her knee between his legs and they were kissing, really hard, not just with their lips but rolling their faces back and forth one against the other. My wife could hardly speak for a couple of hours afterwards. Later she said that she would never waste her sympathy on that woman again.

It's quiet over there. My wife has gone to sleep and so has my arm, which is under her head. I slide it out and open and close my fingers, considering whether to wake her up. I like sleeping in my own bed, and there isn't enough room for the both of us. Finally I decide that it won't hurt anything to change places for one night.

I get up and fuss with the plants for a while, watering them and moving some to the window and some back, I trim the coleus, which is starting to get leggy, and put the cuttings in a glass of water on the sill. All the lights are off next door except the one in their bedroom window. I think about the life they have, and how it goes on and on, until it seems like the life they were meant to live. Everybody is always saying how great it is that human beings are so adaptable, but I don't know. A friend of mine was in the Navy and he told me that in Amsterdam, Holland, they have a whole section of town where you can walk through and from the street you can see women sitting in rooms, waiting. If you want one of them you just go in and pay, and they close the drapes. This is nothing special to the people who live in Holland. In Istanbul, Turkey, my friend saw a man walking down the street with a grand piano on his back. Everyone just moved around him and kept going. It's awful, what we get used to.

I turn off the television and get into my wife's bed. A sweet, heavy smell rises off the sheets. At first it makes me dizzy but after that I like it. It reminds me of gardenias.

The reason I don't watch the rest of the movie is that I can already see how it will end. The citizens will kill each other off, probably about ten feet from the legendary city of gold, and the blind man will stumble in by himself, not knowing that he has made it back to El Dorado.

I could write a better movie than that. My movie would be about a group of explorers, men and women, who leave behind their homes and their jobs and their families – everything they have known. They cross the sea and are shipwrecked on the coast of a country which is not on their maps. One of them drowns. Another gets attacked by a wild animal, and eaten. But the others want to push on. They ford rivers and cross an enormous glacier by dog sled. It takes months. On the glacier they run out of food, and for a while there it looks like they might turn on each other, but they don't. Finally they solve their problem by eating the dogs. That's the sad part of the movie.

At the end we see the explorers sleeping in a meadow filled with white flowers. The blossoms are wet with dew and stick to their bodies, petals of columbine, clematis, blazing star, baby's breath, larkspur, iris, rue – covering them completely, turning them white so that you cannot tell one from another, man from woman, woman from man. The sun comes up. They stand and raise their arms, like white trees in a land where no one has ever been.

BARRY HANNAH

That's True

I'll never forget the summer old Lardner went up to New York with forged credits as a psychiatrist. He'd been studying in med school with designs of becoming a psychiatrist. Then he got into the modern psychiatric scene, had enough of it, and having no other employment for the summer, he went up to New York all fit out with thick glasses and a mustache and an ailing gnarled hand, which he was of course putting on too. He said people in therapy got close to a shrink with an outstanding defect. He had a few contacts, and before you knew it, he was all set up in his office, five phony pieces of paper on the wall.

Old Lardner, I never knew what his real voice was, he had so many, though I knew he came from Louisiana like me. He loved Northerners – Jew, Navajo and nigger alike. He was a broad soul with no spleen in his back pocket for anybody. Except whiners who knew better. You ought to hear some of the tapes he brought back. He never taped anybody without their knowledge of it.

All of them *liked* to be taped, Lardner said.

It was their creativity.

They went like this:

Patient: I feel ugly all the time. I can't quit cigarettes. The two Great Danes I bought won't mate. I'm starting to cry over sentimental things, songs on the radio. Is it basically wrong for a man to like macramé? I never feel intimate with anybody until we talk about Nixon, how awful he was. My kid looks away when I give him an order. I mean a gentle order. Let me take a breath.

Lardner: Jesus Damn Christ! What an *interesting* case! Your story takes the ticket. This is beyond trouble, Mr. _____, this is *art*!

Patient: What? My story *art*?

Lardner: Yes. You *are* ugly. But so very important.

Patient: You think so?

And so on.

The next one might go:

Patient: I'm angry, angry, Doctor Lardner.

Lardner: Why?

Patient: Because I'm a woman. I've taken such evil crap over the years.

Lardner: Why?

Patient: I thought you'd want to know *what*.

Lardner: You got the wrong doctor. Down on Fifth Avenue, about a dozen doors away, there's a good *what* doctor. A little more expensive.

Patient: I'm so angry at men everywhere. Nothing will ever cure me of this hatred.

Lardner: You're wasting money on me. I'm a man.

Patient: But with time, you and I might produce a cure for me.

Lardner: Well, we can start with your basic remedy and work out from there. How about a glass of pure gin on the rocks and a hard dick? (*Sounds of fistfight between Lardner and patient.*) You hit my gnarled hand!

Patient: Oh, I'm so sorry! Christ! I didn't want to.

Lardner: I think you did.

Patient: I . . . yes! I did! We've produced a cure together. You work so fast. (*Sounds of slipped-off panties.*) Have me, have! Let me make up for the hand!

And the only other one I recall:

Patient: It's the end of the world. It's the Big Fight.

I read the *Times* on the subway, and think about my people, the Jews. I think of my good job and prosperity. The oil issue is going to wipe Israel out in ten years. There won't be an Israel. My people will be raped and burned over. And I want to fight. I want to leave Westchester County and fight. I want to bear arms and defend Israel. How can I stand walking around the streets of this town, this loud confusing city, when there are issues so clear-cut?

Lardner: Shit, I don't know. Why don't you fly out tomorrow morning?

When Lardner came back home to the South, he invited me over for a drink in his backyard at Baton Rouge. There'd been a storm in the afternoon and it had made June seem like October all of a sudden when it left. Here he was asking me whether he should go on and finish med school or not, and then he played me the tape recordings.

'The only thing we're sure about anymore is how much money we need,' said I. 'That's about as profound as I ever get. I've got a wife and two kids. Me and the wife drink a great deal in the evenings of Baton Rouge. We're happy. The great questions seemed to have passed us by. I'm a radiologist. All day long I look for shadows. We've got two Chinese elm trees in our backyard and a fat calico named Sidney. Our children are beautiful and I've got stock in Shell.'

'You're right,' said Lardner.

'Every man can be a king if he wants to,' I said. 'That's what my father said. He had harder times than me or you.'

'That's true,' Lardner said.

The last thing I heard about Lardner, he was on a boat out of New Orleans headed for Rio. From there he took a ship to Spain.

I don't know another thing about him.

MAEVE BINCHY

Shepherd's Bush

People looked very weary, May thought, and shabbier than she had remembered Londoners to be. They reminded her a little of those news-reel pictures of crowds during the war or just after it, old raincoats, brave smiles, endless patience. But then this wasn't Regent Street where she had wandered up and down looking at shops on other visits to London, it wasn't the West End with lights all glittering and people getting out of taxis full of excitement and wafts of perfume. This was Shepherd's Bush where people lived. They had probably set out from here early this morning and fought similar crowds on the way to work. The women must have done their shopping in their lunch-hour because most of them were carrying plastic bags of food. It was a London different to the one you see as a tourist.

And she was here for a different reason, although she had once read a cynical article in a magazine which said that girls coming to London for abortions provided a significant part of the city's tourist revenue. It wasn't something you could classify under any terms as a holiday. When she filled in the card at the airport she had written 'Business' in the section where it said 'Purpose of journey'.

The pub where she was to meet Celia was near the tube station. She found it easily and settled herself in. A lot of the accents were Irish, workmen having a pint before they went home to their English wives and their television programmes. Not drunk tonight, it was only Monday, but obviously regulars. Maybe not so welcome as regulars on Friday or Saturday nights, when they would remember they were Irish and sing anti-British songs.

Celia wouldn't agree with her about that. Celia had rose-tinted views about the Irish in London, she thought they were all here from choice, not because there was no work for them at home. She hated stories about the restless Irish, or Irishmen on the lump in the building trade. She said people shouldn't make such a big thing about it all. People who came from much farther away settled in London, it was big enough to absorb everyone. Oh well, she wouldn't bring up the subject, there were enough things to disagree with Celia about ... without searching for more.

Oh why of all people, of all the bloody people in the world, did she have to come to Celia? Why was there nobody else whom she could ask for advice? Celia would give it, she would give a lecture with every piece of information she imparted. She would deliver a speech with every cup of tea, she would be cool, practical and exactly the right person, if she weren't so much the wrong person. It was handing Celia a whole box of ammunition about Andy. From now on Celia could say that Andy was a rat, and May could no longer say she had no facts to go on.

Celia arrived. She was thinner, and looked a little tired. She smiled. Obviously the lectures weren't going to come in the pub. Celia always knew the right place for things. Pubs were for meaningless chats and bright, non-intense conversation. Home was for lectures.

'You're looking marvellous,' Celia said.

It couldn't be true. May looked at her reflection in a glass panel. You couldn't see the dark lines under her eyes there, but you could see the droop of her shoulders, she wasn't a person that could be described as looking marvellous. No, not even in a pub.

'I'm okay,' she said. 'But you've got very slim, how did you do it?'

'No bread, no cakes, no potatoes, no sweets,' said Celia in a business-like way. 'It's the old rule but it's the only rule. You deny yourself everything you want and you lose weight.'

'I know,' said May, absently rubbing her waistline.

'Oh I didn't mean *that*,' cried Celia horrified. 'I didn't mean that at all.'

May felt weary, she hadn't meant that either, she was patting her stomach because she had been putting on weight. The child that she was going to get rid of was still only a speck, it would cause no bulge. She had put on weight because she cooked for Andy three or four times a week in his flat. He was long and lean. He could eat for ever and he wouldn't put on weight. He didn't like eating alone so she ate with him. She reassured Celia that there was no offence and when Celia had gone, twittering with rage at herself, to the counter, May wondered whether she had explored every avenue before coming to Celia and Shepherd's Bush for help.

She had. There were no legal abortions in Dublin, and she did not know of anyone who had ever had an illegal one there. England and the ease of the system were less than an hour away by plane. She didn't want to try and get it on the National Health, she had the money, all she wanted was someone who would introduce her to a doctor, so that she could get it all over with quickly. She needed somebody who knew her, somebody who wouldn't abandon her if things went wrong, somebody who would lie for her, because a few lies would have to be told. May didn't have any other friends in London. There was a girl she had once met on a skiing holiday, but you couldn't impose on a holiday friendship in that way. She knew a man, a very nice, kind man who had stayed in the hotel where she worked and had often begged her to come and stay with him and his wife. But she couldn't go to stay with them for the first time in this predicament, it would be ridiculous. It had to be Celia.

It might be easier if Celia had loved somebody so much that everything else was unimportant. But stop, that wasn't fair. Celia loved that dreary, boring, selfish Martin. She loved him so much that she believed one day he was going to get things organized and make a home for them. Everyone else knew that Martin was the worst possible bet for any punter, a Mammy's boy, who had everything he wanted now, including a visit every two months from Celia, home from London, smartly-dressed, undemanding, saving away for a day that would never come. So Celia did understand something about the nature of love. She never talked about it. People as brisk as Celia don't talk about things like unbrisk attitudes in men, or hurt feelings or broken hearts. Not when it refers to themselves, but they are very good at pointing out the foolish attitudes of others.

Celia was back with the drinks.

'We'll finish them up quickly,' she said.

Why could she never, never take her ease over anything? Things always had to be finished up quickly. It was warm and anonymous in the pub. They could go back to Celia's flat, which May felt sure wouldn't have even a comfortable chair in it, and talk in a business-like way about the rights and wrongs of abortion, the procedure, the money, and how it shouldn't be spent on something so hopeless and destructive. And about Andy. Why wouldn't May tell him? He had a right to know.

The child was half his, and even if he didn't want it he should pay for the abortion. He had plenty of money, he was a hotel manager. May had hardly any, she was a hotel receptionist. May could see it all coming, she dreaded it. She wanted to stay in this warm place until closing-time, and to fall asleep, and wake up there two days later.

Celia made walking-along-the-road conversation on the way to her flat. This road used to be very quiet and full of retired people, now it was all flats and bed-sitters. That road was nice, but noisy, too much through-traffic. The houses in the road over there were going for thirty-five thousand, which was ridiculous, but then you had to remember it was fairly central and they did have little gardens. Finally they were there. A big Victorian house, a clean, polished hall, and three flights of stairs. The flat was much bigger than May expected, and it had a sort of divan on which she sat down immediately and put up her legs, while Celia fussed about a bit, opening a bottle of wine and putting a dish of four small lamb chops into the oven. May braced herself for the lecture.

It wasn't a lecture, it was an information-sheet. She was so relieved that she could feel herself relaxing, and filled up her wineglass again.

'I've arranged with Doctor Harris that you can call to see him tomorrow morning at 11. I told him no lies, just a little less than the truth. I said you were staying with me. If he thinks that means you are staying permanently, that's his mistake not mine. I mentioned that your problem was . . . what it is. I asked him when he thought it would be . . . em . . . done. He said Wednesday or Thursday, but it would all depend. He didn't seem shocked or anything; it's like tonsillitis to him, I suppose. Anyway he was very calm about it. I think you'll find he's a kind person and it won't be upsetting . . . that part of it.'

May was dumbfounded. Where were the accusations, the I-told-you-so sighs, the hope that now, finally, she would finish with Andy? Where was the slight moralistic bit, the heavy wondering whether or not it might be murder? For the first time in the eleven days since she had confirmed she was pregnant, May began to hope that there would be some normality in the world again.

'Will it embarrass you, all this?' she asked. 'I mean, do you feel it will change your relationship with him?'

'In London a doctor isn't an old family friend like at home, May. He's someone you go to, or I've gone to anyway, when I've had to have my ears syringed, needed antibiotics for flu last year, and a medical certificate for the time I sprained my ankle and couldn't go to work. He hardly knows me except as a name on his register. He's nice though, and he doesn't rush you in and out. He's Jewish and small and worried-looking.'

Celia moved around the flat, changing into comfortable sitting-about clothes, looking up what was on television, explaining to May that she must sleep in her room and that she, Celia, would use the divan.

No, honestly, it would be easier that way, she wasn't

being nice, it would be much easier. A girl friend rang and they arranged to play squash together at the weekend. A wrong number rang. A West Indian from the flat downstairs knocked on the door to say he would be having a party on Saturday night and to apologise in advance for any noise. If they liked to bring a bottle of something, they could call in themselves. Celia served dinner. They looked at television for an hour, then went to bed.

May thought what a strange empty life Celia led here far from home, miles from Martin, no real friends, no life at all. Then she thought that Celia might possibly regard her life too as sad, working in a second-rate hotel for five years, having an affair with its manager for three years. A hopeless affair because the manager's wife and four children were a bigger stumbling-block than Martin's mother could ever be. She felt tired and comfortable, and in Celia's funny, characterless bedroom she drifted off and dreamed that Andy had discovered where she was and what she was about to do, and had flown over during the night to tell her that they would get married next morning, and live in England and forget the hotel, the family and what anyone would say.

Tuesday morning. Celia was gone. Dr Harris's address was neatly written on the pad by the phone with instructions how to get there. Also Celia's phone number at work, and a message that May never believed she would hear from Celia. 'Good luck.'

He was small, and Jewish, and worried and kind. His

examination was painless and unembarrassing. He confirmed what she knew already. He wrote down dates, and asked general questions about her health. May wondered whether he had a family, there were no pictures of wife or children in the surgery. But then there were none in Andy's office, either. Perhaps his wife was called Rebecca and she too worried because her husband worked so hard, they might have two children, a boy who was a gifted musician, and a girl who wanted to get married to a Christian. Maybe they all walked along these leafy roads on Saturdays to synagogue and Rebecca cooked all those things like gefilte fish and bagels.

With a start, May told herself to stop dreaming about him. It was a habit she had got into recently, fancying lives for everyone she met, however briefly. She usually gave them happy lives with a bit of problem-to-be-solved thrown in. She wondered what a psychiatrist would make of that. As she was coming back to real life, Dr Harris was saying that if he was going to refer her for a termination he must know why she could not have the baby. He pointed out that she was healthy, and strong, and young. She should have no difficulty with pregnancy or birth. Were there emotional reasons? Yes, it would kill her parents, she wouldn't be able to look after the baby, she didn't want to look after one on her own either, it wouldn't be fair on her or the baby.

'And the father?' Dr Harris asked.

'Is my boss, is heavily married, already has four

babies of his own. It would break up his marriage which he doesn't want to do . . . yet. No, the father wouldn't want me to have it either.'

'Has he said that?' asked Dr Harris as if he already knew the answer.

'I haven't told him, I can't tell him, I won't tell him,' said May.

Dr Harris sighed. He asked a few more questions; he made a telephone call; he wrote out an address. It was a posh address near Harley Street.

'This is Mr White. A well-known surgeon. These are his consulting-rooms, I have made an appointment for you at 2.30 this afternoon. I understand from your friend Miss . . .' He searched his mind and his desk for Celia's name and then gave up. 'I understand anyway that you are not living here, and don't want to try and pretend that you are, so that you want the termination done privately. That's just as well, because it would be difficult to get it done on the National Health. There are many cases that would have to come before you.'

'Oh I have the money,' said May, patting her handbag. She felt nervous but relieved at the same time. Almost exhilarated. It was working, the whole thing was actually moving. God bless Celia.

'It will be around £180 to £200, and in cash, you know that?'

'Yes, it's all here, but why should a well-known surgeon have to be paid in cash, Dr Harris? You know it makes it look a bit illegal and sort of underhand, doesn't it?'

Dr Harris smiled a tired smile. 'You asked me why he has to be paid in cash. Because he says so. Why he says so, I don't know. Maybe it's because some of his clients don't feel too like paying him after the event. It's not like plastic surgery or a broken leg, where they can see the results. In a termination you see no results. Maybe people don't pay so easily then. Maybe also Mr White doesn't have a warm relationship with his Income Tax people. I don't know.'

'Do I owe you anything?' May asked, putting on her coat.

'No, my dear, nothing.' He smiled and showed her to the door.

'It feels wrong. I'm used to paying a doctor at home or they send bills,' she said.

'Send me a picture postcard of your nice country sometime,' he said. 'When my wife was alive she and I spent several happy holidays there before all this business started.' He waved a hand to take in the course of Anglo-Irish politics and difficulties over the last ten years.

May blinked a bit hard and thanked him. She took a taxi which was passing his door and went to Oxford Street. She wanted to see what was in the shops because she was going to pretend that she had spent £200 on clothes and then they had all been lost or stolen. She hadn't yet worked out the details of this deception, which seemed unimportant compared to all the rest that had to be gone through. But she would need to know what was in the shops so that she could say what she was meant to have bought.

Imagining that she had this kind of money to spend, she examined jackets, skirts, sweaters, and the loveliest boots she had ever seen. If only she didn't have to throw this money away, she could have these things. It was her savings over ten months, she put by £30 a month with difficulty. Would Andy have liked her in the boots? She didn't know. He never said much about the way she looked. He saw her mostly in uniform when she could steal time to go to the flat he had for himself in the hotel. On the evenings when he was meant to be working late, and she was in fact cooking for him, she usually wore a dressing-gown, a long velvet one. Perhaps she might have bought a dressing-gown. She examined some, beautiful Indian silks, and a Japanese satin one in pink covered with little black butterflies. Yes, she would tell him she had bought that, he would like the sound of it, and be sorry it had been stolen.

She had a cup of coffee in one of the big shops and watched the other shoppers resting between bouts of buying. She wondered, did any of them look at her, and if so, would they know in a million years that her shopping money would remain in her purse until it was handed over to a Mr White so that he could abort Andy's baby? Why did she use words like that, why did she say things to hurt herself, she must have a very deep-seated sense of guilt. Perhaps, she thought to herself with a bit of humour, she should save another couple of hundred pounds and come over for a few sessions with a Harley Street shrink. That should set her right.

It wasn't a long walk to Mr White's rooms, it wasn't a pleasant welcome. A kind of girl that May had before only seen in the pages of fashion magazines, bored, disdainful, elegant, reluctantly admitted her.

'Oh yes, Dr Harris's patient,' she said, as if May should have come in some tradesman's entrance. She felt furious, and inferior, and sat with her hands in small tight balls, and her eyes unseeing in the waiting-room.

Mr White looked like a caricature of a diplomat. He had elegant grey hair, elegant manicured hands. He moved very gracefully, he talked in practised, concerned clichés, he knew how to put people at their ease, and despite herself, and while still disliking him, May felt safe.

Another examination, another confirmation, more checking of dates. Good, good, she had come in plenty of time, sensible girl. No reasons she would like to discuss about whether this was the right course of action? No? Oh well, grown-up lady, must make up her own mind. Absolutely certain then? Fine, fine. A look at a big leather-bound book on his desk, a look at a small notebook. Leather-bound for the tax people, small notebook for himself, thought May viciously. Splendid, splendid. Tomorrow morning then, not a problem in the world, once she was sure, then he knew this was the best, and wisest thing. Very sad the people who dithered.

May could never imagine this man having dithered in his life. She was asked to see Vanessa on the way out. She knew that the girl would be called something like Vanessa.

Vanessa yawned and took £194 from her. She seemed to have difficulty in finding the six pounds in change. May wondered whether it was meant to be a tip. If so, she would wait for a year until Vanessa found the change. With the notes came a discreet printed card advertising a nursing home on the other side of London.

'Before nine, fasting, just the usual overnight things,' said Vanessa helpfully.

'Tomorrow morning?' checked May.

'Well yes, naturally. You'll be out at eight the following morning. They'll arrange everything like taxis. They have super food,' she added as an afterthought.

'They'd need to have for this money,' said May spiritedly.

'You're not just paying for the food,' said Vanessa wisely.

It was still raining. She rang Celia from a public phonebox. Everything was organized, she told her. Would Celia like to come and have a meal somewhere, and maybe they could go on to a theatre?

Celia was sorry, she had to work late, and she had already bought liver and bacon for supper. Could she meet May at home around nine? There was a great quiz show on telly, it would be a shame to miss it.

May went to a hairdresser and spent four times what she would have spent at home on a hair-do.

She went to a cinema and saw a film which looked as if it were going to be about a lot of sophisticated witty French people on a yacht and turned out to be about a sophisticated witty French girl who fell in love with the deck-hand on the yacht and when she purposely got pregnant, in order that he would marry her, he laughed at her and the witty sophisticated girl threw herself overboard. Great choice that, May said glumly, as she dived into the underground to go back to the smell of liver frying.

Celia asked little about the arrangements for the morning, only practical things like the address so that she could work out how long it would take to get there.

'Would you like me to come and see you?' she asked. 'I expect when it's all over, all finished you know, they'd let you have visitors. I could come after work.'

She emphasized the word 'could' very slightly. May immediately felt mutinous. She would love Celia to come, but not if it was going to be a duty, something she felt she had to do, against her principles, her inclinations.

'No, don't do that,' she said in a falsely bright voice. 'They have telly in the rooms apparently, and anyway, it's not as if I were going to be there for more than twenty-four hours.'

Celia looked relieved. She worked out taxi times and locations and turned on the quiz show.

In the half light May looked at her. She was unbending, Celia was. She would survive everything, even the fact that Martin would never marry her. Christ, the whole thing was a mess. Why did people start life with such hopes, and as early as their mid-twenties become beaten and accepting of things. Was the rest of life going to be like this?

She didn't sleep so well, and it was a relief when Celia shouted that it was seven o'clock.

Wednesday. An ordinary Wednesday for the taxi-driver, who shouted some kind of amiable conversation at her. She missed most of it, because of the noise of the engine, and didn't bother to answer him half the time except with a grunt.

The place had creeper on the walls. It was a big house, with a small garden, and an attractive brass handle on the door. The nurse who opened it was Irish. She checked May's name on a list. Thank God it was O'Connor, there were a million O'Connors. Suppose she had had an unusual name, she'd have been found out immediately.

The bedroom was big and bright. Two beds, flowery covers, nice furniture. A magazine rack, a bookshelf. A television, a bathroom.

The Irish nurse offered her a hanger from the wardrobe for her coat as if this was a pleasant family hotel of great class and comfort. May felt frightened for the first time. She longed to sit down on one of the beds and cry, and for the nurse to put her arm around her and give her a cigarette and say that it would be all right. She hated being so alone.

The nurse was distant.

'The other lady will be in shortly. Her name is Miss Adams. She just went downstairs to say goodbye to her friend. If there's anything you'd like, please ring.'

She was gone, and May paced the room like a captured animal. Was she to undress? It was ridiculous to go to bed. You only went to bed in the day-time if you were ill. She was well, perfectly well.

Miss Adams burst in the door. She was a chubby, pretty girl about twenty-three. She was Australian, and her name was Hell, short for Helen.

'Come on, bedtime,' she said, and they both put on their nightdresses and got into beds facing each other. May had never felt so silly in her whole life.

'Are you sure we're meant to do this?' she asked.

'Positive,' Helen announced. 'I was here last year. They'll be in with the screens for modesty, the examination, and the pre-med. They go mad if you're not in bed. Of course that stupid Paddy of a nurse didn't tell you, they expect you to be inspired.'

Hell was right: In five minutes, the nurse and Mr White came in. A younger nurse carried a screen. Hell was examined first, then May for blood pressure and temperature, and that kind of thing. Mr White was charming. He called her Miss O'Connor, as if he had known her all his life.

He patted her shoulder and told her she didn't have

anything to worry about. The Irish nurse gave her an unsmiling injection which was going to make her drowsy. It didn't immediately.

Hell was doing her nails.

'You were really here last year?' asked May in disbelief.

'Yeah, there's nothing to it. I'll be back at work tomorrow.'

'Why didn't you take the Pill?' May asked.

'Why didn't you?' countered Hell.

'Well, I did for a bit, but I thought it was making me fat, and then anyway, you know, I thought I'd escaped for so long before I started the Pill that it would be all right. I was wrong.'

'I know.' Hell was sympathetic. 'I can't take it. I've got varicose veins already and I don't really understand all those things they give you in the Family Planning clinics, jellies, and rubber things, and diaphragms. It's worse than working out income tax. Anyway, you never have time to set up a scene like that before going to bed with someone, do you? It's like preparing for a battle.'

May laughed.

'It's going to be fine, love,' said Hell. 'Look, I know, I've been here before. Some of my friends have had it done four or five times. I promise you, it's only the people who don't know who worry. This afternoon you'll wonder what you were thinking about to look so white. Now if it had been terrible, would I be here again?'

'But your varicose veins?' said May, feeling a little sleepy.

'Go to sleep, kid,' said Hell. 'We'll have a chat when it's all over.'

Then she was getting onto a trolley, half-asleep, and going down corridors with lovely prints on the walls to a room with a lot of light, and transferring onto another table. She felt as if she could sleep for ever and she hadn't even had the anaesthetic yet. Mr White stood there in a coat brighter than his name. Someone was dressing him up the way they do in films.

She thought about Andy. 'I love you,' she said suddenly.

'Of course you do,' said Mr White, coming over and patting her kindly without a trace of embarrassment.

Then she was being moved again, she thought they hadn't got her right on the operating table, but it wasn't that, it was back into her own bed and more sleep.

There was a tinkle of china. Hell called over from the window.

'Come on, they've brought us some nice soup. Broth they call it.'

May blinked.

'Come on, May. I was done after you and I'm wide awake. Now didn't I tell you there was nothing to it?'

May sat up. No pain, no tearing feeling in her insides. No sickness. 'Are you sure they did me?' she asked.

They both laughed.

They had what the nursing-home called a light lunch. Then they got a menu so that they could choose dinner.

'There are some things that England does really well, and this is one of them,' Hell said approvingly, trying to decide between the delights that were offered. 'They even give us a small carafe of wine. If you want more you have to pay for it. But they kind of disapprove of us getting pissed.'

Hell's friend Charlie was coming in at six when he finished work. Would May be having a friend too, she wondered? No. Celia wouldn't come.

'I don't mean Celia,' said Hell. 'I mean the bloke.'

'He doesn't know, he's in Dublin, and he's married,' said May.

'Well, Charlie's married, but he bloody knows, and he'd know if he were on the moon.'

'It's different.'

'No, it's not different. It's the same for everyone, there are rules, you're a fool to break them. Didn't he pay for it either, this guy?'

'No. I told you he doesn't know.'

'Aren't you noble,' said Hell scornfully. 'Aren't you a real Lady Galahad. Just visiting London for a day or two, darling, just going to see a few friends, see you soon. Love you darling. Is that it?'

'We don't go in for so many darlings as that in Dublin,' said May.

'You don't go in for much common sense either. What will you gain, what will he gain, what will anyone gain?

You come home penniless, a bit lonely. He doesn't know what the hell you've been doing, he isn't extra-sensitive and loving and grateful because he doesn't have anything to be grateful about as far as he's concerned.'

'I couldn't tell him. I couldn't. I couldn't ask him for £200 and say what it was for. That wasn't in the bargain, that was never part of the deal.'

May was almost tearful, mainly from jealousy she thought. She couldn't bear Hell's Charlie to come in, while her Andy was going home to his wife because there would be nobody to cook him something exciting and go to bed with him in his little manager's flat.

'When you go back, tell him. That's my advice,' said Hell. 'Tell him you didn't want to worry him, you did it all on your own because the responsibility was yours since you didn't take the Pill. That's unless you think he'd have wanted it?'

'No, he wouldn't have wanted it.'

'Well then, that's what you do. Don't ask him for the money straight out, just let him know you're broke. He'll react some way then. It's silly not to tell them at all. My sister did that with her bloke back in Melbourne. She never told him at all, and she got upset because he didn't know the sacrifice she had made, and every time she bought a drink or paid for a cinema ticket she got resentful of him. All for no reason, because he didn't bloody know.'

'I might,' said May, but she knew she wouldn't.

Charlie came in. He was great fun, very fond of Hell,

wanting to be sure she was okay, and no problems. He brought a bottle of wine which they shared, and he told them funny stories about what had happened at the office. He was in advertising. He arranged to meet Hell for lunch next day and joked his way out of the room.

'He's a lovely man,' said May.

'Old Charlie's smashing,' agreed Hell. He had gone back home to entertain his wife and six dinner guests. His wife was a marvellous hostess apparently. They were always having dinner parties.

'Do you think he'll ever leave her?' asked May.

'He'd be out of his brains if he did,' said Hell cheerfully.

May was thoughtful. Maybe everyone would be out of their brains if they left good, comfortable, happy home set-ups for whatever the other woman imagined she could offer. She wished she could be as happy as Hell.

'Tell me about your fellow,' Hell said kindly.

May did, the whole long tale. It was great to have somebody to listen, somebody who didn't say she was on a collision course, somebody who didn't purse up lips like Celia, someone who said, 'Go on, what did you do then?'

'He sounds like a great guy,' said Hell, and May smiled happily.

They exchanged addresses, and Hell promised that if ever she came to Ireland she wouldn't ring up the hotel and say, 'Can I talk to May, the girl I had the abortion with last winter?' and they finished Charlie's wine, and went to sleep.

The beds were stripped early next morning when the final examination had been done, and both were pronounced perfect and ready to leave. May wondered fancifully how many strange life stories the room must have seen.

'Do people come here for other reasons apart from ... er, terminations?' she asked the disapproving Irish nurse.

'Oh certainly they do, you couldn't work here otherwise,' said the nurse. 'It would be like a death factory, wouldn't it?'

That puts me in my place, thought May, wondering why she hadn't the courage to say that she was only visiting the home, she didn't earn her living from it.

She let herself into Celia's gloomy flat. It had become gloomy again like the way she had imagined it before she saw it. The warmth of her first night there was gone. She looked around and wondered why Celia had no pictures, no books, no souvenirs.

There was a note on the telephone pad.

'I didn't ring or anything, because I forgot to ask if you had given your real name, and I wouldn't know who to ask for. Hope you feel well again. I'll be getting some chicken pieces so we can have supper together around 8. Ring me if you need me. C.'

May thought for a bit. She went out and bought Celia a casserole dish, a nice one made of cast-iron. It would be useful for all those little high-protein, low-calorie dinners Celia cooked. She also bought a bunch of flowers, but could find no vase when she came back and had to use a big glass instead.

She left a note thanking her for the hospitality, warm enough to sound properly grateful, and a genuinely warm remark about how glad she was that she had been able to do it all through nice Dr Harris. She said nothing about the time in the nursing-home. Celia would prefer not to know. May just said that she was fine, and thought she would go back to Dublin tonight. She rang the airline and booked a plane.

Should she ring Celia and tell her to get only one chicken piece? No, damn Celia, she wasn't going to ring her. She had a fridge, hadn't she?

The plane didn't leave until the early afternoon. For a wild moment she thought of joining Hell and Charlie in the pub where they were meeting, but dismissed the idea. She must now make a list of what clothes she was meant to have bought and work out a story about how they had disappeared. Nothing that would make Andy get in touch with police or airlines to find them for her. It was going to be quite hard, but she'd have to give Andy some explanation of what she'd been doing, wouldn't she? And he would want to know why she had spent all that money. Or would he? Did he even know she had all that money? She couldn't remember telling him. He wasn't very interested in her little savings, they talked more about his investments. And she must remember that if he was busy or cross tonight or tomorrow she wasn't to take it out on him. Like Hell had said, there wasn't any point in her expecting a bit of cosseting when he didn't even know she needed it.

How sad and lonely it would be to live like Celia, to be so suspicious of men, to think so ill of Andy. Celia always said he was selfish and just took what he could get. That was typical of Celia, she understood nothing. Hell had understood more, in a couple of hours, than Celia had in three years. Hell knew what it was like to love someone.

But May didn't think Hell had got it right about telling Andy all about the abortion. Andy might be against that kind of thing. He was very moral in his own way, was Andy.

DONALD
BARTHELME

The King of Jazz

Well I'm the king of jazz now, thought Hokie Mokie to himself as he oiled the slide on his trombone. Hasn't been a 'bone man been king of jazz for many years. But now that Spicy MacLammermoor, the old king, is dead, I guess I'm it. Maybe I better play a few notes out of this window here, to reassure myself.

'Wow!' said somebody standing on the sidewalk. 'Did you hear that?'

'I did,' said his companion.

'Can you distinguish our great homemade American jazz performers, each from the other?'

'Used to could.'

'Then who was that playing?'

'Sounds like Hokie Mokie to me. Those few but perfectly selected notes have the real epiphanic glow.'

'The what?'

'The real epiphanic glow, such as is obtained only by artists of the caliber of Hokie Mokie, who's from Pass Christian, Mississippi. He's the king of jazz, now that Spicy MacLammermoor is gone.'

Hokie Mokie put his trombone in its trombone case and went to a gig. At the gig everyone fell back before him, bowing.

'Hi Bucky! Hi Zoot! Hi Freddie! Hi George! Hi Thad! Hi Roy! Hi Dexter! Hi Jo! Hi Willie! Hi Greens!'

'What we gonna play, Hokie? You the king of jazz now, you gotta decide.'

'How 'bout "Smoke"?'

'Wow!' everybody said. 'Did you hear that? Hokie Mokie can just knock a fella out, just the way he pronounces a word. What a intonation on that boy! God Almighty!'

'I don't want to play "Smoke",' somebody said.

'Would you repeat that stranger?'

'I don't want to play "Smoke". "Smoke" is dull. I don't like the changes. I refuse to play "Smoke"!'

'He refuses to play "Smoke"! But Hokie Mokie is the king of jazz and he says "Smoke"!'

'Man, you from outa town or something? What do you mean you refuse to play "Smoke"? How'd you get on this gig anyhow? Who hired you?'

'I am Hideo Yamaguchi, from Tokyo, Japan.'

'Oh, you're one of those Japanese cats, eh?'

'Yes, I'm the top trombone man in all of Japan.'

'Well you're welcome here until we hear you play. Tell me, is the Tennessee Tea Room still the top jazz place in Tokyo?'

'No, the top jazz place in Tokyo is the Square Box now.'

'That's nice. OK, now we gonna play "Smoke" just like Hokie said. You ready, Hokie? OK, give you four for nothin'. One! Two! Three! Four!'

The two men who had been standing under Hokie's window had followed him into the club. Now they said:

'Good God!'

'Yes, that's Hokie's famous "English sunrise" way of playing. Playing with lots of rays coming out of it, some red rays; some blue rays, some green rays, some green stemming from a violet center, some olive stemming from a tan center – '

'That young Japanese fellow is pretty good, too.'

'Yes, he is pretty good. And he holds his horn in a peculiar way. That's frequently the mark of a superior player.'

'Bent over like that with his head between his knees – good God, he's sensational!'

He's sensational, Hokie thought. Maybe I ought to kill him.

But at that moment somebody came in the door

pushing in front of him a four-and-one-half-octave marimba. Yes, it was Fat Man Jones, and he began to play even before he was fully in the door.

'What're we playing?'

' "Billie's Bounce".'

'That's what I thought it was. What're we in?'

'F.'

'That's what I thought we were in. Didn't you use to play with Maynard?'

'Yeah I was in that band for a while until I was in the hospital.'

'What for?'

'I was tired.'

'What can we add to Hokie's fantastic playing?'

'How 'bout some rain or stars?'

'Maybe that's presumptuous?'

'Ask him if he'd mind.'

'You ask him, I'm scared. You don't fool around with the king of jazz. That young Japanese guy's pretty good, too.'

'He's sensational.'

'You think he's playing in Japanese?'

'Well I don't think it's English.'

This trombone's been makin' my neck green for thirty-five years, Hokie thought. How come I got to stand up to yet another challenge, this late in life?

'Well, Hideo – '

'Yes, Mr. Mokie?'

'You did well on both "Smoke" and "Billie's

Bounce". You're just about as good as me, I regret to say. In fact, I've decided you're *better* than me. It's a hideous thing to contemplate, but there it is. I have only been the king of jazz for twenty-four hours, but the unforgiving logic of this art demands we bow to Truth, when we hear it.'

'Maybe you're mistaken?'

'No, I got ears. I'm not mistaken. Hideo Yamaguchi is the new king of jazz.'

'You want to be king emeritus?'

'No, I'm just going to fold up my horn and steal away. This gig is yours, Hideo. You can pick the next tune.'

'How 'bout. "Cream"?'

'OK, you heard what Hideo said, it's "Cream". You ready, Hideo?'

'Hokie, you don't have to leave. You can play too. Just move a little over to the side there – '

'Thank you, Hideo, that's very gracious of you. I guess I will play a little, since I'm still here. Sotto voce, of course.'

'Hideo is wonderful on "Cream"!'

'Yes, I imagine it's his best tune.'

'What's that sound coming in from the side there?'

'Which side?'

'The left.'

'You mean that sound that sounds like the cutting edge of life? That sounds like polar bears crossing Arctic ice pans? That sounds like a herd of musk ox in full flight? That sounds like male walruses diving to the bottom of the sea? That sounds like fumaroles smoking on the slopes of Mt. Katmai? That sounds like the wild turkey walking through the deep, soft forest? That sounds like beavers chewing trees in an Appalachian marsh? That sounds like an oyster fungus growing on an aspen trunk? That sounds like a mule deer wandering a montane of the Sierra Nevada? That sounds like prairie dogs kissing? That sounds like witch grass tumbling or a river meandering? That sounds like manatees munching seaweed at Cape Sable? That sounds like coatimundis moving in packs across the face of Arkansas? That sounds like – '

'Good God, it's Hokie! Even with a cup mute on, he's blowing Hideo right off the stand!'

'Hideo's playing on his knees now! Good God, he's reaching into his belt for a large steel sword – Stop him!'

'Wow! That was the most exciting "Cream" ever played! Is Hideo all right?'

'Yes, somebody is getting him a glass of water.'

'You're my man, Hokie! That was the dadblangedest thing I ever saw!'

'You're the king of jazz once again!'

'Hokie Mokie is the most happening thing there is!'

'Yes, Mr. Hokie sir, I have to admit it, you blew me right off the stand. I see I have many years of work and study before me still.'

'That's OK, son. Don't think a thing about it. It happens to the best of us. Or it almost happens to the best of us. Now I want everybody to have a good time because we're gonna play "Flats". "Flats" is next.'

'With your permission, sir, I will return to my hotel and pack. I am most grateful for everything I have learned here.'

'That's OK, Hideo. Have a nice day. He-he. Now, "Flats".'

BEVERLEY FARMER

A Man in the Laundrette

She never wants to disturb him but she has to sometimes, as this room in which he studies and writes and reads is the only way in and out of his apartment. Now that he has got up to make coffee in the kitchen, though, she can put on her boots and coat and rummage in the wardrobe for the glossy black garbage bag where they keep their dirty clothes, and not be disturbing him. 'I'll only be an hour or two,' she says quickly when he comes back in. She holds up the bag to show why.

'Are you sure?' His eyebrows lift. 'It must be my turn by now.' They were scrupulous about such matters when she first moved in.

'I'm sure. I must get out more. Meet the people.' She shrugs at his stare. 'I want to see what I can of life in the States, after all.'

'Not to be with me.'

She smiles. 'Of course to be with you. You know that.'

'I thought you had a story you wanted to finish.'

'I had. It's finished. You know you don't have time to go, and I like going.'

He stands there unsmiling, holding the two mugs. 'I made you a coffee,' he says.

'Thanks.' She perches on the bed and drinks little scalding sips while, turned in his chair, he stares out at the sky.

His window is above the street and on brighter afternoons than this it catches the whole heavy sun as it goes down. He always works in front of the window but facing the wall, a dark profile.

He says, 'Look how dark it's getting.'

'It's just clouds,' she says. 'It's only a little after three.'

'Still. Why today? Saturday.'

'Why not? That's your last shirt.'

'It's mostly my clothes, I suppose.' It always is. She washes hers in the bathroom basin and hangs them on the pipes. He has never said that this bothers him; but then she has never asked. He shrugs. 'You don't know your way round too well. That's all.'

'I do! Enough for the laundrette.'

'Well. Okay. You've got Fred's number?'

She nods. Fred, who lives on the floor above, has the only telephone in the building and is sick of having to fetch his neighbours to take calls. She rang Fred's number once. She gets up without finishing her coffee.

'Okay. Take care.' He settles at the table with his back turned to her and to the door and to his bed in which she sleeps at night even now, lying with the arm that shades her eyes chilled and stiff, sallowed by the lamp, while he works late. Sighing, he switches this lamp on now and holds his coffee up to it in both hands, watching the steam fray.

Quietly she shuts the door.

The apartment houses have lamps on already under their green awnings. They are old three-storey brick mansions, red ivy shawling them. Old elms all the way along his street are golden-leaved and full of quick squirrels: the air is bright with leaves falling. The few clumps that were left this morning of the first snow of the season have all dripped away now. As she comes down the stoop a cold wind throws leaves over her, drops of rain as sharp as snow prickle her face. The wind shuffles her and her clumsy bag around the corner, under the viaduct, down block after weedy block of the patched bare roadway. The laundrette seems further away than it should be. Has she lost her way? No, there it is at last on the next corner: D.K.'s Bar and Laundrette. With a shudder, slamming the glass door behind her, she seals herself in the warm steam and rumble, and looks round.

There are more people here than ever before. Saturday would be a busy day, she should have known that. Everywhere solemn grey-haired black couples are sitting in silence side by side, their hands folded. Four small black girls with pigtails and ribbons erect on their furrowed scalps give her gap-toothed smiles. A scowling fat white woman is the only other white. All the washers are going. Worse, the coins in her pocket turn out not to be quarters but Australian coins, useless. All she has in U.S. currency is a couple of dollar notes. There is a hatch for change with a buzzer in one wall, opening, she remembers, into a back room of the bar; but no one answers it when she presses the buzzer. Too shy to ask anyone there for the change, she hurries out to ask in D.K.'s Bar instead. In the dark room into which she falters, wind-whipped, her own head meets her afloat among lamps in mirrors. Eyes in smoky booths turn and stare. She waits, fingering her dollar notes, but no one goes behind the bar. She creeps out again. The wind shoves her into the laundrette.

This time she keeps on pressing and pressing the buzzer until a voice bawls, 'Aw, *shit*,' and the hatch thuds open on the usual surly old Irishman in his grey hat.

'Hul*lo*!' Her voice sounds too bright. 'I thought you weren't *here*!' She hands him her two dollars.

'Always here.' He flicks his cigarette. 'Big fight's on cable.' A roar from the TV set and he jerks away, slapping down her eight quarters, slamming the hatch.

She is in luck. A washer has just been emptied and no one else is claiming it. Redfaced, she tips her clothes in. Once she has got the washer churning she sits on a chair nearby with her garbage bag, fumbling in it for her writing pad and pen. She always writes in the laundrette.

She never wants to disturb him, she scrawls on a new page, *but she has to sometimes, as this room in which he studies and writes and reads is the only way in and out of his apartment.*

A side door opens for a moment on to the layered smoke of the bar. A young black man, hefty in a padded jacket, lurches out almost on top of her and stands swaying. His stained white jeans come closer each time to her bent head. She edges away.

Now that he has got up to make coffee in the kitchen, though, she can put on her boots and coat and rummage in the wardrobe for the glossy black garbage bag where they keep their dirty clothes, and not be disturbing him.

'Pretty handwriting,' purrs a voice in her ear. When she stares up, he smiles. Under his moustache he has front teeth missing, and one eyetooth is a furred brown stump. 'What's *that* say?' A pale fingernail taps her pad.

'Uh, nothing.'

'*Show* me.' He flaps the pad over. Its cover is a photograph of the white-hooded Opera House. 'Sydney, Australia,' he spells out. 'You from Australia?'

'Yes.'

'Stayin' long?'

'Just visiting.'

'I *said* are you stayin' *long*?'

'No.'

'Don't like the U-nited States.'

She shrugs. 'It's time I went home.'

'Home to Australia. Well now. My teacher were from Australia, my music teacher. She were a nice Australian lady. She got me into the Yale School of Music.' He waits.

'That's good.' She gives him a brief smile, hunching over her writing pad.

'I'll only be an hour or two,' she says quickly when he comes back in. She holds up the bag to show why.

'Are you sure?' His eyebrows lift. 'It must be my turn by now.'

'What you writin'?'

'A story.'

'Story, huh? I write songs. I'm a musician. I was four years at the Yale School of Music. That's *good*, is it?' He thrusts his face close to hers and she smells rotting teeth and fumes of something – bourbon, perhaps, or rum. So that's what it is: he is drunk. He has a bunched brown paper bag with a bottle in it, which he unscrews with difficulty and wags at her. 'Have some.' She shakes her head. Shrugging, he throws his head back to swallow, chokes and splutters on the floor. He wipes his lips on the back of his hand, glaring round. Everyone is carefully not looking. One small black girl snorts and they all fall into giggles. He bows to them.

'I work in a piana bar, you listenin', hey *you*, I ain'
talkin' to myself.' She looks up. 'That's *bet*ter. My
mother and father own it so you wanna hear me sing
I get you in for free. Hey, you wanna hear me sing or
don't you?' She nods. 'All *right*.' What he sings in a
slow, hoarse tremolo sounds like a spiritual, though the
few words she picks up make no sense. The black girls
writhe. The couples sitting in front of the dryers
exchange an unwilling smile and shake of the head.

'You like that, huh?' She nods. 'She *like* that. Now I
sing you all another little number I wrote, I write all my
own numbers and I call this little number Calypso
Blues.' Then he sings more, as far as she can tell, of the
same song.

*They were scrupulous about such matters when she
first moved in.*

*'I'm sure. I must get out more. Meet the people.'
She shrugs at his stare. 'I want to see what I can of
life in the States, after all.'*

'Like that one? My mother and father – *hey* – they
real rich peoples, ain' just the piana bar, they got three
houses. Trucks. Boats too. I don' go along with that shit.
Ownin' things, makin' money, that's all shit. What you
say your name was? Hey, *you*. You hear me talkin' to
you?'

'Uh, Anne,'she lies, her head bowed.

'Pretty.' He leans over to finger her hair. 'Long yeller
hair. Real ... pretty.'

'Don't.'

' "I want to see what I can of life in the States after" – after *what*?'

'*All*.' She crams the pad into her garbage bag.

'You sha' or somethin'?'

'What?'

'You sha'? You deaf or somethin'? You *shacked*?'

'Oh! Shacked? Shacked – yes, I am. Yes.' She keeps glancing at the door. The first few times that it was her turn to do the laundry he came along anyway after a while, smiling self-consciously, whispering, 'I missed you.' But not today, she knows. She stares at somebody's clothes flapping and soaring in a dryer. She could take hers home wet, though they would be heavy: but then this man might follow her home.

'So where you live?'

'Never mind,' she mutters.

'What's that?'

'I don't *know*. Oh, down the road.'

'Well, you can tell me.'

'No, I'd – I don't *know* its name.'

'I just wanna talk to you – *Anne*. I just wanna be friends. You don' wanna be friends, that what you sayin'? You think I got somethin' nasty in my mind, well I think *you* do.' He snorts. 'My lady she a white lady like you an' let me tell *you* you ain' nothin' alongside of her. *You* ain' *nothin'*.'

She stares down. He prods her arm. 'Don't,' she says.

'Don't what?'

'Just don't.'

'Hear me, bitch?'

'Don't talk to me like that.'

'Oh, don't talk to you like that? I wanna talk to you, I talk to you how I like, don't you order *me* roun' tell me how I can talk to you.' He jabs his fist at her shoulder then holds it against her ear. 'Go on, look out the door. Expectin' somebody?'

'My friend's coming.'

'Huh. She expectin' her *friend*.' The couples look back gravely. 'My brothers they all gangsters,' he shouts, 'an' one word from me gets anybody I *want* killed. We gonna kill them *all*.' He is sweaty and shaking now. 'We gonna kill them and dig them up and kill them all *over* again. Trouble with you, Miss Australia, you don' like the black peoples, that's trouble with you. Well we gonna kill you *all*.' He drinks and gasps, licking his lips.

The door opens. She jumps up. With a whoop the wind pushes in two Puerto Rican couples with garbage bags. Leaves and papers come rattling over the floor to her feet. One of the Puerto Ricans buzzes and knocks at the hatch for change, but no one opens it; in the end they pool what quarters they find in their pockets, start their washers and sit in a quiet row on a table. Her machine has stopped now. There is a dryer free. She throws the tangled clothes in, twists two quarters in the slot and sits hunched on another chair to wait.

He has lost her. He spits into the corner, staggering, wiping his sweat with a sleeve, then begs a cigarette from the sullen white woman, who turns scornfully away without a word. 'Bitch,' he growls: a jet of spit just misses her boot. One of the Puerto Ricans offers him an open pack. Mumbling, he picks one, gets it lit, splutters it out and squats shakily to pick it up out of his splash of spit. He sucks smoke in, sighs it out. Staring round, he finds her again and stumbles over. 'Where you get to?' He coughs smoke in her face. His bottle is empty: not a drop comes out when he tips it up over his mouth. 'God*dam*,' he wails, and lets it drop on the floor, where it smashes. 'Goddam mothers, you all givin' me *shit*!'

'No one doin' that,' mutters a wrinkled black man.

He has swaggered up close, his fly almost touching her forehead. '*Don't*,' she says despairingly.

'Don't, don't. Why not? I like you, Miss Australia.' He gives a wide grin. 'Gotta go next door for a minute. Wanna come? No? Okay. Don't nobody bother her now. Don't nobody interfere. She *my* lady.'

He stumbles to the side door and opens it on a darkness slashed with red mirrors. Once the door shuts the black couples slump and sigh. One old woman hustles the little black girls out on to the street. An old man leans forward and says, 'He your friend, miss?'

'No! I've never seen him before.'

The old man and his wife roll their eyes, their faces netting with anxious wrinkles. 'You better watch out,' he says.

'What if he follows me home?'

They nod. 'He a load of trouble, that boy. Oh, his poor mother.'

'Maybe he'll stay in there and won't come back?' she says.

'Best thing is you call a cab, go on home. They got a pay phone here.'

'Oh, *where*?'

'In the bar.'

'*Where*!'

The side door slams open, then shut, and they all sit back guiltily. She huddles, not looking round. Her clothes float down in the dryer, so she opens it and stoops into the hot dark barrel to pick them out, tangled still and clinging to each other. Suddenly he is bending over her, his hands braced on the wall above the dryer, his belly thrust hard against her back. She twists angrily out from under him, clutching hot shirts.

'Now stop that! That's enough!'

'Not for me it ain', not yet.'

'Leave me alone!'

'I wanna talk. Wanna talk to you.'

'No! Go away!' She crams the clothes into her garbage bag.

'Hey, you not well, man,' mumbles the old black. 'Better go on home now. Go on home.'

'Who you, man, you gonna tell *me* what to do?' He throws a wide punch and falls to the floor. With a shriek of rage and terror the old woman runs to the side door and pounds on it. It slaps open, just missing her, and two white men tumble in.

'Okay,' one grunts. 'What's trouble here?'

'Where you *been*? You supposed to keep *order*!' she wails, and the old man hushes her. The young man is on his knees, shaking his frizzy head with both his hands.

With gestures of horrified embarrassment to everyone she sees watching her, she swings the glass door open on to the dim street. A man has followed her: one of the two Puerto Ricans. 'Is okay. I see you safe home,' he says, and slings her bag over his shoulder.

'Oh, thank you! But your wife's still in there.'

'My brother is there.' He takes her arm, almost dragging her away.

'He was so drunk,' she says. 'What made him act like that. I mean, why me?'

His fine black hair flaps in the wind. 'You didn't handle him right,' he says.

'What's *right*?'

'You dunno. Everybody see that. Just whatever you did, you got the guy mad, you know?'

They are far enough away to risk looking back. He is out on the road, his body arched, yelling at three white men: the old Irishman in the hat has joined the other two and they are barring his way at the door of the laundrette. There is something of forebearance, even of compunction, in their stance. 'They'll leave him alone, won't they?' she asks.

He nods. 'Looks like they know him.'

He has seen her all the way to the corner before she can persuade him, thanking him fervently, that she can look after herself from here on. He stands guard in the wind, his white face uneasily smiling whenever she turns to grin and wave him on. The wind thrashes her along their street. In the west the clouds are fraying, letting a glint of light through, but the streetlamps are coming on already with a milky fluttering, bluish-white, among the gold tossings of the elms.

A squirrel on their fence fixes one black resentful eye on her: it whirls and stands erect, its hands folded and its muzzle twitching, until abruptly it darts away, stops once to look back, and the silver spray of its tail follows it up an elm.

The lamp is on in his window – none of the windows in these streets has curtains – and he is still in front of it, a shadow. She fumbles with her key. Rushing in, she disturbs him.

'Am I late? Sorry! There was this terrible man in the laundrette.' Panting, she leans against the dim wall to tell him the story. Halfway through she sees that his face is stiff and grey.

'You're thinking I brought it on myself.'

'Didn't you?'

'By going out, you mean? By not wanting to be rude?' He stares. 'No, you wouldn't.'

'What did I do that was wrong?'

'A man can always tell if a woman fancies him.'

'Infallibly?' He shrugs. 'I led him on, is that what you mean?'

'Didn't you?'

'Why would I?'

'You can't seem to help it.'

'Why do you think that?'

'I've seen you in action.'

'*When*?'

'Whenever you talk to a man, it's there.'

'This is sick,' she says. He shakes his head. 'Well, *what's* there?' But he turns back without a word to the lamplit papers on his table.

Shivering, she folds his shirts on the wooden settle in the passage, hangs up his trousers, pairs his socks. Her few things she drops into her suitcase, open on the floor of the wardrobe; she has never properly unpacked. Now she never will. There is no light in this passage, at one end of which is his hood of yellow lamplight and at the other the twin yellow bubbles of hers, wastefully left on while she was out. The tall windows behind her lamps are nailed shut. A crack in one glitters like a blade. Wasps dying of the cold have nested in the shaggy corners. In the panes, as in those of his window, only a greyness like still water is left of the day.

But set at eye level in the wall of the passage where she is standing with her garbage bag is a strip of window overgrown with ivy, one small casement of which she creeps up at night from his bed to prise open, and he later to close: and here a slant of sun strikes. Leaves all the colours of fire flicker and tap the glass.

'Look. You'd think it was stained glass, wouldn't

you? Look,' she is suddenly saying aloud. 'I'll never forget this window.'

He could be a statue or the shadow of one, a hard edge to the lamplight. He gives no sign of having heard.

Wasps are slithering, whining over her window panes. One comes bumbling in hesitant orbits round her head. It has yellow legs and rasps across her papers jerking its long ringed belly. She slaps it with a newspaper and sweeps it on to the floor, afraid to touch it in case a dead wasp can still sting, if you touch the sting. Then she sits down at the table under the lamps with her writing pad and pen and scrawls on, though her hand, she sees, is shaking.

'Not to be with me.'

She smiles. *'Of course to be with you. You know that.'*

'I thought you had a story you wanted to finish.'

'I had. It's finished.'

GRAHAM SWIFT

Seraglio

In Istanbul there are tombs, faced with calligraphic designs, where the dead Sultan rests among the tiny catafalques of younger brothers whom he was obliged, by custom, to murder on his accession. Beauty becomes callous when it is set beside savagery. In the grounds of the Topkapi palace the tourists admire the turquoise tiles of the Harem, the Kiosks of the Sultans, and think of girls with sherbet, turbans, cushions, fountains. 'So were they just kept here?' my wife asks. I read from the guidebook: 'Though the Sultans kept theoretical power over the Harem, by the end of the sixteenth century these women effectively dominated the Sultans.'

It is cold. A chill wind blows from the Bosphorus. We had come on our trip in late March, expecting sunshine and mild heat, and found bright days rent by squalls and hail-storms. When it rains in Istanbul the narrow streets below the Bazaar become torrents, impossible to walk through, on which one expects to see, floating with the debris of the market, dead rats, bloated dogs, the washed up corpses of centuries. The Bazaar itself is a labyrinth with a history of fires. People have entered, they say, and not emerged.

From the grounds of the Topkapi the skyline of the city, like an array of upturned shields and spears, is unreal. The tourists murmur, pass on. Turbans, fountains; the quarters of the Eunuchs; the Pavilion of the Holy Mantle. Images out of the Arabian Nights. Then one discovers, as if stumbling oneself on the scene of the crime, in a glass case in a museum of robes, the spattered kaftan in which Sultan Oman II was assassinated. Rent by dagger thrusts from shoulder to hip. The thin linen fabric could be the corpse itself. The simple white garment, like a bathrobe, the blood-stains, like the brown stains on the gauze of a removed elastoplast, give you the momentary illusion that it is your gown lying there, lent to another, who is murdered in mistake for yourself.

We leave, towards the Blue Mosque, through the Imperial Gate, past the fountain of the Executioner. City of monuments and murder, in which cruelty seems ignored. There are cripples in the streets near the Bazaar, shuffling on leather pads, whom the tourists notice but the inhabitants do not. City of siege and massacre and magnificence. When Mehmet the Conqueror captured the city in 1453 he gave it over to his men, as was the custom, for three days of pillage and slaughter; then set about building new monuments. These things are in the travel books. The English-speaking guides, not using their own language, tell them as if they had never happened. There are miniatures of Mehmet in the Topkapi Museum. A pale, smooth-skinned man, a patron of the arts, with a sensitive gaze and delicate eyebrows, holding a rose to his nostrils . . .

It was after I had been explaining to my wife from the guide-book, over lunch in a restaurant, about Mehmet's rebuilding of the city, that we walked round a corner and saw a taxi – one of those metallic green taxis with black and yellow chequers down the side which cruise round Istanbul like turquoise sharks – drive with almost deliberate casualness into the legs of a man pushing a cart by the kerb. A slight crunch; the man fell, his legs at odd angles, clothes torn, and did not get up. Such things should not happen on holiday. They happen at home – people cluster round and stare – and you accommodate it because you know ordinary life includes such things. On holiday you want to be spared ordinary life.

But then it was not the fact of the accident for which we were unprepared but the reactions of the involved parties. The injured man looked as if he were to blame for having been injured. The taxi driver remained in his car as if his path had been deliberately blocked. People stopped on the pavement and gabbled, but seemed to be talking about something else. A policeman crossed from a traffic island. He had dark glasses and a peaked cap. The taxi driver got out of his car. They spoke languidly to each other and seemed both to have decided to ignore the man on the road. Beneath his dark glasses the policeman's lips moved delicately and almost with a smile, as if he were smelling a flower. We walked on round the corner. I said to my wife, even though I knew she would disapprove of the joke: 'That's why there are so many cripples.'

Our hotel is in the new part of Istanbul, near the Hilton, overlooking the Bosphorus, across which there is a newly built bridge. Standing on the balcony you can look from Europe to Asia. Uskudar, on the other side, is associated with Florence Nightingale. There are few places in the world where, poised on one continent, you can gaze over a strip of water at another.

We had wanted something more exotic. No more Alpine chalets and villas in Spain. We needed yet another holiday, but a different holiday. We had had this need for eight years and it was a need we could afford. We felt we had suffered in the past and so required a perpetual convalescence. But this meant, in time, even our holidays lacked novelty; so we looked for somewhere more exotic. We thought of the East. We imagined a landscape of minarets and domes out of the Arabian Nights. However, I pointed out the political uncertainties of the Middle East to my wife. She is sensitive to such things, to even remote hints of calamity. In London bombs go off in the Hilton and restaurants in Mayfair. Because she has borne one disaster she feels she should be spared all others, and she looks upon me to be her guide in this.

'Well Turkey then – Istanbul,' she said – we had the brochures open on the table, with their photographs of the Blue Mosque – 'that's not the Middle East.' I remarked (facetiously perhaps: I make these digs at my wife and she appreciates them for they reassure her that she is not being treated like something fragile) that the Turks made trouble too; they had invaded Cyprus.

'Don't you remember the Hamiltons' villa? They're still waiting to know what's become of it.'

'But we're not going to Cyprus,' she said. And then, looking at the brochure – as if her adventurousness were being tested and she recognized its limits: 'Besides, Istanbul is in Europe.'

My wife is beautiful. She has a smooth, flawless complexion, subtle, curiously expressive eyebrows, and a slender figure. I think these were the things which made me want to marry her, but though they have preserved themselves well in eight years they no longer have the force of a motive. She looks best in very dark or very pale colours. She is fastidious about perfumes, and tends devotedly our garden in Surrey.

She is lying now on the bed in our hotel bedroom in Istanbul from which you can see Asia, and she is crying.

She is crying because while I have been out taking photos, in the morning light, of the Bosphorus, something has happened – she has been interfered with in some way – between her and one of the hotel porters.

I sit down beside her. I do not know exactly what has happened. It is difficult to elicit details while she is crying. However, I am thinking: She only started to cry when I asked, 'What's wrong?' When I came into the room she was not crying, only sitting stiller and paler than usual. This seems to me like a kind of obstructiveness.

'We must get the manager,' I say, getting up, 'the police even.' I say this bluffly, even a little heartlessly; partly because I believe my wife may be dramatizing, exaggerating (she has been moody, touchy ever since that accident we witnessed: perhaps she is blowing up some small thing, a mistake, nothing at all); partly because I know that if my wife had come out with me to take photos and not remained alone none of this would have occurred; but partly too because as I stare down at her and mention the police, I want her to think of the policeman with his dark glasses and his half-smiling lips and the man with his legs crooked on the road. I see that she does so by the wounded look she gives me. This wounds me in return for having caused it. But I had wanted this too.

'No,' she says, shaking her head, still sobbing. I see that she is not sobered by my remark. Perhaps there is something there. She wants to accuse me, with her look, of being cold and sensible and wanting to pass the matter on, of not caring for her distress itself.

'But you won't tell me exactly what happened,' I say, as if I am being unfairly treated.

She reaches for her handkerchief and blows her nose deliberately. When my wife cries or laughs her eyebrows form little waves. While her face is buried in the handkerchief I look up out of the window. A mosque on the Asian side, its minarets like thin blades, is visible on the skyline. With the morning light behind it, it seems illusory, like a cut-out. I try to recall its name from the guide-book but cannot. I look back at my wife. She has removed the handkerchief from her eyes. I realize she is right in reproaching me for my callousness. But this process of being harsh towards my wife's suffering, as if I blamed her for it, so that I in turn will feel to blame and she will then feel justified in pleading her suffering, is familiar. It is the only way in which we begin to speak freely.

She is about to tell me what happened now. She crushes the handkerchief in her hand. I realize I really have been behaving as if nothing had happened.

When I married my wife I had just landed a highly sought-after job. I am a consultant designer. I had everything and, I told myself, I was in love. In order to prove this to myself I had an affair, six months after my marriage, with a girl I did not love. We made love in hotels. In the West there are no harems. Perhaps my wife found out or guessed what had happened, but she gave no sign and I betrayed nothing. I wonder if a person does not know something has happened, if it is the same as if nothing had happened. My affair did not affect in any way the happiness I felt in my marriage. My wife became pregnant. I was glad of this. I stopped seeing the girl. Then some months later my wife had a miscarriage. She not only lost the baby, but could not have children again.

I blamed her for the miscarriage. I thought, quite without reason, that this was an extreme and unfair means of revenge. But this was only on the surface. I blamed my wife because I knew that, having suffered herself without reason, she wanted to be blamed for it. This is something I understand. And I blamed my wife because I myself felt to blame for what had happened and if I blamed my wife, unjustly, she could then accuse me, and I would feel guilty, as you should when you are to blame. Also I felt that by wronging my wife, by hurting her when she had been hurt already, I would be driven by my remorse to do exactly what was needed in the circumstances: to love her. It was at this time that I realized that my wife's eyebrows had the same attractions as Arabic calligraphy. The truth was we were both crushed by our misfortune, and by hurting each other, shifting the real pain, we protected each other. So I blamed my wife in order to make myself feel bound towards her. Men want power over women in order to be able to let women take this power from them.

This was seven years ago. I do not know if these

reactions have ever ceased. Because we could have no children we made up for it in other ways. We began to take frequent and expensive holidays. We would say as we planned them, to convince ourselves: 'We need a break, we need to get away.' We went out a lot, to restaurants, concerts, cinemas, theatres. We were keen on the arts. We would go to all the new things, but we would seldom discuss, after seeing a play for instance, what we had watched. Because we had no children we could afford this; but if we had had children we could still have afforded it, since as my career advanced my job brought in more.

This became our story: our loss and its recompense. We felt we had justifications, an account of ourselves. As a result we lived on quite neutral terms with each other. For long periods, especially during those weeks before we took a holiday, we seldom made love – or when we did we would do so as if in fact we were not making love at all. We would lie in our bed, close but not touching, like two continents, each with its own customs and history, between which there is no bridge. We turned our backs towards each other as if we were both waiting our moment, hiding a dagger in our hands. But in order for the dagger thrust to be made, history must first stop, the gap between continents must be crossed. So we would lie, unmoving. And the only stroke, the only wound either of us inflicted was when one would turn and touch the other with empty, gentle hands, as though to say, 'See, I have no dagger.'

SERAGLIO

It seemed we went on holiday in order to make love, to stimulate passion (I dreamt, perhaps, long before we actually travelled there, and even though my wife's milky body lay beside me, of the sensuous, uninhibited East). But although our holidays seldom had this effect and were only a kind of make-believe, we did not admit this to each other. We were not like real people. We were like characters in a detective novel. The mystery to be solved in our novel was who killed our baby. But as soon as the murderer was discovered he would kill his discoverer. So the discovery was always avoided. Yet the story had to go on. And this, like all stories, kept us from pain as well as boredom.

'It was the boy – I mean the porter. You know, the one who works on this floor.'

My wife had stopped crying. She is lying on the bed. She wears a dark skirt; her legs are creamy. I know who she is talking about, have half guessed it before she spoke. I have seen him, in a white jacket, collecting laundry and doing jobs in the corridor: one of those thick-faced, crop-haired, rather melancholy-looking young Turks with whom Istanbul abounds and who seem either to have just left or to be about to be conscripted into the army.

'He knocked and came in. He'd come to repair the heater. You know, we complained it was cold at night. He had tools. I went out onto the balcony. When he finished he called out something and I came in. Then he came up to me – and touched me.'

'Touched you? What do you mean – touched you?' I know my wife will not like my inquisitorial tone. I wonder whether she is wondering if in some way I suspect her behaviour.

'Oh, you know,' she says exasperatedly.

'No. It's important I know exactly what happened, if we're – '

'If what?'

She looks at me, her eyebrows wavering.

I realize again that though I am demanding an explanation I really don't want to know what actually happened or, on the other hand, to accept a story. Whether, for example, the Turk touched my wife at all; whether if he did touch her, he only touched her or actually assaulted her in some way, whether my wife evaded, resisted or even encouraged his advances. All these things seem possible. But I do not want to know them. That is why I pretend to want to know them. I see too that my wife does not want to tell me either what really happened or a story. I realize that for eight years, night after night, we have been telling each other the story of our love.

'Well?' I insist.

My wife sits up on the bed. She holds one hand, closed, to her throat. She has this way of seeming to draw in, chastely, the collar of her blouse, even when she is not wearing a blouse or her neck is bare. It started when we lost our baby. It is a way of signalling that she has certain inviolable zones that mustn't be trespassed on. She gets up and walks around the room. She seems overwhelmed and avoids looking out of the window.

'He is probably still out there, lurking in the corridor,' she says as if under siege.

She looks at me expectantly, but cautiously. She is not interested in facts but reactions. I should be angry at the Turk, or she should be angry at me for not being angry at the Turk. The truth is we are trying to make each other angry with each other. We are using the incident to show that we have lost patience with each other.

'Then we must get the manager,' I repeat.

Her expression becomes scornful, as if I am evading the issue.

'You know what will happen if we tell the manager,' she says. 'He will smile and shrug his shoulders.'

I somehow find this quite credible and for this reason want to scoff at it harshly. The manager is a bulky, balding man, with stylish cuff-links and a long, aquiline nose with sensitive nostrils. Every time trips have been arranged for us which have gone wrong or information been given which has proved faulty he has smiled at our complaints and shrugged. He introduces himself to foreign guests as Mehmet, but this is not significant since every second Turk is a Mehmet or Ahmet. I have a picture of him listening to this fresh grievance and raising his hands, palms exposed, as if to show he has no dagger.

My wife stares at me. I feel I am in her power. I know

she is right; that this is not a matter for the authorities. I look out of the window. The sun is glinting on the Bosphorus from behind dark soot-falls of approaching rain. I think of what you read in the guide-books, the Arabian Nights. I should go out and murder this Turk who is hiding in the linen cupboard.

'It's the manager's responsibility,' I say.

She jerks her head aside at this.

'There'd be no point in seeing the manager,' she says.

I turn from the window.

'So actually nothing happened?'

She looks at me as if I have assaulted her.

We both pace about the room. She clasps her arms as if she is cold. Outside the sky is dark. We seem to be entering a labyrinth.

'I want to get away,' she says, crossing her arms so her hands are on her shoulders. 'This place' – she gestures towards the window. 'I want to go home.'

Her skin seems thin and luminous in the fading light.

I am trying to gauge my wife. I am somehow afraid she is in real danger. All right, if you feel that bad, I think. But I say, with almost deliberate casualness: 'That would spoil the holiday, wouldn't it?' What I really think is that my wife should go and I should remain, in this unreal world where, if I had the right sort of dagger, I would use it on myself.

'But we'll go if you feel that bad,' I say.

Outside a heavy shower has begun to fall.

'I'm glad I got those photos then,' I say. I go to the

window where I have put the guide-books on the sill. A curtain of rain veils Asia from Europe. I feel I am to blame for the weather. I explain from the guide-book the places we have not yet visited. Exotic names. I feel the radiator under the window ledge. It is distinctly warmer.

My wife sits down on the bed. She leans forward so that her hair covers her face. She is holding her stomach like someone who has been wounded.

The best way to leave Istanbul must be by ship. So you can lean at the stern and watch that fabulous skyline slowly recede, become merely two-dimensional; that Arabian Nights mirage which when you get close to it turns into a labyrinth. Glinting under the sun of Asia, silhouetted by the sun of Europe. The view from the air in a Turkish Airlines Boeing, when you have had to cancel your flight and book another at short notice, is less fantastic but still memorable. I look out of the port-hole. I am somehow in love with this beautiful city in which you do not feel safe. My wife does not look; she opens a magazine. She is wearing a pale-coloured suit. Other people in the plane glance at her.

All stories are told, like this one, looking back at painful places which have become silhouettes, or looking forward, before you arrive, at scintillating façades which have yet to reveal their dagger thrusts, their hands in hotel bedrooms. They buy the reprieve, or the stay of execution, of distance. London looked inviting from the air, spread out under clear spring sunshine; and one understood the pleasures of tourists staying in hotels in Mayfair, walking in the morning with their cameras and guide-books, past monuments and statues, under plane trees, to see the soldiers at the Palace. One wants the moment of the story to go on for ever, the poise of parting or arriving to be everlasting. So one doesn't have to cross to the other continent, doesn't have to know what really happened, doesn't have to meet the waiting blade.

FRANK
MOORHOUSE

The New York Bell
Captain

DEPOSITION ONE

In New York City, at the old Times Square Hotel, I place
my six bottles of Heineken beer along the window sill
to chill in snow, to save the 50-cent ice charge, to avoid
filling the hand-basin with ice and beer, and to spare
myself the sight of the bell captain's outstretched palm.
I then leave my room to push my way along the Manhattan streets through the muggers, but change my mind

at the hotel door and the snow and return, instead, to drink my Heineken. Reaching the room I find the beer gone from the sill. Instantly, without a flicker of hesitation, I know that the bell captain has swiftly checked my room to find out if I am using the window sill to chill my beer instead of paying him 50 cents plus tip to bring up a plastic bag full of melting ice. Quick work on his part. I open out the window to look for clues and as I do the six bottles of Heineken are swept off the sill down fifteen stories into Fifty-Fourth Street – and the bad end of Fifty-Fourth. I am too apathetic to bother looking down. Already New York is dehumanising me. And I've lost my beer. At first I think it is all my mistake – that when I first looked for the beer I looked at the wrong window. That I then opened the right window in the wrong way and pushed them off. (May be a lot of the so-called muggings in New York are really head injuries from falling bottles from hotel windows sills because hungry-handed bell captains charge too much for ice.) But as I sit there bereft and brooding I arrive at a more convincing conclusion about the beer, the sill, the window. What the bell captain has done is to come into my room, find the bottles, steal one or two or even three and then switch them to where I will sweep the remaining bottles off. This way I will never know if he has been into my room to steal my beer. I will therefore be unable to bring substantiated allegations against him. Alright. This round to the bell captain.

DEPOSITION TWO

I have proved that the bell captain provides ice which is at melting point. I suspected this from the start. The first time I ordered ice I paid him 50 cents, tipped him, checked my wallet, latched and locked the door and propped a chair against it, when I turned around all I had was a plastic bag of ice-water. So I did this. I bought a bag of ice from the drugstore next door to the hotel and sat there in my room and timed its melting against another bag of the bell captain's ice. The results were inconclusive but down in the bell captain's den, I am convinced that they leave the ice out of the freezer to bring it just to melting point and they give this ice to non-tippers or a person who doesn't tip 'enough' for bell captains. I have a frustrated urge to hand them my wallet, to put my wallet in the hand of the bell captain and ask him to take what he thinks is 'fair'. I was told of a man who had no hands and who kept his money in that unused outside breast pocket of his suit (which schoolboys, railway clerks, electricity-meter readers, and eccentrics use sensibly for pens and pencils) so that taxi drivers and so on could help themselves to the money. Poor bastard. Perhaps I should pull my hands into my sleeves and let New York help itself.

DEPOSITION THREE

Anyhow, what can they do to you if you don't tip? What they do in New York is they turn off the heat to your room.

Can they do that? Is that mechanically possible – can they isolate one room out of six hundred and turn off its heat? Well they did it to my room. They must have a control panel down in the bell captain's den.

DEPOSITION FOUR

Every afternoon I have a conversation through the keyhole with the maid who wants me to leave the room so that she can 'change the linen'. When am I going out, she inquires. For 'change the linen' read: Allow the bell captain to come in and prowl about my room and steal my Heineken beer. We come to an arrangement. I take my Heineken in my brief case and sit in the lobby while she 'changes the linen'.

DEPOSITION FIVE

Oh, they know that Francois Blase is just a *nom de voyage*. I know I have not fooled them. The word has gone around too that we are exchange-rate millionaires. Bell captains study the exchange rate. In a ploy to exact larger tips the bell captain has told the doorman to stop opening the door for me, despite a tip of 75 cents the previous evening for bringing up half a dozen Heineken and a packet of crackerjack. When I didn't order ice they knew I was using the window sill.

When I suspect the doorman is not opening the door for me as a reprimand for using the window sill and not buying melted ice from them, I sit in the lobby and count the comings and goings and the times the doorman opens the door. To confirm my suspicions. He opens the door every time. I then rise from my chair in the lobby and go to the door, even saying something genial about the Miami Dolphins and the League to show my immersion in the life of the United States and to show that I bear no ideological or other objections and so on. The bell captain pretends not to hear and the doorman pretends to answer the telephone. I have to open the door myself. The first of twelve comings and goings that the doorman had not opened the door. I 'turn on my heel' and return to my room, deeply miffed.

DEPOSITION SIX

I eat, imprudently, in the lobby restaurant as I do not feel like going out that much – things to do in my room and so on. Obviously the waiter ignores me on the whisper from the bell captain, despite my dollar tip to him for sending a cable home for more money so that I could continue to tip the hotel staff. I eventually have to lean from my chair and grab the waiter's sleeve and jacket with both my hands pulling him to an unsteady halt and me nearly out of my chair. With many smiles, bowing and scrapings, I say that I am going to the theatre and am therefore in a rush. He says what, at 5.45? But anyhow I get some service. Except that what I ask for is off, he says, although I think I see others being served it, and I think he brings me something other than what I ordered, but it takes so long I can't really remember what I ordered. At least I get my Heineken. Of course, I am being penalised for some breach of the hotel customs. I leave a 27-per-cent tip as a gesture of my willingness to 'get along'.

DEPOSITION SEVEN

I eat in the lobby restaurant again, not feeling like going out because I see a blizzard hiding behind the clouds waiting to lash out at me. This time the restaurant pulls a switch in behaviour to throw me into anguish and confusion. On a signal from the bell captain which I did not see, the waiter serves me, this time, *too quickly*. A masquerade – uncivilised haste masquerading as promptness. They want to get me out of the restaurant, get me to rush my food. They don't like me because I dawdle over my food with a book. Hah! They don't like people who read books at dinner. They think, maybe, I am 'parading' my bookishness. So, it's the book-reading that sticks in their gut.

Despite the rushed service, I tip heavily again. I do this for three reasons: to preserve the good name of dinner-table book-readers; to show that I am above pettiness; and to make them think that maybe we are the world's fastest eaters as well as being best at everything else. In short to repay confusion with confusion.

I stand in the lobby picking my teeth, here it is only

6.15 and I've eaten a three-course dinner. I toy with the idea of going out and sparring with the people of New York, turning the table on a few muggers, but decide to go back to my room and have a quiet Heinie and watch colour TV. The bell captain and doorman smile, tip their caps, bow and so on – all unfelt gestures, a debasement of the body-language of service. I know they don't care. The doorman even goes through the motions of opening the lift door, which is automatic. I tip him without looking to see if he smiles or says thankyou, and without consulting my Chamber of Commerce Guide to tipping in automatic lifts.

DEPOSITION EIGHT

A stranger in the lobby asks me for change for the 'valet' slot machine. I at first pretend not to hear, a New York reflex, knowing that as soon as I reach for my money I will betray the amount that I carry, as soon as I speak he will know where I come from and am therefore rich and generous and foolish, and that Francois Blase is a cover, and that whatever I do will reveal me as naive and paranoiac. There is something else, I fear, which I call New York Sleight of Hand, which will make whatever I have disappear. He persists in what appears to be a civilised, middle-class way, so I give him a handful of change. He offers me a note. I wave it away. He thanks me wonderously and goes to the valet machine, looking back at me and back to his handful of money. At first

I feel pleased with myself – it is this sort of gesture that gets us a good name. But when I glance over to the bell captain he appears to be scowling and refuses to meet my eyes. I enter the lift, troubled. In the lift it dawns on me. It is his job to give change and, anyhow, the valet machine is an automation of hotel employment and is probably declared black by the hotel staff. How stupid of me. I have robbed the bell captain of a quarter tip; diminished his role; and threatened his employment. I feel chilly. For these things I will have to pay.

DEPOSITION NINE

When I get to my room the heat is off. Apart from the obvious offences like giving change in the lobby, using the window sill to chill beer, I must have done other offensive things. I rove over my dealings with the hotel staff and my mind recalls to me the automatic lift. One lift is automatic and the other is run by a one-armed black. I have preference for the automatic lift and this must count against me. Maybe I should use the one-armed black lift driver to keep him in employment, as an endorsement of the human element in mechanised society, and as a gesture against discrimination. Maybe I should tip the black lift driver too, although my information from the Chamber of Commerce is that lift drivers are not tipped. Next time, I go by the one-armed black's lift and I see that he is selling the Sunday *New York Times* and I buy a copy from him, although I worry about the newpaper seller in the lobby who is blind and what he will think. The one-armed lift driver charges me 75 cents for the 50-cent paper. With some sort of neurotic reversed-response (like those who smile involuntarily when informed of tragedy), I apologise and thank the one-armed black lift driver. What about the blind paper seller?

DEPOSITION TEN

I am, I tell myself, too passive before the minor oppressions. I am always virtuously assertive about the major oppressions of our times. Apartheid, you name it. But I remain timid before the accumulated indignities which sour the quality of life. I adopt a pretentious inner attitude of 'Pooh, I have not the mental time to worry about the miscellaneous petty injustices of the day-to-day world. My life is dedicated to a larger mission.' So I let waiters off.

I resolve to change this. I go down and confront the manager when my heat is off on the third afternoon. I begin by saying that I know all about Traveller Paranoia and that I have tested myself. I am not suffering from Traveller Paranoia. I want, I tell him, no accusations of that sort.

The depositions of my journal, which I produce as Exhibit A, and the whole heat business, clearly make a case against the bell captain and I call for his dismissal.

I refer the manager to the case of *Jackson v. Horizon Holidays Ltd*. A person who books a holiday at a hotel which falls short of the brochure description can claim damages for vexation and disappointment.

People throughout the world, I thunder, have for too long taken advantage of our open, relaxed, simplified, small-country responses to life. For too long now we have been known as 'easy going'. Because we inhabit a rich, technologically advanced, uncrowded, clean country we are resented and penalised.

I close my case.

'About the economics and geography of your country I know nothing, Mr Blase, but as for the heat – this is a fuel saving measure introduced because of the world fuel situation. Between eleven and three, we turn off the heat. It is the warmest part of the day. Also, most people are usually out of their rooms at around these times.'

I stare at him.

I marvel at the ingenuity of his defence.

Alright, I say, this time I'll accept what you say and, 'turning on my heel', I go back to my room.

I need time to pick apart this carefully prepared explanation.

SUMMING UP

Later, brooding in my cold room, the point of his last remark comes to me, 'most people are usually out of their rooms at around these times'.

What business is it of anyone that I have not left the hotel precincts for five days or so? Do I go out and be mugged on the streets of Manhattan so that the bell captain can have a free hand with the thieving of my Heineken? So they can pick over my luggage. I rent the room. I don't have to go out to see landmarks every day of my life. Anyhow, everything that happens on a journey is 'experience'. It doesn't have to be all landmarks and monuments. Maybe, for all they know, I am exploring the inner spaces of my mind, the subterranean caves of my personality, gazing with new understanting at the ruins and monuments of my own archaeology. The seven wonders of the heart. What would the staff of the old Times Square Hotel know about that? Nothing. Nothing at all.

EVELYN LAU

Glass

She has put her fist through the window of her apartment. As she pulls her arm back, along with half the window, the shards slice across her wrist and the palm of her hand, simple as a knife slicing through uncooked white chicken meat. The blood begins to fill the gash to the brim, spilling over, as she looks down at her hand with detachment. The sound of glass falling fills her ears with wind chimes, the sound of glass spinning in the blue night. Ballerinas of glass cling to her wrist; she plucks them out, lets them fall to the floor.

She walks to the bathroom and holds the cut hand under the tap, filling the sink with diluted blood. She smiles to herself – she always smiles when she feels broken and ground-up, with nothing left except a diamond in her chest. A diamond that nobody can pluck out and possess. A diamond beautiful like herself. She knows she is beautiful, because the sure, sharp mirror tells her so.

I see someone in the mirror, though, who is not beautiful, and that is why she hates me. I am the part of her she wants to kill. She has tried before, but what she doesn't know is that if it wasn't for me she would have died long ago. I won't let her die; even if she doesn't like me, I won't. Maybe that is why she hates me so much. I'm the one who holds her together, and how can I help it if I see bloodshot eyes and the pores of her skin when she bends over the mirror?

The blood mingles in the water in the sink, in sluggish streaks. The water becomes the color of roses. She can hear the glass falling in her apartment; her attention has always been held by bright and flashing things, and she is awed at having created the scattering glass with its private, special orchestra. She loves anything prismatic, fake or real. Chandelier droplets. Diamonds. Treasure buried in white lines ... She wraps her hand in a towel, watching the blue material become tie-dyed with splotches of red. She walks back to the living room and sees the window, an open mouth in the night, dripping glass.

I wish she would pick up the phone and call someone. I want to help her, but she will do whatever she wants to, as she always has. She needs stitches, but although the cut – so clean and deep – was painless, she is terrified of blind needles probing the depth of the wound.

That she is never afraid of anything unusual, but will flee from the ordinary, is a remarkable contradiction. She is all contradictions, her need and her dependency warmly sloshing inside her, and on the surface the frozen lake for others to skate on. I know all this. I don't know why she can't hear my voice. I'm the only one who can love her unconditionally, but she persists in looking outwards.

She stands, holding her hand, near the waterfall of glass. She wants to be with someone brilliant and crazy and artistic like herself. As she thinks this, a smile leaps around her mouth and she spins, dodging the glass that flies into the room. It winks at her lethally from the carpet. She bends over and picks up a piece, stroking it carefully with her finger; it has a sharp, sexy, dangerous curve to it.

Do you see why I am worried about her? Her hand has stopped bleeding, but I don't like the way she acts in times like this, when the white lines seem to tighten their weave around her, when, with her eyes closed, she sees a razor busily cutting, chopping, dividing. But the lines are not the problem; the problem is that she is like a new-born baby who will die without touch. Only my arms can enfold her body, and sometimes, strangely, I want her all to myself. I want it to be just me and her, forever. Like diamonds. Forever. I could rescue her each time from her madness. I could catch the fragments of her and hold them together when she falls and cracks open. Whenever she spins like this, dizzily, I could press each star of her close and protect her.

She stands static, thinking of Allan as the flakes of glass hum in the background. The last time they had been together, she had lain there looking up at him with so much trust in her eyes. He had looked back down at her without smiling, without tenderness, in the 3:00 A.M. dimness. She had seen embarrassment and anger in his face as he thrust himself in and out of her deliberately, one of her white legs stretched up like an arching swan's neck onto his shoulder. Perhaps that trust had frozen him because he could not meet it. Perhaps he could not admire her for this. Perhaps he too only craved things beyond his reach and despised her for giving herself to him. But how else could she have done it? He never phoned, though from the first night he had said he loved her, would have married her if ... if she wasn't so needy? If she didn't pull at him quite so much, trying to take hold of just a corner of him to pull down into her blackness? Allan called himself a marketer of mirages. His phone began ringing every morning at 5:00 with stock-market representatives from New York; he sauntered whistling to his sports car to drive to company meetings. On the evenings when he came to pick her up, jazz on the radio, the web of stars jailed her and she reeled, spinning apart from the speed. Those nights when he buried his head between her thighs for hours, arduous, relentless, she had always felt as if he was trying to take her to some place where she did not belong. Maybe he was searching for the diamond inside her? That was why although in her mind and behind her shut eyes she was looming larger and larger, threatening to branch out, transcend her body, she stayed intact, with her nails digging into the hands on her belly. Their nights grew progressively silent until they never talked anymore; he busily digging with his tongue, she fighting the commands of her body.

No, she could not whirl seductively on the edge of his world. I see that, I see how impossible it all was, and how she had to phone him then, late at night when the white lines had faded and she would speed in a dark cab across the city, looking at the lights colorful and cold. It disturbs me that she was always in such bad shape when she arrived, was always pulling and dragging at his corners. They could have loved each other, measured out equal amounts of light and dark for each other, if she hadn't been on the verge of what she thought was death. If maybe, just once, she had not called him and made herself ugly by whispering *I need you*. Because, though he is the one person who could live with her level of pain, he didn't choose to. I don't think he was contemptuous of her, exactly. It was only that once, just once, he would have liked to see her real smile, not the crazy butterflies that flitted around her mouth. He would have enjoyed that, I think. They could have built something together then, from that one smile.

But she stands now at the jaws of the window, her hand clothed in tie-dyed cotton, listening to the radiant music of falling glass. She pictures Allan in his penthouse bed, with the mountains melting outside the window, the city gathered together and pooled beneath the balcony. The wind is blowing into his apartment, over the crystal ball on his desk, over the bamboo plants, over the waterbed. He is settling under the rose-colored comforter, grateful for the silent phone, the stars floating past the breathing green bamboo, past the pulsating crystal, settling around the mountains.

She stands there, holding her own hand, empty of pain. She watches the glass swoop from the window onto the pavement below, sprawling like dancers in lewd but beautiful positions on the sidewalk. And I hold her hand and tell her that it is better this way, that I am the only one she has, the only one who can keep her safe. She nods, and the diamond glitters in a lump in her chest, intact, and I take her hand and guide her away from the music, down a line of soft white glass.

WILL SELF

A Short History of the
English Novel

'All crap,' said Gerard through a mouthful of hamburger, 'utter shite – and the worst thing is that we're aware of it, we know what's going on. Really, I think, it's the cultural complement to the decline of the economy, in the seventies, coming lolloping along behind.'

We were sitting in Joe Allen and Gerard was holding forth on the sad state of the English novel. This was the only price I had to pay for our monthly lunch together: listening to Gerard sound off.

I came back at him. 'I'm not sure I agree with you on this one, Gerard. Isn't that a perennial gripe, something that comes up time and again? Surely we won't be able to judge the literature of this decade for another thirty or forty years?

'You're bound to say that, being a woman.'

'I'm sorry?'

'Well, insomuch as the novel was very much a feminine form in the first place, and now that our literary culture has begun to fragment, the partisan concerns of minorities are again taking precedence. There isn't really an "English novel" now, there are just women's novels, black novels, gay novels.'

I tuned him out. He was too annoying to listen to. Round about us the lunchtime crowd was thinning. A few advertising and city types sipped their wine and Perrier, nodding over each other's shoulders at the autographed photos that studded the restaurant's walls, as if they were saluting dear old friends.

Gerard and I had been doing these monthly lunches at Joe Allen for about a year. Ours was an odd friendship. For a while he'd been married to a friend of mine but it had been a duff exercise in emotional surgery, both hearts rejecting the other. They hadn't had any children. Some of our mutual acquaintances suspected that they were gay, and that the marriage was one of convenience, a coming together to avoid coming out.

Gerard was also a plump, good-looking man; who despite his stress-filled urban existence still retained the burnish of a country childhood in the pink glow of his cheeks and the chestnut hanks of his thick fringe.

Gerard did something in publishing. That was what

accounted for his willingness to pronounce on the current state of English fiction. It wasn't anything editorial or high profile. Rather, when he talked to me of his work – which he did only infrequently – it was of books as so many units, trafficked hither and thither as if they were boxes of washing powder. And when he spoke of authors, he managed somehow to reduce them to the status of assembly line workers, trampish little automata who were merely bolting the next lump of text on to an endlessly unrolling narrative product.

'... spry old women's sex novels, Welsh novels, the Glasgow Hard Man School, the ex-colonial guilt novel – both perpetrator and victim version ...' He was still droning on.

'What are you driving at, Gerard?'

'Oh come on, you're not going to play devil's advocate on this one, are you? You don't believe in the centrality of the literary tradition in this country any more than I do, now do you?'

'S'pose not.'

'You probably buy two or three of the big prize-winning novels every year and then possibly, just possibly, get round to reading one of them a year or so later. As for anything else, you might skim some thrillers that have been made into TV dramas – or vice versa – or scan something issue-based, or nibble at a plot that hinges on an unusual sexual position, the blurb for which happens to have caught your eye – '

'But, Gerard' – despite myself I was rising to it – 'just

because we don't read that much, aren't absorbed in it, it doesn't mean that important literary production isn't going on – '

'Not that old chestnut!' he snorted. 'I suppose you're going to tell me next that there may be thousands of unbelievably good manuscripts rotting away in attic rooms, only missing out on publication because of the diffidence of their authors or the formulaic, sales-driven narrow-mindedness of publishers, eh?'

'No, Gerard, l wasn't going to argue that – '

'It's like the old joke about LA, that there aren't any waiters in the whole town, just movie stars "resting". I suppose all these bus boys and girls' – he flicked a hand towards the epicene character who had been ministering to our meal – 'are great novelists hanging out to get more material.'

'No, that's not what I meant.'

'Excuse me?' It was the waiter, a lanky blond who had been dangling in the mid-distance, 'Did you want anything else?'

'No, no,' Gerard started shaking his head – but then broke off. 'Actually, now that you're here, would you mind if I asked you a question?'

'Oh Gerard,' I groaned, 'leave the poor boy alone.'

'No, not at all, anything to be of service.' He was bending down towards us, service inscribed all over his soft-skinned face.

'Tell me then, are you happy working here or do you harbour any other ambition?' Gerard put the question as straightforwardly as he could but his plump mouth was twisted with irony.

The waiter thought for a while. I observed his flat fingers, nails bitten to the quick, and his thin nose coped with blue veins at the nostrils' flare. His hair was tied back in a pony-tail and fastened with a thick rubber band.

'Do you mind?' he said at length, pulling half-out one of the free chairs.

'No, no,' I replied, 'of course not.' He sat down and instantly we all became intimates, our three brows forming a tight triangle over the cruets. The waiter put up his hands vertically, holding them like parentheses into which he would insert qualifying words.

'Well,' a self-deprecatory cough, 'it's not that I mind working here – because I don't, but I write a little and I suppose I would like to be published some day.'

I wanted to hoot, to crow, to snort derision, but contented myself with a 'Ha!'.

'Now come on, wait a minute.' Gerard was adding his bracketing hands to the manual quorum. 'OK, this guy is a writer but who's to say what he's doing is good, or original?'

'Gerard! You're being rude – '

'No, really, it doesn't matter, I don't mind. He's got a point.' His secret out, the waiter was more self-possessed. 'I write – that's true. I think the ideas are good. I think the prose is good. But I can't tell if it hangs together.'

'Well, tell us a bit about it. If you can, quote some from memory.' I lit a cigarette and tilted back in my chair.

'It's complex. We know that Eric Gill was something more than an ordinary sexual experimenter. According to his own journal he even had sex with his dog. I'm writing a narrative from the point of view of Gill's dog. The book is called *Fanny Gill or I was Eric Gill's Canine Lover*.' Gerard and I were giggling before he'd finished; and the waiter smiled with us.

'That's very funny,' I said, 'I especially like the play on – '

'Fanny Hill, yeah. Well, I've tried to style it like an eighteenth-century picaresque narrative. You know, with the dog growing up in the country, being introduced to the Gill household by a canine pander. Her loss of virginity and so on.'

'Can you give us a little gobbet then?' asked Gerard. He was still smiling but no longer ironically. The waiter sat back and struck a pose. With his scraped-back hair and long face, he reminded me of some Regency actor-manager.

'Then one night, as I turned and tossed in my basket, the yeasty smell of biscuit and the matted ordure in my coat blanketing my prone form, I became aware of a draught of turpentine, mixed with the lavender of the night air.

'My master the artist and stone carver, stood over me.

' "Come Fanny," he called, slapping his square-cut

hands against his smock, "there's a good little doggie." I trotted after him, out into the darkness. He strode ahead, whilst I meandered in his wake, twisting in the smelly skeins betwixt owl pellet and fox stool. "Come on now!" He was sharp and imperious. A tunnel of light opened up in the darkness. "Come in!" he snapped again, and I obeyed – poor beast – unaware that I had just taken my last stroll as an innocent bitch.'

Later, when we had paid the bill and were walking up Bow Street towards Long Acre, for no reason that I could think of I took Gerard's arm. I'd never touched him before. His body was surprisingly firm, but tinged with dampness like a thick carpet in an old house. I said, trying to purge the triumph from my tone, 'That was really rather good – now wasn't it?'

'Humph! S'pose so, but it was a "gay" novel, not in the mainstream of any literary tradition.'

'How can you say that?' I was incredulous. 'There was nothing obviously gay about it.'

'Really, Geraldine. The idea of using the dog as a sexual object was an allegory for the love that dare not speak its name, only wuffle. Anyway, he himself – the waiter, that is – was an obvious poof.'

We walked on in silence for a while. It was one of those flat, cold London days. The steely air wavered over the bonnets of cars, as if they were some kind of automotive mirage, ready to dissolve into the tarmac desert.

We normally parted at the mouth of the short road

that leads to Covent Garden Piazza. I would stand, watching Gerard's retreating overcoat as he moved past the fire-eaters, the jugglers, the stand-up comedians; and on across the parade ground of flagstones with its man-oeuvring battalions of Benelux au pair girls. But on this occasion I wouldn't let him go.

'Do you have to get back to the office? Is there actu-ally anything pressing for you to do?'

He seemed startled and turning to present the oblong sincerity of his face to me – he almost wrenched my arm. 'Erm . . . well, no. S'pose not.'

'How about a coffee then?'

'Oh all right.'

I was sure he had meant this admission to sound cool, unconcerned, but it had come out as pathetic. Despite all his confident, wordy pronouncements, I was beginning to suspect that Gerard's work might be as meaningless as my own.

As we strolled, still coupled, down Long Acre, the commercial day was getting into its post-prandial lack of swing. The opulent stores with their displays of flash goods belied what was really going on.

'The recession's certainly starting to bite,' Gerard remarked, handing a ten-pence piece to a dosser who sat scrunched up behind a baffler of milk crates, as if he were a photographer at one of life's less sporting events.

'Tell me about it, mate.' The words leaked from the gaps in the dosser's teeth, trickled through the stubble of his chin and flowed across the pavement carrying their barge-load of hopelessness.

The two of us paused again in front of the Hippodrome.

'Well,' said Gerard, 'where shall we have our coffee then? Do you want to go to my club?'

'God, no! Come on, let's go somewhere a little youthful.'

'You lead – I'll follow.'

We passed the Crystal Rooms, where tense loss adjusters rocked on the saddles of stranded motor cycles, which they powered on through pixilated curve after pixilated curve.

At the mouth of Gerrard Street, we passed under the triumphal arch with its coiled and burnished dragons. Around us the Chinese skipped and altercated, as scrutable as ever. Set beside their scooterish bodies, adolescent and wind-cheating, Gerard appeared more than ever to be some Scobie or Brown, lost for ever in the grimy Greeneland of inner London.

Outside the Bar Italia a circle of pari-cropped heads was deliberating over glasses of *caffe latte* held at hammy angles.

'Oh,' said Gerard, 'the Bar Italia. I haven't been here in ages, what fun.' He pushed in front of me into the tiled burrow of the café. Behind the grunting Gaggia a dumpy woman with a hennaed brow puffed and pulled. '*Due espressi*'! Gerard trilled in cod-Italian tones. '*Doppio!*'

'I didn't know you spoke Italian,' I said as we scraped

back two stools from underneath the giant video screen swathing the back of the café.

'Oh well, you know . . .' He trailed off and gazed up as the flat tummy filling the hissing screen rotated in a figure-eight of oozing congress. A special-effect lipoma swelled in its navel and then inflated into the face of a warbling androgyne.

A swarthy young woman with a prominent mole on her upper lip came over and banged two espressos down on the ledge we were sitting against.

'I say,' Gerard exclaimed; coffee now spotted his shirt front like a dalmatian's belly. 'Can't you take a little more care?' The waitress looked at him hard, jaw and brow shaking with anger, as if some prisoners of con-sciousness were attempting to jack-hammer their escape from her skull. She hiccupped, then ran the length of the café and out into the street, sobbing loudly.

'What did I say?' Gerard appealed to the café at large. The group of flat-capped Italian men by the cake display had left off haggling over their pools coupons to stare. The hennaed woman squeezed out from behind the Gaggia and clumped down to where we sat. She started to paw at Gerard's chest with a filthy wadge of J-cloths.

'I so sorry, sir, so sorry . . . '

'Whoa! Hold on – you're making it worse!'

'Iss not her fault, you know, she's a good girl, ve-ery good girl. She have a big sadness this days – '

'Man trouble, I'll be bound.' Gerard smirked. It

looked like he was enjoying his grubby embrocation.

'No, iss not that . . . iss, 'ow you say, a re-jection?'

I sat up straighter. 'A rejection? What sort of rejection?'

The woman left off rubbing Gerard and turned to me. 'She give this thing, this book to some peoples, they no like – '

'Ha, ha! You don't say. My dear Gerard' – I punched him on the upper arm – 'it looks like we have another scrivenous servitor on our hands.'

'This is absurd.' He wasn't amused.

'My friend here is a publisher, he might be able to help your girl, why don't you ask her to join us?'

'Oh really, Geraldine, can't you let this lie? We don't know anything about this girl's book. Madam – '

But she was already gone, stomping back down the mirrored alley and out the door into the street, where I saw her place an arm round the heaving shoulders of our former waitress.

Gerard and I sat in silence. I scrutinised him again. In this surrounding he appeared fogeyish. He seemed aware of it too, his eyes flicking nervously form the carnal cubs swimming on the ethereal video screen to their kittenish domesticated cousins, the jail bait who picked their nails and split their ends all along the coffee bar's counter.

The waitress came back down towards us. She was a striking young woman. Dark but not Neapolitan, with a low brow, roughly cropped hair and deep-set, rather steely eyes that skated away from mine when I tried to meet them.

'Yes? The boss said you wanted to talk to me – look, I'm sorry about the spillage, OK?' She didn't sound sorry. Her tears had evaporated, leaving behind a tidal mark of saline bitterness.

'No, no, it's not that. Here, sit down with us for a minute.' I proffered my pack of cigarettes; she refused with a coltish head jerk. 'Apparently you're a writer of sorts?'

'Not "of sorts". I'm a writer, full stop.'

'Well then,' Gerard chipped in, 'what's the problem with selling your book? Is it a novel?'

'Ye-es. Someone accepted it provisionally, but they want to make all sorts of stupid cuts. I won't stand for it, so now they want to break the contract.'

'Is it your first novel?' asked Gerard.

'The first I've tried to sell – or should I say "sell-out" – not the first I've written.

'And what's the novel about – can you tell us?'

'Look' – she was emphatic, eyes at last meeting mine – 'I've been working here for over a year, doing long hours of mindless skivvying so that I have the mental energy left over for my writing. I don't need some pair of smoothies to come along and show an interest in me.'

'OK, OK,' For some reason Gerard had turned emollient, placatory. 'If you don't want to talk about it, don't, but we are genuinely interested.' This seemed to work, she took a deep breath, accepted one of my cigarettes and lit it with a *fatale*'s flourish.

'All right, I'll tell you. It's set in the future. An old hospital administrator is looking back over her life. In her youth she worked for one of a series of hospitals that were set around the ring road of an English provincial town. These had grown up over the years from being small cottage hospitals serving local areas to becoming the huge separate departments – psychiatry, oncology, obstetrics – of one great regional facility.

'One day a meeting is held of all the Region's administrators, at which it is realised that the town is almost completely encircled by a giant doughnut of health facilities. At my heroine's instigation policies are fomented for using this reified *cordon sanitaire* as a means of filtering out undesirables who want to enter the town and controlling those who already live in it. Periods of enforced hospitalisation are introduced; troublemakers are subjected to "mandatory injury". Gradually the administrators carry out a slow but silent coup against central as well as local government.

'In her description of all these events and the part she played in them, my heroine surveys the whole panorama of such a herstory. From the shifting meaning of hygiene as an ideology – not just a taboo – to the changing gender roles in this bizarre oligopoly – '

'That's brilliant!' I couldn't help breaking in. 'That's one of the most succinct and clearly realised satirical ideas I've heard in a long time – '

'This is not a satire!' she screamed at me. 'That's what these stupid publishers think. I have written this book in the grand tradition of the nineteenth-century English novel. I aim to unite dramatically the formation of individual character to the process of social change. Just because I've cast the plot in the form of an allegory and set it in the future, it has to be regarded as a satire!'

'Sticky bitch,' said Gerard, some time later as we stood on the corner of Old Compton Street. Across the road in the window of the catering supplier's, dummy waiters stood, their arms rigidly crooked, their plastic features permanently distorted into an attitude of receptivity, preparedness to receive orders for second helpings of inertia.

'Come off it, Gerard. The plot sounded good – more than good, great even. And what could be more central to the English literary tradition? She said so herself.'

'Oh yeah, I have nothing but sympathy for her sometime publishers, I know just what authors like that are to deal with. Full of themselves, of their bloody idealism, of their pernickety obsession with detail, in a word: precious. No, two words: precious and pretentious.

'Anyway, I must get – ' but he bit off his get-out clause; someone sitting in the window of Wheeler's – diagonally across the street from us – had caught his eye. 'Oh shit! There's Andersen the MD. Trust him to be having a bloody late lunch. I'll have to say hello to him, or else he'll think that I feel guilty about not being at the office.'

'Oh I see, negative paranoia.'

'Nothing of the sort. Anyway, I'll give you a ring, old
girl – '

'Not so fast, Gerard, I'll come and wait for you. I want
to say goodbye properly.'

'Please yourself,' he shrugged in the copula of our
linked arms.

I stood just inside the entrance while Gerard went and
fawned over his boss. I was losing my respect for him
by the second. Andersen was a middle-aged stuffed suit
with a purple balloon of a head. His companion was
similar. Gerard adopted the half-crouch posture of an
inferior who hasn't been asked to join a table. I couldn't
hear what he was saying. Andersen's companion ges-
tured for the bill, using that universal hand signal of
squiggling with an imaginary pen on the sheet of the air.

The waiter, a saturnine type who had been lingering
by a half-open serving hatch in the oaken mid-ground
of the restaurant, came hustling over to the table, almost
running. Before he reached the table he was already
shouting, 'What are you trying to do! Take the piss!'

'I just want the bill,' said Andersen's companion.
'What on earth's the matter with you?'

'You're taking the piss!' the waiter went on. He was
thin and nervy, more like a semiologist than a servant.
'You know that I'm really a writer, not a waiter at all.
That's why you did that writing gesture in the air. You
heard the talking, talking frankly and honestly to some
of the other customers, so you decided to make fun of

me, to deride me, to put me down!' He turned to address the whole room. The fuddled faces of a few lingering lunchers swung lazily round, their slack mouths O-ing.

'I know who you are!' The waiter's rapier finger pointed at Andersen's companion. 'Mister-bloody-Hargreaves. Mister big fat fucking publisher! I know you as well, Andersen! You're just two amongst a whole school of ignorami, of basking dugongs who think they know what makes a jolly fucking good read. Ha!'

Gerard was backing away from the epicentre of this breakdown in restraint, backing towards me, trying to make himself small and insignificant. 'Let's get the hell out of here,' he said over his shoulder. The waiter had found some uneaten seafood on a plate and was starting to chuck it around: 'flotch!' a bivalve slapped against the flock wallpaper, 'gletch!' a squiggle of calimari wrapped around a lamp bracket.

'I'll give you notes from underwater! I'll give you a bloody lobster quadrille' – he was doing something unspeakable with the remains of a sea bream – 'this is the *fin* of your fucking *siècle*!' He was still ranting as we backed out into the street.

'Jesus Christ.' Gerard had turned pale, he seemed winded. He leant up against the dirty frontage of a porn vendor. 'That was awful, awful.' He shook his head.

'I don't know, I thought there was real vigour there. Reminded me of Henry Miller or the young Donleavy.' Gerard didn't seem to hear me.

'Well, I can't go back to the office now, not after that.'

'Why not?'

'I should have done something, I should have intervened. That man was insane.'

'Gerard, he was just another frustrated writer, it seems the town is full of them.'

'I don't want to go back, I feel jinxed. Tell you what, let's go to my club and have a snifter – would you mind?' I glanced at my watch, it was almost four-thirty.

'No, that's OK, I don't have to clock-on for another hour.'

As we walked down Shaftesbury Avenue and turned into Haymarket the afternoon air began to thicken about us, condensing into an almost palpable miasma that blanked out the upper storeys of the buildings. The rush-hour traffic was building up around us, Homo Sierra, Homo Astra, Homo Daihatsu, and all the other doomsday subspecies, locking the city into their devolutionary steel chain. Tenebrous people thronged the pavements, pacing out their stay in this pedestrian purgatory.

By the time we reached the imposing neo-classical edifice of Gerard's club in Pall Mall, I was ready for more than a snifter.

In the club's great glass-roofed atrium, ancient bishops scuttled to and fro like land crabs. Along the wall free-standing noticeboards covered in green baize were hung with thick curling ribbons of teletext news.

Here and there a bishop stood, arthritic claw firmly clamped to the test score.

I had to lead Gerard up the broad, red-carpeted stairs and drop him into a leather armchair, he was still so sunk in shock. I went off to find a steward. A voice came from behind a tall door that stood ajar at the end of the gallery. Before I could hear anything I caught sight of a strip of nylon jacket, black trouser leg and sandy hair. It was the steward and he was saying, 'Of course, *Poor Fellow My Country* is the longest novel in the English language, and a damn good novel it is too, right?' The meaningless interrogative swoop in pitch – an Australian. 'I'm not trying to do what Xavier Herbert did. What I'm trying to do is invigorate this whole tired tradition, yank it up by the ears. On the surface this is just another vast *Bildungsroman* about a Perth boy who comes to find fame and fortune in London, but underneath that – '

I didn't wait for more. I footed quietly back along the carpet to where Gerard sat and began to pull him to his feet.

'Whoa! What're you doing?'

'Come on, Gerard, we don't want to stay here – '

'Why?'

'I'll explain later – now come on.'

As we paced up St James's Street I told him about the steward.

'You're having me on, it just isn't possible.'

'Believe me, Gerard, you were about to meet another

attendant author. This one was a bit of a dead end, so I thought you could give him a miss.'

'So the gag isn't a gag?' He shook his big head and his thick fringe swished like a heavy drape against his brow.

'No, it isn't a gag, Gerard. Now let's stroll for a while, until it's time for me to go to work.'

We re-crossed Piccadilly and plunged into fine-art land. We wandered about for a bit, staring through window after window at gallery girl after gallery girl, each one more of a hot-house flower than the last.

Eventually we turned the corner of Hay Hill and there we were, on Dover Street, almost opposite the job centre that specialises in catering staff. What a coincidence. Gerard was oblivious as we moved towards the knot of dispirited men and women who stood in front. These were the dregs of the profession, the casual waiters who pick up a shift here and a shift there on a daily basis. This particular bunch were the failures' failures. The ones who hadn't got an evening shift and were now kicking their heels, having a communal complain before bussing off to the 'burbs.

Stupid Gerard, he knocked against one shoulder, caromed off another.

'Oi! Watch your step, mate – can't you look out where you're going?'

'I'm awfully sorry.'

' "Aim offly sorry".' They cruelly parodied his posh accent. I freed my arm from his and walked on, letting him fall away from me like the first stage of a rocket. He dropped into an ocean of Babel.

Terrified Gerard, looking from face to face. Old, young, black, white. Their uniform lapels poking out from their overcoat collars; their aprons dangling from beneath the hems of their macs. They sized him up, assessed him. Would he make good copy?

One of them, young and lean, grabbed him by the arm, detaining him. 'Think we're of no account, eh? Just a bunch of waiters – is that what you think?' Gerard tried to speak but couldn't. His lips were tightly compressed, a red line cancelling out his expression. 'Perhaps you think we should be proud of our work. Well we are matey, we fucking are. We've been watching your kind, noting it all down, putting it in our order pads while you snort in your trough. It may be fragmentary, it may not be prettified, it may not be in the Grand Tradition, but let me tell you,' and with this the young man hit Gerard, quite lightly but in the face, 'it's ours, and we're about ready to publish!'

Then they all waded in.

I was late for work. Marcel, the *maître d'*, tut-tutted as I swung open the door of the staff entrance. 'That's the third time late this week, Geraldine. Hurry up now, and change – we need to lay up.' He minced off down the corridor. I did as he said without rancour. Le Caprice may no longer be the best restaurant in London to eat at, but it's a great place to work. If you're a waiter, that is.

ROBERT
DREWE

Life of a Barbarian

When the earthquake strikes, Michael Pond is trying
to wash away his hangover in the shower. Suddenly
the floor of the shower cabinet slides from under his
feet. As he slips, he twists his back and bumps his
head on the wall. Landing heavily on his buttocks, he
sits staring stupidly at his courtesy toiletries hopping
along the edge of the wash-basin and dropping to the
floor.

Six point five on the Richter scale; the whole hotel is
waving like a blade of grass. Luckily the epicentre is
well north of Tokyo. For a second the earth seems to be
opening beneath Pond, and his runaway razor and tooth-

paste and miniature soaps and smashed bottle of *Eau Sauvage* are portents of the end.

But as time expands and the bathroom keeps undulating he becomes fatalistic. He feels silly, nearly amused, as if he's in an animated cartoon. He can see himself sitting on the floor watching the waving walls with his mouth in a surprised O. He wipes up the broken glass with a towel, and then the past twenty-four hours get too much for him. Still half-wet, he climbs back into bed and collapses.

———

A long flight from Australia, with the usual drinks on the plane and more when they reach the Imperial and check in. Then when Dick Hannam from Trade suggests going out on the town a few of the delegation urge each other along. Pond succumbs.

At one-thirty they end up in this place Dick knows. The mama-san is just closing for the night but she asks them to wait while she organises the girls.

The waiting room takes some of the wind out of their sails. Suddenly it's something like the dentist's, with the seascape prints and stacks of magazines and a big tank of tropical fish in the reception area. But a dentist of dreams. There is a TV set in a corner and an old man is glued to it, watching a game show. Three stony-faced Japanese men, presumably the winning contestants, file past four bare-breasted hostesses. The game-show host, dropping his clipboard to demonstrate, urges the men to tweak the women's nipples. This seems to be their prize.

Pond can't believe what he's seeing. 'Hey!' he says to the others. The prizewinners meanwhile give about five seconds' attention to each nipple, shuffling sideways between the hostesses. While the men are as serious as safe-crackers seeking the right combination, the women look over the prizewinners' earnest heads and twitter at the camera, showing green teeth. The program's color is richly askew. The teeth and flesh of the beaming host-esses, the men's square faces, are different shades of green; the women's lips are black and everyone is dressed in purple.

The woman who leads Pond away is sullen at having to work late. She makes his bath water too hot on purpose and orders him into it with bossy gestures. Like a lobster steaming on a rack, he sits panting on the wooden bath mat while she flicks around the room gathering towels and adjusting water pressures.

When she comes in her white tunic to wash him she is as brisk and efficient as a nurse, not an image or pro-cedure which overly excites him. The room fittings smell of rubber. An antiseptic steam rises from the bath. The sterile surroundings, somewhere between a laboratory and an operating theatre, make Pond feel helpless and alien, like an ape awaiting vivisection.

When she orders him from the bath he stands up and doesn't recognise his flesh. He is astonishingly red and hairy, more gross than he's ever noticed. He sags from the heat. Towering over the grumpy girl, sweat dripping from his chin, he mimes urgent drinking motions. 'Cold water,' he says.

Crossly, she unfurls a hose and mutters something. He drinks from it and runs water over his head. She regains the advantage by towelling him down with rough pats and wipes, without meeting his eyes or showing any expression or touching his face. Then she elbows him across the room towards a white cabinet, repeating a word he doesn't understand. Opening and shutting drawers, she selects the appropriate prophylactic. Then she orders him on to the operating table.

After the earthquake, while Pond sleeps, there is a sudden convulsion, a force, which shakes him and then squeezes the breath out of him. Is it an after-shock? A dream? A seizure? He feels no pain, just a crushing guilty exhaustion which sends him immediately back to sleep.

On waking properly he feels almost normal. The smell of *Eau Sauvage* fills the room. He showers again, dresses and goes down to breakfast. He considers using the stairs in case of another earthquake, but a sign saying *Elevator* in English confronts him so he obeys it. His back is sore from the fall in the shower. Otherwise there is no specific ache. His head is clear; there are no blank spots in his memory.

He is waiting for a taxi to the airport. The cab doesn't

turn up and he begins to panic. Why does this always happen? Taxis are not dependable on the North Shore. The plane leaves soon for Tokyo. Qantas agrees to hold the plane, but only after he mentions names, the mining industry, the fact that it is a government-backed delegation, Japanese trade, a reception to be given by the Japanese Prime Minister and so forth. Qantas says thirty minutes only.

Beth has to drive him and she is in a state. The traffic is sluggish all the way from Wahroonga. He is edgy; Beth's face is stony but tearful. Unsaid sentences hang in the air: he is always going away, the marriage is over. At the airport she turns her mouth from his kiss.

Inside the terminal, despite the rush, he telephones Beth's mother. 'Keep an eye on her,' he says. He is suddenly worried that she might do something. Airline staff shuffle and look at their watches. Economy and business classes have long since boarded. It isn't clear to him that he will see Beth again.

It's a long time since the certainties of his days as a mining engineer. Life was based on precision. Now he is 'management', on the board, and everything is on the verge of unreality. The old engineering phrase *angle of repose* occurs often to him these days. He feels he is living at the maximum angle at which he can exist without sliding.

Things are always on edge, about to tip. Beth, who took it badly when Matthew dropped out of university after only five weeks, takes it worse when he leaves home. She takes it even harder when he hitches north and joins the Hare Krishnas. In no time it is more than just another phase, more than his surfing craze or his post-punk fad or his alternative-farming thing. In no time he has become an initiated 'devotee' and taken a Hare Krishna name which Pond can't bring himself to remember. During their rare conversations he still calls him Matt.

Now Matthew lives mostly in Queensland. When his father phones him the people who answer are politely vague about his whereabouts. Northern New South Wales, they think. Or maybe Darwin. Pond imagines them not passing on his messages. He imagines them hiding behind brocade curtains stifling giggles.

Suddenly people with shaved heads and pony tails begin jigging around the edges of his consciousness. In the street he often hears cymbals and drums in the distance. On city corners he looks for Matthew among the ointment-faced chanters and stompers and then looks away in case he sees him.

Matthew has described his new life as 'moving around a lot, preaching'. Pond finds it hard to imagine his shy and sensitive son 'preaching'. To whom, the other converted? Beth is sure he has ruined his life; Matthew insists he has saved it. Either way, Beth cries every day and seems to hold her husband responsible.

Eventually they have little more to say on the subject of

Matthew. Gradually they stop talking about other painful topics as well. Pond dreads returning to her cold tearful face of an evening. Occasionally a late meeting or an early flight are an excuse to stay in town overnight, at Tattersall's or even the Hilton. It becomes a habit. There is a brief fling with a woman from the office, but she transfers to Melbourne.

On Christmas Eve Matthew phones out of the blue. He is in Sydney on his way somewhere. He might call around tomorrow. That night his parents are so excited and nervous they can't sleep. In his study Pond has a photograph of his son, aged five, sitting on the lowest branch of the jacaranda in the garden, smiling at the camera with his baby teeth. He – the photographer – hadn't noticed the bull ants swarming up the tree. Matthew was stung on the thigh seconds after he took the shot.

On Christmas Eve, unable to sleep, Pond is reading in the study and he glances up suddenly at Matthew about to be stung, happy, at that frozen instant, but about to cry in pain, and he loses his breath, feels an iron bar pressing on his throat. Choking, he weeps to save himself and is surprised at the relief of tears.

When Matthew arrives by taxi next morning there are more surprises. He is taller, fit-looking and politely smiling. There is no odd haircut, no clay markings on his face. His clothes are more conservative than his father's. He carries a briefcase. He looks like a North Shore parent's dream son, or an insurance salesman from 1954.

'That's their latest ruse,' Beth whispers in the kitchen. 'Looking normal.'

Matthew sits in an armchair like a visiting uncle and opens their presents, carefully chosen for their inoffensiveness. He has no presents for them. They wait earnestly for him to reveal his divine afflatus and they laugh at anything approaching a joke. But their son has run out of slang and forgotten old memories. His epiphany seems to have been little more than the joy of Asian lacto-vegetarianism. His talk is of dhal and ghee, the perfect papadom, his voice becoming softer and softer until it stops altogether. He politely pats the dog of his childhood. He flips in a scholarly way through the magazine rack, frowning at garish *Time* and *Vogue*. He peers in the fridge and says, 'Gee, you've got *fruit* in here!'

His parents are conscious of behaving unnaturally but can't help themselves. Beth has a secret cigarette going in the kitchen and she can't stop fidgeting and running back and forth to Matthew with fruity and nutty delicacies. He picks at them suspiciously. Perched on the edge of his chair making conversation, Pond feels like the candidate for a job that has already been filled. He is looking for some sign from this detached young man. Of familiarity, intimacy. Memory would do; he'd be happy with a recognition of past events, of the bull ants on the jacaranda, of Christmases past.

Matthew smiles indulgently at their cups of caffeine,

frowns at his watch, picks up his briefcase and softly says goodbye.

The censors have attacked all the cover girls in the bookshop. Not only the *Playboy* and *Penthouse* bunnies and pets but also the clothed and aloof *Vogue*, *Elle* and *Vanity Fair* models have ugly black smears across their chests and pelvises.

The nuances of Japanese culture are lost on Pond this morning. But at least the Imperial Hotel bookshop hasn't hedged on the central dilemma – the sword is just as evident as the chrysanthemum. He is browsing along the shelves after breakfast, waiting for his companions to assemble in the lobby. The range of books on Mishima's act of harakiri takes up as much shelf space as the ikebana picture books.

His mother's image of Japan is of cherry blossom branches and raked gravel. Perhaps envisioning a serene suburban widowhood spent handfeeding the carp in her kimono, she is attempting to create the vision in her garden at Lane Cove. She has planted miniature bamboo and dug a fish pond. She has bought a truck-load of river pebbles and laid down plastic sheeting to smother the weeds. But unkempt Australia overwhelms the harmony of Nippon. Crows eat the goldfish, while the delicate bamboo indecently thrives, immediately mutating into something thick and coarse, stretching up to the sun and down to the neighbours' sewage pipes.

It is only since his father's death that she feels free to indulge her interest in Japan. His father flew Boston bombers against the Japanese in New Guinea. As his mother grows older and more sentimental she increasingly mentions how brave and dashing he was, her Flight-Lieutenant, how decorated, although he can't recall any such complimentary references while his father was alive.

His father mentions the war only once that he can remember and even this reference is indirect. He is recalling his old flying school days at Point Cook, Victoria. He names a couple of friends. 'We were all pilots later in New Guinea,' he says. He pauses. Will he go on? 'Three Bostons flew into this cloudbank over Wewak. Only one flew out of it.'

But he has his revenge on the economic front. For thirty-five years his father maintains a personal boycott of Japanese products. He deliberately fails to purchase a Toyota or Nissan. (He drives Fords through thick and thin.) Forget Sanyo, he wilfully watches and listens to HMV. When he becomes sick there is a family joke: 'Let's spring it on him now that his pacemaker was made in Japan.'

The air-raid shelter behind the lantana hedge in the back yard: by 1952 it is an underground hideout full of spiders. But it is still a mine of Japanese intelligence. Shored up with war comics, souvenirs and *The Knights of Bushido*. One boy has a Japanese sword, one a pistol holster, another an officer's cap from Singapore. Tales of torture, treachery and obsession. Pearl Harbor. The Burma Railroad. Prison camp executioners. Insane kamikazes. The idea of these manic airmen, grinning human bombs, sends its special thrill of terror through the boys. *Banzai*!

In the hotel bookshop Pond's eyes are drawn to a book on the kamikazes. It's a collection of their last letters, translated into English, called *Voices from the Sea*. The boy in the air-raid shelter eagerly buys it and stuffs it in his briefcase.

He learns that the literal translation of *kamikaze* is *heavenly wind* and that the term acquired its emotive meaning in the thirteenth century. Kublai Khan, grandson of Genghis Khan, had already overthrown the Sung dynasty and conquered China, as well as Turkestan, Manchuria, Korea, Annam and Burma. In 1281 he demanded that Japan too should surrender to him. Japan refused the barbarian's request. Kublai Khan ordered 100,000 warriors and 3,000 ships to conquer Japan. But the Mongols were slaphappy sailors and the enthusiasm of their Chinese and Korean auxiliaries was only lukewarm. The fleet sailed at the height of the typhoon season and, in sight of the Japanese coast, was destroyed in a storm. The *kamikaze*, the *heavenly wind*, had saved the Empire of the Rising Sun.

In spite of the heavenly wind, MacArthur is to be a luckier barbarian than Kublai Khan.

It was after the disastrous Philippines air and naval battle that Vice-Admiral Onishi came up with the idea of using voluntary pilots who had taken a vow of suicide. His scheme was taken up by Tokyo's General Staff as a means of inflicting heavy losses on the American fleet while stirring a despairing population at home with visions of sacrifice and romance.

The kamikazes were made a special corps with their own chief, Vice-Admiral Ugaki, and a distinctive uniform: on the tunic seven buttons decorated with three petals of cherry blossom, on the sleeve the anchor of the navy. A big fuss was made of them – and of their families at home, who were given the title 'Very Honorable'. It was important that a kamikaze's mind should be free of worry about his family.

The people of Japan were told of the kamikazes' existence by special communiqué issued by General Staff headquarters in November 1944. The story of the 'hero-gods' was immediately taken up by the press and then the people.

The official instructions given to the first kamikaze corps pointed out that the Empire stood at the crossroads between victory and defeat. The first suicide unit, triumphing through the power of the spirit, would inspire others to follow its example.

The instructions went on: 'It is out of the question for

you to return alive. Your mission involves certain death. Your bodies will be dead, but not your spirits. The death of a single one of you will be the birth of a million others. Neglect nothing that may affect your training or your health. You must not leave behind you any cause for regret which would follow you into eternity.'

————

Mr Ueda of Tanabe Steel ushers them from the first day's meetings to dinner and then to a men's drinking club, the Big Joy Club. The club has little Australian flags on the bar, and framed photographs of a koala and a frill-necked lizard. The professionally flirtatious hostesses pour them continual glasses of Suntory whisky and bully everyone into singing a song. Pond renders a desultory version of *Waltzing Matilda*. Back at the hotel, although drunk and tired, he is too restless to sleep and stays up reading *Voices from the Sea*.

Most of the 'hero-gods' were recruited from the universities of Tokyo and Kyoto. Secret instructions from the General Staff had recommended that the corps should take either the worst pilots or the youngest ones who had not yet undergone full training. The others, the professionals, were essential for the defence of Japan.

These younger and less capable pilots were given old aircraft which had been stripped of most of their armaments and instruments. They were given only enough fuel for the flight to their target, and they were escorted there by fighters. Their orders were to crash-land on their targets – battleships or, preferably, aircraft carriers.

On the eve of their departure the student pilots were given a funeral banquet. They were dressed in white, the colour of mourning. They symbolically divested themselves of all their worldly goods. They were each given a little white box in which to place cuttings of their hair and fingernails, to be sent to their family to be placed on the family altar in place of their ashes.

Sometimes the last night of the kamikazes degenerated into an orgy. Many of them got drunk on sake to keep their spirits up. Often they were provided with women from the villages around the air base. Even drunk and sated they were rarely able to sleep.

Pond drinks more whisky while he reads, every now and then getting up and dashing water on his face and pacing around the room before returning to the book.

The pilots' letters are mainly in the form of diary entries. One young law student admitted that he wasn't dying voluntarily. 'I am not going to my death without severe regrets,' he wrote. Next day he crashed his aircraft into the sea off Okinawa. No American shipping was nearby.

Another boy wrote proudly that he had just passed his basic flying test. 'I did the test at 7.40. I was very touched as I walked out of the hangar to see the mechanics fussing around my machine. It was a bright morning, the ceiling was at 6,000 feet. I flew round and round for a long time and I enjoyed it in spite of everything.'

Next day this boy's orders came. 'I take off tomorrow morning,' he wrote. 'Tonight the electric light has failed in my room. Oil burns in a tin and the flame throws shadows against the wall. Next door they are rowdy, playing gramophone records and drinking spirits. They probably have the right idea but I prefer to wait quietly.'

He farewelled his parents and asked them to pray for him. 'Twenty-three years of life are approaching their end,' he said. 'I am biting my fingers and the tears are flowing. With my eyes closed I evoke Mother's beloved image. She will never leave me.'

And then he wrote: 'A breath of wind arises. The Kamikaze. It comes to sweep away the sadness of my heart. I write the word "tomorrow" and stare at it. My life will have no tomorrow. My heart has no deviations. You will not receive my ashes; I will substitute my fingernails and my hair.'

After reading the boy's farewell Pond's head spins. The boy's night-light flickers in his mind and his heart races with sympathy and fatigue. The trails of aftershave lingering in the room sting his senses and make him nauseous and thirsty. He drinks a glass of water and tastes chemicals. Pacing the room, he feels alternately drunk and sober and is only slightly surprised to find himself suddenly on his back on the carpet.

Seconds or minutes pass. The cracks in the ceiling

remind him of the rosy broken veins which appeared in the cheeks of Mr Ueda of Tanabe Steel while Mr Ueda was singing, in alternate Japanese and English, *Love Me Tender*. Mr Ueda's romantic intensity and rosy cheeks were not evident during their protracted negotiations earlier in the day. Mr Ueda didn't have a sentimental bone in his body at 3 pm, but at midnight his eyes brimmed. He had his own drink locker at the Big Joy Club and his hostess smacked his cheeky hands and combed his hair for him in front of everyone.

Pond the engineer wonders whether the cracks are old or new. Eventually, making a decision, he gets up and moves to the telephone. Concentrating intently, he makes a call to Beth in Sydney. There is no answer. Then he moves to the window, resting his forehead against the glass and peering down on the bright malls and intersections of the business district. Bright signs flash for Seiko and Honda and Sanyo, and far off there is a neon champagne glass with popping bubbles.

And the window pane bumps against his head – two, three, four times. *Oh, Beth. Oh, Matt.* For a second his chest caves in like an accordion. When his breath comes back he knows he must leave the building, flee the earthquake. He hurries out of the swaying room, down the stairs, seven flights, and through the lobby into the street.

At the curb a taxi waits, quite motionless. The hotel is immobile again and everywhere Pond looks all the building lines remain straight and angles are secure at ninety degrees. The city, the night itself, is also still.

Hazy clouds cover the stars and the moon is a faint milky light.

Pond concentrates on adjusting his thinking. He tries to test the earth's mood and intentions with the soles of his feet. Back and forth he paces in front of the hotel, searching the skyline. Finally he spots the neon champagne glass. Keeping it strictly in view he signals the cab and points it out to the driver.

'Take me to that glass,' he says.

The driver is impassively reading a sex comic. He tears his eyes away to glance vaguely in the direction of the glass, then demands to be paid first. Pond gives him a handful of notes and they set off. Perhaps ten minutes later the cab stops, Pond climbs out and the cab accelerates away.

The buildings are too high for him to find the champagne glass; it's impossible to guess if its bubbles pop above him or not. But across the pavement there is a bar or restaurant displaying the usual plastic replicas of the food available inside: canny likenesses of sushi and shavings of fat-marbled beef and perfectly crafted slices of okra and seaweed and individual grains of rice. And sake, beer and whisky bottles.

Pond pushes at the door. When it resists him he begins thumping. Soon he hears footsteps and a short, thickset man comes to the door, taps his watch and waves him away. When Pond produces a wad of money the man punches his fist threateningly into his palm.

Pond backs away from the door. As he stands

indecisively in the street three men meander towards him, two of them steering and supporting a smaller drunken one whose cheeks, like Mr Ueda's, shine like cherries. They are all wearing business suits and, as they pass, the small man, inevitably, shouts abuse.

One of the more sober men mutters an apology. He is so contrite, bowing slightly, that Pond begins to ask him about the neon champagne glass's whereabouts and, lacking language, mimes the act of drinking. Abruptly the drunken man brushes off his helpers and lurches over to him. His head comes to Pond's chest and his affronted oiled hair rises in a porcupine's spikes. The ground is trembling beneath them; Pond's arms fly out to balance himself against the tremors and immediately the drunk exhales a sour whisky yell and lunges at him.

Caught in the chest, Pond sits down hard. As the spiky-haired man reels above him roaring joyous gibberish, the earth shudders and re-forms itself.

———

Will he and the earth ever stabilise? Taking light and steady breaths, focusing on each action and small accomplishment, he finds that it matters less.

He gets to the nearest intersection and hails a cab. It knows where he is going. At the brothel, in the dream-dentist's waiting room, the mama-san is watching cartoons with the old man. They chuckle without sounds, the laughter compressed into their foreheads and upper lips. A chubby rabbit teases a skinny fox. Both animals are dressed as farmers, in checked shirts and overalls. The rabbit gooses the fox with a pitchfork. Apparently this jab is the latest in a stream of barnyard indignities because the fox chases the rabbit and decapitates him with an axe. The TV color is rich and accurate tonight. Blood spurts from the rabbit's neck-stump; he flops around in dripping circles like a chicken. But there are no cartoon miracles in this place. Bunny's head doesn't pop back as cheeky as ever; the eyes on the severed head roll back; the ears go limp. It's curtains for bunny.

Pond looks at his watch; it's later than he imagined. *Ahem*. He stands up and taps the watch face. The old couple look keenly at him; their grim hesitation is a statement. Finally the mama-san gets up from her chair and pads out of the room. Pond calls after her, hoarse beseeching English hanging in the air: 'Could I have a woman who kisses?'

The shame strikes him at once. The old man turns abruptly back to the television, which is all greens and purples again. Again a game show is taking place. Toothy young men in running-shoes spring about with clipboards under their arms. Purple smiling hostesses move like robots, clutching burning tapers in their talons. Again the line of shuffling males appears, this time ten or twelve of them, company men identically dressed in mauve business suits. Their expressions are serious as they touch their toes; their trouser seats tauten as the camera pans over them and a hostess fussily tucks their jackets out of the way. And then another hostess passes behind them, coy as any magician's assistant, and waves her taper-wand behind each trouser seat.

The old man's chuckling escapes his closed mouth and rises high in his throat. One by one the bending men break wind. The hostess's taper flares and fizzes and individual flames shoot out across the screen.

Once again it is the woman with the nurse's demeanour who sullenly beckons him into her antiseptic, steaming room. He welcomes her like an old friend. Nevertheless, a moment later, his special request is denied.

His hotel stands solidly on its foundations. This is a satisfactory discovery. Pond is relieved to be walking through the lobby of the Imperial. Going up to his room, entering it, he feels that to an extent he is home and this calms him even more. Slowly and methodically he showers and shaves. He even cuts his fingernails and, with the nail scissors, trims his hair in the front where it isn't so grey. He dresses in clean clothes and packs all his belongings in his suitcase.

On hotel stationery he writes a letter to Beth and Matthew and places the cuttings of his hair and fingernails in the envelope. He takes the letter down to the front desk and returns to the security of his room.

Then he lies on the bed, and after thinking for a long while of Beth and Matthew, of life-stages and times when they were all younger, he begins to concentrate on the vibrations passing through and around his body. He is open to all the tremors and changes of the external and internal worlds. He feels all the movements along the fault plane as the daylight gradually comes through the window of his room.

JOAN DIDION

L.A. *Noir*

Around Division 47, Los Angeles Municipal Court, the downtown courtroom where, for eleven weeks during the spring and summer of 1989, a preliminary hearing was held to determine if the charges brought in the 1983 murder of a thirty-three-year-old road-show promoter named Roy Alexander Radin should be dismissed or if the defendants should be bound over to superior court for arraignment and trial, it was said that there were, 'in the works', five movies, four books, and 'countless' pieces about the case. Sometimes it was said that there were four movies and five books 'in the works', or one movie and two books, or two movies and six books. There were in any event, 'big balls' in the air. 'Everybody's working this one,' a reporter covering the trial said one morning as we waited to get patted down at the entrance to the courtroom, a security measure prompted by a telephoned bomb threat and encouraged by the general wish of everyone involved to make this a noticeable case. 'Major money.'

This was curious. Murder cases are generally of interest to the extent that they suggest some anomaly or lesson in the world revealed, but there seemed neither anomalies nor lessons in the murder of Roy Radin, who was last seen alive getting into a limousine to go to dinner at a Beverly Hills restaurant, La Scala, and was next seen decomposed, in a canyon off Interstate 5. Among the defendants actually present for the preliminary hearing was Karen Delayne ('Lanie') Jacobs Greenberger, a fairly attractive hard case late of South Florida, where her husband was said to have been the number-two man in the cocaine operation run by Carlos Lehder, the only major Colombian drug figure to have been tried and convicted in the United States. (Lanie Greenberger herself was said to have done considerable business in this line, and to have had nearly a million dollars in cocaine and cash stolen from her Sherman Oaks house not long before Roy Radin disappeared.) The other defendants present were William Mentzer and Alex Marti, somewhat less attractive hard cases, late of Larry Flynt's security staff. (Larry Flynt is the publisher of *Hustler*, and one of the collateral artifacts that turned up in the Radin case was a million-dollar check Flynt had written in 1983 to the late Mitchell Livingston WerBell III, a former arms dealer who operated a counterterrorism school outside Atlanta and described himself as a retired lieutenant general in the Royal Free Afghan Army. The Los Angeles County Sheriff's Department said that Flynt had written the check to WerBell as payment on a contract to kill Frank Sinatra, Hugh Hefner, Bob Guccione, and Walter Annenberg. Larry Flynt's lawyer said that there had been no contract, and described the check, on which payment was stopped, as a dinner-party joke.) There was also an absent defendant, a third Flynt security man, fighting extradition from Maryland.

In other words this was a genre case, and the genre, L.A. *noir*, was familiar. There is a *noir* case every year or two in Los Angeles. There was for example the Wonderland case, which involved the 1981 bludgeoning to death of four people. The Wonderland case, so called because the bludgeoning took place in a house on Wonderland Avenue in Laurel Canyon, turned, like the Radin case, on a million-dollar cocaine theft, but featured even more deeply *noir* players, including a nightclub entrepreneur and convicted cocaine dealer named Adel Nasrallah, aka 'Eddie Nash'; a pornographic-movie star, now dead of AIDS, named John C. Holmes, aka 'Johnny Wadd'; and a young man named Scott Thorson, who was, at the time he first testified in the case, an inmate in the Los Angeles County Jail (Scott Thorson was, in the natural ecology of the criminal justice system, the star witness for the state in the Wonderland case), and who in 1982 sued Liberace on the grounds that he had been promised $100,000 a year for life in return for his services as Liberace's lover, driver, travel secretary, and animal trainer.

In this context there would have seemed nothing particularly novel about the Radin case. It was true that there were, floating around the edges of the story, several other unnatural deaths, for example that of Lanie Greenberger's husband, Larry Greenberger, aka 'Vinnie De Angelo', who either shot himself or was shot in the head in September of 1988 on the front porch of his house in Okeechobee, Florida, but these deaths were essentially unsurprising. It was also true that the Radin case offered not bad sidebar details. I was interested for example in how much security Larry Flynt apparently had patrolling Doheny Estates, where his house was, and Century City, where the *Hustler* offices were. I was interested in Dean Kahn, who ran the limousine service that provided the stretch Cadillac with smoked windows in which Roy Radin took, in the language of this particular revealed world, his last ride. I was interested in how Roy Radin, before he came to Los Angeles and decided to go to dinner at La Scala, had endeavored to make his way in the world by touring high school auditoriums with Tiny Tim, Frank Fontaine, and a corps of tap-dancing dwarfs.

Still, promoters of tap-dancing dwarfs who get done in by hard cases have not been, historically, the stuff of which five movies, four books, and countless pieces are made. The almost febrile interest in this case derived not from the principals but from what was essentially a cameo role, played by Robert Evans. Robert Evans had been head of production at Paramount during the golden period of *The Godfather* and *Love Story* and *Rosemary's Baby*, had moved on to produce independently such successful motion pictures as *Chinatown* and *Marathon Man*, and was, during what was generally agreed to be a dry spell in his career (he had recently made a forty-five-minute videotape on the life of John Paul II, and had announced that he was writing an autobiography, to be called *The Kid Stays in the Picture*), a district attorney's dream: a quite possibly desperate, quite famously risk-oriented, high-visibility figure with low-life connections.

It was the contention of the Los Angeles County District Attorney's office that Lanie Greenberger had hired her codefendants to kill Roy Radin after he refused to cut her in on his share of the profits from Robert Evans's 1984 picture *The Cotton Club*. It was claimed that Lanie Greenberger had introduced Roy Radin, who wanted to get into the movie business, to Robert Evans. It was claimed that Roy Radin had offered to find, in return for 45 percent of the profits from either one Evans picture (*The Cotton Club*) or three Evans pictures (*The Cotton Club, The Sicilian*, and *The Two Jakes*), 'Puerto Rican investors' willing to put up either thirty-five or fifty million dollars.

–Certain objections leap to the nonprosecutorial mind here (the 'Puerto Rican investors' turned out to be one Puerto Rican banker with 'connections', the money never actually materialized, Roy Radin therefore had no share of the profits, there were no profits in any case), but seem not to have figured in the state's case. The District Attorney's office was also hinting, if not quite contending, that Robert Evans himself had been in on the payoff of Radin's killers, and the DA's office had a protected witness (still another Flynt security man, this one receiving $3,000 a month from the Los Angeles County Sheriff's Department) who had agreed to say in court that one of the defendants, William Mentzer, told him that Lanie Greenberger and Robert Evans had, in the witness's words, 'paid for the contract'. Given the state's own logic, it was hard to know what Robert Evans might have thought to gain by putting out a contract on the goose with the $50 million egg, but the deputy district attorney on the case seemed unwilling to let go of this possibility, and had in fact told reporters that Robert Evans was 'one of the people who we have not eliminated as a suspect'.

Neither, on the other hand, was Robert Evans one of the people they had arrested, a circumstance suggesting certain lacunae in the case from the major-money point of view, and also from the district attorney's. Among people outside the criminal justice system, it was widely if vaguely assumed that Robert Evans was somehow 'on trial' during the summer of 1989. 'Evans Linked for First Time in Court to Radin's Murder,' the headlines were telling them, and, in the past-tense obituary mode, 'Evans' Success Came Early: Career Epitomized Hollywood Dream.'

'Bob always had a premonition that his career would peak before he was fifty and fade downhill,' Peter Bart, who had worked under Evans at Paramount, told the *Los Angeles Times*, again in the obituary mode. 'He lived by it. He was haunted by it ... To those of us who knew him and knew what a good-spirited person he was, it's a terrible sadness.' Here was a case described by the *Times* as 'focused on the dark side of Hollywood deal making', a case offering 'an unsparing look at the film capital's unsavory side', a case everyone was calling just Cotton Club, or even just Cotton, as in ' "Cotton": Big Movie Deal's Sequel Is Murder'.

Inside the system, the fact that no charge had been brought against the single person on the horizon who had a demonstrable connection with *The Cotton Club* was rendering Cotton Club, *qua* Cotton Club, increasingly problematic. Not only was Robert Evans not 'on trial' in Division 47, but what was going on there was not even a 'trial', only a preliminary hearing, intended to determine whether the state had sufficient evidence and cause to prosecute those charged, none of whom was Evans. Since 1978, when a California Supreme Court ruling provided criminal defendants the right to a preliminary hearing even after indictment by a grand jury, preliminary hearings have virtually replaced grand juries as a way of indicting felony suspects in California, and are one of the reasons that criminal cases in Los Angeles now tend to go on for years. The preliminary hearing alone in the McMartin child-abuse case lasted eighteen months.

On the days I dropped by Division 47, the judge, a

young black woman with a shock of gray in her hair, seemed fretful, inattentive. The lawyers seemed weary. The bailiffs discussed their domestic arrangements on the telephone. When Lanie Greenberger entered the courtroom, not exactly walking but undulating forward on the balls of her feet, in a little half-time prance, no one bothered to look up. The courtroom had been full on the day Robert Evans appeared as the first witness for the prosecution and took the Fifth, but in the absence of Evans there were only a few reporters and the usual two or three retirees in the courtroom, perhaps a dozen people in all, reduced to interviewing each other and discussing alternative names for the Night Stalker case, which involved a man named Richard Ramirez who had been accused of thirteen murders and thirty other felonies committed in Los Angeles County during 1984 and 1985. One reporter was calling the Ramirez case, which was then in its sixth month of trial after nine weeks of preliminary hearings and six months of jury selection, Valley Intruder. Another had settled on Serial Killer. 'I still slug it Night Stalker,' a third said, and she turned to me. 'Let me ask you,' she said. 'This is how hard up I am. Is there a story in your being here?'

The preliminary hearing in the Radin case had originally been scheduled for three weeks, and lasted eleven. On July 12, 1989, in Division 47, Judge Patti Jo McKay ruled not only that there was sufficient evidence to bind over Lanie Greenberger, Alex Marti, and William Mentzer for trial but also that the Radin murder may

have been committed for financial gain, which meant
that the defendants could receive, if convicted, penalties
of death. 'Mr. Radin was an obstacle to further negoti-
ation involving *The Cotton Club*,' the prosecuting attorney had argued in closing. 'The deal could not go
through until specific issues such as percentages were
worked out. It was at that time that Mrs. Greenberger
had the motive to murder Mr. Radin.''

I was struck by this as a final argument, because it
seemed to suggest an entire case based on the notion that
an interest in an entirely hypothetical share of the
entirely hypothetical profits from an entirely hypothetical motion picture (at the time Roy Radin was killed,
The Cotton Club had an advertising poster but no shoot-
ing script and no money and no cast and no start date)
was money in the bank. All that had stood between Lanie
Greenberger and Fat City, as the prosecutor saw it, was
boilerplate, a matter of seeing that 'percentages were
worked out'.

The prosecution's certainty on this point puzzled me,
and I asked an acquaintance in the picture business if he
thought there had ever been money to be made from *The
Cotton Club*. He seemed not to believe what I was
asking. There had been 'gross positions', he reminded
me, participants with a piece of the gross rather than the
net. There had been previous investors. There had been
commitments already made on *The Cotton Club*, paper
out all over town. There had been, above all, a $26
million budget going in (it eventually cost $47 million),

and a production team not noted for thrift. 'It had to make a hundred to a hundred forty million, depending on how much got stolen, before anybody saw gross,' he said. 'Net on this baby was dreamland. Which could have been figured out, with no loss of life, by a junior agent just out of the William Morris mailroom.'

There was always in the Cotton Club case a certain dreamland aspect, a looniness that derived in part from the ardent if misplaced faith of everyone involved, from the belief in windfalls, in sudden changes in fortune (five movies and four books would change someone's fortune, a piece of *The Cotton Club* someone else's, a high-visibility case the district attorney's); in killings, both literal and figurative. In fact this kind of faith is not unusual in Los Angeles. In a city not only largely conceived as a series of real estate promotions but largely supported by a series of confidence games, a city even then afloat on motion pictures and junk bonds and the B-2 Stealth bomber, the conviction that something can be made of nothing may be one of the few narratives in which everyone participates. A belief in extreme possibilities colors daily life. Anyone might have woken up one morning and been discovered at Schwab's, or killed at Bob's Big Boy. 'Luck is all around you,' a silky voice says on the California State Lottery's Lotto commercials, against a background track of 'Dream a Little Dream of Me'. 'Imagine winning millions . . . what would you do?'

During the summer of 1989 this shimmer of the possible still lay on Cotton Club, although there seemed, among those dreamers to whom I spoke in both the picture business and the criminal justice business, a certain impatience with the way the case was actually playing out. There was nobody in either business, including the detectives on the case, who could hear the words 'Cotton Club' and not see a possible score, but the material was resistant. It still lacked a bankable element. There was a definite wish to move on, as they say in the picture business, to screenplay. The detectives were keeping in touch with motion picture producers, car phone to car phone, sketching in connecting lines not apparent in the courtroom. 'This friend of mine in the sheriff's office laid it out for me three years ago,' one producer told me. 'The deal was, "This is all about drugs, Bob Evans is involved, we're going to get him." And so forth. He wanted me to have the story when and if the movie was done. He called me a week ago, from his car, wanted to know if I was going to move on it.'

I heard a number of alternative scenarios. 'The story is in this one cop who wouldn't let it go,' I was told by a producer. 'The story is in the peripheral characters,' I was told by a detective I had reached by dialing his car phone. Another producer reported having run into Robert Evans's lawyer, Robert Shapiro, the evening before at Hillcrest Country Club, where the Thomas Hearns–Sugar Ray Leonard fight was being shown closed circuit from Caesars Palace in Las Vegas. 'I asked how our boy was doing,' he said, meaning Evans. 'Shapiro says he's doing fine. Scot-free, he says. Here's the story. A soft guy from our world, just sitting up there in his sixteen-room house keeps getting visits from these detectives. Big guys, Real hard guys. Apes. Waiting for him to crack.'

Here we had the rough line for several quite different stories, but it would have been hard not to notice that each of them depended for its dramatic thrust on the presence of Robert Evans. I mentioned this one day to Marcia Morrissey, who – as co-counsel with the Miami trial lawyer Edward Shohat, who had defended Carlos Lehder – was representing Lanie Greenberger. 'Naturally they all *want* him in,' Marcia Morrissey said.

I asked if she thought the District Attorney's Office would manage to get him in.

Marcia Morrissey rolled her eyes. 'That's what it's called, isn't it? I mean face it. It's called Cotton Club.'

CANDIDA
BAKER

City Lights

The teenager, dressed in a pink paisley mini dress, with a matching headband and feather and teetering on blue platform-heeled shoes, cautiously makes her way through the wind tunnel which runs down beside Central station, where she catches the train to the north side, to the advertising agency where she is currently working as a secretary. It is cold, far too cold for her wardrobe, and there are goosebumps on her arms, so she hurries along, watching the pavements for cracks and assiduously ignoring the derelicts, who are just beginning to wake up.

The wind blows her hair across her face. She can

smell cigarettes from the night before, and it reminds her that again she has only the haziest recollection of how she spent the night after she went home from work to discover her mother passed out drunk on the sofa, and decided to get out. Tonight, she thinks, she will go home early enough to stop her mother from drinking and they will stay home together, have dinner, go to bed. It will be normal. It will be like old times.

'Come over here and warm us up love' . . . Miranda shoots them a glance and as the jeers and catcalls echo after her, hurries on towards her train.

Derek doesn't join in. He's not a joiner, Derek. From his position under one of the arches he only vaguely registers Miranda's presence as a passing blur of pink. Derek has been trying to stand up in order to undo his fly and relieve his bladder, but it is too late, and as the stain and stench of his urine seeping into his trousers reaches him, he knows this is not going to be a good day. 'Fucking cunt,' he says, making futile dabs at his crotch. 'Fucking cunt.'

Miranda is always dazzled by the train journey over the harbour. Even on a grey day like this one, rain clouds rolling in, she still can't believe her luck. Straight out of secretarial college, stints at the Tourist Office, Kleenex and the National Australia Bank behind her, she was told one day to report to a North Sydney advertising agency.

The morning she arrived a bearded man in a leather jacket had looked her up and down. 'I'm trying to work out the square footage of tits in the Miss World competition. What's an average bra size?'

'I don't know,' she said, 'I don't wear bras.'

He looked at her again. 'Neither you do.' He bent back over his calculator and paid her no further attention.

'34C,' shouted a woman from the other side of the open-plan office. 'At least that's what Cosmo says, it's probably 36 if you asked David Jones.'

The bearded man punched some numbers and grunted. 'Jesus fucking Christ, a fucking football field of boobs, that's what we've got if you laid them end to fucking end.'

Miranda wondered if she was in the right place. She waited to be told what to do, for the orders to issue forth.

She was used to the bureaucratic ways of the Tourist Office. 'Only one packet of Tipp-Ex per week, Miss Carson,' the dried-up old husk there had told her. 'Any more than that and you must provide it yourself.'

Walking away with her precious Tipp-Ex she knew perfectly well the dirty old lech was eyeing her backside. By lunchtime she had used the entire packet. She wasn't surprised when she got back from her break to discover that they had complained about her to the employment agency.

'They said your skirt was too short,' said Annabelle from the agency. 'More than six inches above your knee.'

'Did he have a ruler then?' Miranda asked. 'Perhaps it was down his trousers and I didn't spot it.'

Annabelle groaned. 'I'm *trying* to find you a job,' she

said. 'You don't make it easy for me.'

The same woman who had been dishing out bra-size advice now walked up to her. 'Are you working here?'

'I *think* so,' said Miranda.

'Get us a cup of coffee from the cafe up the road then would you?'

And that was it really, on-the-job training. Two months down the track and she was an accomplished dogsbody: lunch orders, taxis, restaurant bookings, flight details, typing, photocopying – anything that came her way. After hours she was one of them, taken to lunch by them, taken to dinner, taken on shoots, bought drinks, and, of course, slept with.

The Wednesday soup-kitchen lady was perturbed that Derek hadn't turned up for his hot meal.

'I think I'll go and take a look,' she said to Mark, her co-worker. 'It's not like him.'

Mark frowned. 'Be careful. You're not supposed to.'

But Stephanie, who had been doing the rounds for many years, felt sure of her ground on this one. 'Don't worry. He's quite safe. Wouldn't hurt a fly.'

But even she was shocked by the state she found him in. He reeked so much it was all she could do to kneel down to check he was alive.

'Derek,' she called. 'Derek . . . can you hear me?'

But Derek did not answer.

What Miranda has discovered is that now she is a

working girl, there is no need to stay home with her drunk mother. There are always men, any number of them, ready to keep her out all night. The ideal companion, she has found, is an older man with his own home and car. Never mind if he's married because he will either take you to a hotel, or if the wife – as he almost inevitably refers to his partner – is away, to his house. She cannot, however, go for a boy her own age (or indeed anyone within the same decade), because then they seem to expect a relationship, and this is the last thing Miranda wants. Relationships, Miranda knows, are messy and confusing. It never occurs to Miranda that she is being exploited by the men she sleeps with. As far as she's concerned it is an equal trade.

But today Miranda has decided she will not end up in the hotel after work. She will go home and cook dinner, and mother and daughter will eat together, maybe play Scrabble or watch television, and then go to bed. Sober and alone, the pair of them.

It takes several men to lift Derek into the ambulance. His lanky frame flops over itself at the slightest opportunity. Stephanie looks on. It is not the first time she has called for help, but it is the first time it has been a matter of life and death. She feels useful, and well . . . needed.

'Good luck, Derek,' she whispers.

In the hospital it takes several nurses to clean him up, and, as he begins to regain consciousness, several orderlies to strap him down so he doesn't do himself an injury while the DT's rage.

'What's your name?' asks the matron at regular intervals.

'I'm a fucking lifeboat,' Derek roars at her. (On a break with her cup of tea, the matron might ponder over this remark, wonder if perhaps it is some long-forgotten memory of a more useful life, or of a childhood on one of Sydney's beaches. Or maybe she will decide it's simply the rantings of a madman.)

Later, he gets crafty.

'What's your name?'

Smiles. 'You know . . . you tell me.'

'Now, now,' says Matron. 'You know the rules.'

Under the arches his companions line up for their soup and bread.

'Give us a buck, missus,' breathes one of them onto Stephanie, and she laughs.

'Come off it,' she says, but friendly – all flushed from her rescue mission. 'You shouldn't ask.'

In the bar it is warm and cozy, and outside the evening rain pours steadily down.

'Well, all right then,' says Miranda, lighting up a ciga-rette. 'Just one.'

In her flat Stephanie begins to prepare her dinner. She wishes there was someone she could tell about her day's excitement. She peels the potato, prepares her lamb chop, turns on the news.

In a house on the other side of the bridge, Miranda's mother lays the table.

In the hospital Derek has settled down and with massive amounts of sedative in him is finally calm enough for the nurses to spoon-feed.

As Miranda gets out of the taxi, she catches her tights and ladders them. 'Fuck,' she says, straightening herself and heading for the front door. She is feeling tiddly, full of bonhomie towards her fellow men – even towards Hans, who has been with the agency for three months and has not yet scored a lay, and who groped her on the way out of the pub, so that she was forced to kick him in the shins. She giggles at the memory. For a minute as she stands outside what was once the family home it seems cheerful, inviting. The lights are on, and as she enters she can hear the television. 'Mum,' she calls out, 'I'm home.'

This is what Derek does once he has come down from the DT's, and is full of baby food and hot sweet tea. He waits until the change of shift – he is an old hand at this – and before the night nurse can fully avail herself of all information regarding the spectrum of illnesses and night noises (oh, the hawking and spitting

243

and tiny bird-like cries) she will be looking after, he escapes. On his way, he finds a full load of laundry waiting in white bags on a trolley. He hauls one into the nearest toilet and fishes out clothes. Clean dry clothes. Not the right size of course but Derek does not notice or care. And dressed in his clean dry clothes, he stalks the hospital corridors to the exit, and sways his stooped frame down the wet street, sniffing like a pointer, nose into the wind for the way home, straight down Oxford Street, into Wentworth Avenue, and home, underneath the arches.

'You're drunk.'

'I am not. Anyway,' Carol hauls herself up in her chair, 'you're late.'

'Well, you didn't have to get drunk.'

'You said you'd be home early, that's what you said.'

'God, you're my mother, not my fucking boyfriend. I had one drink after work. One lousy drink to celebrate the end of the week, and you couldn't even stay sober that long.'

Her mother covers her eyes with her hands. 'Oh, my darling, I'm so miserable. I'm so miserable.'

But Miranda does not hear. She is already halfway up the stairs, full of rage, full of inevitability, heading towards the closet full of silk jackets, suede boots and velvet trousers. She is young. She is sexy. She is alive, tingling with the call of the evening, the drinks to come, the chat, the cigarettes – the hunt.

'I say,' says Stephanie. 'This wild-life documentary is frightfully good. You can't fault David Attenborough.'

With her foot she pushes the rocking chair full of teddy bears, so that they nod, their unblinking eyes fixed on her.

'Oh, yes, frightfully good.'

She thoughtfully sips the one glass of port she allows herself after dinner.

His patch.

'Derek. 'Ere . . . it's Derek.'

'G'day mate. Back from the fucking grave this time.'

Every night they light a fire in an old grate one of them had turned up with from somewhere. Not a night to be out this one, what with the rain and the wind, but under the arches they are dry. Derek's clothes begin to steam a clean antiseptic smell.

'Go on mate, have a swig.'

Derek nods, drinks, feels the liquor like a red-hot poker hit his throat and stomach. The aching familiarity of what he is about to do haunts him for a brief second so that he pauses, just for a moment, bottle to mouth.

In the train, travelling towards the city lights, travelling, as it happens, right over Derek's patch, Miranda looks out into the rainy dark and lights a cigarette. She smiles at her reflection in the mirror, purses her lips to lightly smooth her lipstick. Where will she start? Ah, she thinks, wherever. Wherever will do.

As the train rattles overhead, Derek lifts his bottle to the night sky. As the train rattles overhead a middle-aged woman makes herself hot cocoa and takes her teddy bear to bed. And a daughter heads for the city, and a mother weeps for lost lives.

PETER CAREY

Room No. 5 (Escribo)

I scratch my armpit and listen to the sound, like breakfast cereal. The hotel room has a title, *Escribo*. It was an office. Occasionally there is a rumbling upstairs, a vibration, and water cascades through the ceiling and splashes into the bidet beneath.

Trucks rumble through the town. They are filled with soldiers. It is likely that Timoshenko is finally dying, in which case there may be a coup, or possibly none, possibly a dusty road stretching across the plain and a wrapper from one of those bright green confections lost somewhere among the grasses.

The restaurant smells of piss and is humid. Condensation covers the tiled floor which is streaked with a fine grime. A large footprint with a rubberised pattern repeats itself. Jorge was here yesterday. Jorge may not be important to anything. He is a captain in Timoshenko's army but his ability to affect things is probably small.

Jorge's customs post is six kilometres along the road over the bridge. It will probably rain. If Timoshenko dies things may alter. The wind may blow from a different direction. It may continue hot. The sound of gunfire could be mistaken for thunder, or vice versa. In the urinal humidity of the restaurant possibilities smear into one another. Some young boys drink Coca-Cola and lean against the coffee machine. Outside there are more, revving Zundapps.

You lie on the bed and smile at the ceiling. I wonder what you think. Your smile is permanent and I have given up asking you about it. I have decided that you are smiling about a day five years ago. I have not yet decided what happened on that day. And, as you won't tell me, it is I who must decide, but later. I can think of nothing that might make you smile.

I asked you if you were frightened to die, now. You smiled and said nothing.

I asked the question to stop you smiling.

I don't know who you are. You have not stopped smiling since I found you at Villa Franca. You have not stopped smiling except to make love, and then you frown, as if you had forgotten what you were going to say. Your smile is full and gentle. It is a smile of softness and of complete understanding but you refuse to explain it and I do not know what you understand and you continue to refuse me this.

ROOM NO. 5 (ESCRIBO)

You wish for more yoghurt. Again, for the eighth time today, we leave this room and go to the cafe opposite the Restaurant Centrale. You eat yoghurt. I watch. The soldiers who sit at the other tables watch loudly. They watch us both. You frown, as if making love, eating yoghurt. I cannot bear the sight of it, the yoghurt, the texture of it is repulsive to me, like junket, liver, kidney, brains, Farax, and Heinz baby foods.

Your yoghurt finished, you look at me and smile. Your eyes crease around the edges. The strange thing about your smile is that it has never once become less real or less intense. It is a smile caught from a moment in a still photograph, now extended into an indefinitely long moving film. You look around the cafe. I tell you not to. The soldiers are not schooled in the strange ways of your smile and may misinterpret it. They have already misinterpreted it and sit at tables surrounding us.

If Timoshenko dies they will rape you and shoot me. That is one possibility, have you considered it?

I watch the spider as it crawls up your arm and say nothing. Yot know about it as you know about many things. You insisted on going through the border post ten minutes after me. Is it for that reason, because of your inexplicable behaviour, that they held you there so long. I saw, through the window of the verandah, the officials going through your baggage. They held up your underwear to the light but did not smile. Things are not happening as you might expect.

I wish you to frown at me. What would happen if

I asked you, gruffly, to frown at me here, in public? You would smile, suspecting a joke.

When the soldiers see us walking towards the cafe they call to us. I ask you to translate but you say it is nothing, just a cry. They wait for us to come and eat yoghurt. It is a diversion. While they remain at the cafe there cannot be a general alert. For that reason it is good to see them. They, for their part, are happy to see us. They call out 'Yoguee' as we walk up the hill towards them. When we arrive at the table there are two bowls of yoghurt waiting. For the third time I send one bowl back. The waiter refuses to understand and jokes with the soldiers. You say that his dialect is difficult to catch. It is a diversion.

The heat hangs over the town like a swarm of flies. Trucks rumble over the old stone bridge. It stinks beneath the bridge. If you couldn't smell the stink by the bridge the scene would be picturesque. I have taken photographs there, eliminating the stink. Also a number of candid shots of you. I wish you to appear pensive but you seem unable to portray yourself.

There are some good dirty jokes concerning the Mona Lisa's smile and the reasons behind it. Your smile is not so enigmatic. It is supremely obvious. It is merely its duration that is puzzling.

I do not know you. Your accent is strange and contains Manchester and Knightsbridge, but also something of Texas. You have been to many places but are vague as to why. You have no more money but expect some to arrive at the Banco Nationale any day. We wait for your money, for Timoshenko, for night, for morning, for the ceiling to rumble and the water to pour down. I have put newspaper in the bidet to stop the water from the ceiling splashing. I have begun a letter to my employers in London explaining my absence and there is nothing to stop my finishing it. I have hinted at a crisis but am unable to be more explicit. They, for their part, will interpret it as shyness, discretion, or the result of censorship.

At this moment the letter lies conveniently at the top of my suitcase. If the suitcase is searched the letter will be found easily. It is possibly incriminating, although it is constructed so as to reveal nothing. Knowing nothing, it is possible to reveal everything. That is the danger.

NIGHT

It is night. You lie in the dark with your face hidden in the pillow. You lie naked on top of the blanket; you like the texture of the blanket. It is hot and the blanket is grey and I lie beside you on the sheet, peering at the light entering the room through closed shutters. I have considered it advisable to keep the shutters pulled tight – the room is at street level and has a small balcony that juts out a foot or two above the cobbled roadway.

I touch your thigh with my toe and you make a noise. The noise is muffled by the pillow and I do not understand it.

I sleep.

When I wake you are no longer there. My body is electrified by short pulses of panic. The shutters arc open and a truck drives by, beside the balcony and above it. I hear the driver cough. Men in the back of the truck are singing sadly and softly. I listen to them hit the bump at the beginning of the bridge and hear the hard thump and clatter. The sad singing continues uninterrupted, as if suspended smoothly above the road.

You are no longer there. I dare not look for your bag, but you have left a handkerchief behind. I could rely on you for that, to leave small pieces of things behind you.

It is not the money. I am not concerned with the money. The Banco Nationale has not impressed me with its efficiency and I have no faith in its promises and assurances. They cashed your last traveller's cheque and gave a hundred U.S. dollars instead of ten. You laughed and took the money back, but not from a sense of caution.

In the bank there was an old woman in black who had her money in a partially unravelled sock. You stood behind her and smiled at her when she turned to stare at your dress. If the money were to arrive in an old sock I would have more confidence, but you say it is coming from Zurich and I have little hope. No, it is not the money, which we both undeniably need. The panic is not caused by the thought of you disappearing with or without the money, nor is it caused by the thought of the secret police, although I am not unconcerned by them.

But the panic is there. I fight it consciously. In my

mind I rearrange the filing system in my London office. There are some red tabs I have been anxious to order. I busy myself writing classifications on these red tabs. I write the names of my districts: Manchester, Stockport, Hazel Grove. At Hazel Grove I lose my place. I lie on the sheet covered by small pinpricks of energy and hear a man shout something that sounds like '*Escribo*'. I am sure he could not know the sign on the door of our room. Unless you have told them, and they have shouted it deliberately, to frighten me. For you say nothing of the police or the political situation when I attempt to discuss it. As for the newspapers, you say they are boring, not worth translating, and that, in any case, they are unlikely to report Timoshenko's death immediately. You say you have no idea why they would not let us back across the border last Sunday and claim that you accept their story as reasonable and correct. You have also suggested that it was because 'the border closes on Sunday' but that was not a very good joke. And, by now, it is essential that we wait 'until my cheque comes from Zurich'. You seem bemused, as patient as a sunbather.

Is it because you want to see the ending, how the story works out? Because I remember the way you were in Riano when we went to the cinema to see that American film, something about the FBI. You laughed continually and the audience made small hissing noises at you. But you waited, because you wanted to see the end. Then we went to a cafe for a drink and you sipped your sweet vermouth and I said, 'Wasn't it awful?'

There is a scratching at the door. You enter quietly, wearing my shirt over your dress. I can hear that your feet are bare. And I can smell you, the smell of your pulse. It is as if you opened a window on the inner regions of your soul. The smell is of rain on the wheat plains. Water and sand, seeds, cow dung, spit, wild-flowers, and dry summer grass.

You enter the room softly on your bare feet and I lie on the cool sheet watching you watching me.

I say, where were you.

You say, I went for a walk ... by the river.

I say, it stinks by the river.

You say, I know.

You have nothing but your skirt and my shirt on. You shed them limply and come to my bed, frowning gently.

DAY

The shutters are still open and a small boy watches us. He has climbed up from the roadway onto our small raised balcony. I place a sheet over you and stand up, gesturing to the child that he must go. He refuses to budge, staring fixedly at my cock. He has a large square head and small stupid eyes. Go, I say. But I do not move out onto the balcony where I could be viewed from the street. I could possibly be misinterpreted and that would be unfortunate.

Instead, I close the shutters and wait for him to go.

ROOM NO. 5 (ESCRIBO)

I wait five minutes by the watch on your sleep-limp wrist. He is still there. I make myself comfortable and wait.

He is probably from the police. That amuses me, but not sufficiently, because it is not totally impossible. Things are becoming less and less impossible.

I do not care about the police but would like to know why they refused to let us back across the border last Sunday.

Jorge is a captain in Timoshenko's army at the border post. I am informed of his name because he has been called that, Jorge, by people in the restaurant. Jorge has told you that there is a war across the border. Either that or that the people across the border are anxious to attack this country when Timoshenko dies. Or possibly both things. You say there was a difficulty with the grammar, a doubt about the meaning of a certain verb and one or two words that are phonetically confusing. But you have accepted all three possibilities as being true and reasonable. He bought you a drink and insisted that you sit at his table to drink it. I was more confused than hurt, more anxious than angry. It seemed possible that he was teasing, that he had fabricated or arranged a war to have you sit at his table.

That is why we now eat at the Restaurant Centrale. But sooner or later he will come to buy you a second drink and to announce that the war is continuing indefinitely. I have no plan for dealing with him. He appears to be well covered and practically invulnerable.

In all likelihood I shall watch you both from my table.

Jorge's small spy is still there on the balcony and is peering through the shutters. I turn my back on him and go back to the filing system which is now devoted to the streets of London. I begin to arrange them in alphabetical order but can get no closer to A than Albermarle Street.

Outside the boys are revving up their Zundapps. Trucks continue to pass over the bridge but there seem to be more of them. It is as if they have been brought out by the heat. Today will be most unpleasant. It is hotter now than it was at noon yesterday.

The ceiling rumbles and the water begins to pour through, slowly at first and then in a torrent, I place fresh newspaper inside the bidet and watch Timoshenko's face absorb the water, becoming soggy and grey.

AFTERNOON

I watch you eat your yoghurt. You appraise each spoonful carefully, watching the white sop slide and drip from your spoon. There are beads of perspiration on your lip and you ask me to ask for the water. I have forgotten the word and remember it incorrectly. The waiter appears to understand but brings coffee and you say that coffee will do. Later, when I pay, I notice that he does not include the price of the coffee. Has he forgotten it? Or is it an elaborate joke, to bring coffee, pretending all the time that it is water. After eight days in the town it is not impossible.

ROOM NO. 5 (ESCRIBO)

We leave the cafe and walk up towards the museum. You shade your eyes and say, perhaps it will open today, although you know it will be closed.

After the museum we walk through the same cobbled streets we have walked for eight days, attempting to find new ones. There are no new streets, they are the same. They contain the same grey houses faced with the same ornate ceramic tiles. I photograph the same tiles I photographed yesterday. You take my arm as we enter the square for the last time and say, the money has come, I can feel it.

We walk slowly to the Banco Nationale. It is still early. After we have checked there we will return to our room, there is nothing else.

The money has arrived. You discuss it with the teller. You appear uncertain, moving from one foot to the other as you lean against the counter watching him calculating the exchange on the back of a cigarette packet. The two of you consult frequently. You look at me uncertainly and produce some dark glasses from your handbag. Among your numerous small possessions these are a surprise to me. I thought I could number your possessions and had, one night, compiled a mental list of them. It is called Kim's game, I believe, although I have no idea why.

It is cool and quiet in the bank. You whisper to the teller in his language. The rest of the bank staff sit in shirt sleeves at their desks and watch. Occasionally they say something. A thin-faced clerk addresses a question to me. I shrug and point to you. Everybody laughs and I light a cigarette.

I have no confidence in the money or its ability to get us back across the border. There is a bus later this afternoon.

I ask you to ask the teller about the war across the border. You lean towards him, kicking up your legs behind the counter as you lean. He replies earnestly, removing his heavy glasses and wiping perspiration from his badly shaven face. I notice that he has a small tick in his cheek. He has the appearance of an academic discussing a perplexing problem. When he has finished he replaces his glasses and resumes his calculations.

You say nothing.

I ask you. The anxiety is returning – I cannot connect your behaviour to anything. I am not anxious for the course of the war itself, nor for the sake of the money. I touch your flesh where it is very soft, above the elbow and you jump slightly. I ask you what he has said.

You say, he says everything is OK . . . he heard on the radio that it is OK.

And Timoshenko? I ask you. The clerk looks up when he hears the words but resumes his work immediately. My finger plays with the fabric of your blouse where it clings to your arm. And Timoshenko?

You say, Timoshenko is OK . . . the operation was a success . . .

Did he say?

No, I read it this morning . . . in the newspaper . . . I meant to say. You look at your dusty sandaled foot and scratch the bare calf of your leg. I notice now how you scratch the bare calf of your leg like that. I wonder how such a habit starts. There are many small red scratch marks on your leg. You say, Timoshenko is OK.

I go to stand at the window and look across to our hotel. A number of small boys are fighting on the balcony of our room.

I return to the counter and lean against it as if it were a bar and I were in a western. I lean backwards with my elbows on the bar and watch you sideways. I say, ask him about the border, will they let us across.

He wouldn't know.

I know, I say, it doesn't matter.

BEFORE

In Villa Franca you were in the Banco Nationale when I met you. You wore the same blouse and asked if I would mind you travelling with me. I said, I would be happy for you to. Your eyes were soft and grey, seeming wise and gentle. You had, so it seemed, lived less than a block from me in London. It was difficult to work out the chronology, you appeared to shift around so often.

You said, you don't look as if you work in insurance. And I wasn't sure what you meant.

BORDER

I prepare for Jorge as the bus groans around the mountain road towards the border. It is full of old women and stops constantly to let them off. There are also a few men who wear squat hats, heavy farmers' boots, and black umbrellas. The heat is intense. You gaze out the window and say nothing. We have not discussed the border or any of its implications. I do not believe in the war or Timoshenko.

The border post is at a break in the mountains. There is a small wooden bridge and two buildings that look like filling stations. Soldiers stand around the bridge with machine guns hung casually from their limp shoulders. One kicks a stone. There is a woman and a child sitting in the dust by the customs house steps. The woman waves flies away from her face with a newspaper. The child sits stock still and stares at the bus with dull interest.

There are now only six of us in the bus. Three men with squat hats and black umbrellas and an old woman who carries two chickens by the legs, one in each hand. The chickens appear to be asleep.

We have been here before. Last Sunday. We wait for Jorge and the continuation of his little joke. You sit beside me in the bus and huddle into the window, alone with your reflection in the dusty fly-marked glass. I say, it is OK. You say, yes it is OK. Your eyes hide behind dark glasses and I see only my own face staring at me questioningly.

In the customs shed we form a line. There is an argument about the chickens and one is confiscated. A soldier tethers its feet to the bottom of an old hat stand from which a machine gun hangs heavily.

ROOM NO. 5 (ESCRIBO)

Jorge stands at the head of the line looking along it like a sergeant major. He waves to us and waddles down, a riding crop tucked under his fat folded arm. The riding crop betrays his heroes but looks ludicrous and somehow obscene. He has two broken teeth which appear to be in an advanced state of decay.

You talk to him and he continues to look across at me. Finally you turn to me and say, he says it is OK ... the war was nothing ... an incident ... they often have them.

You do not appear happy. Your forehead is wrinkled with a frown that I yearn to smooth with my palm.

I shake Jorge's hand. I am immediately sorry. The chicken is in danger of upsetting the hatstand. The soldier removes the machine gun and places it on the counter.

AFTER

The bus travels through the flat grey granite as dusk settles. Large rocks pierce the gloomy surface of the earth. There are no trees but a few sheep who prefer the road to the country on either side, possibly because it is softer. It is cooler here on the other side of the border, on this side of the mountains.

Rain begins to fall lightly on the windows, making soft patterns in the dust. I open the window to smell the rain. You are frowning again. I hold my hand out the window until it is wet and then place my palm on your forehead.

PETER CAREY

I say, why do you frown?
You say, because I love you.
I say, why do you smile?
Because I love you.

POSTSCRIPT

In Candalido I ask you about the first time we crossed
the border and why you crossed separately.

You say, it is because of the underwear, because they
always do that . . . at the small border posts . . . take out
the underwear.

I say, why should I mind?
You say, it was dirty.

GABRIEL
GARCÍA
MÁRQUEZ

The Woman Who Came
at Six O'Clock

The swinging door opened. At that hour there was nobody in José's restaurant. It had just struck six and the man knew that the regular customers wouldn't begin to arrive until six-thirty. His clientele was so conservative and regular that the clock hadn't finished striking six when a woman entered, as on every day at that hour, and sat down on the stool without saying anything. She had an unlighted cigarette tight between her lips.

'Hello, queen,' José said when he saw her sit down. Then he went to the other end of the counter, wiping the streaked surface with a dry rag. Whenever anyone came into the restaurant José did the same thing. Even with the woman, with whom he'd almost come to acquire a degree of intimacy, the fat and ruddy restaurant owner put on his daily comedy of a hard-working man. He spoke from the other end of the counter.

'What do you want today?' he said.

'First of all I want to teach you how to be a gentleman,' the woman said. She was sitting at the end of the stools, her elbows on the counter, the extinguished cigarette between her lips. When she spoke, she tightened her mouth so that José would notice the unlighted cigarette.

'I didn't notice,' José said.

'You still haven't learned to notice anything,' said the woman.

The man left the cloth on the counter, walked to the dark cupboards which smelled of tar and dusty wood, and came back immediately with the matches. The woman leaned over to get the light that was burning in the man's rustic, hairy hands. José saw the woman's lush hair, all greased with cheap, thick Vaseline. He saw her uncovered shoulder above the flowered brassiere. He saw the beginning of her twilight breast when the woman raised her head, the lighted butt between her lips now.

'You're beautiful tonight, queen,' José said.

'Stop your nonsense,' the woman said. 'Don't think that's going to help me pay you.'

'That's not what I meant, queen,' José said. 'I'll bet your lunch didn't agree with you today.'

The woman sucked in the first drag of thick smoke, crossed her arms, her elbows still on the counter, and remained looking at the street through the wide restaurant window. She had a melancholy expression. A bored and vulgar melancholy.

'I'll fix you a good steak,' José said.

'I still haven't got any money,' the woman said.

'You haven't had any money for three months and I always fix you something good,' José said.

'Today's different,' said the woman somberly, still looking out at the street.

'Every day's the same,' José said. 'Every day the clock says six, then you come in and say you're hungry as a dog and then I fix you something good. The only difference is this: today you didn't say you were as hungry as a dog but that today is different.'

'And it's true,' the woman said. She turned to look at the man, who was at the other end of the counter checking the refrigerator. She examined him for two or three seconds. Then she looked at the clock over the cupboard. It was three minutes after six. 'It's true, José. Today is different,' she said. She let the smoke out and kept on talking with crisp, impassioned words. 'I didn't come at six today, that's why it's different, José.'

The man looked at the clock.

'I'll cut off my arm if that clock is one minute slow,' he said.

'That's not it, José. I didn't come at six o'clock today,' the woman said.

'It just struck six, queen,' José said. 'When you came in it was just finishing.'

'I've got a quarter of an hour that says I've been here,' the woman said.

José went over to where she was. He put his great puffy face up to the woman while he tugged on one of his eyelids with his index finger.

'Blow on me here,' he said.

The woman threw her head back. She was serious, annoyed, softened, beautified by a cloud of sadness and fatigue.

'Stop your foolishness, José. You know I haven't had a drink for six months.'

'Tell it to somebody else,' he said, 'not to me. I'll bet you've had a pint or two at least.'

'I had a couple of drinks with a friend,' she said.

'Oh, now I understand,' José said.

'There's nothing to understand,' the woman said. 'I've been here for a quarter of an hour.'

The man shrugged his shoulders.

'Well, if that's the way you want it, you've got a quarter of an hour that says you've been here,' he said. 'After all, what difference does it make, ten minutes this way, ten minutes that way?'

'It makes a difference, José,' the woman said. And she stretched her arms over the glass counter with an air of careless abandon. She said: 'And it isn't that I wanted it that way; it's just that I've been here for a quarter of an hour.' She looked at the clock again and corrected herself: 'What am I saying – it's been twenty minutes.'

'O.K., queen,' the man said. 'I'd give you a whole day and the night that goes with it just to see you happy.'

During all this time José had been moving about behind the counter, changing things, taking something from one place and putting it in another. He was playing his role.

'I want to see you happy,' he repeated. He stopped suddenly, turning to where the woman was. 'Do you know that I love you very much?'

The woman looked at him coldly.

'Ye-e-es . . . ? What a discovery, José. Do you think I'd go with you even for a million pesos?'

'I didn't mean that, queen,' José said. 'I repeat, I bet your lunch didn't agree with you.'

'That's not why I said it,' the woman said. And her voice became less indolent. 'No woman could stand a weight like yours, even for a million pesos.'

José blushed. He turned his back to the woman and began to dust the bottles on the shelves. He spoke without turning his head.

'You're unbearable today, queen. I think the best thing is for you to eat your steak and go home to bed.'

'I'm not hungry,' the woman said. She stayed looking

out at the street again, watching the passers-by of the dusking city. For an instant there was a murky silence in the restaurant. A peacefulness broken only by José's fiddling about in the cupboard. Suddenly the woman stopped looking out into the street and spoke with a tender, soft, different voice.

'Do you really love me, Pepillo?'

'I do,' José said dryly, not looking at her.

'In spite of what I've said to you?' the woman asked.

'What did you say to me?' José asked, still without any inflection in his voice, still without looking at her.

'That business about a million pesos,' the woman said.

'I'd already forgotten,' José said.

'So do you love me?' the woman asked.

'Yes,' said José.

There was a pause. José kept moving about, his face turned toward the cabinets, still not looking at the woman. She blew out another mouthful of smoke, rested her bust on the counter, and then, cautiously and roguishly, biting her tongue before saying it, as if speaking on tiptoe:

'Even if you didn't go to bed with me?' she asked.

And only then did José turn to look at her.

'I love you so much that I wouldn't go to bed with you,' he said. Then he walked over to where she was. He stood looking into her face, his powerful arms leaning on the counter in front of her, looking into her eyes. He said: 'I love you so much that every night I'd kill the man who goes with you.'

At the first instant the woman seemed perplexed. Then she looked at the man attentively, with a wavering expression of compassion and mockery. Then she had a moment of brief disconcerted silence: And then she laughed noisily.

'You're jealous, José. That's wild, you're jealous!'

José blushed again with frank, almost shameful timidity, as might have happened to a child who'd revealed all his secrets all of a sudden. He said:

'This afternoon you don't seem to understand anything, queen.' And he wiped himself with the rag. He said:

'This bad life is brutalizing you.'

But now the woman had changed her expression.

'So, then,' she said. And she looked into his eyes again, with a strange glow in her look, confused and challenging at the same time.

'So you're not jealous.'

'In a way I am,' José said 'But it's not the way you think.'

He loosened his collar and continued wiping himself, drying his throat with the cloth.

'So?' the woman asked.

'The fact is I love you so much that I don't like your doing it,' José said.

'What?' the woman asked.

'This business of going with a different man every day,' José said.

'Would you really kill him to stop him from going with me?' the woman asked.

'Not to stop him from going with you, no,' José said. 'I'd kill him because he *went* with you.'

'It's the same thing,' the woman said.

The conversation had reached an exciting density. The woman was speaking in a soft, low, fascinated voice. Her face was almost stuck up against the man's healthy, peaceful face, as he stood motionless, as if bewitched by the vapor of the words.

'That's true,' José said.

'So,' the woman said, and reached out her hand to stroke the man's rough arm. With the other she tossed away her butt. 'So you're capable of killing a man?'

'For what I told you, yes,' José said. And his voice took on an almost dramatic stress.

The woman broke into convulsive laughter, with an obvious mocking intent.

'How awful, José. How awful,' she said, still laughing. 'José killing a man. Who would have known that behind the fat and sanctimonious man who never makes me pay, who cooks me a steak every day and has fun talking to me until I find a man, there lurks a murderer. How awful, José! You scare me!'

José was confused. Maybe he felt a little indignation. Maybe, when the woman started laughing, he felt defrauded.

'You're drunk, silly,' he said. 'Go get some sleep. You don't even feel like eating anything.'

But the woman had stopped laughing now and was serious again, pensive, leaning on the counter. She watched the man go away. She saw him open the refrigerator and close it again without taking anything out. Then she saw him move to the other end of the counter. She watched him polish the shining glass, the same as in the beginning. Then the woman spoke again with the tender and soft tone of when she said: 'Do you really love me, Pepillo?'

'José,' she said.

The man didn't look at her.

'José!'

'Go home and sleep,' José said. 'And take a bath before you go to bed so you can sleep it off.'

'Seriously, José,' the woman said. 'I'm not drunk.'

'Then you've turned stupid,' José said.

'Come here, I've got to talk to you,' the woman said.

The man came over stumbling, halfway between pleasure and mistrust.

'Come closer!'

He stood in front of the woman again. She leaned forward, grabbed him by the hair, but with a gesture of obvious tenderness.

'Tell me again what you said at the start,' she said.

'What do you mean?' José asked. He was trying to look at her with his head turned away, held by the hair.

'That you'd kill a man who went to bed with me,' the woman said.

'I'd kill a man who went to bed with you, queen. That's right,' José said.

The woman let him go.

'In that case you'd defend me if I killed him, right?' she asked affirmatively, pushing José's enormous pig head with a movement of brutal coquettishness. The man didn't answer anything. He smiled.

'Answer me, José,' the woman said. 'Would you defend me if I killed him?'

'That depends,' José said. 'You know it's not as easy as you say.'

'The police wouldn't believe anyone more than you,' the woman said.

José smiled, honored, satisfied. The woman leaned over toward him again, over the counter.

'It's true, José. I'm willing to bet that you've never told a lie in your life,' she said.

'You won't get anywhere this way,' José said.

'Just the same,' the woman said. 'The police know you and they'll believe anything without asking you twice.'

José began pounding on the counter opposite her, not knowing what to say. The woman looked out at the street again. Then she looked at the clock and modified the tone of her voice, as if she were interested in finishing the conversation before the first customers arrived.

'Would you tell a lie for me, José?' she asked. 'Seriously.'

And then José looked at her again, sharply, deeply, as if a tremendous idea had come pounding up in his head. An idea that had entered through one ear, spun about for a moment, vague, confused, and gone out through the other, leaving behind only a warm vestige of terror.

'What have you got yourself into, queen?' José asked. He leaned forward, his arms folded over the counter again. The woman caught the strong and ammonia-smelling vapor of his breathing, which had become difficult because of the pressure that the counter was exercising on the man's stomach.

'This is really serious, queen. What have you got yourself into?' he asked.

The woman made her head spin in the opposite direction.

'Nothing,' she said. 'I was just talking to amuse myself.'

Then she looked at him again.

'Do you know you may not have to kill anybody?'

'I never thought about killing anybody,' José said, distressed.

'No, man,' the woman said. 'I mean nobody goes to bed with me.'

'Oh!' José said. 'Now you're talking straight out. I always thought you had no need to prowl around. I'll make a bet that if you drop all this I'll give you the biggest steak I've got every day, free.'

'Thank you, José,' the woman said. 'But that's not why. It's because I *can't* go to bed with anyone any more.'

'You're getting things all confused again, José said. He was becoming impatient.

'I'm not getting anything confused,' the woman said.

GABRIEL GARCÍA MÁRQUEZ

She stretched out on the seat and José saw her flat, sad breasts underneath her brassiere.

'Tomorrow I'm going away and I promise you I won't come back and bother you ever again. I promise you I'll never go to bed with anyone.'

'Where'd you pick up that fever?' José asked.

'I decided just a minute ago,' the woman said. 'Just a minute ago I realized it's a dirty business.'

José grabbed the cloth again and started to clean the glass in front of her. He spoke without looking at her.

He said:

'Of course, the way you do it it's a dirty business. You should have known that a long time ago.'

'I was getting to know it a long time ago,' the woman said, 'but I was only convinced of it just a little while ago. Men disgust me.'

José smiled. He raised his head to look at her, still smiling, but he saw her concentrated, perplexed, talking with her shoulders raised, twirling on the stool with a taciturn expression, her face gilded by premature autumnal grain.

'Don't you think they ought to lay off a woman who kills a man because after she's been with him she feels disgust with him and everyone who's been with her?'

'There's no reason to go that far,' José said, moved, a thread of pity in his voice.

'What if the woman tells the man he disgusts her while she watches him get dressed because she remembers that she's been rolling around with him all afternoon and feels that neither soap nor sponge can get his smell off her?'

'That all goes away, queen,' José said, a little indifferent now, polishing the counter. 'There's no reason to kill him. Just let him go.'

But the woman kept on talking, and her voice was a uniform, flowing, passionate current.

'But what if the woman tells him he disgusts her and the man stops getting dressed and runs over to her again, kisses her again, does . . . ?'

'No decent man would ever do that,' José says.

'What if he does?' the woman asks, with exasperating anxiety. 'What if the man isn't decent and does it and then the woman feels that he disgusts her so much that she could die, and she knows that the only way to end it all is to stick a knife in under him?'

'That's terrible,' José said. 'Luckily there's no man who would do what you say.'

'Well,' the woman said, completely exasperated now. 'What if he did? Suppose he did.'

'In any case it's not that bad,' José said. He kept on cleaning the counter without changing position, less intent on the conversation now.

The woman pounded the counter with her knuckles. She became affirmative, emphatic.

'You're a savage, José,' she said. 'You don't understand anything.' She grabbed him firmly by the sleeve. 'Come on, tell me that the woman should kill him.'

'O.K.,' José said with a conciliatory bias. 'It's all

probably just the way you say it is.'

'Isn't that self-defence?' the woman asked, grabbing him by the sleeve.

Then José gave her a lukewarm and pleasant look.

'Almost, almost,' he said. And he winked at her, with an expression that was at the same time a cordial comprehension and a fearful compromise of complicity. But the woman was serious. She let go of him.

'Would you tell a lie to defend a woman who does that?' she asked.

'That depends,' said José.

'Depends on what?' the woman asked.

'Depends on the woman,' said José.

'Suppose it's a woman you love a lot,' the woman said. 'Not to be with her, but like you say, you love her a lot.'

'O.K., anything you say, queen,' José said, relaxed, bored.

He'd gone off again. He'd looked at the clock. He'd seen that it was going on half-past six. He'd thought that in a few minutes the restaurant would be filling up with people and maybe that was why he began to polish the glass with greater effort, looking at the street through the window. The woman stayed on her stool, silent, concentrating, watching the man's movements with an air of declining sadness. Watching him as a lamp about to go out might have looked at a man. Suddenly, without reacting, she spoke again with the unctuous voice of servitude.

'José!'

The man looked at her with a thick, sad tenderness, like a maternal ox. He didn't look at her to hear her, just to look at her, to know that she was there, waiting for a look that had no reason to be one of protection or solidarity. Just the look of a plaything.

'I told you I was leaving tomorrow and you didn't say anything,' the woman said.

'Yes,' José said. 'You didn't tell me where.'

'Out there,' the woman said. 'Where there aren't any men who want to sleep with somebody.'

José smiled again.

'Are you really going away?' he asked, as if becoming aware of life, quickly changing the expression on his face.

'That depends on you,' the woman said. 'If you know enough to say what time I got here, I'll go away tomorrow and I'll never get mixed up in this again. Would you like that?'

José gave an affirmative nod, smiling and concrete. The woman leaned over to where he was.

'If I come back here someday I'll get jealous when I find another woman talking to you, at this time and on this same stool.'

'If you come back here you'll have to bring me something,' José said.

'I promise you that I'll look everywhere for the tame bear, bring him to you,' the woman said.

José smiled and waved the cloth through the air that

separated him from the woman, as if he were cleaning an invisible pane of glass. The woman smiled too, with an expression of cordiality and coquetry now. Then the man went away, polishing the glass to the other end of the counter.

'What, then?' José said without looking at her.

'Will you really tell anyone who asks you that I got here at a quarter to six?' the woman said.

'What for?' José said, still without looking at her now, as if he had barely heard her.

'That doesn't matter,' the woman said. 'The thing is that you do it.'

José then saw the first customer come in through the swinging door and walk over to a corner table. He looked at the clock. It was six-thirty on the dot.

'O.K., queen,' he said distractedly. 'Anything you say. I always do whatever you want.'

'Well,' the woman said. 'Start cooking my steak, then.'

The man went to the refrigerator, took out a plate with a piece of meat on it, and left it on the table. Then he lighted the stove.

'I'm going to cook you a good farewell steak, queen,' he said.

'Thank you, Pepillo,' the woman said.

She remained thoughtful as if suddenly she had become sunken in a strange subworld peopled with muddy unknown forms. Across the counter she couldn't hear the noise that the raw meat made when it fell into the burning grease. Afterward she didn't hear the dry and bubbling crackle as José turned the flank over in the frying pan and the succulent smell of the marinated meat by measured moments saturated the air of the restaurant. She remained like that, concentrated, reconcentrated, until she raised her head again, blinking as if she were coming back out of a momentary death. Then she saw the man beside the stove, lighted up by the happy, rising fire.

'Pepillo.'

'What!'

'What are you thinking about?' the woman asked.

'I was wondering whether you could find the little windup bear someplace,' José said.

'Of course I can,' the woman said. 'But what I want is for you to give me everything I asked for as a going-away present.'

José looked at her from the stove.

'How often have I got to tell you?' he said. 'Do you want something besides the best steak I've got?'

'Yes,' the woman said.

'What is it?' José asked.

'I want another quarter of an hour.'

José drew back and looked at the clock. Then he looked at the customer, who was still silent, waiting in the corner, and finally at the meat roasting in the pan. Only then did he speak.

'I really don't understand, queen,' he said.

'Don't be foolish, José,' the woman said. 'Just remember that I've been here since five-thirty.'

JESS MOWRY

Crusader Rabbit

'You could be my dad.'

Jeremy stood, waist-deep in the dumpster, his arms slimed to the elbows from burrowing, and dropped three beer cans to the buckled asphalt.

Raglan lined them up, pop-tops down, and crushed them to crinkled discs under his tattered Nike, then added them to the half-full gunnysack. Finally, he straightened and studied the boy in the dumpster. It wasn't the first time. 'Yeah. I could be.'

Jeremy made no move to climb out, even though the stink seemed to surround him like a bronze-green cloud, wavering upward like the heat-ghosts from other dumpster lids along the narrow alley. The boy wore only ragged jeans, the big Airwalks on his bare feet buried somewhere below. His wiry, dusk-colored body glistened with sweat.

Not for the first time Raglan thought that Jeremy was a beautiful kid, thirteen, small, muscles standing out under tight skin, big hands and feet like puppy paws, and hair like an ebony dandelion puff. A ring glinted gold and and fierce in his left ear, and a red bandana, sodden with sweat, hung loosely around his neck. His eyes were bright obsidian but closed now, the bruise-like marks beneath them were fading, and his teeth flashed strong and white as he panted.

Raglan could have been a larger copy of the boy, twice his age but looking it only in size, and without the earring. There was an old knife slash on his chest; a deep one, with a high ridge of scar.

The Oakland morning fog had burned off hours before, leaving the alley to bake in tar-and-rot smell, yet Raglan neither panted nor sweated. There were three more dumpsters to check out, and the recycle place across town would be closing soon, but Raglan asked, 'Want a smoke?'

Jeremy watched through lowered lashes as Raglan's eyes changed, not so much softening as going light-years away. Jeremy hesitated, his long fingers clenching and unclenching on the dumpster's rusty rim. 'Yeah . . . no. I think it's time.'

Jeremy's movements were stiff and awkward as he tried to climb out. Garbage sucked wetly at his feet. Raglan took the boy, slippery as a seal, under the arms and lifted him over the edge. Together, they walked back to the truck.

It was a '55 GMC one-ton, as rusted and battered as the dumpsters. There were splintery plywood sideboards on the bed. The cab was crammed with things, as self-contained as a Land Rover on safari. Even after two months it still surprised Jeremy sometimes what Raglan could pull out from beneath the seat or the piled mess on the floor ... toilet paper, comic books, or a .45 automatic.

Raglan emptied the gunnysack into an almost full garbage can in the back of the truck, then leaned against the sideboard and started to roll a cigarette from Top tobacco while Jeremy opened the driver's door and slipped a scarred-up *Sesame Street* Band-Aids box from under the floormat. The boy's hands shook slightly. He tried not to hurry as he spread out his things on the seat: a little rock bottle with gray-brown powder in the bottom instead of crack crystals; a puff of cotton; candle stub; flame-tarnished spoon, and needle, its point protected by a chunk of Styrofoam. On the cab floor by the shift lever was a gallon plastic jug from Pay-Less Drugs that used to hold 'fresh spring water from clear mountain streams'. Raglan filled it from gas station hoses, and the water always tasted like rubber. Jeremy got it out, too.

Raglan finished rolling his cigarette, fired it with a Bic, handed the lighter to the boy, then started making another as he smoked. His eyes were still far away.

Jeremy looked up while he worked. 'Yo. I know your ole name. I seen it on your driver license. Why's your street name Raglan?'

Smoke drifted from Raglan's nostrils. He came close to smiling. 'My dad started calling me that. S'pose to be from some old-time cartoon, when he was just a little kid. *Crusader Rabbit*. But I never seen it. The rabbit's homey was a tiger. Raglan T. Tiger. Maybe they was somethin like the Ninja Turtles. Had adventures an' shit. It was a long time ago.'

'Oh.' Jeremy sat on the cab floor. He wrapped a strip of inner-tube around his arm. It was hard to get it right, one-handed. He looked up again. 'Um . . .'

'Yeah.' Raglan knelt and pulled the strip tighter. His eyes were distant again, neither watching nor looking away as the boy put the needle in. 'You got good veins. Your muscles make 'em stand out.'

The boy's eyes shifted from the needle, lowering, and his chest hardened a little. 'I do got some muscles, huh?'

'Yeah. But don't let 'em go to your head.'

Jeremy chewed his lip. 'I used to miss 'em . . . my veins, I mean. A long time ago. An' sometimes I poked right through.'

'Yeah. I done that too. A long time ago.'

The boy's slender body tensed a moment, then he relaxed with a sigh, his face almost peaceful and his eyes closed. But a few seconds later they opened again and searched out Raglan's. It only makes me normal now.'

Raglan nodded. 'Yeah. On two a day, that's all.' He handed Jeremy the other cigarette and fired the lighter.

The boy pulled in smoke, holding it a long time, then puffing out perfect rings and watching them hover in the hot, dead air. 'Next week it only gonna be one.' He held Raglan's eyes. 'It gonna hurt some more, huh?'

'Yeah.'

'Um, when do you stop wantin' it?'

Raglan stood, snagging the water jug and taking a few swallows. Traffic rumbled past the alley. Exhaust fumes drifted in from the street. Flies buzzed in clouds over the dumpsters, and a rat scuttled past in no particular hurry. 'When you decide there's somethin' else you want more.'

Jeremy began putting his things away. The little bottle was empty. It would take most of today's cans to score another for tomorrow. 'Yo. You gotta be my dad, man. Why else would you give a shit?'

'I don't know. You figure it out.' Raglan could have added that, when he'd first found Jeremy, the boy wouldn't have lived another week. But dudes Jeremy's age would think that was bad ... almost cool. Why? Who in hell knew? Raglan didn't remember a lot about being thirteen, but he remembered that.

He dropped his cigarette on the pavement, slipped the sack off the sideboard, and started toward the other dumpsters. There really wasn't much use in checking them: this was the worst part of Oakland, and poor people's garbage was pitiful, everything already scraped bone-bare, rusted or rotted or beaten beyond redemption, and nothing left of any value at all. Jeremy followed, his moves flowing smooth like a black kid's once more.

A few paces in front of the boy, Raglan flipped back

a lid so it clanged against the sooty brick wall. Flies scattered in swarms. For a second or two he just stood and looked at what lay on top of the trash. He'd seen this before, too many times but it was about the only thing he wouldn't accept as just what it is. His hand clamped on Jeremy's shoulder, holding the boy back. But Jeremy saw the baby anyhow.

'Oh . . . God.' It came out a sigh. Jeremy pressed close to Raglan, and Raglan's arm went around him.

'I heard 'bout them,' the boy whispered. 'But I never figured it happen for real.'

'Best take a good look, then.'

But the boy's eyes lifted to Raglan's. 'Why do people do that?'

But Raglan's gaze was distant once more, seeing but not seeing the little honey-brown body, the tiny and perfect fingers and toes. 'I don't know.'

Jeremy swallowed once. His lean chest expanded to pull in air. 'What should we do?'

Raglan's eyes turned hard. He was thinking of cops and their questions, then of a call from some pay phone. There was one at the recycle place. Time was running short. The truck's tank was almost full, but there was food to buy after Jeremy's need, and the cans were the only money. Still he said, 'What do you want to do?'

The boy looked back at the baby. Automatically he waved flies away. 'What do they . . . do with 'em?' He turned to Raglan. 'I mean, is there some little coffin? An' flowers?'

Raglan took his hand off the boy. 'They burn 'em.'
'No!'

'The ones they find. Other times they just get hauled to the dump an' the bulldozers bury 'em with the rest of the garbage. You been to the dump.'

Almost, the boy clamped his hands to his ears, but then his fists clenched. 'No! Goddamn you! Shut up, sucker!' One hand dove for the pocket where he carried the blade.

The boy's chest heaved, muscles standing out stark. His hand poised. Raglan was quiet a minute. Finally he gripped Jeremy's shoulder once more. 'Okay.' Raglan walked back to the truck while Jeremy watched from beside the dumpster, waving away the flies.

Raglan stopped around back. There was a ragged canvas tarp folded behind the cab. On foggy or rainy nights he spread it over the sideboards to make a roof. A piece of that would do. Salty sweat burned Raglan's eyes, and he blinked in the sunlight stabbing down between the buildings. The canvas was oily, and stank. Going around to the cab, he pulled his black T-shirt from behind the seat.

The old GMC was a city truck, an inner-city truck, that measured its moves in blocks, not miles. It burned oil, the radiator leaked, and its tires were worn almost bald. There were two bullet holes in the right front fender. But it managed to maintain a grudging fifty-five, rattling first across the Bay Bridge into San Francisco and then over the Golden Gate, headed north. It had a radio-tape deck, ancient and minus knobs, but Jeremy didn't turn on KSOL or play the old *Dangerous* tape he'd scored in a dumpster and patiently re-wound with a pencil. He stayed silent, just rolling cigarettes for Raglan and himself, and looking once in awhile through the grimy back window at the little black bundle in the bed. Even when they turned off 101 near Navato onto a narrow two-lane leading west Jeremy just stared through the windshield, his eyes a lot like Raglan's even though an open countryside of gentle green hills now spread out around them.

It was early evening with the sunlight slanting gold, when Raglan slowed the truck and searched the roadside ahead. The air was fresh and clean, scented with things that lived and grew, and tasting of the ocean somewhere close at hand. There was a dirt road that Raglan almost missed, hardly more than twin tracks with a strip of yellow dandelions between. It led away toward more low hills, through fields of tall grass and wild mustard flowers. Raglan swung the truck off the asphalt and they rolled slowly to the hills in third gear. Jeremy began to watch the flowered fields passing by, then turned to Raglan. 'Yo. You ever been here before?'

'A long time ago.'

'I never knew there was places like this, pretty, an' without no people an' cars an' shit. Not for real.'

'It real.'

The road entered a cleft between hills, and a little

stream ran down to meet it, sparkling over rocks. For awhile the road followed the splashing water, then turned and wound upward. The truck took the grade growling in second. The road got fainter as it climbed, then finally just ended at the top of the hill. Raglan cut the engine. A hundred feet ahead a cliff dropped off sheer to the sea. Big waves boomed and echoed on rocks somewhere below, wending up silver streamers of spray.

Jeremy seemed to forget why they'd come. He jumped from the truck and ran to the cliff's edge, stopping as close as possible like any boy might. Then he just stood gazing out over the water.

Raglan leaned on the fender and watched.

The boy spread his arms wide for a moment, his head thrown back. Then he looked down at his dirty jeans. Raglan watched a little while longer as the boy stripped to stand naked before the sea and the sun. Then Raglan went to the rear of the truck. There was an old square-nosed cement shovel and an Army trenching tool he used when he cleaned up yards.

Jeremy joined him, glistening with sea spray, but solemn, though his eyes still sparkled a little. Raglan said nothing, just taking the shovel in one hand and the little bundle in the crook of his arm. Jeremy put his jeans on and followed barefoot with the trenching tool.

The ground rose again nearby to a point that looked out over the ocean. They climbed to the top. Raglan cut the sweet-smelling sod into blocks with his shovel, and the earth-scent filled the air. Then they both dug. The sun was almost gone when they finished. Though the evening was growing cooler, Jeremy was sheened in sweat once more. But he picked some of the wild mustard and dandelion flowers and laid them on the little mound.

Far out on the water, the sun grew huge and ruddy as it sank. Raglan built a fire near the truck, and Jeremy unrolled their blankets. He was surprised again when Raglan conjured two dusty cans of Campbell's soup and a pint of Jack Daniels from somewhere in the cab. A little later, when it was dark and still and the food was warm inside them, they sat side by side near the little fire, smoking and sipping the whiskey.

'Is this campin' out?' asked Jeremy.

'Mmm. Yeah. S'pose it is.'

Jeremy passed the bottle back to Raglan, then glanced at the truck: it seemed small by itself on a hilltop. 'Um, we don't got enough gas to get back, huh?'

Raglan stared into the flames. 'Uh-uh. Maybe there's someplace around here that buys cans.'

Jeremy gazed into the fire. 'It gonna hurt a lot, huh?'

'Yeah. I'll be here.'

'I'm still glad we came.'

Jeremy moved close to Raglan, shivering now. 'So, you never seen that Crusader Rabbit. Don't know what he looked like?'

'I think he carried a sword, an' fought dragons.'

'You are my dad, huh?'

ROSE TREMAIN

The Stack

She says to him, 'On your birthday, McCreedy, what d'you want to do?'

She always calls him McCreedy. You'd have thought by now, after being his wife for so long, she'd have started to call him John, but she never does. He calls her Hilda; she calls him McCreedy, like he was a stranger, like he was a footballer she'd seen on the telly.

'I don't know,' he says. 'What'll we do, then?'

'Forty-six,' she says, 'you'd better think of something.'

'Go out . . . ?' he says.

'Out where?'

The pub, he thinks but doesn't say. With the fellas from work. Get the Guinness down. Tell some old Dublin jokes. Laugh till you can't laugh anymore.

'What'd the kids like?' he says.

She lights a ciggie. Her twentieth or thirtieth that Sunday, he's stopped counting. Smoke pours out of her mouth, thick and blue. 'Never mind the kids, McCreedy,' she says. 'It's your fuckin' birthday.'

'Go back to Ireland,' he says. 'That's what I'd like. Go back there for good.'

She stubs out the ciggie. She's always changing her mind about everything, minute to minute. 'When you've got a sensible answer,' she says, 'let me know what it is.'

And she leaves him, click-clack on her worn-out heels, pats her hair tidy, opens the kitchen door, and lets it slam behind her.

McCreedy stares at the ashtray. Time she was dead, he thinks. Time the smoking killed her.

He goes out into the garden where his nine-year-old daughter, Katy, is playing on her own.

Katy and the garden have something in common: they're both small and it looks like they'll never be beautiful, no matter how hard anyone tries. Because Katy resembles her dad. Short neck. Short sight. Pigeon toes. More's the pity.

Now the two of them are in the neglected garden together with the North London September sun quite warm on them, and McCreedy says to the daughter he tries so hard to love, 'What'll we do on my birthday, then, Katy?'

She's playing with her tarty little dolls that have tits and miniature underwear. She holds them by their shapely legs and their golden tresses wave around like flags.

'Dunno,' she says. 'What?'

He sits on a plastic garden chair and she lays her nymphos side by side in a pram. 'Cindy and Barbie are getting stung,' she whines.

'Who's stinging them, darling?'

'Nettles, of course. Cut 'em down, can't you?'

'Oh no,' he says, looking at where they grow so fiercely, crowding out the roses Hilda planted years ago. 'Saving them, sweetheart.'

'Why?'

'For soup. Nettle soup – to make you beautiful.'

She looks at him gravely. For nine years, she's believed everything he's said. Now she's on the precipice of disbelief, almost ready to fly off the edge.

'Will it?' she says.

'Sure it will. You wait and see.'

Later in the day, when his son Michael comes in, McCreedy stops him before he goes up to his room. He's thirteen. On his white neck is a red mark that looks like a love bite.

'What you staring at?' says Michael.

'Nothing,' says McCreedy.

'What, then?'

'Your mother was wondering what we might all do on me birthday. If you had any thoughts about it . . . ?'

Michael shrugs. It's like he knows he's untouchable, invincible: He's the future. He doesn't have to give the present any attention. 'No,' he says. 'Not specially. How old are you anyway?'

'Forty-five. Or it might be a year more.'

'Which?'

'I don't remember.'

'Fuck off, Dad. Everyone remembers their fuckin' age.'

'Well, I don't. Not since I left Ireland. I used to always know it then, but that's long ago.'

'Ask Mum, then. She'll know.'

And Michael goes on up the stairs, scuffing the carpet with the bulbous smelly shoes he wears. No thoughts. No ideas. Not specially.

And again McCreedy is alone.

But they have to do something. Like Christmas, a birthday is there: an obstacle in the road you can't quite squeeze round.

So McCreedy goes to see his friend Spiros, who runs a little restaurant two streets away, and tells him they'll come early Saturday evening, about seven so Katy won't be too tired, and can Spiros do steaks or cutlets because Hilda won't eat any Greek stews or fish.

'No problem,' says Spiros. 'And we make you a cake, John?'

'No,' says McCreedy, 'no bloody cake. Just do some nice meat.'

Spiros takes down a bottle and pours two thimbles of brandy for him and McCreedy. It's five in the afternoon, and they're alone in the place, sitting on stools under the fishing nets that drape the ceiling.

'Commiserations,' says Spiros.

'Ta,' says McCreedy.

They drink and Spiros pours them another. He's a good man, thinks McCreedy. Far from home, like me, but making a go of it. Not complaining. And he does lovely chips.

He tells Hilda it's all booked and arranged, she can take it off her mind, and she looks pleased for once. 'All right,' she says. 'Good. But don't go and spoil it by going out first and getting sloshed, will yer?'

'Why would I?' says McCreedy.

And he wouldn't, he thinks, honest to God, if only the presents had been better. But Hilda has no imagination. Where her imagination should be there's an old tea stain.

Socks, they give him. A Mr. Grumpy T-shirt. Tobacco. Katy draws a house in felt-tip, folds it in half, like a card, forgets to write anything in it.

He has to tell someone how pathetic this seems to him, how the T-shirt is grounds for divorce, isn't it?

'Absolutely,' say his mates in the pub 'Fuckin' socks as well,' they say. 'Socks is grounds.'

They've done the pub up. It feels almost like you're drinking somewhere classy, except it's the same landlord with his face like a dough ball, and the same drinkers, mostly Irish, he's known for fifteen years. And they all, after the first couple of drinks, start to feel comfortable and full of friendliness, and the world outside goes still and quiet. And McCreedy loves this feeling of the quiet outside and the laughter within. It reminds him of something he once had and knows he's lost. It's the best.

He wants to prolong it. Just let everything unwind nice and slowly here. But he tells his mates, 'Kick me out at seven. Make sure I'm gone.'

And they promise. In between pints, they say, 'Plenty of time yet, John, hours of time.' And the pub fills up and starts to get its Saturday-night roar. And a spike-haired girl he's seen before comes up to him for a light and stays by him and he buys her a lager. She smells of leather and her skin's creamy white and she tells him she went to Ireland once and got bitten by a horse. And she shows him the scar of the bite on her shoulder and he touches it and thinks, She's what I'd really like for my birthday.

He's only twenty minutes late at the restaurant. You'd think it was two hours from the look on Hilda's face, and when he says he's sorry she turns her head away, like she can't bear the sight nor smell nor sound of him.

'Well,' he says, 'did you order?'

'Nettle soup,' says Katy, who's wearing a funny little velvet hat. 'I want nettle soup.'

'Fuck off, Katy,' says Michael.

'That's enough, Michael,' Hilda snaps.

She's ordered a gin. She's billowing her smoke out into the room. The menus sit in a pile, pushed aside, like she thinks she isn't going to understand a single thing in them.

McCreedy takes one and opens it. 'Dolmades.' 'Keftedes.' 'Horiatiki.' Excuse me, Spiros. Even the lettering's weird.

'Hey!' he calls, tilting his chair backward and feeling himself almost fall. 'Spiros!'

But Spiros is in the kitchen, as he should have remembered, and it's Elena, Spiros's wife with her mournful face, who comes over with an order pad and McCreedy tells her listen, none of this fancy-sounding stuff, just meat, steak or chops, with chips, O.K., and a pint of Guinness and Coke or something for the kids.

'Lilt,' says Michael.

'Lilt, then, for him,' says McCreedy.

'Which you want?' says Elena.

'One Lilt, one Coke for Katy.'

'Which you want, steak or pork chops, pork kebab?'

'Not pork, do you, Hilda?'

'Steak for me.'

'Steak for her. And me. You want steak, Michael?'

'Yeh.'

'Katy?'

'You said nettle soup would – '

'Not now. Pork or steak?'

She hides under the sad little hat. It's like she's got

no neck at all. And now she's going to start crying.

'It's O.K.,' says McCreedy, 'she'll have steak. Small portion.'

'How you want them – rare, medium, well-done?'

'Well-done,' says Hilda and passes Elena the rest of the menus, like she wants them out of her sight. Then she hands Katy a red paper napkin and she holds it round her mouth like a gag and her tears are just enough to moisten its edge. She glares at McCreedy over the top of it.

McCreedy can't eat the food. It's a good steak. Large and juicy. But he can't get it down.

It's partly the drink he's had, but it's something else as well. It's what his life looks like across this table. Hatred. Indifference. Love. All three staring him in the eye, waiting for him to respond, to act, to assert himself, to be. And he can't. Not anymore. For a long time he could and did. He fought them and held them close. He wept and screamed and tried to think of all the appropriate words of apology and affection. Right up to yesterday. But that's it, over now. They can't see it yet, but he knows it's happened: they've used him up. McCreedy's used up.

He sits in silence while they eat and talk. Katy stares at him under her hat, stuffing chips, one by one. Hilda and Michael blather about Arsenal. Michael snatches Katy's steak and gobbles it down. Hilda sucks the lemon from her gin glass. All McCreedy is doing is waiting for them to finish.

And when they have he begins gathering up the plates. Dinner plates, knives and forks, side plates, veg dishes. One by one, he reaches across the table and piles them into a stack in front of him. It's a neat stack, like Hilda makes at home, with his own uneaten piece of meat transferred to the top plate, and then he sits back and stares at it.

'McCreedy,' says Hilda. 'This is a restaurant.'

'I know it's a restaurant,' he says. Michael is falling around, giggling, scarlet. 'Dad,' he splutters, 'what the fuck you doing?'

'What does it look like?'

'Pass them round again, McCreedy,' snarls Hilda. 'You'll make us the laughing stock.'

'No,' he says.

'Katy,' says Hilda, 'give out the plates again.'

'There's nothing on them,' he says, 'except on mine. Why d'you want them?'

'Jesus Christ!' says Hilda. 'Give us back the plates before that woman comes.'

'No,' he says again. Then he picks up his flab of steak in his fingers and lets it dangle above the stack. He takes a breath.

'See this?' he says. 'This is John McCreedy, aged forty-six today. See it? Chewed and left. Stranded. And this is all your stuff, underneath. Cold and hard and messed up. And I'm telling anyone who wants to listen that I want to get down from here, but I don't for the life of me know how.'

They all three stare at him. They don't know what on earth to make of it all, except it frightens them, it's so dramatic and Irish and odd. Hilda opens her mouth to say it must be the Guinness talking, but no words come out. She begins scrabbling in her bag for a new pack of cigarettes. Michael swears under his breath and gets up and slouches off to the toilet. Katy puts her thumb in her mouth. She watches her father drop the meat and she knows what's going to happen next: McCreedy is going to sweep the stack onto the floor, where it will break into a thousand pieces.

But then Spiros is there at the table. He's smiling. He smells of his charcoal fire, and his face is pink and gleaming. And he laughs good-naturedly at the stack and slaps McCreedy's thin shoulder blades, then snaps his fingers for a waitress to take the pile of plates and dishes away.

He waits a fraction of a second until it's safely gone, and then he says, 'O.K. Serious business now. Some champagne on the house for my old friend John McCreedy and his family, and a beautiful dessert for the princess in the hat.'

B H A R A T I
M U K H E R J E E

Nostalgia

On a cold, snowless evening in December, Dr Manny
Patel, a psychiatric resident at a state hospital in Queens,
New York, looked through the storefront window of the
'New Taj Mahal' and for the first time in thirteen years
felt the papercut-sharp pain of desire. The woman behind
the counter was about twenty, twenty-one, with the
buttery-gold skin and the round voluptuous bosom of a
Bombay film star.

Dr Patel had driven into Manhattan on an impulse. He
had put in one of those afternoons at the hospital that
made him realize it was only the mysteries of metabo-
lism that kept him from unprofessional outbursts. Mr

Horowitz, a three-hundred-and-nineteen-pound readmit-
ted schizophrenic, had convinced himself that he was
Noel Coward and demanded respect from the staff. In
less than half-an-hour, Mr Horowitz had sung twenty
songs, battered a therapy aide's head against a wall,
unbuttoned another patient's blouse in order to bite off
her nipples, struck a Jamaican nurse across the face and
lunged at Dr Patel, calling him in exquisite English,
'Paki scum'. The nurse asked that Mr Horowitz be
placed in the seclusion room, and Dr Patel had agreed.
The seclusion order had to be reviewed by a doctor every
two hours, and Mr Horowitz's order was renewed by Dr
Chuong who had come in two hours late for work.

Dr Patel did not like to lock grown men and women
in a seven-by-nine room, especially one without padding
on its walls. Mr Horowitz had screamed and sung for
almost six hours. Dr Patel had increased his dosage of
Haldol. Mr Horowitz was at war with himself and there
was no truce except through psychopharmacology and
Dr Patel was suspicious of the side effects of such cures.
The Haldol had calmed the prisoner. Perhaps it was
unrealistic to want more.

He was grateful that there were so many helpless,
mentally disabled people (crazies, his wife called them)
in New York state, and that they afforded him and Dr
Chuong and even the Jamaican nurse a nice living. But
he resented being called a 'Paki scum'. Not even a sick
man like Mr Horowitz had the right to do that.

He had chosen to settle in the US. He was not one for

nostalgia; he was not an expatriate but a patriot. His wife, Camille, who had grown up in Camden, New Jersey, did not share his enthusiasm for America, and had made fun of him when he voted for President Reagan. Camille was not a hypocrite; she was a predictable paradox. She could cut him down for wanting to move to a three-hundred-thousand-dollar house with an atrium in the dining hall, and for blowing sixty-two thousand on a red Porsche, while she boycotted South African wines and non-union lettuce. She spent guiltless money at Balducci's and on fitness equipment. So he enjoyed his house, his car, so what? He wanted things. He wanted things for Camille and for their son. He loved his family, and his acquisitiveness was entwined with love.

His son was at Andover, costing nearly twelve thousand dollars a year. When Manny converted the twelve thousand from dollars to rupees, which he often did as he sat in his small, dreary office listening for screams in the hall, the staggering rupee figure reassured him that he had done well in the New World. His son had recently taken to wearing a safety pin through his left earlobe, but nothing the boy could do would diminish his father's love.

He had come to America because of the boy. Well, not exactly *come*, but stayed when his student visa expired. He had met Camille, a nurse, at a teaching hospital and the boy had come along, all eight pounds and ten ounces of him, one balmy summer midnight. He could always go back to Delhi if he wanted to. He had made enough money to retire to India (the conversion into rupees had made him a millionaire several times over). He had bought a condominium in one of the better development 'colonies' of New Delhi, just in case.

America had been very good to him, no question; but there were things that he had given up. There were some boyhood emotions, for instance, that he could no longer retrieve. He lived with the fear that his father would die before he could free himself from the crazies of New York and go home. He missed his parents, especially his father, but he couldn't explain this loss to Camille. She hated her mother who had worked long hours at Korvette's and brought her up alone. Camille's mother now worked at a K-Mart, even though she didn't need the money desperately. Camille's mother was an obsessive-compulsive but that was no reason to hate her. In fact Manny got along with her very well and often had to carry notes between her and her daughter.

His father was now in his seventies, a loud, brash man with blackened teeth. He still operated the moviehouse he owned. The old man didn't trust the manager he kept on the payroll. He didn't trust anyone except his blood relatives. All the ushers in the moviehouse were poor cousins. Manny was an only child. His mother had been deemed barren, but at age forty-three, goddess Parvati had worked a miracle and Manny had been born. He should go back to India. He should look after his parents. Out of a sense of duty to the goddess, if not out of love for his father. Money, luxuries: he could have both in India, too. When he had wanted to go to Johns Hopkins

for medical training, his parents had loved him enough
to let him go. They loved him the same intense, unex-
amined way he loved his own boy. He had let them
down. Perhaps he hadn't really let them down in that he
had done well at medical school, and had a job in the
State set-up in Queens, and played the money market
aggressively with a bit of inside information from Suresh
Khanna who had been a year ahead of him in Delhi's
Modern School and was now with Merrill-Lynch, but he
hadn't reciprocated their devotion.

It was in this mood of regret filtered through longing
that Manny had driven in Manhattan and parked his
Porsche on a side-street outside the Sari Palace which
was a block up from the New Taj Mahal, where behind
the counter he had spied the girl of his dreams.

The girl – the woman, Manny corrected himself
instantly, for Camille didn't tolerate what she called
'masculists' – moved out from behind the counter to
show a customer where in the crowded store the ten-
pound bags of Basmati rice were stacked. She wore a
'Police' T-shirt and navy cords. The cords voluted up
her small, rounded thighs and creased around her crotch
in a delicate burst, like a Japanese fan. He would have
dressed her in a silk sari of peacock blue. He wanted to
wrap her narrow wrists in bracelets of 24-carat gold. He
wanted to decorate her bosom and throat with necklaces
of pearls, rubies, emeralds. She was as lovely and as
removed from him as a goddess. He breathed warm,
worshipful stains on the dingy store window.

She stooped to pick up a sack of rice by its rough jute handles while the customer flitted across the floor to a bin of eggplants. He discerned a touch of indolence in the way she paused before slipping her snake-slim fingers through the sack's hemp loops. She paused again. She tested the strength of the loops. She bent her knees ready to heave the brutish sack of rice. He found himself running into the store. He couldn't let her do it. He couldn't let a goddess do menial chores, then ride home on a subway with a backache.

'Oh, thank you,' she said. She flashed him an indolent glance from under heavily shadowed eyelids, without seeming to turn away from the customer who had expected her to lift the ten-pound sack.

'Where are the fresh eggplants? These are all dried out.'

Manny Patel watched the customer flick the pleats of her Japanese georgette sari irritably over the sturdy tops of her winter boots.

'These things look as if they've been here all week!' the woman continued to complain.

Manny couldn't bear her beauty. Perfect crimson nails raked the top layer of eggplants. 'They came in just two days ago.'

If there had been room for a third pair of hands, he would have come up with plump, seedless, perfect eggplants.

'Ring up the rice, *dal* and spices,' the customer instructed. 'I'll get my vegetables next door.'

'I'll take four eggplants,' Manny Patel said defiantly. 'And two pounds of *bhindi*.' He sorted through wilted piles of okra which Camille wouldn't know how to cook.

'I'll be with you in a minute, sir,' the goddess answered.

When she looked up again, he asked her out for dinner. She only said, 'You really don't have to buy anything, you know.'

She suggested they meet outside the Sari Palace at six-thirty. Her readiness overwhelmed him. Dr Patel had been out of the business of dating for almost thirteen years. At conferences, on trips and on the occasional night in the city when an older self possessed him, he would hire women for the evening, much as he had done in India. They were never precisely the answer, not even to his desire.

Camille had taken charge as soon as she had spotted him in the hospital cafeteria; she had done the pursuing. While he did occasionally flirt with a Filipino nutritionist at the hospital where he now worked, he assumed he did not possess the dexterity to perform the two-step dance of assertiveness and humility required of serious adultery. He left the store flattered but wary. A goddess had found him attractive, but he didn't know her name. He didn't know what kind of family fury she might unleash on him. Still, for the first time in years he felt a kind of agitated discovery, as though if he let up for a minute, his reconstituted, instant American life would not let him back.

His other self, the sober, greedy, scholarly Dr Patel, knew that life didn't change that easily. He had seen enough Horowitzes to know that no matter how astute his own methods might be and no matter how miraculous the discoveries of psychopharmacologists, fate could not be derailed. How did it come about that Mr Horowitz, the son of a successful slacks manufacturer, a good student at the Bronx High School of Science, had ended up obese, disturbed and assaultive, while he, the son of a Gujarati farmer turned entrepreneur, an indifferent student at Modern School and then at St Stephen's in Delhi, was ambitious and acquisitive? All his learning and experience could not answer the simplest questions. He had about an hour and twenty minutes to kill before perfection was to revisit him, this time (he guessed) in full glory.

Dr Patel wandered through 'Little India' – the busy, colourful blocks of Indian shops and restaurants off Lexington in the upper twenties. Men lugged heavy crates out of double-parked pickup trucks, swearing in Punjabi and Hindi. Women with tired, frightened eyes stepped into restaurants, careful not to drop their shopping-sacks from Bloomingdale's and Macy's. The Manhattan air here was fragrant with spices. He followed an attractive mother with two preschoolers into Chandni Chowk, a tea and snacks-stall, to call Camille about the emergency that had come up. Thank god for Mr Horowitz's recidivism. Camille was familiar with the more outrageous doings of Mr Horowitz.

'Why does that man always act up when I have plans?' Camille demanded. '*Amarcord* is at the rep tonight only.'

But Camille seemed in as agreeable a mood as his goddess. She thought she might ask Susan Kwan, the wife of an orthodontist who lived four houses up the block and who had a son by a former marriage also at Andover. Her credulousness depressed Manny. A woman who had lived with a man for almost thirteen years should be able to catch his little lies.

'Mr Horowitz is a dangerous person,' he continued. He could have hung up, but he didn't. He didn't want permission; he wanted sympathy: 'He rushed into my office. He tried to kill me.'

'Maybe psychiatrists at state institutions ought to carry firearms. Have you thought of that, Manny?' she laughed.

Manny Patel flushed. Camille didn't understand how the job was draining him. Mr Horowitz had, for a fact, flopped like a walrus on Dr Patel's desk, demanding a press conference so that the world would know that his civil liberties were being infringed. The moneyless schizos of New York state, Mr Horowitz had screamed, were being held hostage by a bunch of foreign doctors who couldn't speak English. If it hadn't been for the two six-foot orderlies (Dr Patel felt an awakening of respect for big blacks), Mr Horowitz would probably have grabbed him by the throat.

'I could have died today,' he repeated. The realization

dazed him. 'The man tried to strangle me.'

He hung up and ordered a cup of *masala* tea. The sweet, sticky brew calmed him, and the perfumed steam cleared his sinuses. Another man in his position would probably have ordered a double Scotch. In crises, he seemed to regress, to reach automatically for the miracle cures of his Delhi youth, though normally he had no patience with nostalgia. When he had married, he burned his India Society membership card. He was professionally cordial, nothing more, with Indian doctors at the hospital. But he knew he would forever shuttle between the old world and the new. He couldn't pretend he had been reborn when he became an American citizen in a Manhattan courthouse. Rebirth was the privilege of the dead, and of gods and goddesses, and they could leap into your life in myriad, mysterious ways, as a shopgirl, for instance, or as a withered eggplant, just to test you.

At three minutes after six, Dr Patel positioned himself inside his Porsche and watched the front doors of the Sari Palace for his date's arrival. He didn't want to give the appearance of having waited nervously. There was a slight tremor in both his hands.

He was suffering a small attack of anxiety. At thirty-three minutes after six, she appeared in the doorway of the sari-store. She came out of the Sari Palace, not up the street from the New Taj Mahal as he had expected. He slammed shut and locked his car door. Did it mean that she too had come to the rendezvous too early and had spied on him, crouched, anxious, strapped in the

bucket seat of his Porsche? When he caught up with her
by the store window, she was the most beautiful woman
he had ever talked to.

Her name was Padma. She told him that as he fought
for a cab to take them uptown. He didn't ask for, and
she didn't reveal, her last name. Both were aware of the
illicit nature of their meeting. An Indian man his age had
to be married, though he wore no wedding ring. An
immigrant girl from a decent Hindu family – it didn't
matter how long she had lived in America and what rock
groups she was crazy about – would not have said yes
to dinner with a man she didn't know. It was this inar-
ticulate unsanctionedness of the dinner date that made
him feel reckless, a hedonist, a man who might trample
tired ladies carrying shopping-bags in order to steal a
taxi crawling uptown. He wanted to take Padma to an
Indian restaurant so that he would feel he knew what he
was ordering and could bully the *maître d'* a bit, but not
to an Indian restaurant in her neighbourhood. He wanted
a nice Indian restaurant, an upscale one, with tablecloths,
sitar music and air ducts sprayed with the essence of
rose-petals. He chose a new one, Shajahan, on Park
Avenue.

'It's nice. I was going to recommend it,' she said.

Padma. Lotus. The goddess had come to him as a
flower. He wanted to lunge for her hands as soon as they
had been seated at a corner booth, but he knew better
than to frighten her off. He was mortal, he was humble.

The *maitre d'* himself took Dr Patel's order. And with

the *hors d'oeuvres* of *samosas* and *poppadoms* he sent a bottle of Entre Deux Mers on the house. Dr Patel had dined at the Shajahan four or five times already, and each time had brought in a group of six or eight. He had been a little afraid that the *maître d'* might disapprove of his bringing a youngish woman, an Indian and quite obviously not his wife, but the bottle of wine reassured him that the management was not judgemental.

He broke off a sliver of *poppadom* and held it to her lips. She snatched it with an exaggerated flurry of lips and teeth: 'Feeding the performing seal, are you?' She was coy. And amused.

'I didn't mean it that way,' he murmured. Her lips, he noticed, had left a glistening crescent of lipstick on a fingertip. He wiped the finger with his napkin surreptitiously under the table.

She didn't help herself to the *samosas*, and he didn't dare lift a forkful to her mouth. Perhaps she didn't care for *samosas*. Perhaps she wasn't much of an eater. He himself was timid and clumsy, half afraid that if he tried anything playful he might drip mint chutney on her tiger-print chiffon sari.

'Do you mind if I smoke?'

He busied himself with food while she took out a packet of Sobrani and a book of matches. Camille had given up smoking four years before, and now hand-written instructions THANK YOU FOR NOT SMOKING IN THIS HOUSE decorated bureautops and coffee tables. He had never got started because of an allergy.

'Well?' she said. It wasn't quite a question, and it wasn't quite a demand. 'Aren't you going to light it?' And she offered Manny Patel an exquisite profile, cheeks sucked tight and lips squeezed around the filter tip.

The most banal gesture of a goddess can destroy a decent-living mortal. He lit her cigarette, then blew the match out with a gust of unreasonable hope.

The *maître d'* hung around Manny's table almost to the point of neglecting other early diners. He had sad eyes and a bushy moustache. He wore a dark suit, a silvery wide tie kept in place with an elephant-headed god stick-pin, and on his feet which were remarkably large for a short, slight man, scuffed and pointed black shoes.

'I wouldn't recommend the pork vindaloo tonight.' The man's voice was confidential, low. 'We have a substitute cook. But the fish Bengal curry is very good. The lady, I think, is Bengali, no?'

She did not seem surprised. 'How very observant of you, sir,' she smiled.

It was flattering to have the *maître d'* linger and advise. Manny Patel ended up ordering one each of the curries listed under beef, lamb and fowl. He was a guiltlessly meat-eating Gujarati, at least in America. He filled in the rest of the order with two vegetable dishes, one spiced lentil and a vegetable *pillau*. The *raita* was free, as were the two small jars of mango and lemon pickle.

When the food started coming, Padma reluctantly stubbed out her Sobrani. The *maître d'* served them himself, making clucking noises with his tongue against uneven, oversize teeth, and Dr Patel felt obliged to make loud, appreciative moans.

'Is everything fine, doctor sahib? Fish is first class, no? It is not on the regular menu.'

He stayed and made small talk about Americans. He dispatched waiters to other tables, directing them with claps of pinkish palms from the edge of Manny's booth. Padma made an initial show of picking at her vegetable *pillau*. Then she gave up and took out another slim black Sobrani from a tin packet and held her face, uplifted and radiant, close to Manny's so he could light it again for her.

The *maître d'* said, 'I am having a small problem, doctor sahib. Actually the problem is my wife's. She has been in America three years and she is very lonely still. I'm saying to her, you have nice apartment in Rego Park, you have nice furnitures and fridge and stove, I'm driving you here and there in a blue Buick, you're having home-style Indian food, what then is wrong? But I am knowing and you are knowing, doctor sahib, that no Indian lady is happy without having children to bring up. That is why, in my desperation, I brought over my sister's child last June. We want to adopt him, he is very bright and talented and already he is loving this country. But the US government is telling me no. The boy came on a visitor's visa, and now the government is giving me big trouble. They are calling me bad names. Jealous peoples are telling them bad stories. They are saying I'm in the business of moving illegal aliens, can you believe? In the meantime, my wife is crying all day and pulling out her hair. Doctor sahib, you can write that she needs to have the boy here for. her peace of mind and mental stability, no? On official stationery of your hospital, doctor sahib?'

'My hands are tied,' Manny Patel said. 'The US government wouldn't listen to me.'

Padma said nothing. Manny ignored the *maître d'*. A reality was dawning on Manny Patel. It was too beautiful, too exciting to contemplate. He didn't want this night to fall under the pressure of other immigrants' woes.

'But you will write a letter about my wife's mental problems, doctor sahib?' The *maître d'* had summoned up tears. A man in a dark suit weeping in an upscale ethnic restaurant. Manny felt slightly disgraced, he wished the man would go away. 'Official stationery is very necessary to impress the immigration people.'

'Please leave us alone,' snapped Manny Patel. 'If you persist I will never come back.'

The old assurance, the authority of a millionaire in his native culture, was returning. He was sure of himself.

'What do you want to do after dinner?' Padma asked when the *maître d'* scurried away from their booth. Manny could sense him, wounded and scowling, from behind the kitchen door.

'What would you like to do?' He thought of his wife and Mrs Kwan at the Fellini movie. They would probably have a drink at a bar before coming home. Susan

Kwan had delightful legs. He had trouble understanding her husband, but Manny Patel had spent enjoyable hours at the Kwans', watching Mrs Kwan's legs. Padma's legs remained a mystery; he had seen her only in pants or a sari.

'If you are thinking of fucking me,' she said very suddenly, 'I should warn you that I never have an orgasm. You won't have to worry about pleasing me.'

Yes, he thought, it *is* so, just as he had suspected. It was a night in which he could do no wrong. He waved his visa card at the surly *maître d'* and paid the bill. After that Padma let him take her elbow and guide her to the expensive hotel above the restaurant.

An oriental man at the desk asked him, 'Cash or credit card, sir?' He paid for a double occupancy room with cash and signed himself in as Dr Mohan Vakil & wife, 18 Ridgewood Drive, Columbus, Ohio.

He had laid claim to America.

In a dark seventh-floor room off a back corridor, the goddess bared her flesh to a dazed, daunted mortal. She was small. She was perfect. She had saucy breasts, fluted thighs and tiny, taut big toes.

'Hey, you can suck but don't bite, okay?' Padma may have been slow to come, but he was not. He fell on her with a devotee's frenzy.

'Does it bother you?' she asked later, smoking the second Sobrani. She was on her side. Her tummy had a hint of convex opulence. 'About my not getting off?'

He couldn't answer. It was a small price to pay, and

anyway he wasn't paying it. Nothing could diminish the thrill he felt in taking a chance. It wasn't the hotel and this bed; it was having stepped inside the New Taj Mahal and asking her out.

He should probably call home, in case Camille hadn't stopped off for a drink. He should probably get dressed, offer her something generous – as discreetly as possible, for this one had class, real class – then drive himself home. The Indian food, an Indian woman in bed, made him nostalgic. He wished he were in his kitchen, and that his parents were visiting him and that his mother was making him a mug of hot Horlick's and that his son was not so far removed from him in a boarding school.

He wished he had married an Indian woman. One that his father had selected. He wished he had any life but the one he had chosen.

As Dr Patel sat on the edge of the double bed and slid his feet through the legs of his trousers, someone rapped softly on the hotel door, then without waiting for an answer unlocked it with a passkey.

Padma pulled the sheet up to her chin, but did not seem to have been startled.

'She's underage, of course,' the *maître d'* said. 'She is my sister's youngest daughter. I accuse you of rape, doctor sahib. You are of course ruined in this country. You have everything and think you must have more. You are highly immoral.'

He sat on the one chair that wasn't littered with

urgently cast-off clothes, and lit a cigarette. It was rapidly becoming stuffy in the room, and Manny's eyes were running. The man's eyes were malevolent, but the rest of his face remained practised and relaxed. An uncle should have been angrier, Dr Patel thought automatically. He himself should have seen it coming. He had mistaken her independence as a bold sign of honest assimilation. But it was his son who was the traveller over shifting sands, not her.

There was no point in hurrying. Meticulously he put on his trousers, double-checked the zipper, buttoned his shirt, knotted his tie and slipped on his Gucci shoes. *The lady is Bengali, no?* Yes, they knew one another, perhaps even as uncle and niece. Or pimp and hooker. The air here was polluted with criminality. He wondered if his slacks had been made by immigrant women in Mr Horowitz's father's sweat-shop.

'She's got to be at least twenty-three, twenty-four,' Dr Patel said. He stared at her, deliberately insolent. Through the sheets he could make out the upward thrust of her taut big toes. He had kissed those toes only half-an-hour before. He must have been mad.

'I'm telling you she is a minor. I'm intending to make a citizen's arrest. I have her passport in my pocket.'

It took an hour of bickering and threats to settle. He made out a check for seven hundred dollars. He would write a letter on hospital stationery. The uncle made assurances that there were no hidden tapes. Padma went into the bathroom to wash up and dress.

'Why?' Manny shouted, but he knew Padma couldn't hear him over the noise of the gushing faucet.

After the team left him, Manny Patel took off his clothes and went into the bathroom so recently used by the best-looking woman he had ever talked to (or slept with, he could now add). Her perfume, he thought of it as essence of lotus, made him choke.

He pulled himself up, using the edge of the bathtub as a step ladder, until his feet were on the wide edges of the old-fashioned sink. Then, squatting like a villager, squatting the way he had done in his father's home, he defecated into the sink, and with handfuls of his own shit – it felt hot, light, porous, an artist's medium – he wrote WHORE on the mirror and floor.

He spent the night in the hotel room. Just before dawn he took a cab to the parking lot of the Sari Palace. Miraculously, no vandals had touched his Porsche. Feeling lucky, spared somehow in spite of his brush with the deities, he drove home.

Camille had left the porch light on and it glowed pale in the brightening light of the morning. In a few hours Mr Horowitz would start to respond to the increased dosage of Haldol and be let out of the seclusion chamber. At the end of the term, Shawn Patel would come home from Andover and spend all day in the house with earphones tuned to a happier world. And in August, he would take his wife on a cruise through the Caribbean and make up for this night with a second honeymoon.

JOHN CHEEVER

Reunion

The last time I saw my father was in Grand Central
Station. I was going from my grandmother's in the Adi-
rondacks to a cottage on the Cape that my mother had
rented, and I wrote my father that I would be in New
York between trains for an hour and a half and asked if
we could have lunch together. His secretary wrote to say
that he would meet me at the information booth at noon,
and at twelve o'clock sharp I saw him coming through
the crowd. He was a stranger to me – my mother
divorced him three years ago, and I hadn't been with
him since – but as soon as I saw him I felt that he was
my father, my flesh and blood, my future and my doom.
I knew that when I was grown I would be something
like him; I would have to plan my campaigns within his
limitations. He was a big, good-looking man, and I was

terribly happy to see him again. He struck me on the back and shook my hand. 'Hi, Charlie,' he said. 'Hi, boy. I'd like to take you up to my club, but it's in the Sixties, and if you have to catch an early train I guess we'd better get something to eat around here.' He put his arm around me, and I smelled my father the way my mother sniffs a rose. It was a rich compound of whiskey, after-shave lotion, shoe polish, woolens, and the rankness of a mature male. I hoped that someone would see us together. I wished that we could be photographed. I wanted some record of our having been together.

We went out of the station and up a side street to a restaurant. It was still early, and the place was empty. The bartender was quarreling with a delivery boy, and there was one very old waiter in a red coat down by the kitchen door. We sat down, and my father hailed the waiter in a loud voice. '*Kellner!*' he shouted. '*Garçon! Cameriere! You!*' His boisterousness in the empty restaurant seemed out of place. 'Could we have a little service here!' he shouted. 'Chop-chop.' Then he clapped his hands. This caught the waiter's attention, and he shuffled over to our table.

'Were you clapping your hands at me?' he asked.

'Calm down, calm down, *sommelier*,' my father said. 'If it isn't too much to ask of you – if it wouldn't be too much above and beyond the call of duty, we would like a couple of Beefeater Gibsons.'

'I don't like to be clapped at,' the waiter said.

'I should have brought my whistle,' my father said.

'I have a whistle that is audible only to the ears of old waiters. Now, take out your little pad and your little pencil and see if you can get this straight: two Beefeater Gibsons. Repeat after me: two Beefeater Gibsons.'

'I think you'd better go somewhere else,' the waiter said quietly.'

'That,' said my father, 'is one of the most brilliant suggestions I have ever heard. Come on, Charlie, let's get the hell out of here.'

I followed my father out of that restaurant into another. He was not so boisterous this time. Our drinks came, and he cross-questioned me about the baseball season. He then struck the edge of his empty glass with his knife and began shouting again. '*Garçon! Kellner! You!* Could we trouble you to bring us two more of the same.'

'How old is the boy?' the waiter asked.

'That,' my father said, 'is none of your goddamned business.'

'I'm sorry, sir,' the waiter said, 'but I won't serve the boy another drink.'

'Well, I have some news for you,' my father said. 'I have some very interesting news for you. This doesn't happen to be the only restaurant in New York. They've opened another on the corner. Come on, Charlie.'

He paid the bill, and I followed him out of that restaurant into another. Here the waiters wore pink jackets like hunting coats, and there was a lot of horse tack on the walls. We sat down, and my father began to shout again. 'Master of the hounds! Tallyhoo and all that sort of thing. We'd like a little something in the way of a stirrup cup. Namely, two Bibson Geefeaters.'

'Two Bibson Geefeaters?' the waiter asked, smiling.

'You know damned well what I want,' my father said angrily. 'I want two Beefeater Gibsons, and make it snappy. Things have changed in jolly old England. So my friend the duke tells me. Let's see what England can produce in the way of a cocktail.'

'This isn't England,' the waiter said.

'Don't argue with me,' my father said. 'Just do as you're told.'

'I just thought you might like to know where you are,' the waiter said.

'If there is one thing I cannot tolerate,' my father said, 'it is an impudent domestic. Come on, Charlie.'

The fourth place we went to was Italian. '*Buon giorno*,' my father said. '*Per favore, possiamo avere due cocktail americani, forti, forti. Molto gin, poco vermut.*'

'I don't understand Italian,' the waiter said.

'Oh, come off it,' my father said. 'You understand Italian, and you know damned well you do. *Vogliamo due cocktail americani. Subito.*'

The waiter left us and spoke with the captain, who came over to our table and said, 'I'm sorry, sir, but this table is reserved.'

'All right,' my father said. 'Get us another table.'

'All the tables are reserved,' the captain said.

'I get it,' my father said. 'You don't desire our patronage. Is that it? Well, the hell with you. *Vada all' inferno.* Let's go, Charlie.'

'I have to get my train,' I said.

'I'm sorry, sonny,' my father said. 'I'm terribly sorry.' He put his arm around me and pressed me against him. 'I'll walk you back to the station. If there had only been time to go up to my club.'

'That's all right, Daddy,' I said.

'I'll get you a paper,' he said. 'I'll get you a paper to read on the train.'

Then he went up to a newsstand and said, 'Kind sir, will you be good enough to favor me with one of your goddamned, no-good, ten-cent afternoon papers?' The clerk turned away from him and stared at a magazine cover. 'Is it asking too much, kind sir,' my father said, 'is it asking too much for you to sell me one of your disgusting specimens of yellow journalism?'

'I have to go, Daddy,' I said. 'It's late.'

'Now, just wait a second, sonny,' he said. 'Just wait a second. I want to get a rise out of this chap.'

'Goodbye, Daddy,' I said, and I went down the stairs and got my train, and that was the last time I saw my father.

NAGUIB MAHFOUZ

Blessed Night

It was nothing but a single room in the unpretentious Nouri Alley, off Clot Bey Street. In the middle of the room was the bar and the shelf embellished with bottles. It was called The Flower and was passionately patronized by old men addicted to drink. Its barman was advanced in years, excessively quiet, a man who inspired silence and yet effused a cordial friendliness. Unlike other taverns, The Flower dozed in a delightful tranquility. The regulars would converse inwardly, with glances rather than words. On the night that was blessed, the barman departed from his traditional silence.

'Yesterday,' he said, 'I dreamed that a gift would be

presented to a man of good fortune ...'

Safwan's heart broke into a song with gentle lute accompaniment, while alcoholic waves flowed through him like electricity as he congratulated himself with the words 'O blessed, blessed night!' He left the bar, reeling drunk, and plunged into the sublime night under an autumn sky that was not without a twinkling of stars. He made his way toward Nuzha Street, cutting across the square, glowing with an intoxication unadulterated by the least sensation of drowsiness. The street was humbled under the veil of darkness, except for the light from the regularly spaced streetlamps, the shops having closed their doors and given themselves up to sleep. He stood in front of his house: the fourth on the right, Number 42, a single-storied house fronted by an old courtyard of whose garden nothing remained but a solitary towering date palm. Astonished at the dense darkness that surrounded the house, he wondered why his wife had not as usual turned on the light by the front door. It seemed that the house was manifesting itself in a new, gloomily forlorn shape and that it exuded a smell like that of old age. Raising his voice, he called out, 'Hey there!'

From behind the fence there rose before his eyes the form of a man, who coughed and inquired, 'Who are you? What do you want?'

Safwan was startled at the presence of this stranger and asked sharply, 'And who are you? What's brought you to my house?'

'Your house?' said the man in a hoarse, angry voice.

'Who are you?'

'I am the guardian for religious endowment properties.'

'But this is my house.'

'This house has been deserted for ages,' the man scoffed. 'People avoid it because it's rumored to be haunted by spirits.'

Safwan decided he must have lost his way, and hurried back toward the square. He gave it a long comprehensive look, then raised his head to the street sign and read out loud, 'Nuzha.' So again he entered the street and counted off the houses until he arrived at the fourth. There he stood in a state of bewilderment, almost of panic: he could find neither his own house nor the haunted one. Instead he saw an empty space, a stretch of wasteland lying between the other houses. 'Is it my house that I've lost or my mind?' he wondered.

He saw a policeman approaching, examining the locks of the shops. He stood in his path and pointed toward the empty wasteland. 'What do you see there?'

The policeman stared at him suspiciously and muttered, 'As you can see, it's a piece of wasteland where they sometimes set up funeral pavilions.'

'That's just where I should have found my house,' said Safwan. 'I left it there with my wife inside it in the pink of health only this afternoon, so when could it have been pulled down and all the rubble cleared away?'

The policeman concealed an involuntary smile behind a stern official glare and said brusquely, 'Ask that deadly poison in your stomach!'

'You are addressing a former general manager,' said Safwan haughtily. At this the policeman grasped him by the arm and led him off. 'Drunk and disorderly in the public highway!'

He took Safwan to the Daher police station, a short distance away, where he was brought before the officer on a charge of being drunk and disorderly. The officer took pity on him, however, because of his age and his respectable appearance. 'Your identity card?'

Safwan produced it and said, 'I'm quite in my right mind, it's just that there's no trace of my house.'

'Well, now there's a new type of theft!' said the officer, laughing. 'I really don't believe it!'

'But I'm speaking the truth,' said Safwan in alarm.

'The truth's being unfairly treated, but I'll be lenient in deference to your age.' Then he said to the policeman, 'Take him to Number 42 Nuzha Street.'

Accompanied by the policeman, Safwan finally found himself in front of his house as he knew it. Despite his drunken state he was overcome with confusion. He opened the outer door, crossed the courtyard, and put on the light at the entrance, where he was immediately taken aback, for he found himself in an entrance he had never before set eyes on. There was absolutely no connection between it and the entrance of the house in which he had lived for about half a century, and whose furniture and walls were all in a state of decay. He decided to retreat before his mistake was revealed, so he darted into the street, where he stood scrutinizing the house from the outside. It was his house all right, from the point of view of its features and site, and he had opened the door with his own key, no doubt about it. What, then, had changed the inside? He had seen a small chandelier, and the walls had been papered. There was also a new carpet. In a way it was his house, and in another way it was not. And what about his wife, Sadriyya? 'I've been drinking for half a century,' he said aloud, 'so what is it about this blessed night?'

He imagined his seven married daughters looking at him with tearful eyes. He determined, though, to solve the problem by himself, without recourse to the authorities – which would certainly mean exposing himself to the wrath of the law. Going up to the fence, he began clapping his hands, at which the front door was opened by someone whose features he could not make out. A woman's voice could be heard asking, 'What's keeping you outside?'

It seemed, though he could not be certain, that it was the voice of a stranger. 'Whose house is this, please?' he inquired.

'Are you that drunk? It's just too much!'

'I'm Safwan,' he said cautiously.

'Come in or you'll wake the people sleeping.'

'Are you Sadriyya?'

'Heaven help us! There's someone waiting for you inside.'

'At this hour?'

'He's been waiting since ten.'

'Waiting for me?'

She mumbled loudly in exasperation, and he inquired again, 'Are you Sadriyya?'

Her patience at an end, she shouted, 'Heaven help us!'

He advanced, at first stealthily, then without caring, and found himself in the new entrance. He saw that the door of the sitting room was open, with the lights brightly illuminating the interior. As for the woman, she had disappeared. He entered the sitting room, which revealed itself to him in a new garb, as the entrance had. Where had the old room with its ancient furniture gone to? Walls recently painted and a large chandelier from which Spanish-style lamps hung, a blue carpet, a spacious sofa and armchairs: it was a splendid room. In the foreground sat a man he had not seen before: thin, of a dark brown complexion, with a nose reminding one of a parrot's beak, and a certain impetuosity in the eyes. He was wearing a black suit, although autumn was only just coming in. The man addressed him irritably. 'How late you are for our appointment!'

Safwan was both taken aback and angry. 'What appointment? Who are you?'

'That's just what I expected – you'd forgotten!' the man exclaimed. 'It's the same old complaint repeated every single day, whether it's the truth or not. It's no use, it's out of the question ... '

'What is this raving nonsense?' Safwan shouted in exasperation.

Restraining himself, the man said, 'I know you're a man who enjoys his drink and sometimes overdoes it.'

'You're speaking to me as though you were in charge of me, while I don't even know you. I'm amazed you should impose your presence on a house in the absence of its owner.'

He gave a chilly smile. 'Its owner?'

'As though you doubt it!' Safwan said vehemently. 'I see I'll have to call the police.'

'So they can arrest you for being drunk and disorderly – and for fraud?'

'Shut up – you insolent imposter!'

The man struck one palm against the other and said 'You're pretending not to know who I am so as to escape from your commitments. It's out of the question . . .'

'I don't know you and I don't know what you're talking about.'

'Really? Are you alleging you forgot and are therefore innocent? Didn't you agree to sell your house and wife and fix tonight for completing the final formalities?'

Safwan, in a daze, exclaimed, 'What a lying devil you are!'

'As usual. You're all the same – shame on you!' said the other, with a shrug of the shoulders.

'You're clearly mad.'

'I have the proof and witnesses.'

'I've never heard of anyone having done such a thing before.'

'But it happens every moment. You're putting on a good act, even though you're drunk.'

In extreme agitation, Safwan said, 'I demand you leave at once.'

'No, let's conclude the incompleted formalities', said the other in a voice full of confidence.

He got up and went toward the closed door that led to the interior of the house. He rapped on it, then returned to his seat. Immediately there entered a short man with a pug nose and prominent forehead, carrying under his arm a file stuffed with papers. He bowed in greeting and sat down. Safwan directed a venomous glare at him and exclaimed, 'Since when has my house become a shelter for the homeless?'

The first man, introducing the person who had just entered, said, 'The lawyer.'

At which Safwan asked him brusquely, 'And who gave you permission to enter my house?'

'You're in a bad way,' said the lawyer, smiling, 'but may God forgive you. What are you so angry about?'

'What insolence!'

Without paying any attention to what Safwan had said, the lawyer went on. 'The deal is undoubtedly to your advantage.'

'What deal?' asked Safwan in bewilderment.

'You know exactly what I mean, and I would like to tell you that it's useless your thinking of going back on it now. The law is on our side, and common sense too.

Let me ask you: Do you consider this house to be really yours?'

For the first time Safwan felt at a loss. 'Yes and no,' he said.

'Was it in this condition when you left it?'

'Not at all.'

'Then it's another house?'

'Yet it's the same site, number, and street.'

'Ah, those are fortuitous incidentals that don't affect the essential fact – and there's something else.'

He got up, rapped on the door, and returned to his seat. All at once a beautiful middle-aged woman, well dressed and with a mournful mien, entered and seated herself alongside the first man. The lawyer resumed his questioning. 'Do you recognize in this lady your wife?'

It seemed to Safwan that she did possess a certain similarity, but he could not stop himself from saying, 'Not at all.'

'Fine – the house is neither your house, nor the lady your wife. Thus nothing remains but for you to sign the final agreement and then you can be off . . . '

'Off! Where to?'

'My dear sir, don't be stubborn. The deal is wholly to your advantage, and you know it.'

The telephone rang, although it was very late at night. The caller was the barman. Safwan was astonished that the man should be telephoning him for the first time in his life. 'Safwan Bey,' he said, 'Sign without delay.'

'But do you know . . . '

'Sign. It's the chance of a lifetime.'

The receiver was replaced at the other end. Safwan considered the short conversation and found himself relaxing. In a second his state of mind changed utterly, his face took on a cheerful expression, and a sensation of calm spread throughout his body. The feeling of tension left him, and he signed. When he had done so, the lawyer handed him a small but somewhat heavy suitcase and said, 'May the Almighty bless your comings and goings. In this suitcase is all that a happy man needs in this world.'

The first man clapped, and there entered an extremely portly man, with a wide smile and a charming manner. Introducing him to Safwan, the lawyer said, 'This is a trustworthy man and an expert at his work. He will take you to your new abode. It is truly a profitable deal.'

The portly man made his way outside, and Safwan followed him, quiet and calm, his hand gripping the handle of the suitcase. The man walked ahead of him into the night, and Safwan followed. Affected by the fresh air, he staggered and realized that he had not recovered from the intoxication of the blessed night. The man quickened his pace, and the distance between them grew, so Safwan in turn, despite his drunken state, walked faster, his gaze directed toward the specter of the other man, while wondering how it was that he combined such agility with portliness. 'Take it easy, sir!' Safwan called out to him.

But it was as though he had spurred the man on to greater speed, for he broke into strides so rapid that Safwan was forced to hurl himself forward for fear he would lose him, and thus lose his last hope. Frightened he could be incapable of keeping up the pace, he once again called out to the man. 'Take it easy or I'll get lost!'

At this the other, unconcerned about Safwan, began to run. Safwan, in terror, raced ahead, heedless of the consequences. This caused him great distress, but all to no avail, for the man plunged into the darkness and disappeared from sight. Safwan was frightened the man would arrive ahead of him at Yanabi Square, where various roads split up, and he would not know which one the man had taken. He therefore began running as fast as possible, determined to catch up.

His efforts paid off, for once again he caught a glimpse of the specter of the man at the crossroads. He saw him darting forward toward the fields, ignoring the branch roads that turned off to the eastern and western parts of the city. Safwan hurried along behind him and continued running without stopping, and without the least feeling of weakness. His nostrils were filled with delightful aromas that stirred up all kinds of sensations he had never before properly experienced and enjoyed.

When the two of them were alone in the vast void of earth and sky, the portly man gradually began to slow down until he had reverted to a mere brisk trot, then to a walk. Finally he stopped, and Safwan caught up with him and also came to a breathless stop. He looked around at the all-pervading darkness, with the glittering lights of faint stars. 'Where's the new abode?' he asked.

The man maintained his silence. At the same time, Safwan began to feel the incursion of a new weight bearing down upon his shoulders and his whole body. The weight grew heavier and heavier and then rose upward to his head. It seemed to him that his feet would plunge deep into the ground. The pressure became so great that he could no longer bear it and, with a sudden spontaneous burst of energy, he took off his shoes. Then, the pressure working its way upward, he stripped himself of his jacket and trousers and flung them to the ground. This made no real difference, so he rid himself of his underclothes, heedless of the dampness of autumn. He was ablaze with pain and, groaning, he abandoned the suitcase on the ground. At that moment it seemed to him that he had regained his balance, that he was capable of taking the few steps that still remained. He waited for his companion to do something, but the man was sunk in silence. Safwan wanted to converse with him, but talk was impossible, and the overwhelming silence slipped through the pores of his skin to his very heart. It seemed that in a little while he would be hearing the conversation that was passing between the stars.

IRVINE WELSH

Disnae Matter

Ah wis it that Disneyland in Florida, ken. Took hur n
the bairn. Wi me gittin peyed oaf fi Ferranti's, ah thoat
it's either dae somethin wi the dough or pish it doon the
bog it the Willie Muir. Ah saw whit happened tae a loat
ay other cunts; livin like kings fir a while: taxis ivray-
whair, chinkies ivray night, cairry-oots, ye ken the score.
N whit dae they huv tae show fir it? Scottish Fuckin
Fitba Association, that's what, ya cunt.

Now ah wisnae that keen oan Disneyland, bit ah thoat:
fir the bairn's sake, ken? Wish ah hudnae bothered. It
wis shite. Big fuckin queues tae git on aw the rides.
That's awright if ye like that sortay thing, but it's no ma
fuckin scene. The beer ower thair's pish n aw. They go
oan aboot aw thir beer, thir Budweiser n aw that; its like
drinkin fuckin cauld water. One thing ah did like aboot

336

the States though is the scran. Loadsay it, beyond yir wildest dreams, n the service n aw. Ah mind in one place ah sais tae hur: Fill yir fuckin boots while ye kin, hen, cause whin wi git back hame will be livin oafay Mc-Cain's oven chips till fuck knows when.

Anywey, it this fuckin Disneyland shite, this daft cunt in a bear suit jumps oot in front ay us, ken? Wavin ehs airms aboot n that. The bairn starts fuckin screamin, gied ur a real fright, ken? So ah fuckin panels the cunt, punches the fuckin wide-o in the mooth, or whair ah thought ehs mooth wis, under that suit, ken? Too fuckin right! Disneyland or nae fuckin Disneyland, disnae gie the cunt the excuse tae jump oot in front ay the bairn, ken.

Thing is, these polis cunts, fuckin guns n aw ya cunt, nae fuckin joke, ah'm tellin ye, they sais tae ays: Whit's the fucking score here, mate, bit likesay American, ken? So ah goes, noddin ower tae this bear cunt: Cunt jumped oot in front ay the bairn. Well ootay fuckin order. The polis cunt jist says somethin aboot the boy mibbe bein a bit too keen it ehs joab, ken. The other yin sais somethin like: Mibbe the wee lassie's frightened ay bears, ken?

So then this radge in a yellay jaykit comes along. Ah tipples right away thit eh's that bear cunt's gaffer, likesay. Eh apologises tae ays, then turns tae the bear cunt n sais: Wir gaunny hav tae lit ye go mate. They wir jist gaunny, likes, gie the boy ehs fucking cairds like that. This is nae good tae us, eh tells the boy. This perr cunt in the bear suit, eh's goat the head oaf now, likes; the cunt's nearly greetin, gaun oan aboot needin the joab tae pey ehs wey through college. So ah gits a hud ay this radge in the yellay jaykit n sais: Hi mate, yir ootay order here. Thir's nae need tae gie the boy ehs cairds. It's aw sorted oot.

Mean tae say, ah banged the cunt awright, bit ah didnae want the boy tae lose ehs joab, ken. Ah ken whit it's fuckin like. It's aw a great laugh whin they chuck that redundancy poppy it ye, bit that disnae last firivir, ken. Aw they doss cunts thit blow the dough oan nowt. Thuv goat mates they nivir kent they hud – till the fuckin hireys run oot. Anywey, this supervisor radge goes: S'up tae you mate. You're happy, cunt keeps ehs joab. Then eh turns tae the boy n sais: Yir fuckin lucky, ah'm tellin ye. If it wisnae fir the boy here, ken, ye'd be pickin up yir cairds, but this is aw American, likesay, ye ken how aw they doss cunts talk, oan the telly n that.

The cunt ah gubbed, this bear cunt goes: Really sorry, mate, ma fault, ken. So ah jist sais: Sound by me. The polis n the supervisor boy fucked off n the bear cunt turns n sais: Thanks a lot, buddy. Have a nice day. Ah thoat fir a minute, ah'll fucking gie ye nice day, ya cunt, jumpin oot in front ay the fucking bairn. Bit ah jist left it, ken, nae hassle tae nae cunt. Boy's entitled tae keep ehs joab; that wis ma good deed fir the day. Ah jist goes: Aye, you n aw, mate.

DON DeLILLO

The Black-and-White Ball

I.

The first man stood by the window of his stately suite
at the Waldorf. He watched the yellow cabs sink into
soulful dusk, that particular spendthrift light that falls
dyingly on Park Avenue in the hour before people take
leave of the office and become husbands and wives
again, or whatever people become in whatever murmur-
ous words when evenings grow swift and whispered.

The second man sat on the sofa, legs crossed, looking
at Bureau reports.

Edgar said, 'Of course you packed the mask.'

The second man nodded, a gesture that went unseen.

'Junior, the masks.'

'We have them, yes. I'm looking at a security memo
that's a little, actually, rankling.'

'I don't want to hear it. File it somewhere. I feel too good.'

'Protest. Outside the Plaza tonight.'

'What is it the bastards are protesting? Pray tell,' Edgar said in a tone he'd perfected through the years, a tight amusement etched in eleven kinds of irony.

'The war, it seems.'

'The war.'

'Yes, that,' the second man said.

They were staying at the Waldorf Towers, which was J. Edgar Hoover's hotel of choice during his sojourns in New York, but the party was taking place – the ball, the fête, the social event of the season, the decade, the half century no doubt – in the ballroom at the Plaza.

Edgar gazed far up Park, where the earth curved toward Canada, haven for draft dodgers and other misfits. He heard the muted clamor of taxi horns below, a cheerful sound at this protected distance, little toots and beeps that carried a carefree pitch.

'Let's talk about the war tomorrow.'

'A protest by a group we don't know much about.'

'Don't ruin my evening, Junior.'

Clyde Tolson, known as Junior, was Edgar's staunchest aide in the Bureau, his dearest friend and inseparable companion.

They were getting on, of course. Clyde was five years younger than Edgar but not so sharp as he used to be, his flash-card memory a little less prodigious now. But where Edgar was pugnosed and compact, with brows like bat wings, Clyde was long-jawed and tallish, sort of semi-debonair, a fairly gentle fellow who liked conversation – again, unlike his boss, who thought you gave yourself away, word by word, every time you opened your trap to speak.

Edgar held a tumbler of Scotch. He checked the glass for smudges, then sniffed and sipped, feeling the charred fumes prickle his tongue. The handsome suite, the soothing booze, the presence of Junior on the scene, the party that everybody'd been talking about for months, famous long before it happened, the uninvited lapsing into states of acute confusion, insomniac, unable to function – yes, Edgar was feeling pretty good tonight.

Talkative or not, he loved a first-rate party. He loved celebrities in particular, and there would be an abundance of mammal glamour at the Plaza tonight. Personage and flair and wicked wit. A frail and lonely lad still crouched inside the Director's pudgy corpus, and this crypto-schoolboy came to robust life in the presence of show people and other living icons – child stars, ballplayers, prizefighters, even Hollywood horses and dogs.

Celebrated people were master spirits, men and women who spiked the temper of the age. Whatever Edgar's own claim to rank and notoriety, he found himself subject to anal flutters when chatting with a genuine celeb.

Clyde said, 'And this, of course, as well.'

Edgar did not turn to see what the second man was reading. He studied the carpet instead. The carpets at the

Waldorf were thick and lush, nesting grounds for bacteria of every sort.

Clyde said, 'I knew it was a mistake to publicize our methods of ransacking the garbage of organized-crime figures.'

'Makes good copy.'

'And creates a copycat mentality. Now we have a situation that's a public-relations nightmare. To wit, so-called garbage guerrillas are targeting guess whose garbage, Boss?'

'Please. I'm enjoying my drink. A man enjoys a drink when the day winds down.'

'Yours,' Clyde said.

Edgar could not believe he'd heard the fellow correctly.

'This is what our confidential source tells us.' And Clyde rattled the page he was reading for maximum nuisance effect. 'Team of urban guerrillas planning a garbage raid at 4936 Thirtieth Place Northwest, Washington, D.C.'

It was the end of the world, in triplicate.

'When is this supposed to happen?'

'More or less momentarily.'

'You've posted guards?'

'In unmarked cars. But whether we arrest them or not, they will find a way to make public theatre of your garbage.'

'I won't put the garbage out.'

'You have to put it out eventually.'

'I'll put it out and lock it up.'

'How will the garbage collectors collect it?'

Edgar walked over to another window. He needed a change, as they say, of scene.

'Confidential source says they intend to take your garbage on tour. Rent halls in major cities. Get lefty sociologists to analyze the stuff item by item. Get hippies to rub it on their naked bodies. More or less have sex with it. Get poets to write poems about it. In the last city on the tour, they plan to eat it.'

Edgar could see part of the east façade of the Plaza, about a dozen blocks away.

'And expel it,' Clyde said. 'Publicly.'

The great slate roof, the gables and dormers and copper cresting. How odd it seemed that such a taken-for-granted thing, putting out the garbage, could suddenly be a source of the gravest anxiety.

'Do we have a dossier on these guerrillas?'

'Yes.'

'Is it massive?' Edgar said.

In the endless estuarial mingling of paranoia and control, the dossier was an essential device. Edgar had many enemies-for-life, and the way to deal with such people was to compile massive dossiers. Photographs, surveillance reports, detailed allegations, linked names, transcribed tapes – wiretaps, bugs, break-ins. The dossier was a deeper form of truth, transcending facts and actuality. The second you placed an item in the file, a fuzzy photograph, an unfounded rumor, it became promiscuously true. It was a truth without authority and therefore incontestable. Factoids seeped out of the file and crept across the horizon, consuming bodies and minds. The file was everything, the life nothing. And this was the essence of Edgar's revenge. He rearranged the lives of his enemies, their conversations, their relationships, their very memories, and he made these people answerable to the details of his creation.

'We'll arrest them and charge them,' Clyde said. 'That's all we can do.'

Edgar turned from the window, smiling.

'Maybe I can sympathize with the Mafia over this.'

Clyde smiled.

'You were always half a gangster,' he said.

They laughed.

'Remember the tommy guns we carried?' Edgar said.

'When photographers were around.'

They laughed again.

'You were right there alongside me, posed heroically.'

'Edgar and Clyde,' said Clyde.

'Clyde and Edgar,' said Edgar.

Where the current of his need for control met the tide of his paranoia, this was where the dossier was reciprocally satisfying. He fed both forces in a single stroke.

'I liked the thirties,' Edgar said. 'I don't like the sixties. No, not at all.'

The desk at the end of the room was out of the thirties, in a way, equipped with items fashioned to Edgar's specifications. Two nibbed black pens. Two bottles of Skrip Permanent Royal Blue ink, No. 52. Six sharpened Eberhard Faber pencils, No. 2. A pair of five-by-eight linen-finish writing pads, white. A new sixty-watt bulb in the standing lamp. The Director did not want to breathe the dust of old bulbs used to illuminate the reading matter of total strangers. Newspapers, guidebooks, Gideon Bibles, erotic literature, subversive literature, underground literature, literature – whatever people read in hotels, alone, thumbing and breathing.

Clyde checked his watch. Dinner first, the two of them, alone, a practice spanning the decades – then the short ride to the Plaza.

It was called the Black-and-White Ball. A godlike gathering of five hundred, a masked affair, invitation only, dinner jacket and black mask for men, evening gown and white mask for women.

The party was being given by a writer, Truman Capote, for a publisher, Katharine Graham, and the factoidal data generated by the guests would surely bridge the narrowing gap between journalism and fiction.

Edgar had not been invited, initially. But arranging an invitation was not difficult. A word from Edgar to Clyde. A word from Clyde to someone close to Capote. They were in the files, of course, a number of those involved in planning the event – all catalogued and dossiered up to their eyeballs, and none of them eager to offend the Director.

Clyde took a call from the desk. The mask lady was coming up for a fitting.

Edgar noticed that Clyde was wearing a necktie with a driblet design. The little figures made him think of paramecia, sinister organisms with gullets and feeding grooves. At home Edgar sat on a toilet that was raised on a platform, to isolate him from floorbound forms of life. And he'd ordered his lab people to build a clean room at the Bureau with unprecedented standards of hygiene. A white room manned by white-clad technicians, preferably white themselves, who would work in an environment completely free of contaminants, dust, bacteria, and so on, with big white lights shining down, where Edgar himself might like to spend time when he was feeling vulnerable to the forces around him.

She walked in the door, Tanya Berenger, in a maxidress and thrift-shop boots, once a well-known costume designer, now ancient and frowzy, living in a room in a sad hotel off Times Square, a place where the desk clerk sits behind a grille eating a tongue sandwich. People tracked her down, three or four times a year, to do masks for special occasions, and she found fairly steady work doing sadomasochistic accessories for a private club in the Village.

The two men, as always with a female in the room, someone they didn't know, and without others present, and lacking an atmosphere of sociable cheer – well, they tended to become stiff and defensive, as though surprised by an armed intruder.

Clyde did not stray from Edgar's side, sensing a potential for wayward behavior on the woman's part. She wore heavy makeup that she might have poured from a paint can and cooked. Clyde noted how one pocket on her dress drooped just a bit, becoming unseamed.

She spoke to Edgar with a sort of rueful affection.

'You know I can't let you wear one of my masks, dear man, without a consultation. I must put my hands on the living head. Bad enough I had to create my *objet* from a set of written specifications, like I'm a plumber installing a sink already.'

She had a European accent slashed and burned by long-term residence in New York. And her hair had the retouched gloss of a dead crow mounted on a stick.

Of course Clyde had been briefed on Tanya Berenger. She was in the files in a fairly big way. She'd been accused at various times of being a lesbian, a Socialist, a Communist, a dope addict, a divorcée, a Jew, a Catholic, a Negro, an immigrant, and an unwed mother.

Just about everything Edgar distrusted and feared. But she did exquisite masks, and Clyde had been quick to commission her for the job.

He hurried into Edgar's bedroom and fetched the mask.

When she held it in her hands, she looked at Edgar and looked at the mask, weighing the equation, and the Director experienced a queer tension in his chest, wondering whether he was worthy.

She held the object at eye level, six inches from her face, and looked through the eyeholes at Edgar.

And Edgar, in turn, looked at the mask as if it had a life, an identity of its own that he might feel ballsy enough to borrow for a single midnight on the town.

It was a sleek black leather mask with handlebar extensions at the temples and a scatter of shiny sequins around the eyes.

Tanya said, 'You want to put it on or have a conversation with it?'

But he wasn't quite ready.

'Do I want to put it on, Junior?'

'Be brave.'

Tanya said, 'Leather. It's so real, you know? Like wearing someone else's face.'

She fitted the mask over Edgar's head, the padded band not too tight and the leather alive on his skin.

Then she took him by the shoulders and turned him slowly toward the mirror over the desk.

Clyde took the whiskey glass from Edgar's hand.

The mask transformed him. For the first time in some years, he did not see himself as a tenant in an old short pop-over body with an immense and lumpish head.

'I can call you Edgar – this is O.K.? I can tell you how I see you? I see you as as a mature and careful man who has a sexy motorcycle thug writhing to get out. Which the spangles give a crazy twist, you know?'

He felt creamy, dreamy, and drugged.

She made a slight adjustment in the fit, and even as

he cringed at her touch Edgar felt himself tingle thrillingly. She was insidious and corrupt, and it was like hearing your grandmother talk dirty in your ear.

'You are a butch biker to me, you know, riding into town to take over leadership of the sadists and necrophiles.'

Clyde watched in civilized alarm as a cockroach crawled out of Tanya's pocket and moved slowly down her flank. It was Spanish Harlem-sized, with antennae that could pick up the BBC.

'It's a lovely fit, darling. You have savage cheekbones for a full-figured man. I would love to do the total face, you know? Highlights and shadows.'

Clyde took her gently by the arm, concealing her roach side from Edgar's view.

'In fact, shall I tell you something? The ball tonight is a perfect setting for you. Because you are very black-and-white to me. So you'll be totally in character, yes?'

When she was gone, the men busied themselves with practical preparations. Clyde made dinner reservations and set out their evening clothes. Edgar placed the mask on a tabletop and took a bath.

When he was finished, he put on his fluffy white robe and stood by the window, sipping the rest of the drink. He heard a sound above the beeping traffic, something strident rising in the night.

'Junior, that noise. Can you hear it?'

Clyde walked into the room in his shirtsleeves, a shoe-brush in hand.

'Yes, barely.'

'Is it possible?'

'Yes, it could be the protesters at the Plaza.'

'The wind.'

'Yes, the wind is carrying the sound this way.'

They heard the hard rhythmic salvo of voices chanting angry · slogans, again, louder, fading when the wind shifted, then audible once more.

'You know what they want, don't you?' Edgar said.

He thought the old alarums might be sounding once again, figures coming out of the shadows, anarchists, terrorists, revolutionaries, wild-eyed men and women, scruffy and free-fucking, who moved toward armed and organized resistance, trying to break the state and bring about the end of the existing order.

'They want the power to shake the world,' he said. 'It's the old Bolshevik dream, and it's happening here. And you know where it begins, don't you?'

'These are kids, mostly, who lie down in the street and wave flowers at the police,' Clyde said, 'Vietnam is the war, the reality. This is the movie, where the scripts are written and the actors perform. American kids don't want to seize control. They want movies, music.'

Let Junior devise his measured perceptions. He didn't understand that once you patronize the enemy, you begin the process of your own undoing.

'It begins in the inmost person,' Edgar said. 'Once you yield to random sexual urges, you want to see everything come loose. You mistake your own looseness for some political concept, whereas in truth . . .'

He didn't finish the thought. Some thoughts had to remain unspoken, even unfinished in one's own mind. This was the point of his relationship with Clyde. To keep the subject unspoken. To keep the feelings unfelt, the momentary urges unacted-upon. How strange and foolish this would seem to the young people running in the streets, or living six to a room, or three to a bed, and to many other people, for that matter – how sad and rare.

Clyde went back to his duties, leaving the Boss by the window.

Edgar thought there was something noble in a constant companionship that does not fall to baser claims. He assumed Clyde believed likewise. But then Clyde was the second man, wasn't he, and perhaps he only followed Edgar's line of march wherever it led, or didn't.

He heard the chanting intermittently on the wind. Clyde was in the shower now. Edgar turned to see where he'd left the mask and saw himself unexpectedly in a full-length mirror, across the room, in his white robe and soft slippers, and he was startled by the image.

Of course it was him, but him in the guise of a macrocephalic baby, sexless and so just born as to be, in essence, unearthly.

Mother Hoover's cuddled runt.

He crossed the room and picked up the mask. He noted how the stylized handlebars were simple swirls of cut leather designed to fit snugly over the temples.

He heard Clyde come out of the shower.

When they were younger and on vacation together, or away on business, sharing a suite or taking adjoining rooms and keeping the connecting door open so they could talk from their respective beds well into the night, Edgar sometimes managed to angle the mirrors in such a way that he could catch a glimpse – by taking the freestanding antique in an old inn, the cheval glass, for example, and simply moving it to another part of the floor, or opening the medicine cabinet to a certain position when he shaved and letting the mirror absorb the light from the bed in the next room, or leaving a hand mirror propped on a desk – a glimpse, a passing glance, a spy-hole peek at Junior as he busied himself dressing or undressing or taking a bath, the arrangement being such that the moment would seem wholly accidental should the subject realize he was being watched, and an accident not just from his perspective but to Edgar's own mind as well, Junior's likeness being a thing that might simply float across his ken in the normal course of events, away on urgent Bureau business, his companion's body lean and virile, or at a golf resort, or following the ponies west to Del Mar, when they were both a great deal younger.

Junior was going bald now, and bulb-nosed, and he walked with a stoop. But then Junior had always walked with a stoop, in an effort to appear no taller than the Boss.

Edgar was in the bedroom with the door closed. He stood at the mirror, a seventy-one-year-old man wearing nothing but his sequinned biker's mask and his wool-lined slippers, listening to the voices in the street.

II.

The second man made the decision to show up late. It was the kind of firm determination that Clyde Tolson liked to make.

It proved his mettle. And when you're a man who is variously described as dutiful, deferential, obsequious, slavish, and brownnosingly corrupt, in descending order of distinction, you need to make a show of character now and then.

But first Clyde had to convince the Boss that missing an hour or two of party time was not going to haunt the twilight years of his directorate.

An F.B.I. security detail at the Plaza had reported that the protest was growing loud and that the party guests, as they entered, were being cursed in rhyming couplets, exposed to obscene signs and gestures, spat upon at close range, and forced to duck an occasional flying object.

It did not make sense to Clyde to allow the Director to enter a situation – and Edgar finally agreed – in which the dignity of the Bureau might be compromised.

So it was midnight when the two men rolled through the deserted mid-town streets in their bulletproof black Cadillac. They'd had a leisurely dinner, bantering with the wine steward and then enjoying a brandy at the bar with old acquaintances because there were old acquaintances wherever J. Edgar Hoover went, some who were loyal supporters, others residing in the files, a few who were enemies-for-life but didn't know it, and Edgar and Clyde were in a mellow enough mood, despite reports from the site, seated in the plush rear seat, in black tie, of course, and wearing their masks, like a suave and jaunty crime fighter out of the Sunday comics – a master bureaucrat by day who becomes dashing Maskman at night – cruising the streets in formal dress with his trusted right-hand man.

The driver activated the intercom to report that a car was tailing them.

Clyde turned to look while the Director slumped in his seat, getting his head below the window line.

'Little Volkswagen bug,' Clyde said. 'Painted top to bottom in very bright colors. Psychedelic. Big bright swirls and streaks. Can't make out the driver's face.'

The Cadillac coasted slowly past the Plaza. The klieg lights were gone, the media pack was gone, there was no trace of the crush of curious onlookers drawn by news of the event. There were still a few demonstrators – not enough to cause concern, but a few – a scatter of young people in their grimy tie-dyes, and city cops, of course, idler still, showing the eternal laden strain of a big meal hustled down the gullet, where it sits for hours earning overtime.

The car circled the block, purring with bated power, and Clyde checked the other entrances.

The north steps were empty and he tapped on the glass, and the driver pulled up and the two men exited, and suddenly there was the VW, cutting in front, and people came scrambling out, three, four, six, what, seven people – it's a circus car debouching clowns – about nine people tumbling onto the sidewalk and hurrying up the steps to flank the doorway.

All wore masks, the faces of Asian kids, some blood-spattered, others with eyes seamed shut, and they commenced their shouting as Hoover and Tolson moved up the stairs.

The first man was clumsy and slow and the second took his arm to assist, and they made their plodding way toward the entrance.

They heard, 'Society scum!'

They heard, 'A dead Asian baby for every Gucci loafer!'

Clyde wasn't sure the protesters knew who they were. Was Edgar's mask sufficient cover for his gnarled old media mug?

They heard mottoes, slurs, and technical terms.

'Vietnam! Love it or leave it!'

'White killers in black tie!'

A young woman stood at the entrance wearing the mask of a child's shattered face, and she said somewhat softly to Edgar, blocking his way and speaking evenly, whispering, in fact, 'We'll never disappear, old man, until you're in a landfill with your trash.'

Clyde said, 'Coming through,' like a waiter with a

bulky tray, and a couple of minutes later, after a stop in the men's room to collect themselves, the Director and his aide were ready to party.

But first Edgar said, 'Who were those jaspers?'

'Hecklers, that's all. It's public theatre. We'll find out more and place an informant.'

'Did you hear what she said about trash? I think they're connected to the garbage guerrillas.'

'Straighten your mask,' Clyde said.

'I'd like to see them maimed in the slowest possible manner. Over weeks and months, with voice tapes made.'

They walked down the hall to the grand ballroom. They'd walked down five hundred halls on their way to some ceremonial event, some testimonial dinner, one or another ritual salute to Edgar's decades in the Bureau, but they'd never heard a sound as inviting as this.

A subdued roar, a sort of rumble-buzz, with a chandelier jingle in the mix and the dreamy sway of dance music and an element of self-delight – the lure, the enticement of a life defined by its remoteness from the daily drudge of world complaint.

'Tapes of cries and moans,' Edgar said, 'which I would play to help me sleep.'

They moved through the ballroom, they circulated, seeing prominent people everywhere. The room was high and white and primrose gold, flanked by Greek columns that caught the lickery amber light of a thousand candles.

Swan-necked women in textured satin gowns. Masks by Halston, Adolfo, and Saint Laurent. The mother and the sister of one American President and the daughter of another. Crisp little men aswagger with assets. Titled jetsetters, a maharaja and maharani, a Baroness. Somebody in a beaded mask. Famous and raging alcoholic poets. Tough smart stylish women who ran fashion books and designed clothes. Hair by Kenneth – teased, swirled, back combed, and ringleted.

'Did you see?'

'Yes, I did,' Edgar said.

'In the dime-store mask.'

'Yes, decorated with pearls.'

They shook hands here and there, daintily, and dropped a flattering remark to this or that person, and Clyde knew how the Director felt, mixing with people of the rarest social levels, the anointed and predestined, aura'd like Inca kings, but also the talented and the original and the self-made and the born beautiful and the ego-driven and the hard-bargaining, all bearing signs of astral radiance, and the ruthless and brutish as well.

Yes, Edgar was excited.

He stopped to chat with Frank Sinatra and his young actress wife, nymph in a boy's haircut and a butterfly mask.

'Jedgar, you old warhorse. How long has it been?'

'Far too long, my friend.'

'Tempus fugits, don't it, pal?'

'Introduce me to your lovely bride.'

Sinatra was in the files. Many people in the room were in the files. Not a single one of them, Clyde imagined, more accomplished in his occupational strokes than Edgar himself. But Edgar did not carry the glow. Edgar worked in the semidark, manipulating and bringing ruin. He carried the small wan grudging glory of the civil servant. Not the open and confident show, the wide-striding boom of some of these cosmic bravos.

On the stage, under the furled curtain, two bands took turns. A white society band and a black soul group. All musicians masked.

People admired Edgar's leather mask. They told him so. A woman in ostrich feathers ran her tongue over the handlebars. Another woman called him Biker Boy. A gay playwright rolled his eyes.

They found their table and settled in for a spell, sipping champagne and nibbling on buffet tidbits. Clyde uttered the names of people dancing past and Edgar commented on their lives and careers and personal predilections. Whatever anecdotal lore he failed to recall, Clyde was quick to provide.

Andy Warhol walked by wearing a mask that was a photograph of his own face.

A woman asked Edgar to dance, and he flushed and lit a cigarette.

Lord and Lady Somebody held their masks on sticks.

A woman wore a sexy nun's wimple.

A man wore an executioner's hood.

Edgar spoke rapidly in his old staccato voice, like a

radio reporter doing a series of punchy news items. It made Clyde feel good to see the Boss show such animation. They spotted a number of people they knew professionally, Administration faces, past and present, men who held sensitive and critical positions, and Clyde noted how the ballroom seemed to throb with cross-current interests and appetites. Political power mingling lubriciously with art and literature. Domed historians clubbing with the beautiful people of society and fashion. There were diplomats dancing with movie stars, and Nobel laureates telling chummy stories to shipping tycoons, and the demimonde of Broadway and the gossip industry hobnobbing with foreign correspondents.

There was a self-conscious sense of some profound moment in the making. A dreadful prospect, Clyde thought, because it suggested a continuation of the Kennedy years. In which well-founded categories began to seem irrelevant. In which a certain fluid movement became possible. In which sex, drugs, and dirty words began to unstratify the culture.

'I think you ought to dance,' Edgar said.

Clyde looked at him.

'It's a party. Why not? Find a suitable lady and spin her around the floor.'

'I do believe the man is serious.'

'Then come back and tell me what you talked about.'

'Do I remember a single step?'

'You were quite a good dancer, Junior. Go ahead. Do your stuff. It's a party.'

On the floor the guests were doing the twist with all the articulated pantomime of the unfrozen dead come back for a day. Soon the white band re-emerged and the music turned to foxtrots and waltzes. Clyde watched the slowly shuffling mass of careful dancers, barely touching, heedful of hairdos and jewelry and gowns and masks and always on the alert for other fabulous people – heads turning, eyes bright in the great black-and-white gyre.

'Yes, show your true colors,' Edgar said with a twisted grin.

So that was it. Tipsy and bitter. All right, thought Clyde. If this was to be a night in which old restrictions were eased, why not a turn around the floor?

He approached a woman not only masked but wholly medieval, it seemed, a cloth wound about the head and a long plain cloak sashed at the waist and a tight bodice girdled high under her breasts.

She smiled at him, and Clyde said, 'Shall we?'

She was tall and fair and wore no makeup and spoke without awe of the evening and its trappings. A level headed and well-brought-up young lady of the sort that Edgar admired and therefore Clyde as well.

She wore a raven's mask.

Clyde's own mask, an unadorned domino, was in his pocket now.

'Are we using names,' he said, 'or shall we abide by strict rules of anonymity?'

'Are there rules in effect? I wasn't aware.'

'We'll make our own,' he said, surprised by the slightly sexy banter he was generating.

He led her in and out of pairs of bodies ghost-floating to the tune of an old ballad from his youth.

Clyde used to have women friends. But when the Boss started to court other possible protégés, strong-bodied young agents who would serve a social function more than a Bureau function, Clyde knew it was time to submit to Edgar's need for a steadfast and unquestioning friend, a mate of soul and word and unvarying routine. This was a choice that answered Clyde's own deep need for protection, a place on the safe side of the fortified wall.

Power made his suits fit better.

He saw Edgar being photographed with a group at the far end of the ballroom. Clyde recognized most of the people and noticed how eager Edgar seemed to nestle among them.

Edgar's own power had always been double-skinned. He had the power of his office, of course. And also the power that his self-repression gave him. His stern measures as director were given an odd legitimacy by his personal life, the rigor of his insistent celibacy. Clyde believed this, that Edgar had earned his monocratic power through the days and nights of his self-denial, the rejection of unacceptable impulses. The man was consistent. Every official secret in the Bureau had its blood birth in Edgar's own soul.

This was what made him a great man.

Conflict. The nature of his desire and the unremitting attempts he made to expose homosexuals in the government. The secret of his desire and the refusal to yield. Great in his conviction. Great in his harsh judgment and traditional background and early-American righteousness and great in his quibbling fear and dark shame and great and sad and miserable in his dread of physical contact and in a thousand other torments too deep to name.

Clyde would have done whatever the Boss required.

Knelt down.

Bent over.

Spread out.

Reached around.

But the Boss wanted only his company and his loyalty down to the last sentient instant of his dying breath.

Clyde saw another man, and another, in executioner's hoods. And a figure in a white winding-sheet.

'And that man over there. Having his picture snapped,' the young woman said. 'That's the person you were sitting with.'

'Mr. Hoover.'

'Mr. Hoover, yes.'

'And with him, let me see. The wife of a famous poet. The husband of a famous actress. Two unattached composers. A billionaire with a double chin.' Clyde realized he was showing off.

'And you are Mr. Tolson,' said the woman.

And how clever, thought Clyde, who was rarely

recognized in public, and felt a bit flattered, and somewhat unsettled as well.

They were dancing cheek to cheek.

He saw another woman in modified medieval dress, and then a man in a skeleton mask and a woman with a monk's cowl standing on the fringes of the dance floor.

'You know my name,' Clyde said, 'but I'm at a loss, I'm afraid.'

'Which doesn't happen very often, does it? But I thought our rules tended to favor nondisclosure.'

They were dancing to show tunes from the forties. She pressed slightly closer and seemed to breathe rhythmically in his ear.

'Have you ever seen so many men gathered in one place,' she whispered, 'in order to be rich, powerful, and disgusting together? We can look around us, Clyde, and see the business executives, the government officials, the industrialists, the writers, the bankers, the academics, the pig-faced aristocrats in exile, and we can know the soul of one by the bitter wrinkled body of the other and then know all by the soul of the one. Because they're all part of the same motherfucking thing,' she whispered. 'Don't you think?'

Well, she just about took his breath away, whoever she was.

'The same thing. What thing?' he said.

Lynda Bird Johnson danced past with a Secret Service agent.

'The state, the nation, the corporation, the power

structure, the system, the establishment.'

So young and lithe and trite. He felt the electric tension of her thighs and breasts passing through his suit.

'If you kiss me,' she said, 'I'll stick my tongue so far down your throat.'

'Yes?'

'It will pierce your heart.'

Then everything happened at once. Figures in raven faces and skull masks. Figures in white winding-sheets. Monks, nuns, executioners. And he understood of course that the woman in his arms was one of them.

They formed a death rank on the dance floor, halting the music and sending the guests to the fringes. They commanded the room, a masque of silent figures, a plague, a spray of pathogens, and Clyde looked around for Edgar.

The woman slipped away. Then the figures trooped across the floor, draped, masked, sheeted, and cowled. How had they assembled so deftly? How had they entered the ballroom in the first place?

He looked for Edgar.

An executioner and a nun did a pas de deux, a round of simple circling steps, and then the others gradually joined, the skeleton men and raven women, and in the end it was a graceful pavane they did, courtly and deadly and slow, with gestures so deliberate they seemed acted as well as danced, and Clyde saw his young partner move silkenly in their midst.

I will stick my tongue so far down your throat.

The guests watched in a trance – five hundred and forty men and women by actual count, and musicians and waiters and other personnel, all part of the audience for an entertainment other than themselves – hushed and half stunned.

I will pierce your heart.

When they were finished, the troupe stood in a line and removed their headpieces and masks. Then they opened their mouths, saying nothing, and directed hollow stares at the guests. An extended moment, a long gaping silence in the columned hall.

They departed single file.

A couple of minutes later, Clyde found the Boss and they went to the men's room to collect themselves.

'Enjoy your dance, Junior?'

'Turn around.'

'It's all connected. I'm convinced of this. It's all linked in one massive network. The war, the garbage, the promiscuity, the music, the drugs, the hair.'

'There's some dandruff on your jacket,' Clyde said.

Men entered and left, carrying a post-performance buzz into the tiled room. They unzipped and peed. They urinated into mounds of crushed ice garnished with lemon wedges. They unzipped and zipped. They peed, they waggled, and they zipped.

Clyde blew scaly flakes from the Boss's suit and shirt collar.

Back in the ballroom, half the guests were gone. The rest measured out the time so their departure would not seem influenced by the spectacle, the protest, whatever it was – the mockery of their sleek and precious evening.

The society band played some danceable numbers but nobody wanted to dance. Edgar sat, drank, and hated. He had the sheen of Last Things in his eye. Clyde knew this look. It meant the Boss was meditating on his coffin. It gave him dark solace, planning the details of his internment. A lead-lined coffin of a thousand pounds plus. To protect his body from worms, germs, moles, voles, and vandals. They were planning to steal his garbage, so why not his corpse? Lead-lined, yes, to keep him safe from nuclear war, from the blast wave, the shock wave, the fallout.

It was after four in the morning when Clyde led the way down the steps to the Cadillac as the spent trash of a day and a night in a great coastal city went wind-skidding through the streets.

Edgar dead, pray God, not for ten, fifteen, twenty years yet.

Maybe the sixties would be over by then.

The armoured limousine moved slowly back to the Waldorf. Clyde had let that young woman charm and tempt him, and he'd liked it, and he'd been disappointed when he slipped away before the kiss, and he'd been played for a fool in the oldest, weariest way – that radical calculating heartless self-possessed melon-breasted bitch.

Clyde spotted the bug.

He glanced at Edgar, who sat mute and brooding in

his sequinned mask. He'd worn the mask steadily since dinner. A hard man, they said. Cold and laconic. And they made smutty swishy jokes about Edgar and Clyde. But these were not a couple of old queens doddering on. They were men of sovereign authority. And Edgar did not intend to yield control anytime on this earth. This is why he wore the mask – to ease, if only briefly, the burden of control, and maybe to mock, at some level, the painful artifice beneath the shiny leather.

And when Clyde spotted the bug, the poky little Volkswagen with its incandescent doddles and whorls, he decided to say nothing to Edgar. The car was a hundred feet behind them, like a Day-Glo roach, slow and sleepless and clinging.

He said nothing to Edgar because the night had been filled with shock and distress and it was time, finally, for Junior, the life companion and loyal second man, to keep a secret from the Boss.

Notes on the Authors

CANDIDA BAKER was born in London in 1955 into a theatrical and literary family. She visited Australia with the Royal Shakespeare Company production of *The Hollow Crown* in 1975, and emigrated to Sydney in 1977. The author of the novel, *Women and Horses*, a short-story collection, *The Powerful Owl*, the *Yacker* series of interviews with Australian writers, and several books for children, she was previously arts editor of the *Sydney Morning Herald* and is now editor of *The Australian Magazine*.

DONALD BARTHELME was born in 1931 and educated at the University of Houston. A recipient of the National Book Award in 1972 and a member of the American Academy of Arts and Letters, he was the author of the novels *Snow White* (1967), *The Dead Father* (1977) and *Paradise* (1986). His dozen volumes of short fiction include *Unspeakable Practices, Unnatural Acts* (1968), *Sadness* (1972) and *Sixty Stories* (1981). He died in 1989.

MAEVE BINCHY was born in Dublin in 1940 and educated at Holy Child Convent and University College, Dublin, where she took a history degree before becoming a school teacher. In 1969 she joined the *Irish Times*, and has since written newspaper columns from London and all over the world. Her last three novels were number-one bestsellers, and her books have been adapted for television and cinema. Her two plays have been staged at Dublin's Peacock Theatre.

PETER CAREY was born in Bacchus Marsh, Victoria, in 1943, and worked in advertising in Melbourne and Sydney while starting his writing career. He is the author of the short-story collections *The Fat Man in History*, *War Crimes* and *Collected Stories*, and the novels *Bliss*, *Illywhacker* (which was short-listed for the Booker Prize), *The Tax Collector*, *The Unusual Life of Tristan Smith* and *Oscar and Lucinda*, which won the Booker Prize in 1988. His latest novel, *Jack Maggs*, was published in 1997. He now lives in New York.

RON CARLSON teaches at Arizona State University. He is the author of two story collections, *The News of the World* and *Plan B for the Middle Class*, and two novels, *Betrayed by F. Scott Fitzgerald* and *Truants*. His mordant, extremely short fiction has been anthologised in the collections *Sudden Fiction: American Short-Short Stories* and *Micro Fiction*.

JOHN CHEEVER was born in Quincy, Massachussetts, in 1912 and received his only formal education at Thayer Academy. The author of seven collections of stories, most written for the *New Yorker*, and four novels, his vision of the *haute bourgeoisie* of suburban New York, alternately comically affectionate and darkly satiric, brought him the National Book Award and the Pulitzer Prize. He died in 1982.

DON DeLILLO was born in New York City in 1936 and brought up by Italian immigrant parents in the Bronx. He studied history, philosophy and theology at Fordham University before becoming an advertising copywriter at Ogilvy & Mather. His novels, mordant satires of contemporary America, are *Americana, End Zone, Great Jones Street, Ratner's Star, Players, Running Dog, Amazons, The Names, White Noise, Mao II* and *Libra*, a fictional recreation of events leading to the assassination of John F. Kennedy, which won the first annual International Fiction Prize in 1989.

JUNOT DÍAZ was born in Santo Domingo, Dominican Republic, in 1969. He is a graduate of Rutgers University and received his Master of Fine Arts degree from Cornell. His fiction has appeared in *Story*, the *New Yorker*, the *Paris Review, Best American Short Stories 1996* and *African Verse*. His first book, the short-story collection *Drown*, was published in 1996.

JOAN DIDION was born in California's Sacramento Valley in 1934. She graduated from Berkeley in 1956 and, after winning a *Vogue* writing competition, moved to New York to work on the magazine. Her early journalism is collected in *Slouching Towards Bethlehem*; subsequent books of non-fiction are *The White Album, Salvador* and *After Henry*. Her novels, *Run, River, Play It as It Lays, A Book of Common Prayer, Democracy, Miami* and *The Last Thing He Wanted*, examine American cultural and political disintegration. With her husband, John Gregory Dunne, she wrote the film scripts for *Play It as It Lays, Panic in Needle Park, True Confessions* and the Streisand remake of *A Star Is Born*.

BEVERLEY FARMER was born in Melbourne in 1941 and educated at the University of Melbourne. She lived for some years in Greece, which provides the background for much of her fiction. A novelist and short-story writer, she won the Alan Marshall Award in 1981. Her books include *Home Time*, the story collection, *Milk*, which won the New South Wales Premier's Award in 1984, *A Body of Water, The Seal Woman* and *The House in the Light*.

HELEN GARNER was born in 1942 in Geelong, Victoria, and now lives in Sydney. Her first novel, *Monkey Grip*, won Australia's National Book Council Award and became a film, and her story collection, *Postcards from Surfers*, won the New South Wales Premier's Award. She is also the author of the novels *The Children's Bach* and *Cosmo Cosmolino*, the novellas *Honour* and *Other People's Children*, two best-selling works of non-fiction,

The First Stone and *True Stories*, and two screenplays, *The Last Days of Chez Nous* and *Two Friends*.

BARRY HANNAH was born in Clinton, Mississippi, in 1942 and teaches at the University of Mississippi in Oxford. He was awarded the William Faulkner Prize for his first novel, *Geronimo Rex*, and the Arnold Gingrich Short Fiction Award for his story collection, *Airships*. His other books include a novella, *Ray*, the novels *Nightwatchmen* and *The Tennis Handsome*, and the story collection, *Captain Maximus*. He has received a Guggenheim Fellowship and been honoured by the American Academy of Arts and Letters.

NEIL JORDAN, the noted Irish film director and screen-writer, was born in 1950. His films include *The Company of Wolves, Mona Lisa, Michael Collins* and *The Crying Game*, for which he won an Academy Award for Best Original Screenplay and which was nominated for Best Film. He is the author of the story collection, *Night in Tunisia*, which won a Somerset Maugham Award and the *Guardian* Fiction Prize, and two novels, *The Past* and *The Dream of a Beast*.

EVELYN LAU was born in Vancouver in 1971. At the age of seventeen, after living on the streets for two years, she wrote the bestselling *Runaway: Diary of a Street Kid*. In 1992 she became the youngest poet ever nominated for Canada's Governor-General's Award for her second poetry collection, *Oedipal Dreams*. Her book of stories, *Fresh Girls*, published in 1994, was followed in 1995 by a novel, *Other Women*.

NAGUIB MAHFOUZ was born in Cairo in 1911 and began writing when he was seventeen. Since then he has produced over thirty novels, ranging from historical romances to experimental novels, and including his masterwork, *The Cairo Trilogy*, the story of twentieth-century Egypt as seen through the eyes of the Al Jawad family. In 1988 he was awarded the Nobel Prize for Literature. He lives in the Cairo suburb of Agouza.

GABRIEL GARCÍA MÁRQUEZ was born in 1928 in Aracata, Colombia. He attended the National University in Bogotá, became a reporter and worked in Europe and New York as a foreign correspondent. His books include *No One Writes to the Colonel and Other Stories, One Hundred Years of Solitude, The Autumn of the Patriarch, Innocent Erendira and Other Stories, In Evil Hour, Leaf Storm and Other Stories, Chronicle of a Death Foretold, Love in the Time of Cholera* and *The General in His Labyrinth*. Awarded the Nobel Prize for Literature in 1982, he lives in Mexico City.

FRANK MOORHOUSE was born in Nowra, New South Wales, in 1938. His first book of stories, *Futility and Other Animals*, was published in 1969 while he was working as a reporter in Sydney. His other books of stories include *The Americans, Baby, The Electrical Experience, Tales of Mystery and Romance, The Everlasting Secret Family* and *Room Service*. He won the *Age* Book of the Year Award and the Australian Literature Society's Gold Medal for *Forty-Seventeen*. His most recent book is *Grand Days*.

JESS MOWRY was born in Mississippi in 1960. A short-story writer whose urban stories, set in the streets and black housing projects of Oakland, California, were first published in the literary magazine *ZYZZYVA*, he drew wide attention with the publication in 1990 of his novel, *Way Past Cool*. He is also the author of *Six Out Seven, Children of the Night* and *Rats in the Trees*.

BHARATI MUKHERJEE was born in Calcutta in 1942, emigrated to Canada, and now lives and teaches in the United States. She is the author of the novels *Wife* and *The Tiger's Daughter*, two works of non-fiction, *Days and Nights in Calcutta* and *The Sorrow and the Terror*, and two collections of short stories, *Darkness* and *The Middleman and Other Stories*, which won the U.S. National Book Critics' Award in 1988.

JOYCE CAROL OATES was born in 1938 and grew up in the country outside Lockport, New York. She is the author of twenty-two novels and many volumes of short stories, poems, essays and plays, for which she has won several distinguished awards, including the National

Book Award. She lives in Princeton, New Jersey, where she is a Professor in Humanities at Princeton University.

SALMAN RUSHDIE was born in Bombay in 1947. Educated in England, he worked in advertising before turning to fiction writing. He is the author of *Grimus, Midnight's Children, Shame, The Satanic Verses, Haroun and the Sea of Stories, East, West* and *The Moor's Last Sigh*, as well as the essay collection *Imaginary Homelands* and *The Jaguar Smile: A Nicaraguan Journey*. He has won a number of literary prizes, including the Booker Prize in 1981. In 1993, *Midnight's Children* was adjudged the 'Booker of Bookers', the best novel to have won the prize in its first twenty-five years.

WILL SELF was born in London's Old Charing Cross Hospital in 1961, was brought up in East Finchley, and lives in Shepherd's Bush. His collected cartoons were published in 1985, his story cycle, *The Quantity Theory of Insanity*, in 1991 and his twin novellas *Cock* and *Bull* in 1992. His novel *My Idea of Fun* appeared in 1993, followed by the story collection *Grey Area* in 1994.

GRAHAM SWIFT was born in London in 1949. His stories first appeared in *London Magazine*. He is the author of the story collection *Learning to Swim*, and the novels *The Sweet Shop Owner, Shuttlecock, Out of This World, Ever After*, the internationally acclaimed *Water-*

land (which was filmed in 1992) and *Last Orders*, which won the Booker Prize for 1996.

ROSE TREMAIN was born in London in 1943 and educated at Crofton Grange School, the Sorbonne in Paris, and the University of East Anglia, where she studied English literature with Angus Wilson. She is the author of nine works of fiction, including *Restoration*, which was shortlisted for the Booker Prize, and made into a film starring Meg Ryan and Hugh Grant. She has also written many plays for radio and television, a history of the women's suffrage movement and an illustrated biography of Stalin.

JOHN UPDIKE was born in Shillington, Pennsylvania, in 1932 and attended Harvard and the Ruskin School of Drawing and Fine Art at Oxford. From 1955 to 1957 he was on the staff of the *New Yorker*, to which he has contributed numerous short stories, essays and poems. His many novels include *The Poorhouse Fair, Rabbit, Run, The Centaur, Of the Farm, Rabbit Redux, Couples, The Coup, Rabbit is Rich* (winner of the 1982 Pulitzer Prize), *The Witches of Eastwick* and *Roger's Version*. His story collections include *The Same Door, Pigeon Feathers, The Music School, Museums and Women, Your Lover Just Called* and *Problems*.

IRVINE WELSH was born in 1960 and lives in Edinburgh. His first book, *Trainspotting*, published in 1993, was a bestselling novel, reached the short list for the Booker Prize, and became an international cult success when it was filmed in 1995. His short-story collection, *The Acid House*, was published to wide critical acclaim in 1994. His new novel is *Marabou Stork Nightmares*.

TOBIAS WOLFF was born in Alabama in 1945, grew up in the Cascade Mountains of Washington State and was educated at Oxford and Stanford. His short stories place him in the strong American myth-making tradition of Hemingway, Fitzgerald, Jack London and Mark Twain. *This Boy's Life*, his evocative memoir of an unusual childhood, has been made into a film starring Robert De Niro, Ellen Barkin and Leonardo DiCaprio.

BANANA YOSHIMOTO was born in 1964 and lives in Tokyo. In addition to *Kitchen* and *NP*, she is the author of two collections of essays, *Pineapple Pudding* and *Song from Banana*. Her stories, novels and essays have won prizes both in Japan and abroad. 'Newlywed', a short story in her recent collection, *Lizard*, was first se-rialised on posters aboard Tokyo's Higashi Nippon Railway commuter trains.

Acknowledgements

I wish to thank Katie Purvis, Katherine Steward, Miriam Cannell, Annabelle Furphy and Peg McColl, whose tireless efforts eased the process of bringing together cities, stories, writers and, especially, copyright permissions from all over the world. Thanks, too, to Julie Gibbs for her enthusiastic support for the project.

Candida Baker 'City Lights' © 1997 by Candida Baker. **Donald Barthelme** 'The King of Jazz' from *Great Days* by Donald Barthelme © 1979 by Donald Barthelme. Reprinted by permission of The Wylie Agency. **Maeve Binchy** 'Shepherd's Bush' from *London Transport* by Maeve Binchy © 1983 by Maeve Binchy. Reprinted by permission of Dell Books, a division of Bantam Doubleday Dell Publishing Group, Inc., Random House UK and Christine Green. **Peter Carey** 'Room No. 5 (Escribo)' from *Peter Carey: Collected Stories* © 1994 by Peter Carey. Reprinted by permission of University of Queensland Press and Rogers, Coleridge & White Ltd. **Ron Carlson** 'Reading the Paper' © 1988 by Ron Carlson. Originally appeared in *Sudden Fiction* (Penguin, 1988). Reprinted by permission of Brandt & Brandt Literary Agents, Inc. **John Cheever** 'Reunion' from *The Stories of John Cheever* by John Cheever © 1962 by John Cheever. Reprinted by permission of Wylie, Aitken & Stone and Alfred A. Knopf, Inc. **Don DeLillo** 'The Black-and-White Ball' from *Underworld* by Don DeLillo © 1996, 1997 by Don DeLillo. First published in *The New Yorker*, December 23–30, 1996. Reprinted by permission of Scribner, a division of Simon & Schuster, and Macmillan. **Junot Díaz** 'How to Date a Brown Girl' by Junot Díaz © 1996 by Junot Díaz. Reprinted by permission of Faber & Faber and Riverhead Books, a division of the Putnam Publishing Group. **Joan Didion** 'L.A. *Noir*' from *After Henry* by Joan Didion © 1992 by Joan Didion. Reprinted by permission of Simon & Schuster. **Robert Drewe** 'Life of a Barbarian' from *The Bay of Contented Men* by Robert Drewe © 1989 by Robert Drewe. Reprinted by permission of Pan Macmillan Australia Pty Ltd. **Beverley Farmer** 'A Man in the Laundrette' from *Home Time* by Beverley Farmer © 1985 by Beverley Farmer. Reprinted by permission of Penguin Books Australia Ltd. **Helen Garner** 'In Paris' from *Postcards from Surfers* by Helen Garner © 1985 by Helen Garner. Reprinted by permission of Penguin Books Australia Ltd. **Barry Hannah** 'That's True' from *Airships* by Barry Hannah © 1978 by Barry Hannah. Reprinted by permission of The Wallace Literary Agency and Alfred A. Knopf, Inc. **Neil Jordan** 'Last Rites' from *Night in Tunisia* and *The Neil Jordan Reader* by Neil Jordan © 1976, 1983, 1993 by Neil Jordan. Reprinted by permission of Casarotto Company Ltd in association with Lutyens & Rubinstein and Vintage Books, a division of Random House, Inc. **Evelyn Lau** 'Glass' from *Fresh Girls and Other Stories* by Evelyn Lau © 1993, 1995 by Evelyn Lau. Reprinted by permission of Reed Books, HarperCollins Publishers Ltd and Hyperion. **Naguib Mahfouz** 'Blessed Night' from *The Time and the Place and Other Stories* by Naguib Mahfouz © 1991 by the American University in Cairo Press. Used by permission of Doubleday, a division of Bantam Doubleday Dell Publishing Group, Inc. **Gabriel García Márquez** 'The Woman Who Came at Six O'Clock' from *Leaf Storm and Other Stories* by Gabriel García Márquez © 1972 by Gabriel García Márquez. Reprinted by permission of Random House UK and HarperCollins Publishers Ltd. **Frank Moorhouse** 'The New York

ACKNOWLEDGEMENTS

Bell Captain' from *Room Service* by Frank Moorhouse © 1987 by Frank Moorhouse. Reprinted by permission of Penguin Books Australia Ltd. **Jess Mowry** 'Crusader Rabbit' by Jess Mowry from *Cowboys, Indians and Commuters: The Penguin Book of New American Voices* © 1994 by Viking. Reprinted by permission of Jess Mowry. **Bharati Mukherjee** 'Nostalgia' by Bharati Mukherjee from *The Penguin Book of Modern Indian Short Stories* © 1989 by Penguin Books. Reprinted by permission of Janklow & Nesbit Associates. **Joyce Carol Oates** 'Happy' from *Raven's Wing* by Joyce Carol Oates © 1986 by The Ontario Review. Used by permission of Blanche C. Gregory, Inc. and Dutton Signet, a division of Penguin Books USA, Inc. **Salman Rushdie** 'The Free Radio' from *East West: Stories* by Salman Rushdie © 1994 by Salman Rushdie. Reprinted by permission of Random House UK and Pantheon Books, a division of Random House, Inc. **Will Self** 'A Short History of the English Novel' from *Grey Area* by Will Self © 1994 by Will Self. Reprinted by permission of Bloomsbury Publishing Pty Ltd and Grove/Atlantic, Inc. **Graham Swift** 'Seraglio' from *Learning to Swim* by Graham Swift © 1982 by Graham Swift. Reprinted by permission of Macmillan and A. P. Watt Ltd. **Rose Tremain** 'The Stack' by Rose Tremain, first published in *The New Yorker* © 1996 by Rose Tremain. Reprinted by permission of Richard Scott Simon Ltd, part of Sheil Land Associates, 43 Doughty Street, London WC1N 2LF. **John Updike** 'The City' from *Trust Me* by John Updike (Penguin Books, 1988) © 1987 by John Updike. Reprinted by permission of Penguin UK and Alfred A. Knopf, Inc. **Irvine Welsh** 'Disnae Matter' from *The Acid House* by Irvine Welsh © 1995 by Irvine Welsh. Reprinted by permission of Random House UK. **Tobias Wolff** 'Next Door' from *Hunters in the Snow* by Tobias Wolff © 1981 by Tobias Wolff. Reprinted by permission of the author, c/o Rogers, Coleridge & White Ltd, 20 Powis Mews, London W11 1JN in association with

ACKNOWLEDGEMENTS

International Creative Management Inc., 40 West 57th Street, New York, NY 10019, USA, and Alfred A. Knopf, Inc. **Banana Yoshimoto** 'Newlywed' from *Lizard* by Banana Yoshimoto © 1993 by Banana Yoshimoto. Reprinted by permission of Grove/Atlantic Inc.

Visit Penguin on the Internet
and browse at your leisure

- ◆ preview sample extracts of our forthcoming books
- ◆ read about your favourite authors
- ◆ investigate over 10,000 titles
- ◆ enter one of our literary quizzes
- ◆ win some fantastic prizes in our competitions
- ◆ e-mail us with your comments and book reviews
- ◆ instantly order any Penguin book

and masses more!

'To be recommended without reservation ... a rich and rewarding on-line experience' – Internet Magazine

READ MORE IN PENGUIN

In every corner of the world, on every subject under the sun, Penguin represents quality and variety – the very best in publishing today.

For complete information about books available from Penguin – including Puffins, Penguin Classics and Arkana – and how to order them, write to us at the appropriate address below. Please note that for copyright reasons the selection of books varies from country to country.

In the United Kingdom: Please write to *Dept. EP, Penguin Books Ltd, Bath Road, Harmondsworth, West Drayton, Middlesex UB7 ODA*

In the United States: Please write to *Consumer Sales, Penguin Putnam Inc., P.O. Box 999, Dept. 17109, Bergenfield, New Jersey 07621-0120.* VISA and MasterCard holders call 1-800-253-6476 to order Penguin titles

In Canada: Please write to *Penguin Books Canada Ltd, 10 Alcorn Avenue, Suite 300, Toronto, Ontario M4V 3B2*

In Australia: Please write to *Penguin Books Australia Ltd, P.O. Box 257, Ringwood, Victoria 3134*

In New Zealand: Please write to *Penguin Books (NZ) Ltd, Private Bag 102902, North Shore Mail Centre, Auckland 10*

In India: Please write to *Penguin Books India Pvt Ltd, 210 Chiranjiv Tower, 43 Nehru Place, New Delhi 110 019*

In the Netherlands: Please write to *Penguin Books Netherlands bv, Postbus 3507, NL-1001 AH Amsterdam*

In Germany: Please write to *Penguin Books Deutschland GmbH, Metzlerstrasse 26, 60594 Frankfurt am Main*

In Spain: Please write to *Penguin Books S. A., Bravo Murillo 19, 1° B, 28015 Madrid*

In Italy: Please write to *Penguin Italia s.r.l., Via Benedetto Croce 2, 20094 Corsico, Milano*

In France: Please write to *Penguin France, Le Carré Wilson, 62 rue Benjamin Baillaud, 31500 Toulouse*

In Japan: Please write to *Penguin Books Japan Ltd, Kaneko Building, 2-3-25 Koraku, Bunkyo-Ku, Tokyo 112*

In South Africa: Please write to *Penguin Books South Africa (Pty) Ltd, Private Bag X14, Parkview, 2122 Johannesburg*

READ MORE IN PENGUIN

A SELECTION OF OMNIBUSES

The Penguin Book of Classic Fantasy by Women
Edited by A. Susan Williams

This wide-ranging and nerve-tingling collection assembles short stories written by women from 1806 to the Second World War. From George Eliot on clairvoyance to C. L. Moore on aliens or Virginia Woolf on psychological spectres, here is every aspect of fantasy from some of the best-known writers of their day.

The Penguin Collection

This collection of writing by twelve acclaimed authors represents the finest in modern fiction, and celebrates sixty years of Penguin Books. Among the stories assembled here are ones by William Boyd, Donna Tartt, John Updike and Barbara Vine.

V. I. Warshawski   Sara Paretsky

In *Indemnity Only*, *Deadlock* and *Killing Orders*, Sara Paretsky demonstrates the skill that makes tough female private eye Warshawski one of the most witty, slick and imaginative sleuths on the street today.

A David Lodge Trilogy   David Lodge

His three brilliant comic novels revolving around the University of Rummidge and the eventful lives of its role-swapping academics. Collected here are: *Changing Places*, *Small World* and *Nice Work*.

The Rabbit Novels   John Updike

'One of the finest literary achievements to have come out of the US since the war ... It is in their particularity, in the way they capture the minutiae of the world ... that [the Rabbit] books are most lovable' – *Irish Times*

READ MORE IN PENGUIN

A SELECTION OF OMNIBUSES

Zuckerman Bound Philip Roth

The Zuckerman trilogy – *The Ghost Writer*, *Zuckerman Unbound* and *The Anatomy Lesson* – and the novella-length epilogue, *The Prague Orgy*, are here collected in a single volume. Brilliantly diverse and intricately designed, together they form a wholly original and richly comic investigation into the unforeseen consequences of art.

The Collected Stories of Colette Colette

The hundred short stories collected here include such masterpieces as 'Bella-Vista', 'The Tender Shoot' and 'Le Képi', Colette's subtle and ruthless rendering of a woman's belated sexual awakening. 'A perfectionist in her every word' – *Spectator*

The Collected Stories Muriel Spark

'Muriel Spark has made herself a mistress at writing stories which seem to trip blithely and bitchily along life's way until the reader is suddenly pulled up with a shock recognition of death and judgment, heaven and hell' – *London Review of Books*

The Complete Saki

Macabre, acid and very funny, Saki's work drives a knife into the upper crust of English Edwardian life. Here are the effete and dashing heroes, the tea on the lawn, the smell of gunshot, the half-felt menace of disturbing undercurrents ... all in this magnificent omnibus.

The Penguin Book of Gay Short Stories
Edited by David Leavitt and Mark Mitchell

The diversity – and unity – of gay love and experience in the twentieth century is celebrated in this collection of thirty-nine stories. 'The book is like a long, enjoyable party, at which the celebrated ... rub shoulders with the neglected' – *The Times Literary Supplement*

READ MORE IN PENGUIN

A SELECTION OF OMNIBUSES

Italian Folktales Italo Calvino

Greeted with overwhelming enthusiasm and praise, Calvino's anthology is already a classic. These tales have been gathered from every region of Italy and retold in Calvino's own inspired and sensuous language. 'A magic book' – *Time*

The Penguin Book of Lesbian Short Stories
Edited by Margaret Reynolds

'Its historical sweep is its joy, a century's worth of polymorphous protagonists, from lady companions and *salonières* to pathological inverts and victims of sexology; from butch-femme stereotypes to nineties bad girls' – *Guardian*

On the Edge of the Great Rift Paul Theroux
Three Novels of Africa

In *Fong and the Indians*, Sam Fong, a Chinese immigrant in a ramshackle East African country, is reduced to making friends with the enemy. Miss Poole runs a school in the Kenyan bush in *Girls at Play*, and in *Jungle Lovers*, the fortunes of a dedicated insurance salesman and a ruthless terrorist become strangely interwoven.

The Levant Trilogy Olivia Manning
The Danger Tree • The Battle Lost and Won • The Sum of Things

'Her lucid and unsentimental style conveys the full force of ordinary reality with its small betrayals and frustrations but, at the back of it, images of another and more enduring life emerge' – *The Times*

The Complete Enderby Anthony Burgess

In these four collected novels Enderby – poet and social critic, comrade and Catholic – is endlessly hounded by women. He may be found hiding in the lavatory where much of his best work is composed, or perhaps in Rome, brainwashed into respectability by a glamorous wife, aftershave and the *dolce vita*.